ALSO BY PRU SCHUYLER

THE WICKED TRILOGY

The Wicked Truth

The Wicked Love

The Wicked Ending

NIGHTHAWKS SERIES

Find Me in the Rain

Find Me on the Ice

Find Me Under the Stars

Not My Coach (Novella)

MRS. CLAUS STANDALONE DUET

Stealing Mrs. Claus

Becoming Mrs. Claus

HEAU HOCKEY LEGENDS SERIES

Saving the Beast

Saving THE BEAST

PRU SCHUYLER

Saving
THE BEAST

Hockey Terms

Apple
An assist

Barn
The home rink of a team

Breakaway
When there are no opponents between the offensive player and the goalie, this is usually very fast-paced as the offensive player wants an attempt to score before the defense catches up.

Check
A number of defensive moves aimed to disrupt the player with the puck, doing so by crashing into the opponent with their body

Chippy
Often used to describe a game or moment where the aggression in the game heightens, typically resulting in more shoving, checking, chirping, and fighting.

Chirping

a term for 'trash talk' often used in hockey. Chirping can get under the opponents skin and distract them.

Dangle

Completely embarrassing the opponent with impressive stick handling offensively. Practically "dangling" the puck in front of them but they can't get to it.

Defender

A hockey position that is responsible for preventing the other team from scoring, as well as other tasks.

Deke

'faking' an opponent out using a deceptive movement in order to get them out of the way of a pass, or to bypass them altogether

Fivehole

The gap between a goalie's legs, typically referring to scoring.

Hat Trick

When a player scores three goals in one game, often celebrated by the fans throwing their hats onto the ice

Michigan

A Michigan is a lacrosse style goal where the player picks the puck up on their stick, skates around the back of the net, and throws it into the net to score.

Penalty

A punishment imposed by a referee for breaking a rule.

Power play

When a team has more players than their opponent on the ice as an outcome of the other team committing a penalty.

Sin bin

Also known as the penalty box. An area where players are sent, off of the ice, to serve the allotted time from the committed penalty

SCAN ME TO PLAY

Amazon

Spotify

Playlist

Till Forever Falls Apart, Ashe + Finneas

Run Like a River, Jamica

The Love I Give, RHODES

The Archer, Taylor Swift

Stargazing, Myles Smith

Venus, Zara Larson

Mirrorball, Taylor Swift

Skin and Bones, David Kushner

Long Live, Taylor Swift (Taylor's Version)

Forever and a Day, Benson Boone

The Prophecy, Taylor Swift

Something There, Emma Watson & Dan Stevens
& Ewan Mcgregor & Ian McKellen & Emma
Thompson & Nathan Mack & Gugu Mbatha-Raw

For the readers who first fell in love with fairy tales from the Little Golden Books.

For my incredible mother, who showed me the magic of fairy tales from a young age and who always nurtured my wildly imaginative mind, I love you.

author's note

This story isn't a romantic tale of a cursed beast that transforms into a handsome prince because his sweet, endearing captive falls in love with him.

This is the story about a stubborn girl named Blair Adams, who is struggling to make her dreams come true, and Griffin Hawthorne, a hockey player who would rather have everything stay the way it is—with the past in the past and his heart in a cage.

H E A
University

Dear Reader,

It is with great pleasure that we announce your acceptance into Happily Ever After University. As the most elite school in the country, we are proud to have selected you out of hundreds of thousands of applicants.

As a HEAU student, be prepared to immerse yourself in the lux campus culture. You will have the opportunity to study in our breathtaking castles alongside the brightest students and highest-regarded faculty. You will also spend time in beautiful blossoming flower gardens, hedge-lined student quads, vine-covered gazebos, and state-of-the-art facilities.

Along with your course load, there are endless extracurriculars to indulge in, including cheering on our Legend's hockey team at the astounding Kensington arena.

Based on your application, it is clear that you are driven and dedicated. We have no doubt that you will be an excellent fit for our student body, and we look forward to having you join our campus in the near future.

Welcome to Happily Ever After University.

Sincerely,
Dean of Admissions.

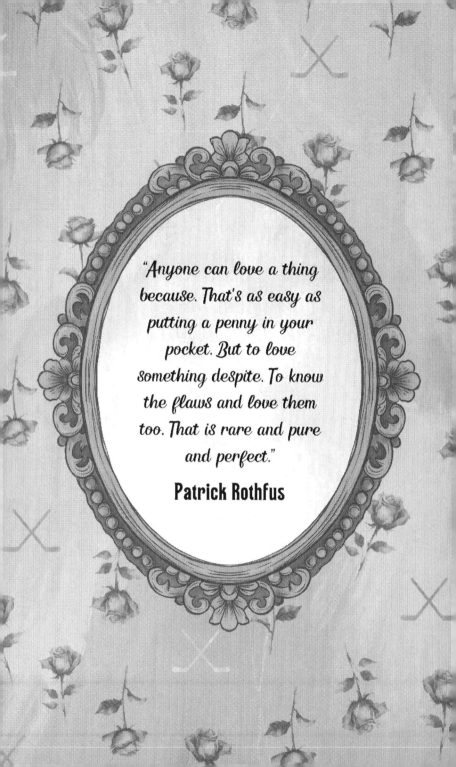

"Anyone can love a thing because. That's as easy as putting a penny in your pocket. But to love something despite. To know the flaws and love them too. That is rare and pure and perfect."

Patrick Rothfus

chapter one
blair

There's one thing that people don't tell you about dreams as a kid. Eventually, you wake up from them.

Getting accepted into Happily Ever After University has been my dream since I was a little girl. I spent countless hours fantasizing about wandering the ornate buildings and lounging in the lush flower gardens.

Once I knew that it existed, I refused to settle for anything else. If I could get into that school, I thought that any problem that arose in my life wouldn't matter because HEAU would become the solution.

I remember seeing their advertisements on TV, and it looked like they'd plucked the place straight out of a fairy tale with every building carefully crafted like a castle. Magnificent architecture, tall towers, long corridors, the highest ceilings, a bell tower in the center of the campus, and seemingly unlimited chandeliers that hung in every room.

Every inch of the campus is whimsical and magical. Tall hedges line most of the walkways while overflowing beds of colorful flowers decorate the outside of each building, making the air smell like heaven when they bloom. They even have gigantic marble water fountains in the courtyards.

The campus is almost completely isolated from society, hidden away in the wealthy, luxurious town of Evermore, Washington. I think to be a resident, you have to come from money. I swear the only vehicles I ever see are luxury sports cars and SUVs. Although most residents never drive a day because their chauffeurs take them everywhere.

Tucked in the furthest corner of Evermore, amid a handful of industrial factories, are the only housing options in the entire town for those not dripping in wealth. That's where my dad and I found a house when we moved here a few months ago.

It's hard not to gaze upon the self-proclaimed elite with raging envy when they have the world and all its treasures at their fingertips. My father and I were not dealt the same hand of cards. Not a day has gone by when I haven't watched my dad work himself into the ground to provide for us. He has sacrificed so much to ensure I can chase my dreams, and I refuse to let him down.

When I got that golden acceptance, I felt like nothing else could ever top that moment. But that piece of paper left a cut, a gaping hole in my plans. Everything would have been fine had I gotten a full scholarship, but the school only granted a partial one, leaving an enormous amount of debt to be paid out of pocket.

It didn't make sense that they hadn't chosen me for the

full ride. I had the application full of volunteer hours, extracurriculars, perfect grades, and the tug-at-your-heart story. I know everyone who applied probably felt the same way I did, expecting to be chosen. However, it was slipping through my fingertips after the years I spent meticulously shaping my high school career to get accepted into HEAU.

I'm tenacious and a hard worker; I have been my whole life, although I didn't have much choice. My father has stretched every dollar he's earned since I was born to help keep us afloat, and once I could contribute, I did my part to help. I've worked part-time jobs since I was old enough to help pay our bills. That's why getting a full scholarship was so critical; I wasn't sure if I would still be able to continue my education without it.

My father had been so excited when I told him I was a shoo-in for the scholarship that I couldn't bring myself to tell him the truth when I got the unfortunate news. I knew I had to find a way to make everything work. I couldn't live with myself if I had to settle for a different school. I couldn't even accept that as a possibility.

After discovering that I would only receive half, I applied for every scholarship I could find online. I got selected for many of those, which helps, but that money is still just tiny drops in the gigantic pond. I needed to find a job that would allow me to continue pitching in financially with my father while also making school payments.

After scouring the hiring sites and postings, I found the one job that would give me everything I would need. Even if it was somewhat out of my comfort zone, I was so desperate that I had no choice but to accept it—a job as a bartender and server at The Fallen Petal, a strip club.

Even though I bring home a few hundred every night, my father and I are always playing catch-up on bills, including the tuition he doesn't know I have to pay. It's the best money I've ever made; even if it comes at the cost of lying to my father, it's worth it. He would probably strangle me if he found out I work there. He always supports me, but I think it's just one of those things a father doesn't want to picture his daughter doing.

I don't strip down completely. Instead, I wear booty shorts, short skirts, and tight and revealing tops while I serve. The more scandalous, the more tips.

My father thinks I work at a restaurant on campus as a bartender. Allowing him to believe this is just easier for the both of us.

But I wish I had the confidence to get onstage. I would never have to worry about money again. Those girls bring in the big bucks. But I can't bring myself to do it, as much as I need the money. The thought of dancing onstage in front of a crowd is terrifying.

I like to stay out of that spotlight as much as I can. I make the drinks, help serve the customers, flirt until my cheeks hurt from fake smiling, and help keep an eye on the girls. If anyone gets too rough or handsy, we alert our security, and they handle it.

Honestly, this job has become my second home, as wild as it sounds. All of my coworkers are so supportive, and vice versa, like a little family. Of course, I don't want to work here forever, but I owe the club a lot because it's helping me pursue my real passion in the long run —literature.

I've always wanted to work in the publishing world. I know I'm not cut out to be the one writing the stories. Is that a skill you can learn, or is it one you're born with? Are writers born capable of creating entire lives in their heads, or do they have to teach themselves how to do it?

Those questions have always tickled my brain. If you have to be born with it, then I think I'm screwed. I can write a fifty-page paper about any topic we discuss in class, but I usually use the materials provided to bring it to life, not generating ideas from thin air. That's why I will go into another side of the industry as a literary agent.

I would still experience the whirlwind and whimsical world of books, but from a different perspective. I get to hype the author's work up and find publishers who believe in their stories as much as I do. I would be like a real-life fairy godmother, helping authors' dreams come true.

I can picture it so clearly in my head that I can practically taste the crisp, clean air of my oversize office and the scent of hardwood from my desk. The sunshine fills the room through the large windows, and bookshelves line every wall. I'll do anything to make that dream a reality, and getting into this school was only the first step.

HEAU has the most renowned programs in the world, and they are the most elite. It's a relatively small campus because of that. Their acceptance rate is around point-one percent of applicants, so when I was selected, I made it my mission to see it through. I can't deny fate. They'd chosen me out of hundreds of thousands of applications. I'm destined to be here.

It's well known that if you graduate from HEAU, you will succeed in whatever path you desire. It's like a winning lottery ticket for life. The name Happily Ever After holds true, granting that to every graduating student. That's why I work as hard as I do day and night. Failure truly is not an option.

Susie, my coworker, shouts over the deafening music, yanking me from my thoughts as I walk toward the back room of The Fallen Petal, where we keep our belongings in the staff lounge, "Are you heading out?"

I open the door, and we step through. The music dies down as we shut the door behind us, sighing in unison at the peaceful quietness.

Nodding, I answer her as my feet scream for relief from these heels, "Yeah. When are you off?"

"I'm leaving now. My sitter called and has to go for some family emergency, so I have to go relieve her," she says with her back to me as she gets dressed.

Her daughter, Melody, is the sweetest and most polite five-year-old I've ever met. Susie hates being here late nearly every night and missing tucking her into bed, but she does this for her daughter and their future.

"You know I can always watch her if I'm off," I offer genuinely.

She doesn't have a lot of friends or family around here

to help her, but she has employees here who would do just about anything for her.

She glares at me over her shoulder. "You know I won't let you. I have it handled." She spins around and sits down on the bench, tying her shoes. "Besides, it's not like you don't already have enough on your plate."

Rolling my eyes, I throw my coat and sweats over my uniform, consisting of a pleather miniskirt, stockings, and a lace tank top. "Yeah. But I can always use extra cash."

She hooks her arm through her purse, and I grab my own as she says, "Margo wants you onstage. You could be making four times what you're pulling right now."

Margo manages the dancers and their schedules and helps with wardrobes. She has nothing to do with the bar side of the club.

My cheeks flush at the thought of being on that stage. "Yeah, I don't know. I don't think people would want to see me dancing onstage."

Walking over to me, she boops my nose and says, "If you're onstage and practically naked, you could stand there and do nothing and still make more than you do now, working your ass off nightly."

She's right; I know. But I can't hype myself up enough to do it.

"Yeah. For now, I'm good with bartending and serving. Besides, I wouldn't want you guys completely out of work if I started dancing," I tease her with feigned confidence.

"Oh, yeah, hot stuff?" She laughs and pulls the door open, music enveloping us as we leave the building, waving goodbye to the bouncers and staff.

Wrapping my fingers around my Taser in my purse, I

part ways with Susie and say, "Good night! Get home safe!"

"You too!" she shouts as she gets into her car.

I check my phone to see if my Uber is almost here.

"Seems busy in there tonight," Jared, one of our bouncers, says as I see my Uber is one minute out.

Nodding, I continue our small talk. "Yeah, busier than usual for a Thursday night, I'd say."

The black Chevy Cruze pulls up in front of us, and once I match the license plate to the one showing on my phone, I step forward.

"You have a good night, Blair." He smiles and gets the car door for me.

Grinning back at him and his chivalry, I say, "You too."

He shuts the door behind me once I'm inside the car, and the driver greets me instantly.

"Good evening. Do you have a music preference?" the clean-cut guy asks me as he drives the car and pulls away.

"No. Whatever you prefer is just fine by me," I say quietly, pulling out my phone and opening my e-book.

I'm currently reading a contemporary romance book that follows a girl named Avery Fox. She's a premed student who has to move in with her brother and his rock-star bandmates. Rock star plus nerd means I'm obsessed. As a self-identified nerd, I love seeing the hot guy in romance books get that girl. Because in real life, that is not realistic. Not that a nerdy girl couldn't get a jock or rock star, but from my personal experience, it never works out because their egos usually outweigh their personalities and good looks.

My ex, Grant Gustavson, is proof of that. He's the backup quarterback for the HEAU Legends football team. The mascot for our school is the Legends, represented by a dragon. He was also the quarterback at our high school. For three years, he did his best to convince me to date him, but I always turned him down. I didn't see how he and I would be a good match. That didn't stop him from leaving gifts in my locker, notes on my desk, and chasing away any other guy who showed interest in me.

At the beginning of our senior year, I gave in. We dated for two months. But when I couldn't take any more of his self-centered behavior, I ended our barely beginning relationship. He still won't let it go. He seems to think that I didn't really mean it. But that makes sense because it's not like my words mean anything to him.

When high school ended, I wrote him off for good. But then I ran into him at the end of summer, right before classes at HEAU started. It was move-in day at the dorms, and I volunteered as a student worker to get some volunteer hours. Surprisingly, it was kind of nice to see a familiar face, even if it was Grant.

Grant was helping his friend Felix move in, and he made sure to spend equal time helping Felix as he did flirting with me. I figured that a date wouldn't hurt anything. Maybe he was different. Maybe he grew up since our senior year.

I, in fact, was terribly wrong.

It took all of three-weeks for me to realize that no matter what, we were never going to last. He was going to earn the title of *ex-boyfriend* permanently.

I'd had other boyfriends in high school from other

schools, and unfortunately, they all checked a box for some sport. It is becoming a horrible pattern at this point. I lost my virginity to a basketball player named Chad Summers. It was in the summertime between sophomore and junior years.

At the time, I thought it was so romantic. Chad laid a bunch of blankets and pillows out in the bed of his pickup truck, and we parked in a field under the stars. What no one tells you about that cute plan is the bug bites that you get *everywhere*.

Chad told me he was also a virgin and that he loved me. I didn't realize that you could be a virgin more than once because I later found out he'd lost his virginity fourteen times that summer—thirteen of them not with me.

I was willing to give Grant another chance when I saw him again. I was settling into Evermore, ready to start my life and career and potentially find my college sweetheart. So, I might have ignored a few red flags along the way, chasing the high of a happily ever after.

His lust and so-called love blinded me. The first red flag should have been when he told me he never stopped loving me after only dating for one date. He had told me in high school that he loved me, but that felt like a lifetime ago. At first, he was so fun to be around, and I felt comfortable with him. But his clingy lust quickly morphed into a smothering, overbearing obsession. He wanted to manage my every minute of every day to revolve solely around him.

He pretended to listen to what I had to say before cutting me off and completely changing the subject. He never really heard me. He just waited for me to finish so he could finally talk. Anything I was genuinely interested in; he couldn't care less about. Unless we were conversing about football, football practice, football games, or his dream to go pro, he made no effort whatsoever.

He became possessive, accusing me of cheating on him when I so much as looked at another guy, even going so far as beating a guy up who had winked at me. He also demanded to know where I was at all times, and at first, I thought it was cute; he was protective of me.

Then, he would somehow appear at places I was— the bookstore, library, mall, etc. He would say he was at practice, and then I would see him clear as day minutes later. It became creepy and started to make me uneasy. I had no idea how I didn't see this behavior in high school. Maybe I was just in denial, wanting the relationship to be better than it really was. Regardless, I knew his second chance had to come to an end.

On our three-week anniversary, he picked me up to take me to dinner, and I knew I had to end it. We weren't healthy, and I sure as hell wasn't happy.

He had other ideas for us. I showed up with his broken heart on a plate, and he showed up with a diamond engagement ring. After three weeks! When he pulled it out and set it on the table, I literally laughed in his face, at my limit for his ridiculousness. I hadn't meant to laugh, but I was so shocked that he even thought that was a possibility in our relationship.

I stood up immediately and told him that we weren't working out. He really couldn't take the hint. Over and over, he told me how we belonged together and that, no matter what, we would end up together. The days following the breakup were tense. Nonstop texts from him, calls at all hours, and voice mails as long as the phone would let him record. Eventually, his texts begging me to be with him and to love him turned into mean and menacing lashes. He went from calling me the love of his life to calling me a bitch, slut, whore. Then, he would apologize, say he didn't mean it, and again tell me he loved me. The whiplash he gave me still hurts my damn neck.

It's been about a month since our breakup, and I still get texts from him, but they are far more sporadic. Sometimes nice, sometimes mean, but completely unpredictable. I don't respond; it would just make things worse. And for some reason, I can't bring myself to block him. I will. But it's become entertainment for Lumi, my best friend, and me, like a comedy segment in our everyday lives. *What did Grant say today?*

The driver pulls up in front of my house and turns down the music. "Feel free to grab a water bottle or candy."

Realizing I haven't even read a word in my book, I close the app and respond, "I'm okay. Thank you."

"Have a good night." He smiles kindly, and I grab my bag.

"Thanks. You too."

I'm tired, and I can't wait to dive-bomb into my bed. Nothing makes your bed feel comfier than utter exhaustion.

Quietly unlocking the door, I open it and enter the silent house. My dad is fast asleep at this hour, as he works early tomorrow morning at the factory where he recently got a job. He's worked in warehouse factories for years, and luckily, there was an opening here when we moved. He knows I get home late from bartending, and I do my best not to wake him. Although he always says that he doesn't get to sleep until he knows I'm home safe.

Kicking my shoes off, I tiptoe into the kitchen and examine the endless bills hanging by magnets on the fridge. Checking the overdue dates, I select the one that needs to be paid first and pull it off the door. Taking the cash out of my bag from my tips tonight, I attach all but fifty dollars to the electric bill and set it on the counter for my dad to take.

I know it hurts him to have my help, but he needs it, and I don't want to see him or our house go under. I wish we made better money. We are constantly playing catch-up on invoices and never ahead. It's draining, more so than I'll ever admit. But if this is how we must do it, then so be it because I'm not giving up on my future anytime soon. I will work every day and night if it means I get to stay in school at HEAU.

hat trick

When a player scores three goals in one game, often celebrated by the fans throwing their hats onto the ice

chapter two
griffin

"**W**hy are you acting like such a little pussy?" I shout as fire races through my veins, wanting nothing more than to drop my gloves and beat this prick into the ice.

My team and coaches would be pissed off if I chose to do that. It's a tied game against our rival team, the Knights, and I can't risk getting my ass put in the penalty box because of my temper.

The guy begging to get his teeth knocked in says something under his breath, and it takes a lot of willpower not to retaliate. Our coach calls a time-out, and I skate over to the bench. I lean against the boards, and he nods at me, his way of acknowledging my use of self-control … for once.

Coach talks to us about what we need to improve in order to take the lead. My job? Being a bit of a pest on the ice, riling the other guys up, getting their blood boiling, and pushing them to make mistakes. Once you get into someone's head, you can ruin their game. Over the next five minutes, that is exactly what I do, and it works because we score again, taking the lead.

Number thirty-eight on the Knights is about to fucking snap as I pick his pockets, stealing the puck away, and dish it to Malik Ravenwell, a foreword on my team. My legs are completely dead, and I'm dying to get off the ice. I'm hurting my team more than helping them right now.

Right before I reach the bench, I'm shoved hard from behind and into the boards, hitting it awkwardly because I wasn't expecting to be plowed into while changing out. My fists clench, and Coach nods at me, cocking his head to the side at number thirty-eight. I hate to admit that even without his approval, I planned on beating the ever-living shit out of this kid.

My blood pumps hard, and my heart races excitedly as I spin around. "I have been waiting all fucking night for this," I growl and spit on the ice.

"Waiting to get your ass kicked? I would love to do the honors," he chirps, and I don't hesitate to drop my gloves.

As a smile tugs at my lips, I welcome the adrenaline spiking in my veins and grab on to the collar of his jersey. I rear back and punch him straight in the ribs. He bends over, somehow surprised that I hit him.

Taking advantage of him bending at his waist, I rip his helmet off as he thrashes and fights to grab on to any part of me. It's too late though. There's not enough time for him to recover. He lost this fight the second he decided to start it.

My knuckles crash into his cheek, the side of his head, any part of him I can reach. He's so discombobulated that he can't land a single punch. It's okay; I'm doing it enough for the both of us.

The ref skates over and waits for us to stop—or rather for me to end it. But I'm not done yet. Letting up, I let thirty-eight hit me across the jaw to give the illusion of a fair fight. But the pain only eggs me on more. From the smile forming on this idiot's face, he thinks he actually earned it. How sad.

A smirk kicks the corner of my lips up, and I watch the moment thirty-eight realizes he is thoroughly fucked. He's the biggest guy on their team, and he probably thought he could take me. God, I love proving people wrong.

Pulling my elbow back, I smash my fist into his face over and over and over until he falls to the ground and red speckles the ice around us.

"Is this where you'll do the honors of kicking my ass?" I deeply snarl as I stand to my feet, victorious.

"All right, that's enough, Hawthorne," the ref warns me as he grabs my shoulders and starts skating backward, pulling me along with him.

Thirty-eight stays quiet—the first smart thing he's done tonight. He holds his side, and I wonder if maybe I shouldn't have gone so hard. But if I'm frank, I don't care; it's part of the game. Something comes over me when I start a fight, and I can't stop myself.

As the blood pounding in my ears begins to settle, I hear the crowd and my team shouting my nickname, one I earned from mercilessly dominating the ice.

The Beast.

"Beast!"

"Beast!"

"Beast!"

"Beast!"

The crowd bellows, the entire arena vibrating with praise for taking him down. Adrenaline courses through me, and my spine tingles at the sensations.

Fucking hell, I love hockey.

One of the linesmen skates over, handing me my equipment.

"Thank you," I grumble as I grab my stick, gloves, and helmet.

"Just couldn't help yourself, huh?" He laughs as he escorts me to my bench.

Shrugging, I laugh. "More like the other way around. He kept pushing me, and in my defense, he started it. I was just giving him what he wanted."

"Right." He chuckles, releasing me as I step through the board door, my team whistling for me.

They all pat me on the back and sing their praises, along with the crowd, as I walk through the tunnel to the locker room. I'm done in this game, and I won't be allowed back onto the ice.

When you drop gloves and fight in college hockey, it's an automatic game misconduct penalty, meaning I'm out for this game and, unfortunately, the next. Sometimes, the referees play nice and only give me misconduct. But my reputation doesn't usually encourage much grace.

Our team scores again, and by the end of the third period, we're crushing the Knights four to two, increasing our win streak to five games since the season started only a week and a half ago. No one expected our team to be dominating this early on in the season because we are relatively young in terms of strong talent.

The seniors are usually on the first line because they are the most talented players with the most experience, but for some reason, when us first-year students we came in, we took over. It's not like the rest of the team isn't talented because they are. We're just better.

The plus side of hockey is that different lines get time on the ice, so we aren't taking too much away from them. But they respect our grind and the fact that we are winning. They want that above anything else. The more we win, the more scouting our team gets from the pro league. And that is the most important part of it all. That's the dream for any one of us—getting to the big show.

But HEAU gets noticed by everyone. It doesn't matter what industry you're in; if you can get into this school, you're pretty much set for any goal you have in life. It doesn't mean every college hockey player attending HEAU gets to go pro. But it does mean they have a hell of a better chance than at any other university. I have no doubt that Malik and I will go pro after college.

Malik Ravenwell is my best friend on the team. We understand each other without having to say too many words. We know that we haven't had the best cards dealt to us our whole lives, but we still worked our asses off and got here.

He's a little shit with a hell of a reputation, but if you knew his story, you'd know that his coolness and harshness are just armor that he had to build around himself to survive. I know that because I had to do the same. But even I had more support than him, growing up.

After my family left when I was fifteen, I was practically all alone. But I still had Mrs. Pottinger, and her son, Charlie. Although I haven't called them by those names in years. I only refer to them as Mrs. Potts and Chip. Mrs. Potts was my family's chef and maid. She still technically is, I suppose, but rarely do I allow her to do anything for me.

She has tried to convince me more times than I can count to stop paying her, but that will never happen. I might not let her do any cleaning for me, but that doesn't mean I will stop taking care of her and Chip. I want them to have everything they need.

When I finally get home and step inside the quiet house, each step feels heavier than the last. My body is exhausted from tonight, more so than usual. But that probably has to do with the fucking stress headache I'm going to have to deal with tomorrow.

I'm smart, even more so than I let on. But for some goddamn reason, I am nearly failing my English class. My head coach and teacher are threatening that if my grade doesn't start to climb, my ass won't be taking the ice anymore. Which is a big fucking problem. Mainly because I plan to be playing professionally after this. If I'm not on the ice, I'm not getting seen.

I have a meeting with a tutor at the school's library at ten tomorrow morning. Hopefully, whoever it is can make enough of a difference. I've never struggled with my

English classes, and I don't quite understand why this curriculum doesn't click with my brain. I just need someone to fix it so I can get on with the season without the looming cloud of failure over my head.

Quietly, I walk through the foyer and reach the large sitting room, dropping my bags next to the oversize velvet sofa, hearing an echo through the house as they hit the ground. I meander into the kitchen, and something on the island catches my eye. The aroma of sweet chocolate invades my nose.

Flicking a light on, I see a Tupperware of chocolate chip cookies with a note propped up beside them. It reads, *Congrats on another win, Griff. We were cheering you on. Love, Mary and Chip.*

Lifting the transparent lid of the container, I snatch a cookie out and take a bite.

Fuck. These cookies are so good. I don't know how she keeps them so soft with a crispness on the outside. Regardless, they're perfect every time. Putting the lid on the Tupperware, I chug a glass of water before walking out of the kitchen, shutting the light off behind me.

This house has been in my family for a few generations, and it's breathtaking, but it's just too much for three people to live in. There are twenty beds, twelve and a half baths, an in-home movie theater, a basement that my parents transformed into an inside faux ice rink, a playroom filled with every toy a kid could want in a vaulted room with skylights. For God's sake, there are wings in our house. My room is on the upper level in the east wing. Chip and Mrs. Pottinger reside on the main floor in the east wing. The west wing is closed off, completely untouched.

My teammates have been begging me to let them move in, but I know better than that. They would throw the biggest party and get me in so much fucking trouble. On top of it, I hate having my space invaded. I don't mind parties, as long as they aren't in my house.

Running my fingers along the cool railing, I ascend the marble steps, veering left toward the east wing. Pushing the double-door entrance open, I step into the hallway and hear the doors click shut behind me, sealing me in my personal slice of paradise.

Over the years, I have turned this part of the house into my safe haven. No one comes in here, not Chip, not Mrs. Potts, just me. I like knowing that it's just mine and only mine.

Twisting the gold handle, I push the door open to my room, shutting it behind me. I drop my sweats, tear off my T-shirt, and throw them in my hamper across the room. Grabbing the corner of my comforter and sheets, I pull them back and slide between them in only boxers, loving the cooling touch of the golden silk.

Powering the TV on, I turn on whatever professional game is playing, happy to fall asleep to the sound of pucks and skates on the ice.

You've got to be fucking kidding me.

I'm meeting up with my tutor right now at the library, and the second I see her, I know this isn't going to work out. I recognize her not just from campus, but also from games, where she practically presses her tits against the glass to get our attention.

Rubbing the back of my neck, I approach her table, and her smile widens as I wrap my hands around the back of an empty chair, leaning against it. She's practically drooling. Although this is nice for my ego, it's not doing shit for my grades.

"Oh my God, I didn't know you would be my new student!" she squeals and feigns naivety because I know damn well she was aware it was me coming.

She's wearing a low-cut tank top that plunges far below the average neckline, a full face of makeup, and a pleather skirt with heels. I don't know about you, but I don't typically see many people dressed like that for a tutoring session. I'm not saying it's impossible, but it's more improbable. She knows what she's trying to do. But it's just not going to work on me.

"Yeah …" I trail off and take a seat across from her.

It's not that I'm not into her; sure, she's cute. But I don't have the time for the clinginess oozing out of her every pore. When my hand doesn't do the job, I occasionally hook up with someone, but it's rare. I can count on two fingers the number of partners I've had. It's harder to make that list than it is to get into this school, and that's saying something. No offense to her, but she isn't the type of girl I want to fuck. She is the girl who has aspirations of being a WAG—a partner of a pro athlete—and I have zero intentions of granting that wish to her.

"So, I know a bit about what you need help with. Your professor passed that along. But what are you looking to get out of this?" She bats her eyelashes at me and leans forward against the desk between us.

Annoyance quickly turns into anger at the amount of my time she is wasting right now. This whole fucking meeting is pointless. Taking a slow inhale, I try to calm my racing heart and growing rage.

My temper hasn't always been my greatest source of control. But I'm trying not to completely jump to conclusions about her ability to do her job. If she has what it takes to fix my problems and focus on the tasks at hand, I will put up with a little flirtation.

"Just to get my grade up so it doesn't affect my playing time," I say coolly.

She pushes the tip of the pen between her lips and hums, "Mmhmm."

Jesus Christ, could she be more obvious?

"I've been struggling with the work for the final," I admit, giving her everything she needs to know in order to do her job.

"Yeah, totally," she sighs. "Do you have any distractions impeding you from fully focusing?"

"Like what?" I ask, rolling my eyes at where I think this is heading.

She smirks and asks, "Like a job? A girlfriend?"

And *there* it is.

"We're done here." I laugh and push off of the chair.

Her jaw drops, and her eyes widen. "W-what?"

It's hilarious that she doesn't understand why she's being fired.

Slowly, I step around the table, holding her eye contact the entire time. Placing my hand down on the tabletop, my arm muscles rippling, I inch forward and close the distance between us, feeling her breath on my lips. She is practically panting; she wants this so badly. Maybe I would consider her if I didn't need help and was looking for a hookup. But hockey is too important to me, and some random girl isn't going to mess with my future.

Inching forward, I lean further down, feeling the slightest graze of her lips. Her eyes drift shut, and I whisper, "I'm not fucking you."

Her eyes fly open, and she scoffs like that isn't what she wants. Her shoulders fall, and she stutters, "I-I w-was not trying to fuck you, Griffin."

"Is that why you were going to kiss me and are completely out of breath right now? Sure." I chuckle and push off the table, standing up straight. "Nice meeting you …"

I would say her name, but I didn't even catch it, or maybe I don't remember it. Oh well, I don't have time to learn it because I'm now back at square one.

Coach might kill me for firing her, but he can get over it because I'm not putting up with that shit for the remainder of the semester. Fucking hell, now, I have to find a new tutor.

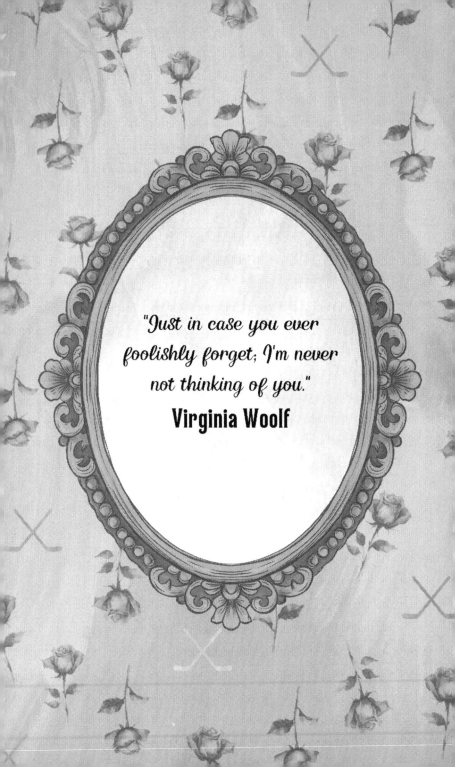

"Just in case you ever foolishly forget; I'm never not thinking of you."

Virginia Woolf

chapter three
blair

"Thank you. I really needed this," I praise Lumi. With a proud smile, he hands over the delicious liquid energy from Cogsworth Coffee. "You are welcome, my love."

I'm exhausted this morning. I picked up a shift last night at the club for my coworker Grace, who called out sick. I should have been out of there by one a.m., but didn't leave until about two thirty. Don't get me wrong; I made a lot of extra tips from how busy it was, but I'm dead right now.

Sipping on my hot mocha latte, we walk into our eight a.m. English class and up the stairs to our seats near the top of the bowl. It's the best seat in any class. Far enough from the professor that you can people-watch when classmates are entertaining and the teacher is boring, but not too far back that the teacher thinks you're screwing off. It's the perfect middle ground. But I don't think it would matter where I sat. Dr. Schrute knows that I take every class very seriously.

I can't afford to fuck around because I can't bear to lose my partial scholarship. That being said, I also don't need to pay attention to every word Dr. Schrute says because I've already studied and read at least the upcoming five chapters. I'm always ahead. It helps to know the information before digging deeper into it because I grasp it even more the second time and am better off.

We're early, as usual. I don't love the idea of having everyone's eyes on me, so if I'm the first to arrive and the last to leave, I can avoid walking in front of everyone.

It's also why I took college Speech while still in high school. Instead of getting up in front of a few hundred people to give a speech, I had to give it in front of forty. I would have hated to have to take it any other way. Attention is the last thing I crave, and I avoid the spotlight at all costs.

I might be a nerd and proud, but I'm not the raise-my-hand-and-answer-every-question kind of nerd. I would rather quietly be the smartest person in the room, harnessing my brain like a secret weapon.

Dr. Schrute spends the next hour talking about Jennette McCurdy's autobiography *I'm Glad My Mom's Dead* and how we could find inspiration for our final project. I've already read it. It was incredible and heartbreaking at the same time. I can't imagine being raised by a mom who doesn't truly love or care for you.

My mom tragically passed away when I was only three years old. I have almost no memory of her, but when I was growing up, my dad told me stories. He loved her so deeply and always reminded me of her. I wish we'd had more time together. I wish I remembered more of her, but I never suffered in her absence. My dad ensured that, filling my childhood with laughter and love.

Our final project for the year is to write a twenty-page autobiography about our past, present, and future. I've already started it, practically finished, even though I still have nearly four months to turn it in.

Dr. Schrute leaves the last ten minutes for us to discuss the book with our seatmates, which, of course, almost no one does, each little group falling into a conversation of their own. Lumi bumps my arm and pulls my head out of the book I'm buried in.

"What?" I ask, not tearing my gaze from the movie playing out in the pages before me.

"Did you hear what he just said?" Lumi aggressively whispers at me, looking down at a group of guys a few rows down from us.

"No. And why would I care what a few jocks are talking about?" I scoff and ignore him, trying to get back into my book.

Lumi's voice is the opposite of a whisper as he rises to his feet and announces to the entire goddamn class, "Blair could tutor you."

My hand lashes out and slaps his arm hard, leaving my fingers tingling. I hiss, "What the hell are you doing?"

Panic blooms in my chest and snakes around my throat.

"Shh. I'm helping you live out here in the real world

with the rest of us," he murmurs as the entire room faces us, including the row Lumi was eavesdropping on.

God really dumped an entire bottle of sexy into our university's hockey team. That whole goddamn group is too hot for their own good. I recognize them from the posters plastered all over campus. *The HEAU Hockey Legends*.

The one with black hair and almost-purple eyes checks me out, and I consider throwing my book at him, but I wouldn't want to do that to the poor book.

The guy next to him turns and glances up at us. His hazel eyes lock on mine, and I swear I can see fucking sunshine shimmering in them. His overgrown brown hair flows off his head with such ease, perfectly messy. My chest clenches, and I try to ignore my innate attraction to the giant before me.

Why am I so bothered by how hot he is? Because I know his type. I hate that I'm captivated by him, and I've heard enough about him to have an opinion. Rich. Vain. Quick-tempered. An asshole. He is the type of guy who uses his charm and appeal to get whatever he wants in life.

The purple-eyed guy and the brunette guy rise from their seats. Turning to us, they give us their unwanted, undivided attention. The black-haired one seems amused, and the other one, who I recognize, looks rather annoyed. Griffin Hawthorne, the legend of all Legends.

I have had no choice but to overhear from squealing girls on campus that he's hot, which, to be fair, is true. He's rich as hell. He's undoubtedly going to go pro after college, and he's already being looked at by multiple pro teams. He lives in a mansion near campus that no one besides a few select teammates have stepped foot in. And he is completely unattainable, which means every girl wants him. No offense to him, but I'm not one of them. I don't have time for distractions when I barely have time to sleep.

Griffin's thick eyebrows pinch together as he opens his mouth; a deep, gruff voice that tingles my spine asks, "You're a tutor?"

"Nope," I answer before looking away and quickly throwing my stuff into my backpack.

Lumi grabs my arm as I try to walk by him, and he says loud enough for the entire room to hear, "She might not tutor officially, but I bet that she has the highest percentage in this class."

Curiosity forces Griffin's gaze to stay on me. "What's your grade?" he asks me as I sling my backpack over my shoulder.

Remaining silent, I debate on bolting straight out of the room and pretending this conversation isn't happening. Or to toot my own horn for once.

Lumi answers before I can make a decision, "One hundred percent."

Griffin's face distorts with doubt, and he squints, studying me skeptically. "Bullshit. No fucking way."

Shrugging, I slip past Lumi and step into the aisle to descend the stairs. But Griffin rushes out of his row and blocks my path.

"Jesus ..." I scoff, a bit startled at how the hell he got here so fast.

Standing my ground, I look straight up at him and

relax my face, attempting to hide that my heart is trying to break through my ribs right now from all the onlookers.

"You have a perfect grade?" he questions, looking down at me with an intense stare. It's intimidating, but I've never been one to fold under pressure.

Swallowing my fear, I lower my shoulders. At this point, we are the center of attention. I imagine I'm at work, where I fake confidence.

"Yes, I do. Now, if you will excuse me," I say, meeting his stare. "I have somewhere to be."

He ignores me completely, and I roll my eyes at his unwavering stance.

"Dr. Schrute, is she serious? Is that even possible?" Griffin turns and asks our professor, who has a big grin and is apparently enjoying our conversation.

Proudly, he says, "It is very possible, and I won't disclose a student's grades without their consent."

Griffin faces me again, and from the challenge in his eyes, I can tell he's not just going to let this go, and I don't feel like being in this standoff all day long.

Grinning, I look around Griffin and monotonically say, "Please just tell him so we can get this over with and I can leave."

Dr. Schrute nods with my consent and confesses, "Yes, she has a perfect grade in my class. Blair, I know you haven't done it before, but I fully believe you would make an excellent tutor."

What is this? A prank show? Even Dr. Schrute is in on it.

Griffin turns back to me with hope in his hazel eyes.

Unfortunately for him, I am going to squash it. This whole situation is draining, and I still have a long day ahead of me. I have another class and a mountain of homework, and I work tonight on top of it all.

"That is kind of you, Dr. Schrute. But I don't have time to tutor anyone."

My gaze flicks up to Griffin, and the look in his eyes sends shivers through me. He's looking at me like I'm a puzzle he needs to solve.

"Excuse me," I say, descending a few more steps until only one remains between us, and he suddenly seems even bigger than before.

He is taller than I realized, towering over me, even with the extra inches I'm getting from the step.

Griffin smirks and doesn't budge an inch. "Come on. You have to be a tutor. It's unfair to your classmates to not help those less brain fortunate than you."

"Like I said"—my grip tightens on my backpack strap as my confidence wavers—"I'm not a tutor. You'll have to find someone else. I'm sorry."

Stepping forward, I place my hand on his side, feeling his muscles tighten and ripple beneath my fingers, and push my way through, knowing that I only get past him because he's letting me.

Moving down the stairs quickly, I exit the classroom and hear Lumi behind me, hot on my heels.

"You are crazy for not taking that offer," he grumbles while catching up to me.

Rolling my eyes, I feel someone brush against my other side, and I sigh. How naive of me to think that conversation was over.

"I'll pay you," Griffin blurts out, slowing down to match my stride.

Fuck.

There are a million reasons I shouldn't take this job. I really don't have time to be a tutor right now. I've never done it before; I wouldn't even know where to start. But that one green reason is almost enough to convince me it's a good idea. It's unbelievable what you might consider reasonable when you are as desperate for cash as I am.

"I don't need one hundred percent in this class; I just need to maintain above a C," he says, trying to make it seem better—and I hate to admit that he's succeeding.

My pride gets the better of me even though the extra money does sound great. "I'm sorry, but I can't help you."

He strides ahead and spins around, stepping in front of me with his hands up, blocking my way.

Why won't he drop this?

"I'm not interested," I say, filling the silence between us.

"Look, I've already had to fire a tutor for being a flirt and just wanting to get in my pants, refusing to focus on the work. If you think this is a game to get you in my bed, it's not. I need to get my grades up, and my future depends on them. Name your price, and I'll pay you. I just need someone to help me out, and as you said"—he looks at Lumi and then back at me—"you're the best in the class. Which means I need you."

Lumi obnoxiously clears his throat next to me, and it takes everything in me not to slap him silly.

I wasn't even considering him trying to make a move on me because I have zero intention of pursuing that.

Clearly, he's not attempting to get into my pants, or he wouldn't have fired his last tutor for trying that exact thing.

No strings. No flirting. Just business. I can do that. But my time is worth the money.

I throw out a crazy number, hoping we can negotiate for at least a fifth of the amount. "Five hundred dollars a session."

He doesn't blink before saying, "Done."

"Fine," I huff, flushed because he actually just agreed to that price.

This money will help out a lot. It should keep us afloat so we can stop drowning in bills—at least for a while. Hopefully, he's a slow learner, so I can stretch this extra income out a bit longer and rake in the money all semester long.

He holds his hand out between us with his empty palm up. Staring at it briefly, I slide my hand in his and shake it gently.

He busts out laughing and says, "Your phone. Give me your phone."

Oh.

My face burns, and I pull my cell out of my pocket and unlock it, opening up a new text while trying to ignore the growing lump in my throat from the embarrassment.

Handing it to him, I glance up. "Here."

He takes it from me, still grinning as he types into it. A second later, his phone chimes.

"I'll be out of town the rest of this week for games, but I'll let you know when I'm back, and we can meet up for our first session. Does that work?" he asks before looking over my head and nodding at someone behind me.

Turning, I see three other hockey players waiting for him. When I spin back around, he hands me my phone, and I take it, saving his contact information under Griffin.

"Sounds good, yeah," I mumble, still in a bit of shock that I agreed to this at all.

"Thank you. Seriously, I owe you," he says before walking away.

Did he forget that he's paying me for this? He won't owe me anything as long as he holds up his end of our deal.

The club is packed tonight as I walk into the building. I still have to change and slap a little makeup on before my shift starts, and I only have about five minutes. Somehow, Griffin holding me up after class earlier made every single part of my day run later than planned.

Entering the back room, I throw my backpack in my locker and pull out my outfit for tonight—a super-short skirt that shows the bottom of my butt cheeks and a strappy black top that tucks into my skirt. If it wasn't for it being so low-cut, I wouldn't have worn it, but the more skin you show, the more money you make. It's simple.

The strappy, long-sleeved top hugs my arms and chest as I put it on, followed by the metallic black skirt and stockings that stop at my upper thighs, held up by tiny suspenders connected to my shirt beneath the skirt.

Throwing on some blush, mascara, smoky eye shadow, and red lipstick, I give myself a pep talk in the mirror before I have to face the vultures.

"You've got this, babe! Look at you! You're hot! Go get those tips!" I whisper-shout at myself.

As much as I usually don't love social interaction at all, it's different when it comes to this. It's like I get to play a character that doesn't shy away from the spotlight and attention. I have to be flirty and sweet, even when I don't want to because that's how you get the cash these guys are happy to hand out.

Shutting my locker, I slide on a pair of black heels and step out of the quietness and into the chaos that awaits me.

The music is constantly blaring, and somehow, after a minute or so, I manage to tune it out. But I think that comes with the territory of working in this environment all the time. As I approach the bar, a hand wraps around my waist, and I cringe inside, trying not to show it.

"Hey, baby, how much for a lap dance from your pretty little self?" The middle-aged guy slurs his words.

Smiling sweetly, I fully slip into character. I giggle and say, "Oh, honey, you got the wrong girl. I just make the drinks here. But that girl right there? That's Daisy. I'm sure she would love to give you a dance."

Standing only a few feet away, Daisy hears me and sashays over, wearing only a bikini bottom and colored pasties. "I'm Daisy. How can I be of service?"

"Oh, oh, oh," he whistles. "Damn, you are fine, Ms. Daisy."

His hand drifts off my waist and onto hers as she leads him toward an empty seat.

Stepping behind the bar, I finally take a breath and exhale after that guy's sleazy hand is gone from my body.

"Hey, B!" Erica calls out as she makes a round of shots.

Erica has been here forever. She's the one who trained me, and she also manages the bar side of the club. She's tall, blonde, and gorgeous. She taught me all the tips and tricks on how to milk every dollar from the suckers who walk in here. She's also like the mom of the bartenders, always making sure that the customers aren't too handsy and that we are always taken care of.

"Hey, Tia!" I answer back, using her fake name at work, as someone approaches the bar top.

"Hey, can I get two tall Bud Lights, please?" the scruffy younger guy asks me as I meet his eyes.

"You got it!" I smile and grab two glasses, pouring perfect beers before sliding them across the counter to him. "Sixteen dollars."

He slides a twenty and a five to me and winks. "Keep the change."

Pretending every tip is the best and biggest one I've ever gotten, I smile and praise his generosity. "Oh my gosh, thank you so much!"

He nods proudly, grabs his glasses, and walks away.

I repeat variations of that exact interaction with guys all night until exhaustion weighs on my eyes and my shift ends. Six hours of work, and I made two hundred ninety-eight dollars. It's not my best earnings for a night, but it's still nearly three hundred dollars, which I didn't have when I walked in here.

It takes all of two minutes for me to pass out when I get home, ready to do the same thing all over again tomorrow.

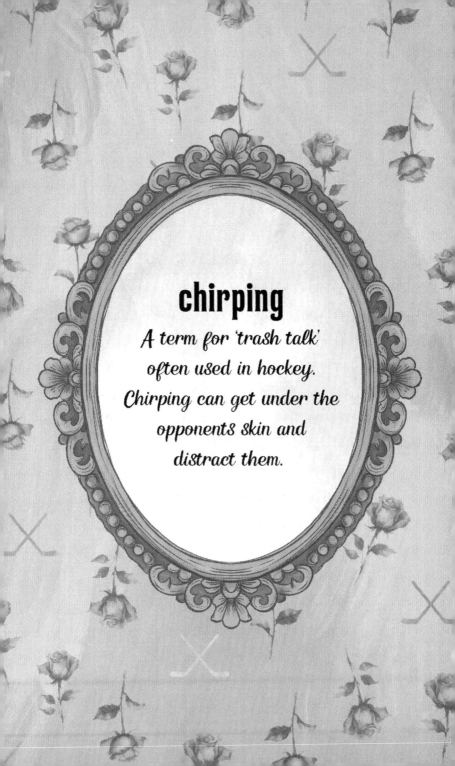

chirping

A term for 'trash talk'
often used in hockey.
Chirping can get under the
opponents skin and
distract them.

chapter four
griffin

"Fire your new tutor yet?" Malik laughs as I skate up next to him, my legs burning with each stride, completely gassed.

"Not yet." I smirk and bump my shoulder into his as I glide past him. "But we haven't even had a session yet."

"There's still time," he snarks and pushes away, scooping a puck up with this stick.

"Ha-ha," I mock him, picking his pocket and stealing the puck.

Coach blows his whistle, and the team skates over to him, silent and ready for his instruction. We leave tomorrow for a doubleheader weekend against our biggest rival, the Knights, and everyone is wound a bit tighter because of it. They nearly beat us the last time we faced them in their barn, and we don't want that to happen again. The problem is, our teams are so goddamn similar in talent, grit, and dedication. We might as well be fighting for our lives when we play against each other. We are both out for blood.

"All right, boys, the bus leaves tomorrow at eight a.m. Please do not give me a reason to bench you for being late; I want every one of you on the ice tomorrow night. Am I understood?" He pauses for our response.

We answer him with a slew of, "Yes, sir," and, "Yes, Coach."

"Good. See you boys tomorrow. Bruce, take us out," he instructs our assistant coach, who steps forward from his command.

"Legends on three. One. Two. Three," he shouts over us.

"LEGENDS!" we shout in unison.

I wanted to be on this dream team since I was old enough to understand college hockey. The best of the best go to school and play here. They truly are making legends here with legacies that will live forever on and off the ice. The diplomas they give out at graduation should be a golden check with a blank line that you can fill in with whatever you want. Because having this school on your résumé is the only thing you need to do whatever the fuck you want in life. All I've ever really wanted is to make it to the big show—the National Hockey League—and this school will get me there.

Now, all I have to do is not get benched for bad grades. I've always coasted through school with minimal effort and never had any issues. Until now, that is. I swear this professor has it out for me. Okay, maybe that's a bit of a stretch. But I don't see why opening up about my feelings will help me in the long run. It sure isn't going to help me play hockey.

The professor decided to focus this entire semester on autobiographies and self-reflection, and our main project requires us to write a twenty-page paper about our past, present, and future. Our assignments and homework are pieces of the final project's puzzle.

I'm a smart guy. I really am. But there is something about digging into the past that makes me want to take a skate blade to the throat.

Hopefully, this new tutor of mine will make everything easier. Honestly, I'm looking forward to having a session with her. For one, she's more intelligent than everyone else in the class. Second, she literally ran away from me because she didn't want to tutor me so badly. That might make someone else shy away from wanting to work with her, but not me. I usually have the opposite problem with tutors, like the last one I just fired.

Her immediate disdain was precisely what I wanted to see because if she's going to make my grade better, then we both need to be able to focus, which seems to be her top priority.

Five hundred dollars is a bit fucking steep, but I'd have agreed to a thousand if she requested it. There isn't an amount I wouldn't dole out to get my grade up. Money isn't an issue; I'm not worried about it, and she needs it. We're a match made in heaven.

"What's the jail time for murder?" Malik catches his breath, heaving as he skates up beside me next to the bench for a time-out.

"Pretty sure it's prison time, but more years than that shithead is worth," I scoff, trying to encourage him to cool off before he takes the head off of Knights' number twenty-nine.

"Did you see him? He was trying to split my ribs in fucking half with his stick and elbow." Malik is starting to turn red with every breath, and if I cared, I would be concerned for that player's well-being because he fucked with the wrong guy.

Malik is malicious without provocation. But twenty-nine has been spending the entire last period poking the bear, and he's about to get fucking mauled to death. As entertaining as a pissed-off Malik is, we have to win this game, and we need him to stay on the ice, meaning he can't end up in the penalty box as long as we can help it.

Coach spends the next minute talking us through a couple of errors and corrections we can make in our play. We need to tighten our passes up, and we need to be quicker with them too. We are hesitating with our decisions, allowing the Knights a chance to step in and steal the puck before we make our move.

The ref blows the whistle, and we skate over to the dot on the ice just outside our offensive zone for puck drop.

46

The second the puck hits the ice, Dean Kensington dishes the puck back to Asher Kensington, who takes off into the zone. Speeding up, I cut off their defender, opening the lane up for Elias Lancaster, our center, who doesn't waste a second of the opportunity and sinks it into the net, right through the goalie's five-hole. We hold them off from scoring the rest of the game while getting two more goals of our own, sealing the win in our books.

Leaning my head on the chair of my seat in this comfy charter bus, I pull my phone out and start typing to my new tutor.

> Hey, are you free tomorrow for our first session?

I don't even know what our meetings will look like. I hope she'll go over the previous tests and assignments, tell me where the hell I went wrong, and then tell me how to do better next time. When she explains everything, I need her to treat me like I'm five years old.

I dread discussing the parts of class I've been avoiding —the self-reflection and digging into our pasts. I don't want to do any digging. Keep the shovels far away from me. I live in the present. I don't fantasize about what's to come, and I definitely don't spend time visiting ghosts. I don't want to start now.

I mean, I guess I could lie about everything in my papers and assignments. I could make up a story and pretend that it's real. No one would know the difference. That's probably a better option than the half-assed work I've been submitting.

My phone vibrates.

> Tutor: Yes, I am. What time would you like to meet up?

I respond immediately.

> Preferably not before 10 a.m. so I can at least sleep in.

> Tutor: Would noon work?

> Nope. I have weight lifting. Then practice at 5. By then, I'll be starving and will need to eat, or my brain will be worthless. How about, like, 7:30?

> Tutor: Are you serious? That's so late.

> It's not that late, but it's funny that you think so. I'll pay you extra tomorrow if you can make 8 p.m. work. Six hundred.

> Tutor: Fine. 8 p.m. Sharp. Where do you want to meet?

I should offer the library, but it will be closed for the night by then. We could meet at a coffee shop or diner, but I don't want to have to deal with any HEAU hockey fans or puck bunnies. So, I offer the one place I typically keep to myself.

> Here's my address. Don't worry. I'll be ready and set up at my dining table.

> Tutor: There is no way in hell I'm going to your house. You could be a creep for all I know.

I chuckle, taken aback by her response. She seemed so meek and shy in person, and for her to be snarky behind a screen is a pleasant surprise. I like this side of her. I need someone to tell me like it is.

> I'm not a creep, thank you very much.

> Tutor: Oh, perfect. Then, I won't worry at all.

Am I talking to the same girl who sits quietly in the back of class? What the hell is going on?

> If it makes you feel better, bring a friend. They can hang out while we work.

She doesn't answer right away, and I swipe out of our messages and get distracted playing a game on my phone while waiting. Before I know it, two hours have passed when she finally gets back to me.

> Tutor: Deal. See you then.

Sweet! I don't know why that felt more victorious than

our win tonight. Maybe it's because I won't get to keep winning on the ice if I don't start performing off of it.

I like her message and return to my phone, falling asleep a few minutes later.

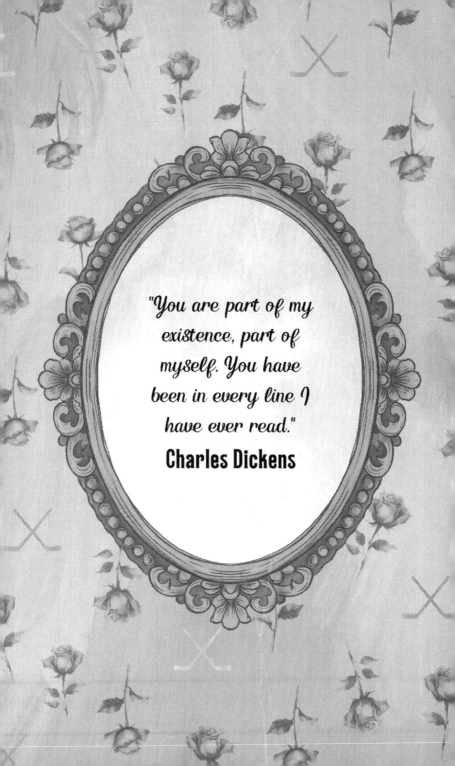

"You are part of my existence, part of myself. You have been in every line I have ever read."

Charles Dickens

chapter five
blair

"Shut up. Shut the fuck up right now," Lumi whisper-shouts at me as we near our destination and turn into a never-ending private driveway lined with tall green hedges.

"Holy shit." The words fall from my parted lips of their own accord as I try to keep my jaw off of the ground.

A gigantic house starts coming into view—and I use the word *house* loosely. Let's call it what it is—a mansion. Well, technically, from how much land it's sitting on, it would properly be called a manor. *Hawthorne Manor.* It's three stories of beautiful light-brown bricks. Lumi pulls into the circular driveway with the most enormous fountain I've ever seen in the center of it. This place is bigger than some of our buildings on campus, and that's really saying something.

Arched windows cover the front of the house, and I

would be lying if I said I wasn't dying to see every inch inside of this place. It's unreal.

"Am I dreaming right now?" Lumi breathily asks.

"If you are, I'm in it with you. But seriously, is this guy in the mob or something? Are his parents royalty?" Word vomit flows from my mouth, and I catch myself, taking a breath and calming down.

I've just never seen anything like this. Of course, I've seen photos of places similar, but to see it in real life is entirely different. It has a presence of its own. It's impressive and *intimidating*.

One of the front double doors opens, and Griffin steps out, wearing joggers, a Legends T-shirt, and a backward hat. He smiles as he raises his hand and waves. The hem of his shirt lifts off of his defined lower abs, and I have to physically stop myself from staring. It doesn't matter if I want to acknowledge it or not; he's hot. That's not even an opinion; it's just plain fact.

Still in shock, I lift my hand and wave back.

Lumi reaches over and gently grabs my arm, pulling my attention his way. "Real question: what are the chances that you think he could be gay?"

"What?" I chuckle, taken entirely by surprise at his question, although I should know better by now. "I don't know. Find out for yourself."

He sighs and looks past me, admiring Griffin. "If I knew it wouldn't jeopardize this job for you, I so would."

"Fair point," I say and grab my backpack. "Let's get this over with."

"Show some enthusiasm. The entire campus would kill

to be you right now," Lumi mumbles as I throw the door open and step into the dark and cool evening air.

Lumi begged me to dress up for this tutoring session, but I absolutely did *not* take his advice. I dressed comfortably, donning a pair of yoga pants and an oversize HEAU T-shirt. I'm already completely out of my element, and I don't want to make it worse by wearing something revealing and tight.

"Hey, glad you found the place okay," Griffin calls out, jogging down the fifteen steps to the first landing and then down the final ten steps to us.

At least I'll get a little workout from climbing these stairs when I come here.

"Yeah, super easy. Your house is amazing, by the way," Lumi gushes, not holding back any sweetness in his voice.

"Thanks," he mumbles and rubs the back of his neck.

Is that *humility* showing?

I can't imagine that someone living in a house like this can even be humble. He has the world at his fingertips, and I guess, now, I have him wrapped around mine until this is all said and done. Maybe I should have asked for more than five hundred.

"I can take that for you." Griffin gestures toward my backpack.

I sling it over my shoulder. "I'm good. Thanks."

He smiles and lifts his hands in defeat before spinning on his heel and starting back up the stairs, Lumi hot on his tail.

Maybe Lumi wasn't the best person to bring with me. I laugh to myself. Any red flags Griffin has will seem bright green to Lumi.

Thank God for all the time I spend on my feet at work because these stairs are kind of a bitch. Griffin takes them two at a time, and Lumi, now out of breath, drifts back to walk alongside me.

"It, like, has to be big, right?" Lumi murmurs and nudges my shoulder with his.

"What does?" I ask as my eyebrows pinch together.

He stops dead in his tracks and glares at me, then smirks, and it clicks.

"Stop that!" I whisper-scold him, slapping his arm.

He smiles and catches back up to me as we reach the front door Griffin is holding open for us.

"Thank you," I say as I pass through the threshold and inhale sharply, examining the entryway.

Dark natural hardwood lines every inch of the floor I can see. To my left, a massive sitting room with furniture that looks like it's never been used fills the modern and classy room, a giant rug nearly covering the center of it. To my right, the most extensive and elaborate kitchen I've ever seen takes up the entire space, continuing around a corner, seemingly endless. Vault ceilings and a hundred windows must illuminate the house with natural light during the day.

But the most magnificent part is the white marble staircase that splits in two directions, and I can't see where they end. I want to explore this place and map it out because I am definitely going to get lost.

"So, Griffin, what the hell do your parents do for a living? Also, are they looking to adopt an adult?" Lumi asks, and reality slaps me in the face, pulling me out of my stupor.

Oh my God, he is so going to get me fired.

Griffin chuckles hauntingly, looking off to the side as he answers, "My mom invented a sports drink and founded the company behind it, and my dad invented a gadget that the military uses."

"What drink?" Lumi's nosy-ass asks.

"Elixir," he murmurs.

Lumi digs a bottle from his backpack. "You mean this?"

Griffin nods, glancing away.

Elixir is the most popular sports drink in the entire world. They are the sponsored beverage for, like, every professional sport. Griffin's not just rich. He's *rich*, rich.

"Well, that's amazing. Your parents sound like the ultimate power couple." Lumi chuckles before mumbling, "Although they could still very well be in the mob."

Griffin doesn't laugh, and Lumi's face falls flat instantly, like there might be any truth in his wild accusation.

"Please don't kill me," Lumi begs, and Griffin's stone-like demeanor cracks with a smile.

"My family is not in the mob, I can assure you," he says, grinning as he stalks across the wide-open corridor and turns, walking through an archway.

"Don't touch anything and behave!" I scold Lumi as we trail behind Griffin, following him into the next room.

Jesus Christ.

This dining room is larger than my entire house.

"Will this work?" Griffin asks, gesturing to the large oak table that seats fourteen people.

"Yeah," I answer and drop my bag on the table in front of the chair closest to me.

"Sweet. I'll be right back," Griffin says and walks back out of the room.

Lumi stops him. "Can I get a glass of water?"

He nods. "Be my guest."

Lumi blushes, and I roll my eyes as he kindly replies, "Sweet. Thank you! And where can I find a living room with a TV?"

"You passed it when we walked in. Follow me. I'll show you. I have to use the remote to bring it up," Griffin says casually, as if any of that made sense.

"I'm sorry?" Lumi voices the confusion for the both of us.

"It rises out of the entertainment center," he says quizzically, as if everyone's TV does that.

"Oh, right. Of course it does." Lumi smiles and follows a befuddled Griffin.

Leaving me to peaceful silence, I begin unloading my backpack and setting my stuff up. I can't imagine living her. I would never have stress or sadness.

An aching pain twists my chest. I wish my life were this easy. A bitter resentment toward Griffin and the life he was born into tugs my lips downward.

He is taking all of this for granted. I know he has hockey, but aside from that, he has all the time in the world to focus on his grades, yet he's still failing. If I didn't have to work almost full-time just to stay in school, I would have one hundred percent in every one of my classes, not just English.

"All right, do you need anything? Water?" Griffin's

deep voice slices through my silent suffering, and I try not to let my sudden jealousy affect my reaction.

"I'm okay. Thank you." I smile politely as he sets his stack of papers, laptop, and pens down beside mine.

"Cool," he says, pulling out his chair and taking a seat.

I follow suit and drag the heavy wooden chair back before sinking down onto the cushioned pillow.

I'm prepared; of course I am. I might not have tutored someone before, but that doesn't mean I can't do it perfectly. If I set my mind to it, I can do anything, including turning this jock into the smartest guy on the team.

Having already drafted an entire plan for how tonight will go, I turn toward him and ask, "Do you have the assignments and papers that we've done so far? I want to review them and see what you need to improve."

He nods and starts his computer. "I'll email them to you."

As he compiles his documents into a digital folder, I can't help but realize how gigantic this man is. As I sit next to him, he is towering over me. Not only that, but everything about him is ... big. His arms bulge in his shirt, so thick that I could probably wrap only half of my hand around one of them. It's like every inch of him was created with extra parts.

I'm not ogling him. I'm just stating the obvious.

"Email?" he asks.

"Blair Adams at H-E-A-U dot U-S," I respond, and he types it in.

"Sent."

My laptop dings a second later, and I pull up his email

and see fourteen attachments. I want to go over these later when I can really dig into them. It would be weird if he sat silently while I pored over his work for an hour.

"Thank you," I mumble and add the email to a new folder titled *Griffin Tutor*.

"Now what?" he asks, incessantly tapping his pen.

Pulling a printed version of our study guide for Friday's test out of my backpack, I set it between us.

"Have you filled out your study guide yet?" I ask.

His eyes widen, and his face contorts into shock, similar to what deer look like when they are blinded by headlights.

"I'll take that as a no." I chuckle and pull the stapled study guide I prepared from my bag. "This is a copy, so you can keep it. We have a quiz on Friday. Read this until you have practically memorized it. Mark up and highlight the parts you feel we should review further."

"Yes, ma'am," he says with a smile and slides the packet fully in front of him, immediately circling a thousand things on the first page.

In the meantime, I pull up my current draft of our next paper due. We have to write a five-page paper about our goals for the near and far future and the plans we want to accomplish. I'm nearly finished with mine, but I feel like it's missing that perfect conclusion that ties the paper up in a bow. I just haven't quite figured out what that will be. It's not due until the end of the month, so I still have over two weeks before I have to submit it.

Once Griffin finishes decorating every page with question marks, he says, "Okay, I think I'm done."

Griffin genuinely seems to understand most of the

guide when I finish word-vomiting and peppering him with follow-up questions. Glancing up at him, I find him staring intently at me, smiling proudly from ear to ear.

"What?" I murmur.

"Nothing. It's just the first time this semester that I don't feel like a complete idiot in this class." He hesitates and studies me briefly. "So, thank you," he says excitedly, kicking back in his chair.

"You're welcome. We still have a ways to go, but you have promise," I say honestly.

Part of me expected him to ask me to help him cheat or do his homework for him. But he actually seems to want to put in the work, and I respect that.

Checking the time on my laptop, I gasp. "Shit, it's already almost ten."

"Yeah?" Griffin asks, confused.

"I have to get going. But I think we should meet up again before Friday to make sure you're good to go for the test. I also want to see your draft for the paper due at the end of the month," I request as I shove all of my stuff into my backpack.

He rubs the back of his neck again, and I fear I know the response that's coming, so I beat him to it.

"You haven't started?"

He points at me and shyly says, "That would be correct."

"Okay, there's still time. But you need to start drafting it," I say before taking off out of the room and walking toward the entrance. "Try to have your bullet points done by our next session so we can plan when you'll actually write it out."

"Umm, okay. Yeah, sounds good," he agrees, walking beside me calmly with long strides as I practically jog.

"Lumi!" I call out as we approach the living room.

The couch comes into view, and I spot Lumi passed the fuck out, drooling on one of the lavish throw pillows.

"Lumi, wake up. We've got to go, like, now," I ramble.

His eyes fly open, and he jumps up, immediately checking his phone. "Oh shit. Yeah, we do."

He wipes his mouth, and his face bursts into flames. "So sorry about that," he apologizes and wipes his drool off of the pillow.

Griffin chuckles. "Don't worry about it."

My chest tightens as I look at the elaborate wood clock above the ornate doorframe. I hate being late to anything, and I have ten minutes to make a thirteen-minute drive to the club before my shift starts.

"I'll text you to schedule the next one. Let me know what days or times work better," I inform him as I throw his door open and step outside.

"Wait!" Griffin calls out, and I spin around, watching him pull his wallet from his pocket. "I owe you." He whips out six one-hundred-dollar bills and extends his arm. "Worth every penny. Seriously, thank you."

"No problem." I smile, grab the cash, and take off down the steps toward Lumi's car with him right beside me.

Throwing the door open, I hop in and text my boss.

I'm so sorry. I'm running a few minutes late. I will be there as soon as I possibly can.

Boss Lady: It's okay. See you soon.

Lumi starts the car, and we take off around the fountain, following the circle driveway to go out the way we came. Stealing one last glance at the front doors, I look for Griffin, but he's already gone.

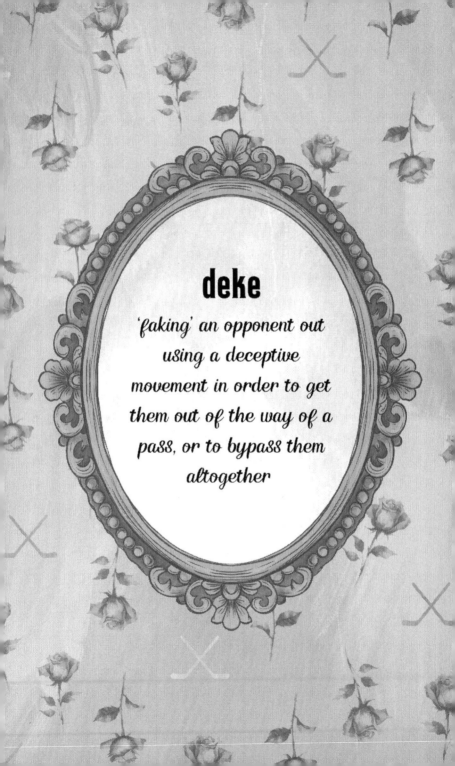

deke

'faking' an opponent out using a deceptive movement in order to get them out of the way of a pass, or to bypass them altogether

chapter six
griffin

"Good morning, Griffin." Mrs. Potts beams as I walk into the kitchen. "How did your first study session go?"

Yawning, I stretch my arms up and sit down on the barstool at the island. "Good morning. It was really good. I think I found the perfect tutor."

"That's great news." She smiles. "Perhaps I should bake her some cookies."

Thankfully, Mrs. Potts and Chip were at dinner last night when Blair and Lumi came over. It's not that I don't think they wouldn't get along. To be honest, I don't care if they do. I just didn't want to deal with the possible judgment when I would have to explain that I have a chef and maid.

Unless you live in this world, it's looked at as lazy or snobby. But no one would understand that Mrs. Potts and Chip aren't just my staff, they're practically family.

She sets a plate of scrambled eggs, toast, and bacon in front of me.

"Thank you very much. And she'd be lucky if you did. They're the best."

"You're too sweet, Griffin," she hums and finishes loading the dishwasher.

A light pitter-patter sounds through the house, growing louder by the second. Chip bursts into the room in his Buzz Lightyear pajamas with the world's craziest bedhead.

"Good morning, Chocolate Chip." I chuckle as he races straight toward the plate of bacon by the stove.

"You must have smelled it, huh?" Mrs. Potts giggles and brushes his hair with her fingers.

He grabs a piece and quickly takes a bite.

He nods and smiles, every inch of his face lighting up with happiness.

Chip has nonspeaking autism. So, we never expect him to answer our questions with anything other than his physical reactions. But he's so expressive that we know exactly what he's communicating.

"What are you guys doing today?" I shovel more of this delicious breakfast into my mouth.

"I'm going to take Chip to the art museum in town to look at the paintings." She glances at Chip with the warmest and kindest eyes. "One day, yours will be in there too, honey. You're so talented."

Chip smiles bashfully.

"Well, take lots of pictures. I want to see them when I get back from practice later."

"You've got it!" Mrs. Potts says. "There's a salad and

sandwich in the fridge if you need any snacks or quick meals today."

"You're the best. Thank you," I say genuinely before taking the final bite of my breakfast.

She walks over and takes the plate from me even though I glare at her while she does it. It's an ongoing battle that neither of us will ever win. She always wants to do more for me, and I want her to stop waiting on me.

She's worked for my family since I was born. She is family and always will be. The same goes for Chip. There are very few things I let Mrs. Potts do for me, cooking and dishes being the only things. Other than that, I don't let her wait on me.

"I've got to get to class. But I hope you guys have the best day at the museum." I mess Chip's hair up even more with my fingers before dismissing myself from the kitchen.

Mrs. Potts's sweet voice carries through the house as she continues to tell Chip about the day she has planned for the both of them. She homeschools Chip, and they are practically inseparable—unless, of course, I steal him away for a boys' day. We are due for one of those soon. Once my grades are under control, that will be my next priority.

My morning classes are about as exciting as a dentist appointment. I have Microeconomics first and then go straight into Algebra. My brain is nothing but mush by the time I'm rolling into the weight room to meet with my team.

"Finally, you have decided to grace us with your presence. We're almost done with rep one," Malik teases as I slide my backpack into my gym locker and pull my hoodie off over my head, tossing it on top of my bag.

"Shut up, Malik. You needed the extra rep anyway," I jab back at him.

He laughs in defeat as he switches places with Asher on the bench and slides under the bar. Asher is one of our forwards. His brother, Dean, is a defender. They are a real dynamic duo and completely unstoppable when they are on the ice together.

Malik finishes his reps and hops off the bench. "All right, your turn."

Stretching my arms out, I loosen them up just a little before grabbing a fifty-pound weight and adding it to Malik's set.

"Oh, okay, Griff, you want today to be a competition. I see," he huffs and puffs out his chest, crossing his arms.

Chuckling, I slide under the bar and wrap my hands around the metal. "Not a competition, buddy. It's not my fault that you couldn't handle my max weight even if you tried."

"Yeah, because I wasn't born like a fucking brute," Malik retorts as he moves in to spot me. "Now, let's go. Give me eight."

Tightening my core, I push the bar up and off of the rest and position it above my chest. As slow as I can manage, I lower it to my pecs before gently guiding it back up.

"There's one. Let's go, baby. Now, number two," Malik shouts, pumping me up.

"Ugh," I grunt as I push through my second rep.

"Two!" Malik counts off.

I fight my way through to number seven before I really start struggling. My arms are burning like they're drenched in gasoline and lit on fire.

"Don't quit on me now, Beast. You earned that name; now, fucking prove it," he screams at me, and it's just the boost I need.

"Erghhhh!" I scream back at him as I use every ounce of strength I have remaining to push that bar up one more time.

"Yes! That's what I'm talking about!" Malik cheers as he helps me rack it.

My breathing is rough and ragged as I sit up and take a couple of deep inhales to calm my racing heart. Hopping up, I walk over to my bag and grab my water bottle while Dean moves beneath the bar for his turn.

We spend the next hour or so going through our usual weights routine, hyping each other up and pushing ourselves to our absolute limit. We end the workout with a quick mile run, and by the time we're done, my adrenaline is spiking and pulsing through my veins with vigor.

As we walk to the parking lot, I pull my phone out and text Blair to see when she wants to meet before the test on Friday.

> Hey, I'm free tomorrow after six if you want to come over for another session.

"Who are you texting?" Malik bumps into me and

looks at my phone. "Ohhh, the new tutor. How good is she during those *sessions*?" He chuckles.

Rolling my eyes, I tuck my phone away in my pocket before saying, "First off, we really are just studying. No funny business."

"But that's the funnest business." Malik smirks. "She's cute though—in a sexy-nerd way, you know?"

"Yeah, I guess I haven't noticed," I admit, lying straight through my teeth.

"I'll catch you later." He laughs and walks away, but not before calling out, "Griff, you're full of shit."

Of course I've noticed those big doe brown eyes and how she bites down on her bottom lip when she's focusing on something, but I'm not even going to allow myself to think of her in any way other than my tutor. I don't have time for that, and neither does she. Our relationship is simply a business transaction.

My phone vibrates, and I yank it out of my pocket.

> Tutor: Tomorrow at six works. I have to leave by eight, just FYI.

> Sounds good. See you then.

If we're meeting tomorrow, I guess I have to study on my own so I don't look like a complete lost cause when she comes over.

After two hours of educational torture, I decide I'm done for the night. My brain is completely dead right now.

Maybe I should do a little digging on Blair; after all, she will be spending time in my home. I look her up on every social media platform, but I only find one account that hasn't been updated or posted on in a couple of years, so that's not very helpful.

I've never met a college girl who doesn't live on social media, so what's her deal? Too focused on her studies?

Stop right there.

Who cares what she does during her free time? She's just my tutor, and it's none of my business.

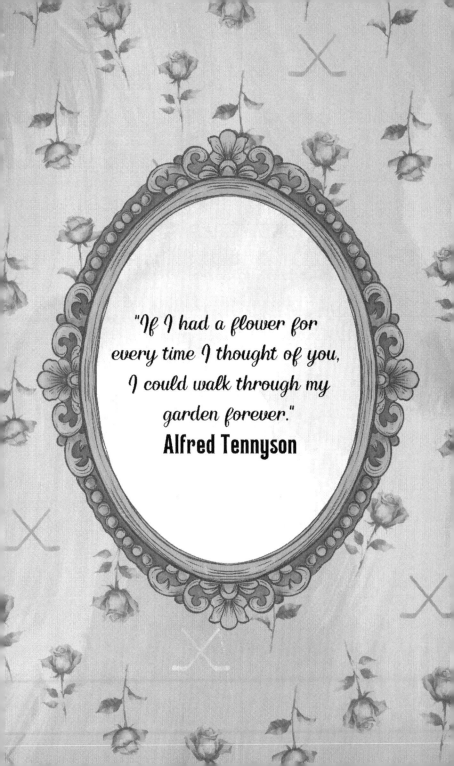

"If I had a flower for every time I thought of you, I could walk through my garden forever."
Alfred Tennyson

chapter seven
blair

S eeing Hawthorne Manor at sunset is a whole new experience. The orange and pink colors in the sky cast the most stunning glow on all of the light brick and large windows. It's really magical.

A cool breeze ruffles the bottom of my short skirt. The oversize cream sweater holds the skirt in place, so at least I'm not flashing anyone. However, there isn't exactly anyone to flash.

I wonder where Griffin's parents are. Does he have any siblings? Do they live here too?

Honestly, I don't believe a soul lives here at all because of how tidy and clean the house is.

I'm barely up the first set of stairs when the double front doors open.

"Hey," Griffin says, and tingles shimmy down my back from his sultry tone.

"Hi!" I chime, immediately wanting to slap myself for how high-pitched it came out.

He stretches his arms across the double doors, and, dear God, it's unreal how fit he is. His arms bulge in his sleeves, his veins snaking down his forearms. I would have to be blind to not appreciate the artistry in his body and the hours he pours into his training for these results. It's admirable, and it's fucking hot.

But it doesn't matter how hot he is. I don't date jocks, not after Grant, who still won't leave me alone. Grant is an overachieving narcissist who likes me more when my lips are sealed than when I express a sliver of thought.

I don't know how I was dumb enough to give him a second chance. I was out of my damn mind. Thinking back to high school, I was thankful when he committed to a school in California for football; I would finally be free of his constant love-bombing texts and late-night calls with never-ending voice mails. Then, Mr. Vain himself showed up at HEAU. And I fell for his sweet words all over again, letting him take me out. He said he was offered a scholarship here and had a gut feeling that he just had to take it. Lucky me. His unwanted affection comes in waves. I know I should just block him and kill the connection altogether. I just … I don't know why I haven't done it yet.

"Blair?" Griffin's deep voice invades my train of thought, completely taking over.

Reality clicks back into place, and I realize we are at his dining table. I was really zoned out; it felt like a dream, walking through here.

Goddamn Grant, at it again, making everything about him.

Clearing my throat, I begin unloading my backpack on the table. "Shit, sorry. I was thinking about …" I trail off. "It doesn't matter. How are you feeling about the study guide?"

His laptop and papers are already set up, including a glass of water for each of us.

He takes a seat while filling me in on his progress. "Pretty good. I was up late last night studying. I think I'm going to ace it."

My eyes widen with shock from his profound confidence. "Really? An A, huh?"

His glare tugs my lips up. "Yes, smarty-pants, an A."

Holding my hands up in defeat, I chuckle. "Good. I'm an even better tutor than I thought."

"Now, who's being cocky?" He scoffs.

A smile stretches across my face, and I quickly kill it, forcing myself to get back on task. But I don't miss the almost-indiscernible pout of his full lips.

"I made a practice test for you to take," I announce as I take the test out of a folder in my bag and slide it over to him.

He pushes the glass of water closer to me and murmurs, "I made *you* this glass of water."

My snarkiness yet again slips past my lips without my intent. "How do I know you didn't roofie it?"

He chokes on his own gulp of water and laughs before setting his cup down and picking mine up. "Fair point." He takes a gigantic mouthful of my water and swallows it. And another, nearly emptying the glass. "See, it's not roofie—"

His eyes roll into his head before his head crashes down to the table, and the sound startles me cold.

"Oh my God, Griffin!" I shout and slap his cheek.

"Ha! Gotcha!" He flies up, laughing, and I almost hit him again for pulling that. "I love how your concern shows itself in violence."

"I was just going to get my money and go. It wouldn't have been my fault if you'd drugged yourself." I shrug, biting down on my bottom lip.

He huffs and shows off those perfect pearly whites again. "Ha-ha. Very funny."

"I'm not a nurse. I'm here to help you with English. I did my part. Now, you do yours and take your test," I order him and grab my glass of water from his hand, my fingers grazing his as I take it.

He smirks. "Fine. Just don't slap me again."

I stand up and head for the kitchen. "I'll be right back. Don't cheat."

He gasps as if I hurt his feelings, but I ignore him and trek onward.

Wandering through the enormous house, I walk into the kitchen and nearly shout as chills race down my arms.

A little blond boy sits on the kitchen island, eating milk and cookies.

"Hello there. Sorry. I wasn't expecting anyone to be in here," I say softly, smiling gently at him. "My name's Blair."

I think the kid has to be, like, nine. Maybe ten?

He stares at me with kindness twinkling in his bright blue eyes, but doesn't respond.

"I'm just going to get some water quickly if you don't mind." I grin and stroll up to the automatic dispenser on the fridge and fill my cup back up.

"Chip, are you ready to start the movie?" an overly

sweet voice sings through the kitchen right before a woman walks in with a smile stretched ear to ear. "Oh, I'm sorry. I didn't know you were here. You must be Blair!" she chimes and walks over to me. Without hesitation, she pulls me into a gentle hug. "It is lovely to meet you, dear."

Embracing her softly while balancing the water in the cup, I murmur, "It's nice to meet you too, Mrs. Hawthorne."

A warm spice and honey aroma drifts through the air and invades my nose as she pulls away, chuckling softly. "I am not Mrs. Hawthorne. My name is Mary Pottinger. Feel free to call me Mrs. Potts. I am the Hawthornes' live-in maid and chef."

You've got to be kidding me.

"Chip, have you met Griffin's new tutor?" She directs her attention to the little boy watching us with the biggest chocolaty smile.

He nods and shovels another cookie into his mouth.

"All right, Chip, that's enough for one night. You're going to get a thousand cavities," Mrs. Potts says before walking to the kitchen island, pulling the plate of cookies away from him, and stowing them on top of the fridge.

Chip dismisses himself without a word and scurries away. He must be Griffin's little brother.

As if she can read my mind, Mrs. Potts introduces Chip. "Chip is my son. Don't take it personally when he doesn't respond to anything you say. He is nonverbal."

That makes me feel better about him not answering me. I thought maybe he just didn't like me. But I suppose I am a stranger who just barged into his kitchen after all.

"That makes a lot of sense as to why he didn't answer me earlier."

"He's a sweet boy. He's talented, too, with his art. Once you better understand how to communicate with him, you will be able to do so for hours on end." She giggles. "The hard part is getting him to stop."

While I appreciate the thought, I can't think of why I would spend a lot of time with Chip. Once I'm done tutoring Griffin, we will return to our little worlds. Perhaps mine is more *little* than his.

"So, do you work with many students?" she asks me, and she steals a cookie from the plate. "Shh. Don't tell Chip."

My chest floods with warmth at the genuine goodness that exudes from Mrs. Potts. "Your secret is safe with me. And, no, Griffin is my only student."

She finishes her bite of chocolate deliciousness and whispers, "That's probably for the best. He never was very good at sharing. Oh my goodness, I couldn't even count the number of nannies and staff he ran off when he was a little boy."

I chuckle at her comment. "I don't know why that doesn't surprise me."

She lowers her voice and caresses my arm. "He wasn't always so … distant. He used to be the type of kid to make friends in seconds. He was outgoing and playful, loving every second of life with the biggest smile always plastered on his face." Her eyes seem to gloss over as she remembers that time.

My heart aches, and my curiosity is piqued. "What changed?"

"A lot. Sometimes, I wonder if we'll ever see that side of him again. He's built so many walls around himself to protect his heart. After what happened with—"

"Yeah, yeah. Enough with the stories." Griffin's deep voice slices through the room, and I jump at the intrusion.

The hair on my neck rises as he steps directly behind me.

As I turn around, I take a small step back.

His gaze lowers until it's locked on to mine, and he murmurs, "I've finished the test."

It wasn't too invasive of a practice run. But even then, he finished that much faster than I'd expected. Mrs. Potts and I got carried away, talking about Griffin's childhood. I will need to hear the rest of that story.

"Well, duty calls," I utter before spinning on my heel with my full water in hand, following Griffin back into the dining room.

"I see you met the rest of the crew," he says as he finds his seat and kicks back, crossing his hands behind his head.

The motion causes his shirt to lift up and exposes a couple of inches of solid, deeply grooved muscles and his V-line. I knew he was ripped, but *holy shit.*

He clears his throat, and my eyes fly to his. The corner of Griffin's lips tip up, and now, the only person I would like to slap is myself.

Get it together. It's just abs on some boy's body. Oh well. Who cares?

Squinting in annoyance at his mere existence at this moment and at the damn agreement we made, I set my water on the table and take my seat.

"I did. They are very nice," I say without meeting his eyes. Grabbing the test, I put it in front of me.

"They are," he responds, and I wait for him to tell me more, but he remains silent.

Where are his parents if that's the rest of his crew? Do millionaires leave their homes and travel all the time?

Stopping my brain from running rampant with assumptions, I uncap my red pen and begin grading his answers. After going through each page carefully, I'm actually … impressed. He really did study for this, and it definitely shows.

"All right, results are in. You got …" I trail off, and he slams his eyes shut in anticipation. "A perfect score!"

He flies out of his seat and jumps up, his eyes widening and face lifting with excitement. "You're lying!"

"Nope!" Rising to my feet, I circle the one hundred percent on the top of the page and turn it around to show him. "You did it!"

He rushes forward, and I gasp as he lifts me into the air and spins me around. "Ahh!"

After a full three-sixty twirl, he apologizes and slowly lowers me to the ground with mere inches between us. "Oh shit, sorry." His cheeks burn bright red, and he shyly smiles. "I got a bit carried away."

"Yeah." I grin as I feel my heart racing and my breath quickening. "I can see that."

Stepping back, I try to ignore the way I liked being in his arms, the way it made me giddy, like that feeling I got as a little girl, dreaming about fairy tales.

I beg that damn feeling to go away. But it's too late; the cage is open, and butterflies are flying free.

Attempting to disregard the fluttering in my stomach, I say, "D-don't forget that there will be a short essay part on the test that you will have to do. Have you prepared the bullet points for your final yet?"

He looks away. "Shit. I was kind of hoping you had forgotten about that."

"Well, I will take that response as a no. But as your tutor, I have to remind you that in order to get your grade up and keep it up, you cannot afford to purposefully forget things," I say to him as I pack my things up in my bag. "You'll do great on the test. You'll do splendidly on the essay portion. Unfortunately, I can't help you with that because the only person who truly knows yourself is you."

"That was"—he hesitates—"kind of deep."

"And true," I respond, grabbing my phone and throwing my bag over my shoulder.

Ugh. The text notification makes me squirm.

> Grant: I miss you, baby. When are you going to stop playing these games? You know we are meant to be together. I love you.

I swipe the notification away the second I'm done reading it and look up from the screen to find Griffin with concern etched into his features.

"Everything okay?" he asks quietly.

Shrugging like it's no big deal, I grin. "It's nothing, really. I have to get going though; my ride's here. I'll see you tomorrow in class."

"Yeah, see you then. Good night, Blair." His voice is

lower and thicker somehow, like the emotion that wasn't there before is now gently tucked beneath every word.

"Good night," I murmur before spinning on my heel and walking away.

Griffin clears his throat, and I realize he's trailing behind me.

Griffin's words spew out of his mouth as he attempts to fill the silence. "I'll walk you out."

"Okay, thank you," I say, slightly distracted by the vibration from my phone in my hand.

It's a text from Grant—*again*.

> Grant: I miss you. Seriously, I need to see you, Blair Bear.

Absolutely not, especially if I can help it. I ignore the feeling of my skin crawling off of my body, pull open the front door, and step into the crisp fall air.

"Lumi's not picking you up tonight?" Griffin asks as he follows me onto the porch, stopping beside me and quickly typing into his phone.

"Not tonight. I just got an Uber. I'll see you tomorrow." I look up at him and smile, and my breath catches in my throat.

He is aggravatingly beautiful in a way that isn't fair to the rest of humanity.

He smiles back at me, and I feel a burn ignite in my cheeks. Before any shade of red can shine through, I look away and begin descending the stairs.

"See you tomorrow," he calls out, but my attention is already drifting to my phone once again.

It's a notification that Griffin sent my payment—the easiest money I've ever made.

The club is packed tonight, but it doesn't stop me from gossiping with my coworkers.

"Scarlet, it's been a month. You barely know the guy."

I scoff at what she said.

Scarlet is one of the dancers here and is very popular, earning more than almost everyone else. But she gets too attached to these boyfriends that she dates for a short period and lets whoever her new guy is completely change her personality. The man of the month wants her to stop working here, specifically to stop dancing. For one, she loves it, so screw whatever he wants. Two, she isn't going to find a job that would pay her nearly the same money she's making now—at least not a legal job.

She never likes being alone and would rather be with a guy undeserving of her than being single. I wish she could see how amazing she is. Screw any guy who demeans her. I understand that being a stripper isn't a career that you can keep your entire life. But she's nineteen and having the time of her life.

Maybe after they're together for six months and they sit down and discuss it, concluding that he doesn't want her to do it anymore and she's okay with it, then quit. But a month? You don't know anything about someone after a month—at least not anything that counts.

"I knoooow." She drags the O out while pouting.

"Do what you want, Scar. But make sure that *you* are the reason you're making the decision, not him," I shout over the music.

"You always give the best advice." She blows me an air kiss and shimmies away, leaving a trail of body glitter in her path.

A cool shiver runs down my shoulders, and the hair on the back of my neck rises, as if someone is watching me. Discreetly, I scan the club with batted eyelashes and a sickeningly sweet smile. I glance at the entrance, and my blood runs cold.

Grant.

This isn't the first time he's been here. He and his football buddies come by occasionally, stay for a few beers, then leave. Usually, I don't care when he comes in because he knows the rules and mostly minds his business. He knows that pissing me off at work isn't in his favor of winning me over.

The Fallen Petal has one rule that must be obeyed above all else—the *no partner* rule. Of course, we are allowed to date, but our partners cannot show up at the club and make a big scene. It often deters the clientele and is unprofessional. There is zero tolerance, and if it happens, you are fired on the spot.

Grant's presence isn't what makes me feel uneasy; it's the anger in his eyes that I don't recall seeing there before that chills me to the bone, like staring into a dark forest, not knowing what monsters lurk in the shadows.

fivehole

*The gap between a
goalie's legs, typically
referring to scoring.*

chapter eight
griffin

I have more nerves this morning for my test than I do for most of my hockey games. I want to do more than pass; I want to ace it. Proving not only to myself, but also to Blair that I can succeed in this class.

I even looked up things you should do before an exam to mentally prepare. I went to bed at a decent time and made myself eggs, sausage, and toast for breakfast. Now, I'm rolling into class ten minutes early. I'm not exactly sure how this is supposed to help, but I'm not in any position to question the test gods right now.

If I don't pass this exam, my ass is going to get benched for who knows how long. I can't afford that, and neither can my team. We are a perfectly well-oiled machine; if one part is removed, we will fall apart. Maybe that's a bit dramatic, but you get the damn point. Perhaps the team would be just fine, but I definitely wouldn't be.

"Mr. Hawthorne, you're not late today. I'm glad to see

your tutor has been rubbing off on you." Dr. Schrute greets me with a big smile as he writes on the whiteboard.

"Yeah, she's good at her job," I tell him truthfully as I walk toward the stairs to take my usual seat.

As I walk up the first couple of steps, I glance up and lock eyes with Blair. How have I not noticed her the last few months that we've been in class together?

I think even if I were blind, I would know how stunning she is because her beauty radiates from every pore of her being, like a force you can't help but be drawn to.

Locking my gaze on to hers, I continue to climb the stairs until I reach my row and stop. Her face warms, and her lips purse while she holds my stare, seemingly refusing to be the first to break the staring contest.

Oh, it's on.

"Excuse me," someone whispers behind me, and without blinking, I scoot into my row while looking straight at Blair, who's talking to Lumi.

Lumi leans over and whispers in her ear, and Blair's cheeks redden immediately.

"Is there a reason you are eye-fucking your tutor right now? Can I join?" the deep voice says in my ear, not nearly as quiet as I would like.

"Fuck off, Malik. It's a simple stare-down, nothing more."

Proving my point to him, I break the eye contact and find my seat.

Blair's smirk falls when I end our little game, and I can't ignore how my chest twists in pain at her disappointment. I want to know what she's thinking right now. I'm two seconds from going up there and finding out, but Dr. Schrute has other plans.

"Good morning, class. You know what today is, and for your sake, I hope you have prepared thoroughly." He chuckles like he doesn't hold my entire future in the palm of his hand. "Before we begin, phones, study guides, and everything else must be cleared off your desk, aside from a pen. Thank you."

Checking my phone one last time, I see a text from Blair.

Tutor: Good luck. You're going to do great.

With a shit-eating grin warming my face, I shove my phone in my backpack and tuck it beneath my legs. I take a deep breath and exhale. I've got this. I went through Blair's study guide until I had it practically memorized. The only part I'm semi-nervous about is the essay question, but I guess I'll worry about that when I get to it.

"Take one and pass it down your row, please. When you are finished, bring them up front. Good luck," Dr. Schrute announces to the class as he hands a stack of tests to the first person in each row.

"Thanks," I mumble to Malik as he hands me the stack, and I take one off of the top and pass them along.

"You got this, man." He hypes me up, and I'm grateful for the mini pep talk.

After filling in the top of the test with my name and the date, I read question one.

What did one toilet say to the other?

Is this seriously a test question? At least he has a sense of humor.

The multiple choice options include, *You look like shit*, *You're full of shit*, or *You look flushed*. All of the answers seem like they could be correct, so which one do I pick?

"There isn't a wrong answer for question one; don't panic. I want you to pick which answer you would finish the joke with. It's just for fun." Dr. Schrute chuckles.

If I wasn't failing this class, I would think it's funny. But I'm too stressed out to think about a toilet joke right now; I'll come back to it.

Reading the following question, I know the answer before I finish reading the choices. Pride and joy pump through my veins as I circle the correct response and move on to the next question.

Before I know it, I've finished all of the multiple choice and fill-in-the-blank portions, and now, all that remains is the essay. I wish coming up with the words were my struggle. I don't have a lack of ideas. I have a lack of vulnerability. Why couldn't Dr. Schrute pick any other damn thing to focus on this semester that isn't ourselves?

Tell me about a childhood memory you will always cherish and how that moment still impacts you today.

I had the best childhood with loving parents and the sweetest little brother, but that doesn't mean I want to share anything about them with a professor who won't understand how even thinking about them burns a hole in my chest.

They left me long ago, and they still refuse to return. Maybe I was too selfish, or perhaps they just got sick of me and left. Regardless, it's only been Mrs. Potts, Chip, and me since I was fifteen. Any good childhood memory that I have will forever be overshadowed by the day they abandoned me.

Writing rapidly, I pour words onto the page that will tug at Dr. Schrute's heartstrings and hopefully give me an A. It might not be a real story—at least not one I have ever experienced—but it sounds real enough to be believable.

I talk about how, as a young boy, I met a hockey player who changed what I wanted in life. Meeting my hero made me realize that I could become that hero for another little kid one day. By the time I finish constructing this adorable little lie, I'm even questioning whether it actually happened. It might be a fake story, but it's structured properly, it has no spelling errors, and it's grammatically correct, so I'm happy with it.

A warmth spreads through my chest as I take a deep inhale and slowly dispel it, feeling every muscle in my body relax. There's no way that I won't get a near-perfect grade on this test. Setting my pen down, I flip the packet back to the front page and realize I have one more question to answer. I fill in a new answer to Dr. Schrute's toilet joke—*You're full of shit.*

I gather my things and rise from my seat, making my way to the stairs to turn my test in. Glancing up at where Blair sits, I find her scribbling like a maniac on her paper, like she can't write fast enough for what she wants to say. I wonder what childhood memory she's spilling onto the pages. Her eyebrows furrow with focus, and she bites her bottom lip between her teeth. She looks cute like that.

As if she can feel my stare, her eyes flick up and land

directly on mine. It takes her a second to react, and she gives me a shy thumbs-up. Smirking, I reciprocate it and hold my thumb up.

She goes back to her work, rapidly writing. Her face finds that adorable balance of stress and concentration. I descend the stairs to Dr. Schrute's desk and, for once this semester, confidently drop my answers into the bin.

"Thank you," he whispers, and I nod in response before walking out of the room, the door clicking shut behind me.

He usually has grades posted by the end of the day, so fingers crossed, I'll find out before tonight's game because I don't want anything but hockey on my mind when I take the ice.

Lingering in the hallway, I wait to see if Blair comes out so I can ask her how she thinks she did, although I imagine I could answer that myself. I only have a few minutes before I have to dip and head to the pregame skate, so hopefully, she finishes quickly.

I count tiles on the floor as time seems to drag out forever while I wait for her to walk out of class. I jump slightly as the door finally swings open, but it's not her. It's Lumi.

"Hey, man," I greet him. "How'd it go?"

"Good, I think," he says with pep. "You?"

Yawning, I respond, "That's awesome. I think I di—"

Blair walking out of the room takes my full attention, cutting me off mid-sentence.

"There you are. I never finish before you," Lumi teases her as she types angrily into her phone.

What the hell is that about?

"I know. I couldn't get focused right away, which is weird for me, but I got there eventually," she mumbles and looks up, her eyes widening when she sees me. "You're still here?"

Glancing away, I clear my throat and calmly say, "Yeah, I was waiting for Malik to finish up."

Lumi side-eyes me, and I ignore him.

"So, how'd it go?" she asks enthusiastically.

Wringing the straps of my backpack on my chest, I proudly say, "I think I fucking killed it."

"Yes! I knew you could do it. You just needed a good study guide and some pointers," she praises me, and I lap up the compliments.

"Good thing I found the best tutor in the class," I respond kindly, and she smiles softly in return. "I've got a game tonight. I'm not sure what you guys are up to. But it would be cool if you guys came." I say before adding, "Unless you already have really important plans."

"We don't!" Lumi practically shouts, and Blair turns bright red.

"Perfect. Game's at seven," I respond without leaving a moment for Blair to turn down my invite. "I've got to head to the rink. I'll see you guys later."

As I step away from them, Blair speaks up with a glimmer in her eyes. "I thought you were waiting for Malik?"

Shit.

Rubbing the back of my neck, I say, "Yeah, I was. But he's taking too goddamn long, and I don't want to be late."

"Fair enough. I usually have the same problem with Lumi." She laughs as he glares at her.

I chuckle and smile before turning around and walking toward the exit. I really do hope they come out tonight. It would be cool to have someone I actually know in the crowd. Mrs. Potts and Chip attend a game every so often, but Chip isn't the biggest fan of the loudness.

My phone buzzes as I enter the locker room, and I pull it out to find a text from Blair as I sit down in front of my locker.

> Tutor: I'm just letting you know we are coming tonight. Hope you don't suck.

I wish she would let some of this sass shine outside of our texts.

Biting down on my cheek to stifle my smile and laugh, I type out my response.

> What do you even know about hockey? You won't be able to tell if I'm doing well or not.

> Tutor: A bunch of oversize humans wear blades on their feet, chase after a rubber ball with a stick, and rage out when things don't go their way. I feel like that sums it up.

A laugh bursts out of me, and I quickly respond, feeling electricity begin to pulse through my veins at our back-and-forth banter.

> Okay, that is wrong on so many levels. In the vaguest of ways, I suppose you're right, but also, you know nothing about hockey.

An idea jumps into my head, and I type it out before I can even think it through and she can respond.

> You help me with our class, and I'll help you better understand hockey.

> Tutor: Success in class is essential. Me understanding a sport? Not so much.

> Think of it as an addendum to our original deal. No negotiation. I want it written into stone.

> Tutor: Is that blackmail? That I have to learn hockey or our deal is off?

> Yep.

She must be contemplating my offer deeply because she doesn't answer me nearly as fast this time. Glancing up from my phone, I nearly shit myself.

My entire team is silent and facing me with a variety of smirks and smiles on their faces.

I huff. "What the fuck are you guys doing?"

They explode with laughter like they couldn't keep it

inside themselves for a second longer. Malik is bent over at his waist, cackling so hard that it sounds like it hurts.

Malik is still heaving from his laughter as he forces the words out. "Don't worry; I took photos so we could look back at this moment."

Knowing he's baiting me for his punch line, I follow along so we can get this over with. "What moment?"

Asher stalks over to me, chuckling, and throws his arm over my shoulders. "Proud of you, man. Finally growing up."

"Will someone tell me what the fuck is going on?" I demand, my voice powerful enough to chill some of the craziness down.

Malik turns his phone around and shows me a picture of myself sitting on the bench with my face buried in my phone, and quite literally, I have the biggest smile I've ever seen in a photo of myself. Granted, most pictures of me are of me playing hockey, and I tend not to smile on the ice unless we score or I'm about to beat someone's ass.

Playing it cool, I shrug it off. "What about it?"

Malik squints with a knowing smirk. "Are we going to have to drag every single word out of you? Who were you talking to? Who's got you smiling like that, Griff?"

These boys know me well, and I'd trust them with my life, but for some reason, I lie, "No one. I found a bunch of funny memes and shit."

"All in favor of accepting Griffin's answer, say aye," Malik calls out loudly to the team.

Silence falls upon us.

He continues, "All those opposed to his bullshit answer and still waiting for some truth, say aye."

"AYE!" everyone screams.

Why in the hell are they like this?

"Try again," Malik says. "Who were you texting? Was it that hot little nerd from our English class?"

Clenching my jaw, I tilt my head, my blood boiling at his nickname for her. "Yeah, it was. And? She's my tutor. I was telling her how good I did on the test. And Malik?"

"Yeah?"

"Don't call her that," I order him.

The guys look at each other, seemingly assessing whether or not they are happy with this response, but a majority of them are clearly not pleased. But by the glare on my face right now, they back down and remain quiet.

Dean breaks the silence and asks, "And how did our boy do on the test?"

Looking back down at my phone, I see Blair responded, but I swipe out of our messages before I can read it and pull up my grades, specifically my English class, and find the most recent entry from tonight.

Holy shit.

"I got ninety-two percent!" I cheer like we just won a championship game because, fuck, it feels that good right now.

The room explodes in chants, hoots, and hollers as we celebrate my small victory.

"That's what I'm talking about, Griffin. The mother-fucking BEEEAST!" Dean growls out.

I can't believe I got an A on my test. Like, I'd thought I was going to, but, damn, to see that really happen is something else altogether.

"Now, let's go get a W, boys!" I shout, and the group gets distracted with gearing up for our game.

Taking one more second, I open Blair's text.

Tutor: I'm not going to cheer. I'm going to be straight-faced the entire time.

Grinning, I text her back one last time before storing my phone away.

I wouldn't have it any other way.

In a matter of a half hour, we are warming up on the ice as the arena fills in around us. I would be lying if I said I'm not trying to spot her in the crowd as I skate around. Of course, I'm not making it obvious, just taking little glances now and then. But I haven't seen her yet.

Warm-ups quickly come to an end. After a twenty-minute break, the starting lineup is announced for the visiting team, the Pirates, and finally, it's our turn.

"Let's meet the starting lineup for your HEAU Legends!" the announcer's voice booms into the mic. "Starting in goal, number thirty, Finn Rutherford!"

Our other starting defender, Dean Kensington is shouted into the mic, and he skates out as the entire building comes to life with the energy and cheers of our fans.

I'm up next.

"On defense, number seventy-five, Griffinnnn Hawthorne!" He drags the IN out in *Griffin*.

I fly onto the ice.

As our fans do every game, they roar my nickname. "Beast."

Goose bumps scatter across my body as I take my place next to Dean on the blue line, practically vibrating as adrenaline pumps through my veins.

Nothing makes me feel more at home than being on the ice.

Our forwards are announced next, Malik Ravenwell and Asher Kensington, followed by our center, Elias Lancaster.

I rock back and forth on my skates as the anthem starts, and thankfully, the singer tonight is fast-paced. It's the worst when they are torturously slow and it feels like it lasts forever.

"And the home of the brave," the singer finishes, and the lights turn on as the air electrifies.

The crowd cheers and claps as we line up for puck drop, and I take one last glance around the rink to see if I spot Blair and Lumi. But I fail to locate them and have to forget it, needing to get my head in the game.

"Let's go, boys!" I huff and ready myself, bending at the waist with my stick on the ground.

Chaos ensues as the puck drops between one of the Pirates and Asher, one of our best players in winning face-offs.

Asher dishes the puck between his legs, and it flies backward to Elias. With a flick of the wrist, he passes it across the center line to Malik, who, with a quick deke, gets around the defender and races toward the goal on a breakaway.

Drifting to the left side of the net, he pushes his stick far left before bringing it across his body lightning fast and shooting it. Unfortunately, their goalie seems to have magical fucking reflexes and snatches the puck out of midair, killing the play.

A goal on the opening puck drop would have been insane, but maybe another time.

The rest of the first period flies by without either team getting a point on the board, and I have yet to grant myself a moment of time to search for Blair. But that changes when we retake the ice for the start of the second.

Our line is first to start, and while we wait for the other team to be ready, I look into the crowd.

Nope. Nope. Not her. Definitely not him. Not her. Nop—

As the hairs rise on the back of my neck, I can almost sense her for a mere second before my eyes lock with hers and her lips part with a gasp. Two rows up from behind the penalty box, she watches me. Her luscious hair cascades down her shoulders in loose curls, and her cheeks are rosy from the chill of the arena.

The usual smirk that tips her plump lips up is gone and replaced by a vulnerability she hasn't let me see before. My skates guide me toward her, but before I get lost in whatever fantasy my mind is stirring up, I get ripped back to reality.

"Griffin. Hey! Let's go!" Malik whistles at me, and I line up, doing my best to push Blair out of my mind.

After we score, I can't help but turn to her and see her reaction. When a player gets in my face and wants to fight,

I'm unable to resist glancing at her to see the fire in her eyes, and as the game comes to an end, I'm incapable of doing anything other than watch her cheer us on in victory, knowing that I'm completely fucked because I have feelings for my tutor.

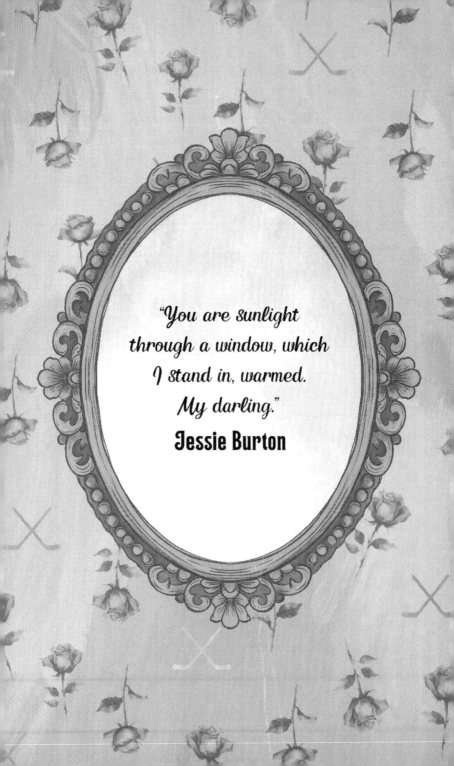

"You are sunlight
through a window, which
I stand in, warmed.
My darling."

Jessie Burton

chapter nine
blair

When I was a little girl, wanting to grow up too fast, I never realized that part of adulthood is dealing with never-ending piles of laundry. Like, how in the world does one never fully complete that task? It's the same thing with dishes, and I'm tired of this cycle. Maybe I should get us paper plates. At least then, I would never have to worry about a sink full of dishes again.

My entire morning has been spent returning our house to clean and orderly. When I finally finish deep-cleaning every room in our house, I reward myself with an iced coffee and five minutes of reading. Between work, school, and now tutoring, I never have time to read recreationally. Five minutes turns into ten minutes and then an hour. It's not my fault I get lost in the pages and can't escape even if I try.

Unfortunately, I can't mentally live inside of fictional worlds forever, and I have to face reality. I work tonight, and I know every dime will need to go toward our bills. My dad does the best he can. But since we moved and he accepted a new job at a different factory, he hasn't been making as much money, which is now even tighter than before.

I walk into the kitchen to see what still needs to be paid to keep us afloat. I like to keep all the bills pinned to the fridge with magnets so it's constantly in my face and reminding me to work harder and harder. Right now, we have two overdue payments that are top priority—electric and Wi-Fi.

Spinning around, I spot the shoebox I forgot to put back under my dad's bed while I was cleaning. Grabbing it, I meander to my dad's room and kneel beside the bed, sliding it underneath. Something fights me from pushing it back. Lifting the blanket, I find a shoebox in the way—looks like with work boots, based on the photo on the box—and push it, nearly launching it across the floor because it's a lot lighter than I expected.

Lying down on my stomach, I wiggle under the frame, grab on to the box, and pull it out. Sitting up, I crisscross my legs and set it in my lap, carefully placing my hands on the lid. I bet it's full of old photos. It wouldn't be the first time I found a bunch of pictures and memorabilia in a box.

When I lift the lid off of the box, my body chills, and my chest tightens so much that I can't breathe. The lid quivers in my hand as I fully process what I'm looking at.

Stacks of folded papers fill every inch of the box, all stamped with red ink. It's packed to the brim with late bills that I didn't even know existed. Pinching my brows together, I read where they are from and become even more confused. They're all medical bills, but that doesn't make sense. Dad hasn't said anything about going to the doctor. I know he hasn't been feeling one hundred percent lately, but he hasn't had an appointment on our shared calendar for months, so where is all of this coming from?

My ears begin to ring, and I feel like I'm going to be sick. Kicking my foot out, I come into contact with the little trash can by his bed. Dammit.

The full bin topples over, and all the contents spill out, including the endless wrappers of M&M's that typically fill his garbage. But beneath it is a bunch of tissues with …

Is that dried blood?

What the hell is going on?

Tears pool in my eyes as more and more uncertainty unfolds in front me. We're barely doing okay with the bills we already have, let alone the box full in front of me on top of it. Oh my God, I'm going to have to drop out of school. We can't afford to have me funneling a bunch of my income toward tuition. We can't even afford to stay on top of mortgage payments.

My breathing quickens, and I start rocking back and forth. This can't be happening. I thought I'd found a way to make this all work out. I thought I was so close to ensuring that after I graduate, we wouldn't have to worry about this level of struggling again. But maybe dreams aren't always meant to come true.

The sound of our front door unlocking pulls me from my stupor. I should stand up, cover the box, shove it beneath the bed, and pretend this never happened. But I'm frozen, and I can't move.

Footsteps sound down the hallway, growing louder with each step and thump of my heart.

"Blair? Are you home?" my father calls out, his voice sounding weaker than I recall before.

My lips part, but not a single word leaves my mouth.

"Oh, there you are …" He trails off as he steps into the room.

Forcing my gaze to leave the box of debt, I tilt my head up and turn, meeting his watery eyes.

"I can explain, honey."

He holds his hands up like he's trying to calm a wild animal, and I'm sure that, in a way, I probably resemble one right now.

My voice is frail as I tell him, "Explain it then. Please."

Walking over, he sits down on the bed and taps the spot next to him. Somehow, I order my body to move, and it obeys, my shaky muscles lifting me to my feet. Sitting on the bed next to him, I take a deep breath.

"I'm sorry I've been keeping this from you. I didn't want to, but I was nervous to tell you," he says with a quivering bottom lip.

"Why would you be nervous? It's just me. You and me against the world, remember?" Reaching out, I take his hand and mine.

He wipes my tears away with his free hand and smiles without any ounce of happiness. "I remember. But I also know that you already have a ton of pressure on your shoulders. It isn't your responsibility to put food on the table and help pay bills. Yet you've sacrificed your entire life to help because I could never do it alone. I didn't want to add more burdens to your already-full plate."

My heart begins tearing in two, and a lump rises in my throat, cutting my airway off. "What burdens?"

He hesitates and strokes the back of my hand with his thumb. "I'm sick, honey. From all those years of working in factories. My lungs aren't doing so well anymore."

"Well, what does that mean? Are the doctors fixing it?" The words race out of my mouth.

"It means I have lung cancer. The doctors caught it fairly early, so we should be able to beat it. I'm going to be just fine, honey."

But what if he's not? What if they can't treat it completely? What if—

I throw my arms around his neck, and sobs burst out of me. He wraps his arms around me and pulls me closer, and I feel like a little girl in her daddy's arms. In some ways, I'll forever be his little girl. But I'm not a child anymore.

Money might not be the most important thing in life, but, boy, it sure does make a difference in how that life is lived. Right now, we need all the money we can get, and I know I could start tripling my income if I just got over my fears.

This evening is a blur. I'm merely a spectator in my own mind and body, moving through the motions of pouring drinks and giggling at guys' terrible jokes and pickup lines. I've been at work for two hours, and I have one hundred fifty dollars in tips to show for it. That might seem like a good start, and I suppose it is if I were just a college student looking for some spending money. But that barely puts a dent in the debts my dad and I owe.

"Dammit!" I whisper angrily and slap my hand on the bar top, my outcry completely drowned out by the blaring music and booming bass.

Erica bumps my hip with hers and leans into my ear. "Are you all right?"

Nodding, I continue to pour out shots and load them onto a tray. As I lift it up, Erica snatches it from me.

"What are you do—"

She cuts me off, "I've got it. Go take a second in the back."

Her soft gaze and smile are the only encouragement I need to do just that.

Thank you, I mouth, fighting the burn behind my eyes that's threatening to ruin my makeup.

She nods and winks at me before plastering a customer-service smile on and walking out from behind the bar with the tray of shots in her hands. Her swinging hips grab the attention of every person she passes, and I slip away while they're distracted.

The silence makes my ears ring as I enter our back room and shut the door behind me. My long sigh breaks the quietness around me as I slump onto one of the couches. A door opens around the corner. I hear Margo talking fast, but I can't make out what she's saying. Her heels click, growing louder with each step she takes until entering the large lounge area.

Surprise strikes her face as she meets my gaze and

barks into her phone. "Hold that thought. I'll deal with you later." She hangs up and slides the phone into her pocket. "Blair, right?"

"Umm, yeah …" I trail off, wondering why she's even asking.

Her face lights up, and she rushes over to the chair across from me. "Do you have any interest in dancing?"

My throat tightens at her question, and my chest twists with vulnerability. The thought of being onstage makes me feel nauseous.

"Oh, I don't know if that's really my thing." My voice is shaky and hesitant.

She clasps her hands together. "If it's the nudity, don't stress about that; you can keep everything covered."

I bite down sharply on my bottom lip, and the pressure begins to burn as I process what she's saying right now.

I'm not actually considering this, am I?

Kudos to the girls who dance. I will be the first person to cheer them on, but I physically don't know if my anxiety will let me get on that stage.

She smiles sympathetically and stands up. "I don't want to pressure you. But if you decide to, I need to fill a few time slots. So, I need to know within the next five to ten minutes."

My palms start sweating as I nod. "O-okay." As Margo is about to leave, I stop her. "Can I ask a question?"

She perks up instantly. "Yes, of course."

My eyes fall to my lap. I can't bear to hold her stare as my ego sinks to the floor. I'd love to stay behind the bar, but I desperately need the extra cash. "H-how much would I make?"

"That would depend on how long you're onstage and if the crowd likes what they see," she states casually.

Music floods the room as the door opens, and Chantel, one of the main dancers, walks in.

"Chantel, how much did you make from your last dance?" Margo asks her, and Chantel sashays over to us.

Her lips tip up, and a gleam of curiosity flashes in her eyes. "Blair, are you considering getting onstage? Oh my God! Yes, please! You would kill it out there!"

"Chantel, focus, please." Margo laughs.

She waves her hands. "Yeah, yeah. So, off the last dance, I made about five hundred dollars in tips, give or take. Average-size crowd, average excitement. But as a newcomer, you would rake in the cash."

Five hundred for one dance? That's more than I would make all night from bartending. Maybe letting go of this fear will feel freeing. It will be like taking ahold of a small piece of control in the chaos that has become my life.

Meeting Margo's eyes confidently, I say, "I'm in."

Margo claps and cheers, "Fuck yes! Chantel, get her ready. She's taking the stage in an hour. I'll get your announcer card ready. Do you want to go by Blair?"

When I stand to my feet, a bizarre wave of excitement tingles across my skin. "No. I'll go by Belle."

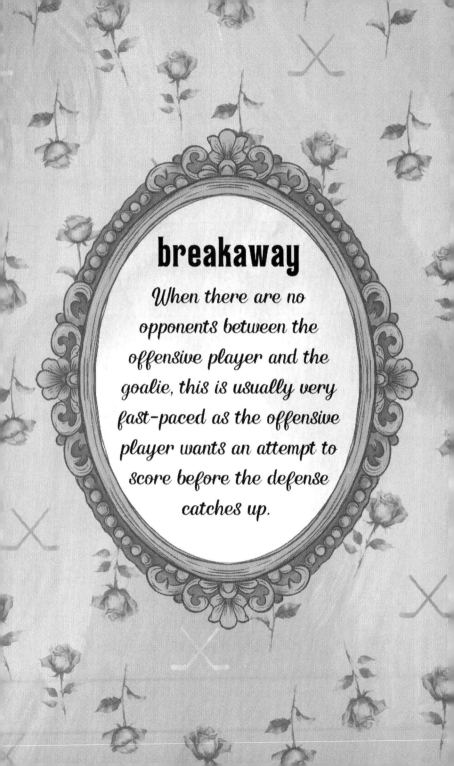

breakaway

When there are no opponents between the offensive player and the goalie, this is usually very fast-paced as the offensive player wants an attempt to score before the defense catches up.

chapter ten
griffin

My body is aching as I step out of the shower, dry off, and quickly change into a T-shirt, a hoodie, and sweats. Nothing sounds better than crawling into bed right now and taking the fattest nap ever.

"We have to go. Come on!" Malik begs the handful of Legends players remaining in the locker room. "For Ollie!"

Ollie Andrews is a forward for the Legends hockey team. But he got really hurt at the end of last season and is still recovering.

"Oh God, what are you planning?" I laugh as I walk across the room to my locker and sit down on the bench.

Malik fills me in on what I missed. "Ollie just got out of his toxic-ass relationship with that girl who's been sleeping around like her life depended on it."

"Oh, he finally escaped her, huh?" I ask Malik, and slide my tennis shoes on.

Ollie walks over, his face bright red from all the attention. "Yeah, I'm finally free. Malik is trying to convince me to go to the strip club to celebrate."

"Hear me out," Malik interrupts with his hands up, ready to plead his case. "Ollie said he's never been to one, and I feel like it's a rite of passage. And I offered to pay for a lap dance because he deserves it after putting up with Becky for so fucking long. Besides, I've never been to one here, so I wouldn't mind checking it out anyway." He looks at Ollie. "Come on, man. Let loose for once. One dance, and then we can go if you want."

Ollie gets lost in thought. Malik's eyes shoot to mine, and a smirk tips his lips. I know that look, and smart decisions never follow it.

"Okay, fine. One dance, and then we go," Ollie gives in, and honestly, I'm surprised he fought it as long as he did because we all know Malik wasn't going to give up until he got his way.

"Fuck yeah!" Malik's face lights up with victory. "Griff, you in?"

Eh, I have no interest in strip clubs. Besides, after one lap dance, it would drive me insane to watch her do it to someone else. I can't help it; I just don't like to share anything, even if it's a stripper I'll never see again.

Blair's innocent gaze and plump lips flash in my mind, and I try to push the incoming thought away, but it's too late. I wonder what she would look like, giving a lap dance. She's got a killer body. I can tell from how her clothes hug her, outlining her soft curves.

Fuck. I can't think about her this way. I need our relationship to be strictly business—at least until the end of the semester. Maybe I need a little distraction. Even as I nod my head, agreeing to go with them to the club, I can't get the image of Blair out of my mind.

The place is packed when we arrive. I hadn't even heard of this place before Malik brought it up, but everyone else in town seems to know what The Fallen Petal is. After paying the cover fee and getting inside, we find seats near the stage and wait for a server.

Malik looks like a kid in a candy store, eyeing up every server and dancer as they pass by, and Ollie looks absolutely terrified; they're the funniest pair to look at.

"Hello, boys. Can I get a drink for you?" A bubbly blonde, wearing a bikini top and a pleather skirt, approaches us.

Malik sits forward. "You know, I have a thing for blondes …" He trails off and reads her name tag. "I'll have a rum and Coke, please, Tia."

Tia bats her eyelashes. "Well, I have a thing for good manners."

Ollie laughs and says, "Then, Malik isn't the guy for you."

I'm glad he could lighten up some and enjoy himself.

"No?" She giggles, and Malik slaps Ollie's arm hard. "Rum and Coke for you. What about you, sweetheart?"

Ollie's face reddens, and he stutters as he answers her, "S-surprise me."

"You got it." She winks at him, and I'm worried he might burst into flames from how red-hot his face is right now. "And for you?"

"I'll just take a tall Bud Light, please," I answer politely.

Her stare lingers on me longer than the others, not in a flirty way, but quizzically, like she knows me, but just can't place it. But a moment later, she looks back at the others and says, "I'll have those right out."

We all thank her as she walks away, and now, I wonder if maybe I know her from somewhere. But I don't think so.

Within two minutes, she is already back with our drinks. Malik and Ollie start talking about something, but it's too loud for me to hear clearly.

The speakers vibrate through the large room like someone is tapping the microphone. Looking around, I don't see whoever it is.

Someone clears their throat into the mic. "All right, everyone, we have a special treat for you tonight. We have a dancer making her debut onstage ..." She trails off before singing into the mic, "Right. Now!"

The crowd erupts into applause and screams of praise as a light show begins on the stage. Any empty seat around us is full within seconds as guys practically foam at the mouth for what's about to come. It's fucking gross, like I know the girls need these guys to get their money, but ... I don't know ... something about the look in their eyes is rubbing me the wrong way.

"Put your hands together for her first dance, the lovely

Belle!" the announcer cheers as a girl stumbles backward onto the stage, wearing a gold outfit.

God, there's something so familiar about her ...

I can't focus on anything other than how nervous she seems, but as soon as the music starts pulsing through the room, her hips start to sway, and she finds her groove. Money starts flooding the stage until bills almost cover the floor.

My eyes freely roam her body, traveling over the soft curves of her hips and ass. From this angle, I can see her full breasts spilling out of the side of her bra.

The music builds, speeding up as it races to the beat drop. The dancer is tuned completely into the song and her body, and it's mesmerizing to watch, almost hypnotic.

She kicks her leg out to the side, bends over, and sensually runs her fingers up her bare leg, flipping her hair as she stands up fully. As the pulsing music thumps louder, she turns around right on the beat drop, and my soul is sucked from my body.

My lungs deflate, and I do my best to keep my jaw off of the floor as the shock settles.

My blood heats instantly, and I suddenly become very aware of how many other men are in here, eyeing her up like a piece of meat.

Malik leans over Ollie with a shit-eating grin and shouts, "Hey, isn't that your tutor?"

I snap.

"Close your fucking eyes," I bark at him.

I'm already on my feet and charging the stage before realizing what I'm doing. My heart is pumping ferociously, and I feel like it might break every one of my ribs.

Grabbing the shirt from the back of my neck, I yank it over my head.

Murmurs break out among the crowd, getting Blair's attention, but I think the lights are too bright in her face to see me. That changes a second later when I jump onto the stage and stride toward her.

Everyone starts shouting at me, but I ignore them.

As I pass beneath the blinding lights, she finally sees me, and her eyes widen with shock and embarrassment. Her face shifts through a thousand emotions before landing on rage.

Her eyebrows pinch together, and her lips twist. "What the *fuck* are you doing, Griffin?"

Fucking hell. If I was mad before because everyone got to see her like this, then I'm livid now because seeing her up close is about to bring me to my goddamn knees. I try not to focus on how perfect every inch of her body is. I have to force myself to pay attention and not get distracted by trying to memorize her every curve.

I don't care if she's my tutor. I don't care if she loves this job. No one gets to see her like this. Besides, if she needed the extra money, she should've asked, and instead of doing this, I would have helped her. I need her to be at her best to help me be at mine.

That's the only reason, right?

Closing the distance between us, I pull my shirt over her head and down past her arms.

"Griffin! What the fuck?!" she yells at me and steps forward, slapping my chest as hard as she can, but I ignore her. "Get out of here!"

"No," I answer and meet her stare.

A gleam of dread strikes her pretty brown eyes.

"Yes! You need to leave!" she orders and crosses her arms.

God, she looks good in my shirt.

Jesus, get it together.

Grinning, I say, "Fine. Let's go."

"What? You're insane—ahh!" she squeals as I bend down and pick her up, throwing her over my shoulder with ease.

"If I'm leaving, then you're coming with me," I growl and squeeze her tighter against me as I walk toward the edge of the stage, where I find Malik and Ollie looking at me with their jaws on the floor.

The crowd is quickly dispersing, and I see two security guards racing toward me.

"Let her go! NOW!" one of the roid-ragers shouts at me as he approaches the stage.

"Blair, tell them it's fine," I murmur to her and spin around so she can face them and tell them to fuck off.

"I'm so sorry! Please tell Margo this is all just one big misunderstanding!" she pleads with them.

"Blair, do you know this guy?" one of them asks, and I suddenly hate the thought of them being all first-name friendly.

"Unfortunately, yes. He's harmless, I promise. I think he thinks this is some kind of game." She continues to try to excuse my behavior.

"Harmless?" I laugh. "I know a lot of people who would disagree with that statement."

Although I've probably overstepped, I don't care. I know that I don't want these guys eye-fucking her any longer. But maybe this isn't the way to handle it. Maybe it's none of my business. Although, at this point, it's too fucking late.

Blair digs her fingers into my ribs, and I grunt with pain and oblige to her silent request, slowly lowering her to the ground. As she slides down my torso, I do my best to pretend like it doesn't feel like fucking heaven, having her pressed against me.

As her feet hit the ground, she stares up at me with such rage. My God, she looks hot when she's pissed off.

A tall lady rushes us, looking murderously at me, "What in the hell is happening out here?"

"Margo, I'm so sorry. This was all just a mistake. I'm sorry! Please give me a second chance," she apologizes to the older lady, who looks so mad she could kill.

She looks up at me and shakes her head before shifting her attention to Blair. "Blair, I'm disappointed. You had a real opportunity here. But I'm sorry. You know the rules. It's a zero-tolerance policy."

Blair clasps her hands together. "Please, please, please don't do this! I just tutor him. He's not my boyfriend. I can promise it won't happen again."

"I can't promise that," I declare, stepping beside Blair and staring down at the lady that's scolding Blair like a child.

"My hands are tied. You know the rules. I'm sorry. I'll have Tia gather your things and bring your tips outside. You're fired, effective immediately," she says before turning away. "Tia, grab all of her things and meet her outside. Security, please escort them out."

"No! Please, no! I really need this job! Please, Margo, give me another chance!" Her voice is so raw and ragged that it cuts me like a knife, and I wish I could fix this for her.

One of the big guys with a security T-shirt grabs Blair's arm and starts yanking her toward the front doors.

"No, wait! Stop! Oww!" she yelps, and I immediately intervene.

Reaching out, I squeeze the guy's wrist, pressing between his tendons until he releases her. "Don't fucking touch her!"

Blair walks away as the guy gets in my face, challenging me with his stance. He shoves me lightly, and a growl-laugh bubbles from deep within me.

"I promise that you don't want to do that. Consider it a favor that I don't beat your ass for touching her."

"You are un-*fucking*-believable!" she screams at me before rushing toward the exit. "Leave me alone!"

Without hesitating, I bump Roid-Rage here with my shoulder and chase after her, bursting through the doors right behind her and bursting into the cool evening air.

"Blair, wait!" I call out.

"No, go fuck yourself, Griffin!" she yells without turning around and continues stomping farther away from me, her heels clicking on the pavement.

Speeding up, I jump in front of her and gently grab her shoulders. "Hey, I'm sorry! Just stop, please!"

The light from a lamppost illuminates her face, and

my heart breaks as I realize she's crying, her tears striking my heart like a wake-up call.

Shit. What have I done?

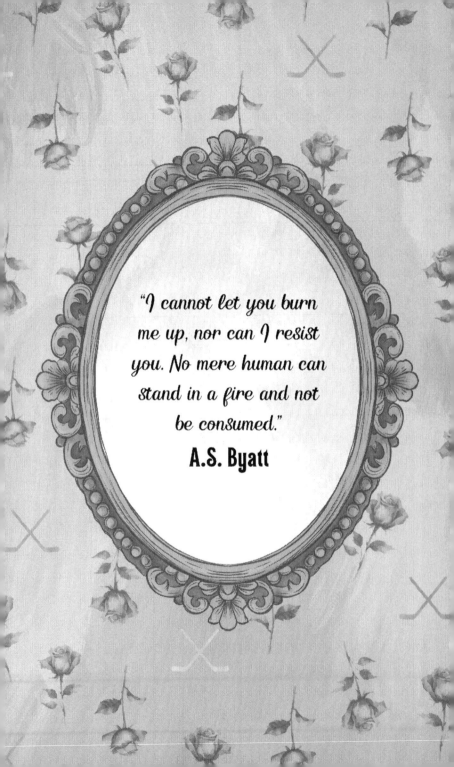

"I cannot let you burn me up, nor can I resist you. No mere human can stand in a fire and not be consumed."

A.S. Byatt

chapter eleven
blair

I've never felt this level of anger and frustration before.

"I'm sorry!" Griffin pleads, which only pisses me off more.

Placing my hands on his bare, stupidly defined chest, I shove him as hard as I can. "You being sorry means nothing to me right now!"

"Oh, the little reader's got some spice!" The black-haired and purple-eyed guy I recognize from class whistles behind me, and I begin to question how hard disposing of a body might be.

Griffin's eyes flick up, and he glares at Malik with a look that runs a shiver down my spine.

"Come with me. Let's talk in my truck." Griffin directs his attention back at me, and I wonder how men have such audacity.

Are they born with it? Or is it a skill they acquire over time? Regardless, it's baffling.

I can't even look at him right now, I am so angry. "I'm not going to go talk with you in your truck, Griffin. And good luck with your classes. You're going to need to find another tutor."

Fuck, I really shouldn't have done that. I can't afford to lose that job too.

But, God, Griffin's look of defeat and shock is a little worth it. He deserves to feel as helpless as I do right now.

"I'll pay you more! Name your price, and it's yours," Griffin counters, and I hate that I don't have a choice but to accept.

Purple-Eyes cuts through the silence. "Ooh, do you get dances for the extra money? If so, can I schedule some tutoring sessions with you too, Blair?"

"Malik," Griffin deeply snaps, silencing him immediately.

I never wanted to dance in the first place, and now, it's being thrown in my face like some kind of joke.

Without a word, I stride past Griffin and try to distance myself from them as much as possible.

"Blair, please stop. Let me fix this," Griffin pleads as he catches up to me with ease. "Please."

"No. I think you've already done enough, don't you?" I snap.

Griffin slides his finger beneath my chin and lifts my face up to him, but I turn away. "What can I do?"

"Leave me alone," I retort, staring at his chest.

"No can do. I need you." His voice is soft, and I hate that part of me falls for it—that charm that all jocks use to manipulate people.

"You don't understand, Griffin; you can't possibly

realize the damage you just caused me." My throat tightens as the back of my eyes burn.

I can't help but to think of my dad and how much he needs help right now or the bills on the fridge that still need to be paid for the month.

He cups my face and brushes my cheeks with his thumbs. "Then, tell me, please."

Closing my eyes, I have no choice but to tell him the truth because I'm afraid he's the only person who can make this better. "You didn't cost me some job. You cost me my house payment, electricity, my tuition … my father's treatment. I worked full-time there because I had to keep the heat on in our home and still go to school. You just ruined my life and didn't even realize it."

"Look at me," he whispers and tilts my head up. "I said I wanted to fix it, and I'm going to. I promise." His eyes light up. "How about a new business deal?"

"Like what?" I ask, scared it might actually include occasional dances from the gleam in his eyes.

"I'll pay for everything," he says casually, like he isn't offering to give me hundreds of thousands of dollars.

Feeling doubtful of his good intentions, I ask, "And why would you want to do that?"

"Because making it to the pro league is all that I care about, and I can't do it if I'm failing my classes and benched from playing." He hesitates and licks his bottom lip before sucking it between his teeth. "I will give you everything you need and want in exchange for one simple thing."

"And what's that?" My voice trembles.

He smirks. "You move in with me for the remainder of

the semester so that whenever I need your help, you're there to assist me. My little live-in tutor."

"That's the craziest thing I've ever heard. I can't live with you! I barely know you!" I scoff, completely taken aback by his offer.

I can't just move in with Griffin Hawthorne. That's literally insane.

"That's my offer. I'll pay for everything you need. You underestimate my love for hockey and the amount of money I have. You might need the money, but I desperately need you."

My cheeks warm at how his voice softens when he says he needs me, although I know he needs my brain, which is kind of ironic if you think about it because usually, guys want to use you for your body, not for your mind. Regardless, right now, he doesn't deserve to make me blush.

The brushing of his thumbs slows down, and if I wasn't gloriously pissed off at him, I would find it cute. But right now, his touch is only making me angrier.

Backing out of his grasp, I sigh. "I don't know."

"You don't know?" His brows furrow, like he's confused as to why I could somehow not be jumping at his offer.

I cross my arms over my chest. "Yes, Griffin! I don't know if I can move in with a practical stranger and agree to live with him for months so that he can use my brain whenever he pleases in exchange for money. What if you're secretly a serial killer or something? These are things that have to be considered!"

He chuckles, and I squint my eyes at him, wiping the smug smile off of his face.

"I'm not a killer."

"That's exactly what one would say, don't you think?" I snark at him.

"Okay, fair. But I promise you I'm not." He steps closer, and I back away again.

"Did you know I worked here? Did you do this on purpose so you could manipulate me into being your kidnapped tutor?" Each word makes me realize how horrible of a possibility that is.

What if this was his plan all along?

He throws his hands in the air. "Are you crazy? Of course I didn't plan this! How could you even think that?"

"Because I don't know you, and now, it seems like everything is working out for you, but I suppose when you have enough money to throw around, all of your problems disappear, right?"

He leans down, and his warm breath hits my face as his demeanor turns cold. "I have enough money to burn it for fun, but it doesn't make my demons any weaker or my loneliness any less agonizing. You're right. You don't know me at all."

I'm exhausted and defeated, and I don't want to do this anymore. I've figured it out on my own for this long, and I'll do it again.

Holding his stare, I murmur, "Goodbye, Griffin."

I turn around and walk away from him, determined to walk home in these heels and his T-shirt at this point.

"Where are you going?" I hear his heavy steps follow me, and I can't resist rolling my eyes. "Dear God, let me drive you home."

"No, thank you," I sing.

"Stop being so stubborn, Blair! Let me give you a ride," he begs. "Please."

My feet are already killing me, and I'm twenty miles from my house. Slowly, I turn around with defeat etched into my face and a slump in my shoulders.

"Blair!" Erica, aka Tia, calls out to me from the club, and I just now realize how far we have wandered from the entrance.

Waving to her, I say, "I'm coming!"

Malik and the other guy walk over to her, and she smiles up at them.

He says something to her, and she voluntarily hands over my purse and backpack.

"Hey!" I shout at them, and Malik laughs.

"Don't worry; everything's in safe hands," he says reassuringly.

My pace quickens, and as I pass Griffin, he reaches his hand out, and his fingers graze my side, but I ignore him.

"Girl, I am going to miss you." Erica frowns.

Taking a deep breath for the first time in the last hour, I throw my arms around her, feeling the shirt lift above my ass.

She pulls me in tightly and kisses my cheek as she releases me. "Coffee date soon?"

I nod. "Yes, please."

Margo's head pops through the door, and she yells, "Erica, we need you back in here. Chat with her when you're not on the clock."

She ducks back inside, and I grumble, "Was she always such a hard-ass?"

Erica laughs. "When you're not on her good side? Yes. See you later, B."

"Bye," I practically whisper as I fully come to terms with what just happened and realize that I will miss working with some of the staff.

It's hard not to build relationships with the people around you, especially when you're stuck with them for hours at a time. I don't think I ever appreciated how much I'd come to care for them until now, knowing that I'll never have potlucks with them in the back room, bathroom parties before our shifts, or dance lessons on the slow nights. It's all just gone now.

"She's a cutie," Malik says into my ear, and I drop my elbow backward into his side as I spin around. His eyes light up, and he says, "Griffin, I like this one. Would you be willing to share?"

Griffin strolls up, and a coolness whips through the air. His nostrils flare, and his chest heaves as he stomps beside me and slides a hand around my waist. "No. She's already spoken for."

Forcing myself out of Griffin's tight grasp, I groan. "Oh my God, can we stop with the pissing contest? Break out the rulers already, and we'll see who's bigger."

"No need to do that, sweetheart. Mine's bigger." Malik winks.

"Good for you, buddy. Now, give me my stuff," I demand, holding my hands out.

Malik and Griffin apparently solve the pissing match they were knee-deep in not a second ago. Now, they are smiling at each other, making me feel like prey stuck between two oversize predators.

"Here you go," Malik says, holding my stuff out toward me.

I reach for it, and he yanks it away and tosses it to Griffin.

You have got to be kidding me.

"Griffin," I scold him like the child he is acting like. "Give me my shit."

"After I give you a ride home, it's all yours." He smiles proudly about finding a new way to make me go along with his plan.

I wish I could say no and call an Uber. But if my dad is awake, he can't exactly catch me coming home in a metallic-gold bikini set, a T-shirt, and heels. I need my bag.

"Fine, you win. Let's get this over with." I sigh and feel the slightest twinge of relaxation settle into my shoulders, knowing this night is almost over.

"Right this way." Griffin beams.

With my arms crossed, I follow him.

"Good night, Blair!" Malik calls out sweetly.

Lifting my hand up, I flip him off and hold it in the air for him to see clearly.

He and the other guy burst out laughing.

Silence surrounds us as we walk to the car. Griffin opens the door for me and holds his hand out to help me into his truck. Taking his hand, I hop onto the leather seat, and he closes the door behind me.

He slides into the driver's seat and starts the truck. He presses some buttons, and moments later, my backside warms up from the heated seat.

"Thank you," I force out with a grunt.

He types into his phone and then holds it out for me. "I need your address."

I take the phone and enter it in the Maps app before handing it back to him.

"What kind of music do you like?" Griffin asks as he pulls out of the parking space.

"Doesn't matter to me. Anything's fine," I answer and lean my head against the window.

He turns the volume on the radio up, and Taylor Swift's "Love Story" plays softly through the speakers.

I don't know what it is about music, but I swear it always makes me feel every emotion I'm trying to ignore. And right now, the floodgates have opened, drowning me in agony.

I'm so tired, tired of trying to stretch every second of every day so I can make enough money to just survive. Until now, I don't think that I've even allowed myself to feel the burnout that's been there for quite a while.

My chest heaves, and a sob breaks free. I lean further into the window, hoping Griffin didn't notice. Thankfully, he doesn't say anything, so I assume that he didn't hear.

He hums along to "Love Story," and as mad and drained as I am, I can't help but grin at the fact that he knows the song.

My eyes shut, and I drift into sleep for just a few minutes, where my problems fade away. But the serenity doesn't last long.

Griffin nudges my shoulder, and I sit up, my eyes dry.

"We're here," he announces.

Mindlessly digging in my backpack, I pull out my

leggings. Kicking my heels off, I slide the leggings on and step into my tennis shoes, stowing the heels in my bag.

I slide my backpack on and throw my purse over my shoulder.

"My deal still stands, but I need an answer as soon as possible in case I have to start at square one again and find another tutor," he says before opening his door and stepping out.

What in the hell is he doing? He walks around the front of the truck, but I open it and hop down to the ground before he can reach the door.

I don't have anything left to say to him right now, and all I want is to crawl into bed and pretend this night never happened.

Griffin laughs as I step past him and head to my house.

"Good night, Blair," he calls out.

With the least effort required, I force a response. "Night."

With the stealth I've acquired from the countless nights of entering the house at late hours, I go inside silently, shutting the door behind me.

I tiptoe down the hallway toward my room.

The most aggressive cough I've ever heard roars from my father's bedroom, and my heart breaks. How can I help him now without my job?

My eyes well up as I hear my father settle back down. I take the last few steps to my room and sneak inside, dropping my bags next to my desk.

Flopping onto my bed, I stare at the ceiling and contemplate how I got here. I wouldn't need extra money if I had just gotten a full scholarship. If my dad hadn't been stuck at those damn factories for years, maybe he wouldn't have gotten lung cancer. What-ifs continue to bounce through my mind, but I know they are pointless. No what-if will solve all of my problems.

I hate that I have no other choice at this point. In order to ensure my dad gets his treatment and I get to stay in school, I have to make a deal with The Beast.

Sliding off of my bed, I dig my phone out of my purse and text him.

> Fine. We have a deal. But you must promise that my dad will be taken care of, no matter what.

Bubbles appear before his text comes through.

> Griffin: I promise far more than that.

Tossing my phone on the bed, I quickly change into PJs, throwing Griffin's T-shirt and the rest of my outfit in the laundry bin.

My phone dings. Once. Twice. Three times.

What else does he have to say tonight?

Shutting my light off, I grab my phone and expect to see Griffin's name appear. Somehow, a worse fate has found me.

> Grant: I can't believe you let him touch you like that. I know that dance was only for me. What a pleasant surprise from you, my Blair Bear.

Attachments load immediately, and I gasp at what I see. Photos of me thrown over Griffin's shoulder at The Fallen Petal tonight.

That fucking prick. I didn't even notice him there. Usually, I can feel his presence like a hand choking my throat.

I can't handle anything else tonight. I feel like a bomb; everything is burning the fuse, and I'm about to blow.

> I am not yours, Grant. Get it through that thick skull of yours. Leave me alone!

Grant: I love this game we play, Blair Bear.

dangle

Completely embarrassing the opponent with impressive stick handling offensively. Practically "dangling" the puck in front of them but they can't get to it.

chapter twelve
griffin

Practice is usually the one place that makes me forget about any outside stressors. But right now, it's not doing anything to get Blair out of my mind. We've been scrimmaging for a half hour, and my thoughts are everywhere but on the puck.

She's moving in today, and I can't stop fucking thinking about it. I still can't believe I offered my home to her, but as much as she felt like she didn't have a choice, I felt the same. I need her to help me with English, but now, I might as well have her help me with any and every class I might have issues with going forward. I mean, Lord knows I'm paying her enough for help in more than one class. As long as she's willing, of course.

It's only for a few months. As long as this semester ends with her still enrolled at HEAU and making sure I don't fail any of my classes, I'll be content.

My chest tightens, and my lungs burn. I can't help but acknowledge that I might want more from her. But I have to concentrate on what I've been working toward my whole life—to secure my future and get my spot in the pro league. That's what has to be my top priority. I can't have gone this far, only to lose focus now.

I can't let any funny business happen during her stay, not with me and sure as shit not with anyone else. Neither she nor I can afford any distractions, including anyone trying to distract her *from* me.

Malik sprays me with his skates, and ice tears me from my stupor, and I lock on to my target.

"Really?" I scoff, pinching my eyebrows.

Shrugging, he winks. "What? You weren't paying attention anyway. I'm surprised you noticed."

"You're such a fucker." I chuckle.

Malik huffs and grabs his bottle, spraying water into his mouth and then on his face to cool off. "Finally, we get a break. Is Coach trying to kill us today or what? I'm tired as shit right now."

Holding his stare, I say with a deadpan voice, "Maybe it's because you were up all night, sending me shit on socials until I had to turn my sound off because my phone was dinging every five seconds."

He scoffs and throws his hand up. "Look, it's not my fault you don't appreciate all the time I dedicate to sending you funny shit."

"Riiight. Sure, bud." I laugh.

"Fuck you." Malik grins and skates back to center ice, where Coach is waiting to start the next drill.

Taking a few gulps of water, I toss my bottle back on the bench and skate out to join the huddle.

Skating up behind Malik, I smack his ass with my stick, and he fake moans loud as hell.

"Don't stop now," Malik says in a super-high-pitched voice.

Rearing my stick back, I prepare to hit him five times harder than before and swing through, smacking him on the left side of his ass.

"Ahh!" Malik moans, and our team bursts out in laughter. "Speaking of moaning, have you heard what your tutor sounds like yet? Because I bet she makes the sweetest soun—"

Jabbing my stick into his ribs hard enough to hurt him but not do any real damage, I cut his sentence off and skate right in front of him, putting my face in his.

He's wincing as I hold his stare and growl, "Don't." He smirks, and I make sure he knows how serious I am. "Don't talk about her. Don't make a move on her. Don't mess with her. Don't think about her. Nothing. Got it?"

"Anything else, Dad?" he asks sarcastically.

Lifting my arms, I place my hands on his chest and shove him. Hard. "Malik, I'm dead fucking serious. In fact …"

Skating to the front of the group, I announce, "Excuse me, I need to make something clear."

The team faces me and goes silent.

"Blair Adams, my new tutor, is off-limits to everyone! She is not to be pursued romantically. She is not to be messed with in any capacity. Am I clear?"

"You got it, man," Asher calls out first, followed by everyone else's agreement, everyone except Malik.

"Don't make me beat compliance out of you, Mal," I warn jokingly … well, mostly jokingly.

He rolls his eyes. "Jesus, yes, I'll leave your little book-worm alone."

"All right, set up for breakaways. One-on-two," Coach announces, drifting the focus back to practice. "Griffin and Dean on defense."

Dean and I set up on defense while half of the group splits to the other zone, and lines form at the center line. The first person in our line, Asher, skates forward. Coach tosses a puck onto the ice, and Asher grabs it with his stick and starts racing toward us.

Skating backward, I watch him like a hawk, looking for the slightest shift in his body to tell me where he's going. He drifts left toward Dean. Of course, he wants to make his brother look bad if possible. With stunning finesse and quick wrist movements, he passes the puck through Dean's legs and catches it on his stick again, skating past Dean with a gigantic smile on his face. But he's not in the clear yet.

Digging into the ice, I skate in front of Asher and see a weak spot in his plan. As he skates to the side and pulls back slightly, I charge him and poke the puck out of the way.

"Dammit!" Asher shouts, and I shrug like it was the easiest thing in the world.

"Ha-ha!" Dean laughs at Asher as he skates up next to me.

Asher grimaces at him.

"I went by you like nothing. Maybe lose some of that confidence," Asher chirps at Dean.

"No, thanks." Dean grins.

The three active players rotate. I skate to the back of the long line, Dean takes my spot, Asher takes Dean's spot, and a new player takes Asher's.

Malik is a few people in front of me. I tap him with my stick, and he turns around and sighs dramatically.

"What do you want?"

"You're helping me tonight with moving Blair in. You owe me," I tell him, not taking no for an answer.

"Ugh, fine!" he huffs.

"Thanks." I chuckle.

"No problem, buddy." He smiles and skates forward as the drill shifts players again.

Mrs. Potts is getting her room ready right now, and I'm picking her up after practice. I wonder if she'll like my home. Will she be comfortable? Maybe even happy?

I can't stop running what-ifs through my mind the rest of the time on the ice, and it doesn't stop until I'm pulling up to her house.

My heart feels like it's running a marathon, and my palms are sweating. I hate feeling nervous. It feels a lot like vulnerability, a sense of lacking control.

"Be on good behavior, Mal," I warn him as I back up into the driveway of house 1091.

"Psh. I'm a fucking angel, thank you very much," he says defensively, and I can't help but wonder if he has ever taken a single thing in his life seriously.

A flash of blue catches the corner of my eye, and I turn, my mouth drying at the sight of Blair in a light-blue sweater and leggings. She hasn't looked over yet, which seems intentional from the curled lips as she stares aggressively *away* from us. Her profile is stunning. From her plump and often-pouting lips to the smooth curve of her nose, she's—

Get yourself together.

Forcing myself out of my truck, I open the door and walk over to her. "I brought Malik to help carry anything you need."

She still won't meet my eye as she coolly says, "Thank you. But there's no need. I just have this suitcase."

She rolls it over to me, and I push it to Malik, who then rolls it gently and loads it into my truck while I debate on what the hell to say next. I've never been one who had to force conversation with a girl, nor have I wanted to. But something about Blair being mad at me makes my gut twist and my heart ache.

Pinching myself, I try to calm my racing heart. I don't know when or how she got this far under my skin, but she burrowed herself in. I know her cold-shoulder is out of anger at our deal, so I let her take the lead.

"I'll be right back," she announces and retreats back inside.

"Okay." The word is a whisper on my breath as I fight the urge to follow her.

Running my hand down my face, I sigh loudly. Maybe I should just check to ensure she doesn't need help with anything else. I know she said that her suitcase was the only thing, but just in case, I should probably go in there.

My emotions have always been the one part of myself that I've struggled to control. No matter what I'm feeling, my emotion pulls the strings of my actions like a puppeteer. Right now, all I feel is confusion because I shouldn't care that she's upset with me, but I do.

As I step toward her house, the front door swings open, and she walks through with a backpack on her shoulders and a grocery bag full of envelopes, which I'm assuming are bills, in her hand. Instead of her turning every bill over to me to pay, I set up a checking account that she can use to pay whatever she needs. It might seem excessive, but honestly, it's just laziness. I don't want to have to send her money or pay every bill she gives me. I'll just transfer a lump sum after she gives me an initial estimate, and then she can take it from there.

"Is your dad home?" I ask, wondering why that's any of my business.

She looks at me for the first time with teary eyes, and I feel my heart contract with pain. "Why? Do you want to meet him and ask for his blessing before you kidnap his daughter?"

Malik laughs audibly and immediately clears his throat like he's trying to cover it up.

"What? I am not kidnapping you! You literally agreed to move in." My words fly out of my mouth hastily because I cannot believe she just referred to her moving in as kidnapping.

"It doesn't matter. No, he's not home." Her gaze drops to my chest, and she clenches her jaw. "But I'm ready. Can we go? I want to get unpacked. I have a lot of homework to do."

Running my hand through my hair, I nod. "Yeah, of course."

Pulling open the passenger front door, I hold it for her, but she ignores me and opens the back door, hopping inside. Stifling a laugh, I bite down on my bottom lip as Malik pretends it was for him all along.

"Thanks, babe." He makes a kissing sound, and I slam the door shut the second he's in.

Fucking hell, maybe this was a really terrible idea. I probably could have found another tutor to help me, but I don't think I want one that isn't Blair. For her intelligence, of course, and no other reason—like me dying to know what she tastes like, what her body feels like pressed against mine, and what beautiful fucking sounds she could make from my touch. Nope, definitely not that.

The ride to my place would be quiet and tense if it wasn't for Malik giving us a concert the entire drive. Sometimes, I wonder how he has the seemingly unlimited energy of a toddler. But I also know that he's only like that with certain people. He's the type of person who only lets people see his true self if he's really comfortable with you. To most of the world, he comes across as an arrogant asshole, which he is, but there's more to him than his scowl.

Asher and Dean should already be parked in my driveway when we arrive. They're picking Malik up and giving him a ride back to his car so I can stay here and help Blair settle in.

When I park, Malik jumps out and frolics over to the guys. I can't help but notice that Blair hasn't opened her door yet.

"What's wrong?" I ask her, wiping my hands on my sweats.

She scoffs, "Griffin, why are we doing this? There must be a thousand other solutions."

Her genuine question catches me off guard. My lips part, and I lick my bottom lip as I look in my rearview mirror and find her staring out of the window, her face pinched with frustration.

"Name one," I challenge because I can't think of one possible alternative that would give each of us a better outcome.

The silence stretches between us, and she sighs. "I can't."

It's the truth. No job could possibly offer her the amount of money I will end up paying her, and I could never find a tutor who is serious enough about helping me that they'd move into my house with me. There really is no better scenario.

Trying to ease the situation, I attempt to level the playing field of suffering. "Look, I know this isn't ideal for you. To be honest, it's not for me either. I'm very protective about who comes into my house, and like you said, we don't know each other, not really. Mrs. Potts and Chip are my family, and I invited you to live not only with me, but with them. If I had another choice that would benefit me as much as this will, I would take it."

I hear her suck in a breath, but she stays quiet.

"They're leaving. They were just here to pick Malik up. The front door of the house will be unlocked if you want to wait in here until they leave," I tell her as I open my door and get out.

Opening the driver's-side back door, I grab my backpack,, and walk over to where the guys are talking outside the twins' car.

"How's the girlfriend?" Asher teases, and all it takes is one serious glance from me for his lips to seal shut.

A pulse of anger shocks my system like a strike of lightning. Blair is clearly going through enough without them picking on her to her face or behind her back.

Meeting Asher's challenging stare, I bite out, "For one, she's not my girlfriend, and you know that. Secondly, keep any talk of her out of your mouth. I like you, Ash, but don't think you're safe from me because we're on the same team. I meant it—she's off-limits to any and *all* bullshit."

"Okay, okay." He holds his hands up in defeat. "My bad. I'll chill out."

"Good. Glad to hear it," I acknowledge his agreement, but do nothing more to continue this conversation. "You guys get out of here. I'll see you at practice tomorrow."

"All right," Dean says and opens the driver's door. "See you tomorrow, man."

"Try not to dream of me tonight." Malik blows me a kiss and slides into the back seat, laughing.

Someday, I really need to put that little fuck in his place, but he's just so damn funny that I can't help but laugh along with him.

They drive away, and I decide to give Blair a moment alone before coming inside. I walk up the stairs, and unlock my front door. She'll come inside eventually.

I set her bag by the door. My stomach grumbles as I inhale something that smells amazing, and I head into the kitchen to see what Mrs. Potts is cooking up.

Her wide eyes find me the second I enter the room, and she whispers, "Is she here?"

"Yeah, she's still in my truck." I chuckle. "She'll probably be in soon."

Mrs. Potts is whisking something in a bowl as she asks, "What is she doing?"

I pull one of the barstools out from the island and sit down on it, leaning my arms against the counter. "I have no clue."

She is just as confused as I am but leaves it be. "Are you hungry? I'm making bacon cheeseburgers with Parmesan fries and garlic aioli."

My mouth waters instantly, and I think I could eat a thousand burgers right now; I'm so hungry. "Yes, I'm starving."

"Good. Because there will be plenty!" she cheers, and my heart warms that she is making me a plate, no matter what my answer might have been.

I hear the click of the front door shutting and excuse myself. "I'll be back."

She chortles, and I wish I knew what she was thinking. She's probably asking herself the same thing I was earlier —what the hell am I doing?

"Hello?" Blair's soft and sultry voice carries through the entryway.

Turning the corner, I walk toward the front door and answer, "Right here."

She stands in the center of the open space with reddened eyes, and I resist the urge to swipe any remaining tears from her face as I wander closer to her.

She offers a soft smile that doesn't show any true happiness. "Where should I ..."

"Yeah, I'll show you," I respond to her unfinished question because I assume she's asking where her room is.

"Cool. Thanks." She grabs the handle on her suitcase and drags it behind her.

"You'll be in the east wing with me. Mrs. Potts and Chip live downstairs, and I don't want to intrude on any of their space, so I had her prepare one of the rooms upstairs," I tell her, hoping she doesn't freak out that her room will be closer to mine.

Although I didn't exactly want to give up any of the rooms in my wing of the house, I really didn't want to do it to Mrs. Potts and Chip. Besides, now I don't have to trek through the house when I have a question on any homework.

"O-okay," she murmurs and follows me as I head to the split staircase.

Spinning around, I look down at her and hold my hand out. "I'll take that for you."

Without giving her much of an option, I grab the suitcase from her before she can protest and continue to lead the way up the staircase.

She doesn't fight me on it, so I take that as a win.

When we reach the landing, where we'll either veer left into the east wing or right into the west wing, I decide now is the best time to tell her the one rule I have.

"One quick thing." I stop.

She steps beside me and looks up at me. "Yeah?"

"You can go anywhere in this house; explore at your whim. But the west wing is off-limits. No exceptions.

Okay?" I ask her, my jaw clenching from discussing the west wing at all.

"Okay, but wh—"

I cut her off, "It's not anything bad. It's just full of really valuable family stuff, and I don't want anything to get broken."

She squints. "I'm not going to break anything."

Rubbing my face, I grit out, "I know. But it's still off-limits, okay? This isn't fucking debatable!" *Fuck*. I didn't mean to snap at her. "I'm sorry for yelling. Everything in there is just very important to my family and me, and we can't risk anything happening to it."

"Yeah, fine. I won't go in there." Her face is cold, like a sheet of armor has slid into place, and I hate that it's there because of me.

"Thank you. Your room is right down here." I step forward and lead her through the double-door entrance into the east wing.

My bedroom is the third door on the right, and hers is directly across from it.

"This is it." I open the door for her and step inside.

"Oh my God." Her surprise slips past her anger as she enters the room.

A tall four-poster bed sits against the back wall, full of the best down pillows, silk sheets, and comforters one can buy. A soft, glowing chandelier cascades down from the high vaulted ceiling, casting the prettiest glow on her face.

One corner of the room has a sofa and coffee table with a lifting lid for a makeshift desk. If she wants an actual one, we can do that, but I tried not to change too much here since there wasn't much time to get it ready.

Handcrafted dressers sit opposite the bed, and she could use more clothes by the looks of the one small suitcase. Maybe I'll add that to her list of bills that will be covered. Anything she needs to make this stay more comfortable, she can have, simple as that.

"Make yourself at home. Let me know after you get a chance to settle in if you want to change anything," I offer and look down at her. The slightest ounce of peace calms her, and my shoulders instantly relax at the sight. "Dinner will be ready soon, if it's not already now. If you're hungry, of course."

Fuck, I feel like I'm trying to talk to a wild animal. I want to talk to her enough to make her feel welcome, but not too much to scare her off. I have no idea how to act around her right now.

Backtracking out of the room, I step through the threshold and say, "But, yeah, just let me know if you need anything else."

She walks over to the door and says, "Thanks," before shutting it in my face.

Exhaling, I breathe normally again, the quickness of it diminishing from being near her. Hell, I was afraid to breathe too loudly and make the situation worse.

The scent of bacon invades my nose again, and I follow the trail of it back downstairs. With two plates full, Mrs. Potts and Chip are already digging into their food when I enter the dining room. There is plenty left over for Blair when she comes down.

But as time passes by and she doesn't show, I realize she doesn't intend to join us. Being the good host I am, I load a plate up and bring it with me upstairs when I head to bed.

Knocking on her door, I call out, "Hey, I've got dinner for you."

"No, thank you!" she shouts, and it sounds all muffled through the door.

God, she is so stubborn.

"Okay, well, I'll leave it out here if you change your mind!" I shout back at her and gently set the plate on the floor outside of her door.

Turning around, I open my door and walk in, shutting it behind me. Grabbing the neck of my shirt from the back, I pull it over my head and toss it into the hamper, along with my sweats. Turning my TV on and my light off, I slide into bed and find one of the pro games.

A few minutes later, I hear Blair's door shut across the hall. My lips tip up, and I can't do anything to stifle the full-blown smile from taking over my face.

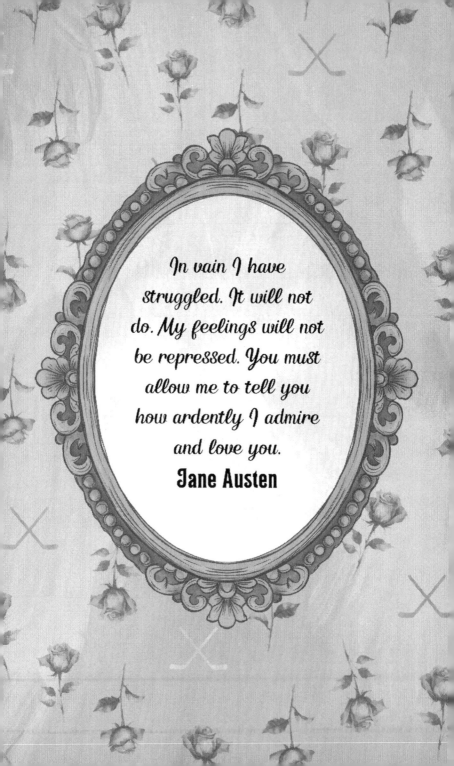

In vain I have struggled. It will not do. My feelings will not be repressed. You must allow me to tell you how ardently I admire and love you.

Jane Austen

chapter thirteen
blair

I'm struggling with deciding if I enjoy or hate my new living situation. I've never imagined living in a place like this. In every regard, it is lush and lavish. Its beauty is unmatched—from the unbelievably comfortable bed and elegant décor to the vault ceilings and dazzling chandeliers.

If I pretend just for a moment that this is my bedroom and always has been, I feel like a princess in her castle who takes on the world without limits. A girl who isn't afraid of going after what she wants and settles for nothing less than perfection in every aspect of life. But the only way I can live like that is between the pages of my books.

Before I let reality sink in, I open my copy of *The Piece That Fits*. The main male character, Liam Lockwood, has Avery, the main female character, pushed back against the wall and is growling something sexy into her ear. I'm eating up every single second.

I wonder what it would be like to be cornered by Griffin as he fights the urge to kiss me.

Nope. I am not doing that.

Forcing my mind and eyes on my book, I continue reading for what feels like minutes. But when I check my phone, I realize that hours have passed, and my mouth is painstakingly dry.

Sliding out of the high-rise bed, I fall a few inches to the floor and step into my fuzzy slippers. A chill runs through my body, and I grab my university sweatshirt and throw it over my matching tank top and short set before stealthily slipping out of my room.

Soft, glowing lights from the golden sconces illuminate the hallway as I wander past the double-door entrance to the top of the staircase.

Descending the stairs, I trail my hand down the cool banister. I can't imagine what it was like growing up in this house.

I wonder where his family is now. I know he mentioned they're gone, and I'm sure with this kind of money, they could live on their own island for all I know. But are they loving? Are they kind? Or are they cold and calculated and only had a child because they felt it was a box they should check?

I don't think I've let myself wonder anything about Griffin because I didn't want to know him—at least not really. It's easier to imagine that he and Grant are cut from the same cloth. But I know they are not even close to being the same. Griffin might have forcefully encouraged me to move in with him, but he's never treated me as an object, like Grant.

Did little Griffin have the best childhood filled with elaborate birthday parties and love?

How has it taken me this long to even ask those questions?

My chest convulses as I come to the realization that I've been disconnected from everything around me.

I pride myself on my empathy and my kindness. I love that I wear my heart on my sleeve. But I think after Grant and the overwhelming financial stress, I tucked my heart away into a little lock box that only I could reach. Because I couldn't trust anyone not to break it. I wouldn't be able to survive it. I'm not sure much has changed, but I know I don't want to live without feeling anything, regardless of how much it might hurt.

"Oh my God!" I screech as I step on the landing and turn, coming face-to-face with Griffin. "Warn a girl!"

His smile takes over his face as he tries his best not to laugh. "I figured that you could hear me walking. Maybe you should have better awareness of your surroundings."

My mouth waters as I become acutely aware of the "surroundings" standing feet away from me.

His wet hair is messy, sexy, and sticking to his forehead. Not to mention the fact that he's only wearing gray sweatpants. Every inch of his thick, muscular chest and stomach are glistening with sweat.

No man should be allowed to look like that. It's … distracting. Plus, he has light-brown chest hair that I find annoyingly sexy and a trail that runs down his lower stomach, disappearing beneath the gray sweats like a path I should *not* want to travel down.

Griffin clears his throat, and I about throw myself off

of the top of these stairs from the embarrassment that electrifies my body, warming every inch of my skin.

Frustrated with myself for checking him out so obviously and for getting called out on it, I cross my arms over my chest and roll my eyes.

"I can do a spin if you want to get the full view," Griffin offers with a smirk.

Yes, please.

"No, thank you. I've already seen more than I wanted to," I snark at him and descend two steps closer. "Now, if you'll excuse me."

"Of course. Let me get out of your way on this ten-foot-wide staircase." He laughs and steps up closer to me; goose bumps erupt down my shoulders as only three marble steps remain between us.

Our eyes are almost level right now, and I don't plan on losing this high ground until I know I've won.

Glancing away, I try to reel in my racing heart and calm my erratic breathing. I feel his stare scorching a trail down my body, drawing my gaze back to the real-life Greek god. I suddenly feel like an ice bath in the Antarctic would do nothing to cool me off.

Now, it's me that catches him. I clear my throat. His eyes shoot up to mine, and his cheeks flush the lightest shade of pink.

"Have a good night, warden," I tease and descend the few steps between us as he chuckles.

Reaching out, I pat his warm chest and feel his laughter, halting a millisecond later as he looks down at my hand.

His fingers near my leg stretch out and trail up my thigh, my breathing becomes shallow as he nears my hip.

Curiosity gets the better of me. "Do you always work out at one in the morning?"

He looks away, all tension between us snapping as he sighs, his face darkening. "Not usually. But I couldn't fall asleep, so I went for a quick run."

"Why couldn't you sleep?" The question falls past my lips before I can remind myself that it's none of my damn business. But it's too late.

He laughs humorlessly. "You don't need to be haunted by my demons."

Shrugging, I sit down on the cool steps and gesture beside me. "I think that's my call to make."

He scoffs and sits beside me, resting his clasped hands between his knees. "All right then." He pauses. "I've had difficulty sleeping for a few years now."

I remain silent, giving him the space to fill if he wishes to continue.

He glances over at me and cautiously looks me in the eye, like he's contemplating how much of himself he's willing to share. I don't blame him for hesitating. I'm the same way.

"I've got pills and melatonin that can help. But I don't like how groggy I always feel coming off of them in the morning. Plus, I don't always hate that I have a hard time sleeping." His voice softens, almost inaudible. "Sometimes, I think I deserve it."

For what?

"Why would you say that?"

Griffin drops his head into his hands and runs his fingers through his hair. "It's a long story."

Shrugging, I say, "I've never been one to shy away from a long story."

Griffin smiles, but it never reaches his eyes.

"I doubt you deserve it, Griffin," I whisper to him, staring at the ground and avoiding his gaze. "You seem like a decent guy."

He bumps my shoulder with his. "Just decent?"

My chest flutters at his flirty tone, but I try to ignore the giddiness now dancing through me. "Ehh. Pretty decent. Is that better?"

He laughs, one that lights up his face and crinkles his eyes. "I'll take it."

"Good," I say sassily.

"And why are *you* wandering the house at one a.m.? Shouldn't you be holed up in your room, refusing to come out?" He smirks.

"Well, I got lost in a book for a while. I'm grabbing some water before I go to bed," I answer truthfully.

"Does that help you sleep? The reading, not the water."

"Depends on how good the book is and how far along I am in it. Because sometimes, I start a book with the thought in mind to only read a chapter or two, but then I get completely sucked in and can't stop until I finish it. It's like I get addicted to the story. I swear some authors weave crack between the lines of their books. You can't ever get enough." I have to stop myself and take a breath. "Sorry, I got carried away."

When I glance at Griffin, he looks at me with soft,

twinkling eyes. "Don't apologize." He hesitates. "Would you share one of your favorite books with me sometime?"

Nodding, I gulp, feeling naked under his stare. "Yeah."

As we sit in silence, looking at each other, the world around us seems to fall away.

Sitting up, I am a second away from standing and heading down to the kitchen.

But Griffin stops me, asking, "Are you doing okay? I know this is a big change."

Tilting my head side to side, I sigh, "Yeah. I think so. I'll let you know in a few days once I've decided if you're the best or worst housemate to have."

This earns a chuckle from him. "All right. I'll be awaiting your decision."

Grinning, I wrap my arm around my legs, tucking them into my chest and resting my head on my knees.

"Do you need anything? We can change anything in your room if you want. Just let me know," Griffin says and pushes to his feet.

"No, I'm okay. I'll tell you if that changes," I answer him.

My stomach flutters as he offers me his hands. I slide mine into his, and he gently pulls me to my feet.

"Have a good night, warden. I hope you get some good sleep. Your studies will thank you for it." I smirk and inch my hands out of his before moving down the stairs.

Griffin chuckles. "Good night, my little prisoner."

I scoff and smile. How ridiculous of a nickname. It's horrible.

I love it.

Aside from the deafening thump of my heart, I remain

quiet as I walk into the kitchen, refocused on the mission —getting a glass of water. After looking through, like, thirty cabinets, I can tell you where everything else is in this kitchen, except for the glasses. Finally, I locate them and fill one with water, chugging it immediately before refilling it with one thought in my mind.

Griffin is starting to surprise me.

I don't know how I'm possibly going to be able to get to sleep after our little conversation.

Getting Lumi to pick me up this morning for class took a lot of bribing. I know Griffin would offer to drive me, but I have no desire to be in close quarters with him right now. I might do something stupid, like flirt with him.

I'm two steps from the front door when Griffin's voice stops me dead in my tracks.

"Hey, wait up."

Mouthing the word, *Shit*, I squeeze the straps of my backpack tighter and spin around to face him.

The bottom half of his torso is exposed as he finishes sliding his shirt into place, and I try not to drool.

"Good morning." I smile up at him as he reaches me.

His brows pinch, and he cocks his head to the side. "Are you leaving?"

Rocking back and forth on the balls of my feet, I nod shyly. "Yeah. Lumi's picking me up for class."

My answer does nothing to ease the confusion etched into his features. "You mean the class we have *together*?"

Biting down on my lip, I nod. "Yeah, that's the one."

He takes a small step toward me, and I realize butterflies don't just flutter in your stomach. They can break free and invade every body part, making you feel like your feet are lifting off of the ground.

"You didn't want to ask me for a ride?" His voice is pained, but his soft, smiling lips tell a different story—a confusing one.

This is exactly what I was trying to avoid, hence my trying to sneak out. But, no, that would be too much to ask.

"I didn't want to bother you, and Lumi used to pick me up for classes every day anyway, so it's not unusual that he's doing it now." I word-vomit my excuse at him.

"Uh-huh, sure." He studies me for a moment before grinning. "See you there then."

"Yeah, see you," I respond and leave this conversation as fast as I can, walking through the door and shutting it behind me.

A cool breeze filters through my coffee-colored sweater, sending chills down my spine. I stride down the stairs and slide into Lumi's front passenger seat.

He's staring at me with two coffees in his hands and a look of impatient intrigue, resembling a bomb with a lit fuse about to blow. I know he's been dying to know all the details since I moved in with Griffin.

I've kind of been avoiding his calls and keeping my texts short because I haven't really decided what I was going to say. Should I tell him about the midnight run-in on the stairs? Should I tell him I couldn't get that moment out of my mind all night and still can't?

"You're in trouble," Lumi scolds me as he juts an inviting cup of coffee at me.

Any thoughts of keeping anything from him go out the window the second he greets me and hands me the warmest cup of happiness. I don't know why I'm constantly trying to create walls between myself and the world. There's no reason to have any barrier between Lumi and me because we are platonic soulmates. Yet I still struggle sometimes to open myself up fully to him.

I squeeze my lips together to suppress a smile. "I know. I know. I know. I'm sorry!"

"You should be." He glares and pulls out of the driveway. "To make it up to me, you can invite me to be your new roommate."

"Oh my God …" I trail off, laughing. "You're ridiculous."

His phone rings, and he checks the screen. "We are not finished with this conversation. But I have to answer this. It's my mom."

I tune him out and scroll mindlessly through socials as he talks to his mom, and thankfully, his mom is a chatterbox, saving me from the nonstop questions that are bound to flow from Lumi the second he gets the chance.

"All right, Mom, we just got to campus, so I'll have to call you later," he says, pulling into a parking spot and shutting his car off.

As I step outside, I inhale deeply. There's a crispness to the air that I don't remember being there lately; the feel and scent of fall is upon us.

It hasn't taken over the tall green hedges, the flower beds that are full to the brim, or the giant oak trees that decorate campus, but soon, this place will be decorated in the most beautiful shades of oranges, reds, and yellows.

We wander down the cobblestone sidewalks toward the quad closest to our class.

"So, tell me everything. Are you like a pretty little princess in her new castle?" He takes a sip of his coffee. "Are you sharing a bed with the sexy beast? Have you seen his *little beast?*"

"Lumi!" I scoff and feel my cheeks light on fire.

Lumi stops dead in his tracks and scoffs. "What is that?"

Planting my feet, I purse my lips. "What?"

He waves his finger in my face, circling the air. "That. The coyness and the blush. Am I sensing something there that wasn't there before?"

"Stop it!" I swat his finger out of the air and glance around to see if anyone is looking.

He gasps, "Oh my God. You like him!"

Slapping my hand over his mouth, I whisper-shout, "Shut up! Keep your damn voice down!"

His lips move beneath my hand, and muffled sounds fight to break free. I pull my hand away while keeping a firm stare locked on his overly excited gaze.

"You like him, Blair. Just admit it!" he murmurs aggressively.

"I will admit nothing because there's nothing to admit!" My words, laced with lies, fly out of my mouth as I spot Griffin sauntering over to us. "I swear to God I'll kill you if you say anything. Now, act normal."

My face is relaxed, and I have a playful smile. It is like our conversation didn't revolve around the giant who's approaching us in three, two, one.

"Hey, what's up?" I ask while pinching Lumi's side to remind him to behave.

"Oww," he shouts, and Griffin laughs.

"What were you guys talking about?" Griffin asks, his eyes narrowing on me with the most intense stare.

I feel like every cell in my body is starting to vibrate.

"Lumi's love life. We were trying to plan out what we should do to find him a guy worth dating." The words continue to flow from my lips with ease.

"Maybe you and Blair could double date with me and whoever I find," Lumi barges in, and I stare at him. "Then, I could get your opinion on him in the moment."

Griffin bites down on his bottom lip, and I mirror his action involuntarily. "Umm … yeah, all right. Just let me know when."

"I'm sure we will be all right. It wouldn't be the first time I third-wheeled for Lumi," I retort, hating the rabbit hole we are now wandering down.

"What about your place?" Lumi asks Griffin, and this time, I really do elbow him.

"Don't mind him. He's uncultured, and he doesn't know how to stay inside of *boundaries*." I emphasize the last word and glance at him.

"Yeah, I'm sorry. I don't like having a lot of guests at my place," Griffin responds.

My shoulders slump, and I sigh, not realizing that I was a bit excited at the possibility of him saying yes. It would have been fun to have Lumi's dating chaos at the house.

"Yeah, of course. We can figure something out. No big deal," I say, desperate to change the subject.

"Let me know what you come up with, and I'll see if I'm free." He inches closer to me, and the air between us draws taut.

"Will do," I say confidently.

Someone calls Griffin's name, and he breaks the tension as he turns and starts walking away toward Malik. "I'll see you in class."

Fight or flight has never so strongly invaded my senses as it is right now.

Lumi leans down and whispers, "I don't know whether to laugh or cry about what just happened. You need to work on your game, babe."

"Oh my God. That is the absolute furthest thing from the top of my priority list," I assure him with false confidence and a racing heart.

He rubs his temple with his hand and sighs, "On the plus side, he seems like he's down to tag along on a little double date."

"It's not a date. Just friends hanging out," I murmur.

"Mmhmm." He scoffs. "Well, it will definitely be a date for me."

"And we will be there to support you, *not* on a date. Just two people at the same place at the same time together."

"Right," he bellows. "Totally normal. You're ridiculous."

We start heading to class, and I smile. "You love me."

He shrugs. "I sure do."

Chuckling, I lead us to our seats and unpack my backpack to prepare for the lecture.

"Excuse me." A deep, familiar voice sends shivers up my spine.

I look up and find Griffin staring down at me with parted lips and a playful gaze.

"Is that seat taken?"

He glances at the empty one next to me, and Lumi answers his question before I get a chance.

"Nope. No one sits there!" he boasts.

Griffin smiles at his enthusiasm, "Good. Regardless if it was, I was going to take it. It's only right that I get to sit next to *my* tutor."

"Well, isn't that rude if it's someone else's seat?" I sneer as I fight back the smile from tipping my lips up.

He walks past me and sits down, his size making the chair look small. He sets his bag down and gets his notebook and pen out before leaning over.

His whisper sends electrifying tingles from my ear down my neck, landing dead center in my core. "What are they going to do? Fight me?" A deep, suppressed laugh that vibrates against my ear makes me acutely aware of how close he is to me. "They can try."

Is he doing this on purpose to get a rise out of me? Because it's totally working, and I hate it.

"All right, class, I've got a surprise for you today." Dr. Schrute speaks into the mic, and the class quiets down. "A pop quiz. I'll hand them out, and once you're finished, you'll be free to go for the day."

My stomach sinks to the floor. *Oh my God, is Griffin ready for a pop quiz?*

"Are you okay?" Griffin's warm voice caresses my concerns, and I do my best to swallow my fear and not vocalize it.

"Yeah. I'm okay. Are *you?*" I ask nervously.

He winks at me. "Are you kidding? I'm going to kill this quiz."

Smiling at him, I try to feign confidence. I am confident in him, but far less confident in myself as a tutor. Am I actually doing a good job, teaching him everything he needs to know?

At the end of this arrangement, he needs a good passing grade, and I need the money.

What if he ends up failing and fires me? What will I do then?

My anxiety terrorizes me the entire time as I answer each and every question on the quiz with ease and accuracy.

Please, dear God, let him pass this.

I finish first in the class. Rising to my feet, I grab my bag and whisper, "I'll be outside." Although I'm unsure if I was directing that at Lumi or Griffin.

Descending the stairs, I turn my paper in to Dr. Schrute, who smiles and thanks me, and I head to the hallway to wait.

As I sit down in one of the comfy study chairs outside of the room, my nerves are at an all-time high. Each second feels like a minute, and time drags on forever.

Malik walks into the hallway with a smile on his face and spots me immediately. "Hey, bookworm."

"Malik," I greet him indifferently because I have yet to decide whether I like him or not.

"Kind of a cold tone you've got there, but whatever," he sighs. "How do you think you did?"

"Oh, I got every question right," I state.

He grins, his lips dripping with arrogance. "Good for you. I did too."

"Really?" I scoff, doubting him.

He shrugs. "Yes, really. Smart-ass."

"Rude. But good for you," I applaud him.

The door opens again, and my heart rate spikes as I anticipate who will walk through it. A few girls I don't know saunter out and immediately look at Malik, smiling and waving at him. He grins at them and winks, sending them into a giggling fit as they walk away.

Dear God, he is unbearable to be around.

The door cracks and slowly opens. My palms start sweating, and my breathing quickens. The second I see it's Griffin, I stand up, eager to hear how he did.

The door closes behind him, and he finds me immediately. A look of sadness stretches tightly across his face. Shit.

I walk cautiously up to him and ask, "How d-did it go?"

He strikes. His hands fly out and grab my waist, and he lifts me into the air and spins me around. I shriek as he swings me around like a doll, and I can't help giggling as I fly through the air in circles.

He slows down and pulls me against him while lowering me to the ground. Our bodies slide together, and my heart is out of control as his arm circles around my back. He holds me in place for just a second, our faces inches apart. His hooded gaze darts to my lips and then back to my eyes.

Right as I think he's about to lean in, he lowers me fully to the ground and steps back, putting distance between us.

He smiles shyly at me as I try to figure out what the hell just happened.

"I fucking aced that shit! All thanks to you!" he praises me, and somehow, I feel even warmer inside than before.

Pretending that moment between us didn't just happen, I boast, "Well, of course you did. I'm amazing at my job."

He smirks. "Most of it was stuff we covered in that study guide anyway, and I memorized that like the back of my hand. If that was a glimpse of the test, I will ace that shit too." His eyes drift to where Malik is standing, and he does that weird, silent *what's up* head-nod thing.

"Glad you did good, bro," Malik praises him, and for the tiniest moment, I don't dislike Malik for the support he gives Griffin. "Ready for weights?"

"Yeah, we'd better get going." Griffin looks at me. "Let me know when you want to leave campus. I'll give you a ride home."

I nod and say, "Yeah, I'll text you," while doing my best to ignore the butterflies going insane in my chest.

He smiles before turning on his heel and walking away with Malik, and I watch them until they turn the corner and are out of sight.

I'll wait for Lumi to come out of class so he can finish freaking out about Griffin. I know he will want to talk about the fact that he sat next to me, and he's going to lose it when I tell him he spun me around in the hallway. But I can't stop thinking about the fact that Griffin called his house my home. I know he means to his house, but I can't lie and say it doesn't feel strange to hear it aloud.

But the part that's stirring inside of me that I can't shake is that I don't know where my home is right now. It will always be with my dad. It has been my whole life. But that doesn't change the fact that I feel a bit lost. It doesn't matter though, knowing that my dad is getting the best health care money can buy. He wasn't necessarily excited about my new living arrangements. I told him it was a job opportunity and a way for us to afford everything we need. It's a blessing. He saw it that way at least, and I'm glad he did.

A house is where you store your possessions and sleep. It's a noun, and right now, my house is Griffin's. But a home is the one place you have no doubt in your mind you belong. It's your safe haven. It's where you laugh, cry, and love. It's where you can let your heart out of its cage to explore fearlessly.

I think it's best not to consider Griffin's house my home because I'm scared that once I let my heart out of its confines, it won't ever be the same. It will wind up finding happiness once and for all in the arms of the guy I shouldn't be developing feelings for, or it will end up shattered in pieces, and I'll be left trying to put it back together.

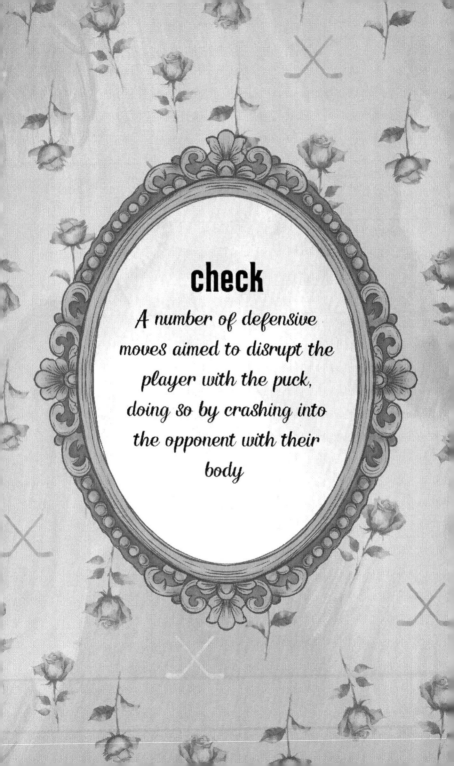

check

A number of defensive moves aimed to disrupt the player with the puck, doing so by crashing into the opponent with their body

chapter fourteen
griffin

It's been three weeks since Blair moved in, and I'm losing my goddamn mind. When I ran into her on the stairs that night, it was like seeing the real her for the first time. She was relaxed and honest. It was nice talking with her, even if I avoided opening up to her. It's not personal. There are parts of myself that I haven't faced in a long time.

A flash of her hand on my chest burns into my vision. Something changed that night, and tension started humming beneath the surface in the air between us. I saw it in the flush of her body and the hunger in her eyes.

Then, I almost kissed her in the hallway after class, and I haven't been able to stop thinking about it since.

I know we started working with each other because we understood the lines of our relationship and weren't going to cross it. But I don't know if I can keep up my end of that deal. Although Blair hasn't made a direct move and, at times, seems to be fighting her gravitation toward me, I know she still feels whatever fire we ignited that night on the stairs.

She's been all business since our almost kiss in the hallway, and she's trying her hardest not to look at me while we spend hours studying. She's also been putting more physical distance between us during study sessions. Maybe I should try harder not to flirt with her, but I can't fucking help it when she smiles and giggles at a joke I make. It's addictive.

She's been practically locked in her room every day and night, only coming out to grab a plate of food, make some excuse about how busy she is, and then disappear again back upstairs. I know Mrs. Potts wants to spend more time with her. She can't stop telling me how much she likes having another girl in the house. Mrs. Potts has also been baking up a storm, and I'm worried that if she doesn't slow down, I'm going to gain a hundred pounds.

I'll admit, it feels a bit ironic for initially wanting a tutor who didn't want to get in my pants, and now, I can't stop thinking about what it would be like to glide hers down over her hips and throw them onto the floor. Or how her lips would feel as we fought for air between desperate, messy kisses.

Fucking hell, I just need to jerk off before I break all the unspoken rules we set.

Maybe she doesn't like me at all, and she's just trying to get through our time together as fast as she can. I just know that whenever our deal ends and she leaves, I won't be able to let her go completely. But for right now, I need to get it together. Because I still have a grade that threatens to end my career.

For the time being, I'll stay professional. I'll behave for the duration of our little agreement, and then when she moves out, all bets are off.

If you had asked me at the beginning of this semester if I would be developing a plan to win over my tutor, I would have laughed because I don't have the time or energy, but she makes me want to find it.

She is a good tutor, and I'm so much better off with her helping me. I've gotten nearly perfect scores on our quizzes and assignments. The only thing I'm still struggling with is the writing assignments where we talk about ourselves. I hate talking about my feelings, especially regarding my past. It's nobody's business but mine, so I've been lying this whole time. But the more and more time I spend with Blair, the guiltier I feel about lying.

No one will know the difference if I sell my words as the truth. But I don't want Blair to like a made-up version of myself.

It's so much easier to write about a version of Griffin Hawthorne, who's had the perfect life, filled with happy memories, than to dig up the truth. But maybe that's how I've been getting by for so long—by pretending everything is peachy and perfect. I don't know what's happening to me. Before Blair, I was content with the lies I shared with Dr. Schrute and the rest of the world. Now, a pit the size of a black hole has settled into my stomach, making me queasy every time I bend the truth.

Dangling a puck with my stick, I slide gently it across the ice before catching it again and pushing it the other way.

"Hey, bro." Asher rips me from my thoughts and skates over, passing a puck back and forth to himself.

Using my stick, I steal it from him before sliding it back his way. Drifting backward on my skates, I put a little distance between us, and he passes it back to me.

"There's a party tonight at the baseball house. Do you want to go?" he asks, slapping the puck over to me.

In all honesty, I don't feel like partying, but maybe getting out of the house and away from Blair could be a good move right now. "Sure, yeah. What time?"

Asher's eyes light up, and I try not to laugh. I don't go out a ton, so when I do, the guys get really excited about it.

"Fuck yeah!" Asher cheers.

Picking the puck up on his stick, he chucks it at Dean. "Hey, Griff's in tonight."

Spinning around, he's grinning from ear to ear. "Sweet! Mal, you in?"

Malik skates up behind me. Throwing an arm over my shoulders, he stops at my side. "A party? Always in."

By the time warm-ups are done, I think the party might be overrun tonight due to the number of hockey players going. Coach skates out to us, and we huddle around him, waiting for his instruction. He has us start with breakout stickhandling drills to warm our hands up and get ready.

We break out into four groups, each stationed at one of the red dots in the offensive and defensive zones. Three players are inside of the circle, stickhandling to themselves while constantly skating around, but never leaving the confines of the red-painted circle. Then, three other players are outside of the circle, trying to pass through the chaos of the circle to each other. It helps us be better at passing through groups of players in a tight area. After running this drill for about five minutes, the outer and inner groups switch, and we start again.

We run through a few more stickhandling drills before we start scrimmaging, and that's what we spend the next hour doing—running our five-on-five lines against each other. We end practice with a shoot-out on each end of the ice.

After a quick change, I'm stuck debating whether to hang out around campus or go home.

Blair only has one class on Wednesdays, and it's done around eleven a.m. She's been stubbornly adamant about Lumi driving her everywhere—or perhaps adamant about not riding with me. She should be home by now unless she's doing something else today. The idea of her meeting up with someone and hanging out makes my blood boil. I can't imagine she has time to entertain anyone who isn't Lumi or me, but I still can't shake the skin-crawling invasive thought that another guy could be spending today with her. Shit, maybe I should just stay home and skip the party.

"Hey, sweet cheeks." Malik smiles as he walks out of the locker room, finding me lost in my mind. "What's happening in that big brain of yours? You look constipated."

I snort. "Thanks, buddy. What time is that party tonight again?"

"Starts at seven, but we'll probably head over at about

eight thirty or nine. Why?" he asks hesitantly and sighs. "Don't tell me you're thinking about backing out."

I assure him, "No, I'm not. I was just wondering. I'm going to run home, try to get some homework done quickly, and I'll meet you guys there."

He studies me curiously for a moment before slowly saying, "Okay. That sounds good. Pick me up?"

He's such a fucking passenger princess, and he never wants to drive himself anywhere. At this point, it's kind of our thing.

"Yeah, I've got you. I'll let you know when I leave."

He stretches his hand out, and we do our handshake before I walk away, forcing myself not to run out of the building in a hurry to get home. I'm just going to do some homework and maybe take a nap. That's it. I don't even care if Blair is there or not. My chest constricts immediately at the thought.

Fucking hell, I can't even lie to myself anymore when it comes to her.

The house is completely silent when I get home. No Mrs. Potts, Chip, or Blair to be found. I know that Mrs. Potts and Chip were going on a homeschool field trip today to the zoo, but I really thought that Blair would be here, and I can't help but feel the disappointment weighing me down more and more with each empty room I find.

Eventually, I give up and decide to shower quickly because I feel gross and sweaty from practice. Walking into my en suite bathroom, I strip out of my clothes and start the water, finding the perfect temp before hopping in.

God, there is almost no greater feeling than a long, hot

shower, and by the time I'm done with my routine, the bathroom is full of steam. I wrap a towel around my hips and open my bathroom door; cool air chills the water beading down my chest.

Shit. I forgot to grab clothes from my closet.

A shiver runs down my spine. There's a rather small closet in my bedroom that I only use to store my hockey gear. I keep my clothes in one of the bedrooms, which I converted into one big closet.

As I open the door and step into the hallway, I smack straight into Blair, holding a hand up like she was about to knock. She reaches out, grabbing on to my torso to get balance. My eyes slam shut as I bite the inside of my cheek to stop myself from doing something I might regret. Like tugging her into my room, grabbing her face, and kiss—

"Sorry, I was just …" She trails off as her eyes fall to the towel hanging low on my hips.

The heaviness in her gaze is not helping me stay under control.

Her lips part as she studies every inch of my bare skin. Her scorching gaze warms me to the core. My cock twitches, and as the towel lifts, her eyes widen, and her cheeks flush the prettiest shade of pink.

Fucking hell, I need to get out of here before I drop the towel altogether.

Her breathing is shallow as I do something I definitely shouldn't do. Reaching out, I gently tuck her hair behind her ear, exposing that intense blush even more. Her tongue wets her bottom lip, and I bite the inside of my cheek again, hard enough to stop me from pushing her against the wall and finding out how sweet her mouth tastes.

My entire body is on fire, every inch sparking with desire. Shutting my eyes, I hear our breathing fill the silence, heavy, needy, and panting. It's not just me. She's right there with me, waiting to see if one of us makes a move.

And I do the hardest thing I've ever done.

Stepping aside, I walk the four steps down the hallway to my closet and shut myself inside. I'm hard as hell from the almost kiss we had and the thought of finally giving in to whatever is growing between us.

Dropping my towel, I pump my dick from tip to base as the image of her heated cheeks and lust-blown pupils flashes in my mind. Rolling my head back, I imagine her hand wrapped around me.

"Fuck!" I whisper and release my dick.

I can't imagine what it will be like when I part those pretty lips with my tongue and show her exactly how I feel. But until it's her bringing me over the edge, I'm not doing it. It's not a matter of if, but when. Because sooner or later, neither one of us will be strong enough to stay away. As out of control she feels in life, she has the reins when it comes to me.

My emotions have always been a beast of their own to conquer, and plenty of times, they still get the best of me. But I don't want them to control me when it comes to Blair. I won't let them.

When I'm dressed and ready to emerge from my hiding spot in the closet, I tiptoe into the hallway and quickly dart back into my bedroom. I crash onto my bed and type rapidly into my phone, pressing Call on one of my dad's old friend's contacts.

David answers on the second ring. "Hello? Griffin, is this really you?"

"Yeah. Is now a bad time?" I ask, my nerves twisting and knotting together with unease.

I haven't spoken to David since my family left, and that was years ago. I don't know if David hates me for what I did, but I'm hoping after all this time, maybe he's forgiven me.

"No, not at all." His voice is kind, and my shoulders relax. "What's up? How have you been?"

"I'm doing fine. Thank you. How are you and your family?" I ask in return.

"Doing really well. Thanks for asking. You guys have been doing great this season. You've turned into quite the player over the years," he praises me, and my chest warms with his compliment.

I can't believe he's been watching me play. He has no idea how much that means to me. The crowd might be packed with Legends fans at every game, but it can still feel pretty empty when I don't know a single face.

"Thank you, seriously." I pause, "I'm calling because I have a big favor to ask of you."

Two hours into the party, I know I've accepted too many shots and drinks. I'm fucked up right now. The party itself is pretty laid-back, especially for it being hosted by the baseball team. They are notorious for their parties.

I've been sitting on the couch next to Malik for a little while. A cute blonde sits down beside me with a shy smile.

"Hi," she says softly. "Is this seat taken?"

Her hand slides onto my thigh, and I tense up. I scoot closer to Malik, and the room spins a bit as I settle into the cushion.

"Yes, it is," I respond, my words a slurry mess.

Her hand is still on my thigh, and with each second that passes, it's pissing me off more and more.

"Are you here with anyone?" she asks, batting her eyelashes at me and clearly not taking any hints that I'm not interested.

Malik stretches his arm around my shoulders and leans forward, saying, "Yeah, he's here with me."

She squints her eyes and purses her lips. "Sure. Whatever."

She finally gets it and stomps away, and I'm instantly relieved.

"Thank you," I murmur to Malik as my head rolls back onto the top of the cushion behind me and I stare up at the ceiling before closing my eyes. "Wake me up in five. I need to rest my eyes for a minute."

He laughs, but it sounds so far away as I become one with the couch. "Let's get you home, buddy."

"Holy shit, I don't think I've ever seen him this drunk," someone who sounds an awful lot like my teammate Asher says.

I'm too busy watching the light show behind my

eyelids to respond, so Mal does it for me. "Yeah, I know. I'm going to get him home."

"Are you good to drive?"

"Yeah. I had one earlier, but once this guy started chugging like his life depended on it, I stopped so I could get him home." Malik chuckles. "It's kind of fun, being on the other side of this and watching all of the drunk people for once."

I start laughing at Malik because that guy is so goddamn funny, and he should know that. Laughter continues to bubble out of me as someone helps me stand up, and my legs are like wobbly noodles as I try to step forward.

As if I can time-travel, I'm suddenly in Malik's car.

I blink again, and we're in my driveway.

Is time moving that fast, or am I developing superpowers?

He parks and helps me out of the car, practically dragging me up the stairs to my front door.

"Where are your keys?" Malik asks.

I dig in my pocket, somehow helpful enough to find them.

"Here you go." I smile as I drop the keys right as he's about to grab them. "Shit. Sorry."

"Jesus, Griff, you're obliterated right now." He makes a weird noise between a sigh and a giggle as he picks them up and unlocks the door. "Let's get you inside."

"Whatever you say, buddy," I sing to him.

He throws my arm around his shoulders, and we waddle inside.

"I should go to bed. I'm so tired," I groan as he kicks the door shut behind us.

Without a word, he helps me to the couch, and I crash onto it, never happier to be lying down in my life.

"Fuck. This is the comfiest couch. It's like it's made out of clouds or shit."

He bursts out laughing. "You're hilarious right now. I'm really hoping it's clouds though. I've sat on that couch before, and I'll be pissed off if it's made of shit. I totally should've recorded you."

"Yeah, yeah, yeah ..." I grin, sinking deeper into the cushions.

"I'm going to leave your phone and keys on the table next to you, all right?" he asks. I hear the clang of my keys hitting the table beside me. "Let's sit your head up in case you get nauseous. Lift."

It takes all my power to lift my head as he slides two throw pillows under it, propping me up.

"Thanks, Mal. Love you, man."

He chuckles. "You too, buddy. I'll see you tomorrow."

I hear the front door click shut, and just as I'm about to fall asleep, I hear someone walking across the foyer.

Sitting up, I force myself to my feet and mindlessly wander toward the noise. "Malik? Did you forget something?"

I follow the footsteps into the kitchen, and someone who is definitely not Malik answers me.

"Griffin?"

Blair.

My heart jumps in my throat, and blood pounds in my ears, pulsing like the beat of a song that only plays for her.

I never want it to stop. She's frozen with a cup in her hand that's half full of ice.

She rocks back and forth on her feet, and a shiver runs through me. I love making her nervous.

"Fuck." My voice is gruff and dry.

The delicate pink silk tank top does nothing to hide the peaks of her nipples pushing against it. I wonder what kind of sound she would make if I took one of them into my mouth. Don't get me started on the matching shorts. They are clinging to her hips, wrapped tightly around her, as desperately as I wish to be.

Her long hair is falling over her shoulders. This is the first time I've seen her hair not tied half up with a black bow. It looks good. It would look even better wrapped around my hand though.

Her lips part, and she studies me. Part of me worries that I said any of that out loud and not just in my mind. Her eyes are hooded, and she's looking at me with a hunger that wasn't there before. Or maybe that's just my stare reflecting back at me.

When I take a small step toward her, she grins and bites down on the inside of her cheek. As I step toward her again, she sets the glass of ice down on the island and backs against it.

She's only a few feet from me, and I'm more intoxicated by the thought of finally kissing her than I am from any of the alcohol I had tonight.

She sucks her bottom lip between her teeth, and my body twitches. With every step I take, I watch her chest rise and fall faster and faster. By the time I reach her and cage her in with my arms, I can hear her panting, and I would be a liar if I said that it wasn't driving me crazy.

Every day since I met her, I swear she gets more and more stunning. I don't know if it's because she's opening up little by little, and I'm falling for who she is as a person, and it's reflected in how I see her. If I'm finally noticing the little things about her—like the freckles that softly paint the bridge of her nose and her cheeks, the gold flecks around the pupils in her eyes, the way her face scrunches up when she laughs, the way she tries to walks through campus without attracting attention even though it's impossible to not stop in your tracks and notice her. Or the cute way she tucks her tongue between her bottom teeth and cheek when she's intensely focused. Or perhaps it's all of the above.

The words slip past my lips without thought. "You're so beautiful, Blair."

Without thinking, I reach out and gently cup her jaw. She inhales sharply and settles into my touch. Painstakingly slow, I run my thumb along her bottom lip, memorizing how velvety it feels and how badly I want to do this repeatedly.

Ever so slightly, I lean down and freeze the second I feel her warm breath caressing my lips. I want nothing more in the world than to keep going, especially when she's looking at me like *this*—like it's all she wants too.

I rest my forehead against hers, and even that tiny contact makes my legs feel weak.

Her voice is a breathy whisper. "You're drunk, Griffin."

Tilting her head up with my hand, I stare down into her hooded, lust-filled eyes as I brush my nose against hers, and fight the unbearable urge to steal a kiss. "That doesn't change the fact that you are so goddamn perfect."

She murmurs my name with such desperation that my shoulders quiver. "Griffin."

Wetting my lips, I want nothing more than to lift her onto this counter and kiss her into oblivion. She pushes against me, her breasts grazing my chest, and my dick throbs against my zipper. Fuck, I want her so goddamn bad.

But I don't want her to question my intentions when I first claim her lips with mine. There will be no room for doubt in her mind that I mean business, and there will be no going back. Because once I get a taste of her, there's no way I'm letting her go.

Swiping my thumb once more across her bottom lip, I pull away before pressing my lips against her forehead. "Good night, Blair."

Pushing off of the counter, I spin around and head upstairs to crawl into bed.

After I slide between the sheets, I touch my tingling lips and fall asleep, thinking of what it will be like when she's mine.

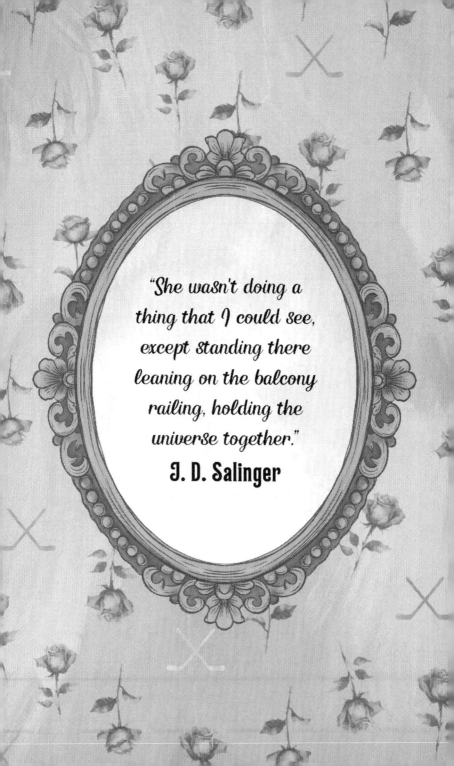

"She wasn't doing a thing that I could see, except standing there leaning on the balcony railing, holding the universe together."

J. D. Salinger

chapter fifteen
blair

My dad called me last night and told me that he's being transferred to a private hospital to be personally treated by one of the best doctors in the country, Dr. David Cole. I don't know what strings Griffin had to pull to make that happen, but I am forever grateful.

My father means the world to me. I know he's across the country in Georgia, getting treatment, but he feels worlds away. I miss him so much. But I wouldn't really change a thing because at least now, he's getting the treatment he deserves. All because of Griffin.

Please tell me how I'm supposed to sit across the table from him this afternoon without thinking about our near kiss in the kitchen two nights ago. This will be the first time we've seen each other since then, and my stomach is churning at the thought.

Will he bring it up? Will he pretend it didn't happen?

He was pretty drunk that night. Will he remember it at all?

Part of me is considering texting him and telling him I don't feel well, but unfortunately, I don't think that'd go over well since I'm a terrible liar—there's also the fact that he could literally walk into my bedroom and check on me and I'm indeed not sick.

The vibration of my phone gives me a second of reprieve, and I read Lumi's message.

> Lumi: Do not under any circumstances make plans for tonight.

Oh God, what does he have up his sleeve?

> Why?

> Lumi: It's a surprise. Just be ready to leave by seven—hair, makeup, etc. Everything aside from your outfit.

This is bizarre, but it's hard to worry when it comes to Lumi. He always has everyone's best interests at heart.

> Okay … I will. But again, I will ask you, why???

> Lumi: To get you out of the house and have some fun. Don't you have a tutoring session you should be in right now?

> Lumi, I will stay home if you don't tell me what you're planning.

Lumi: You are no fun! There's a costume party at the baseball house tonight, and I'm bringing you as my plus-one.

Your plus-one? Who invited you?

Lumi: A baseball player from my Econ class.

Is he cute? Did he like invite you, invite you? Or was it more like, swing by if you're bored?

Lumi: A mix of both? I'm not sure. He's, like, a seven, but I'm hoping this is my in to meet a ten.

Wait, did you say costume party??

Lumi: Yes. Why? I can put together some cute outfits for us since I know you have a date with Griffin today.

It's not a date. It's a study session. And don't worry about putting something together for me. I can handle my own. I've got a ton of clothes from working at the club that can easily pass as a slutty costume.

Lumi: Okay, I can't wait to see what you come up with!

What are you dressing up as?

Lumi: A Ken doll.

> Okay, but, like, that's actually perfect. You'd better send me pictures of yours! Do you already have your clothes picked out?

> Lumi: Going shopping now.

> Okay, I can't wait to see it!

> Lumi: Me too, LOL.

As much as I love the idea of staying in bed and doing nothing but reading tonight, I wouldn't mind a night out to clear my head because being in the room across the hall from Griffin has my mind cloudy with thoughts, including flashbacks of him in nothing but a towel. Knowing he's feet away from me is aggravating because finishing what we started the other night would be so easy. But I can't. Dear God, I cannot do that. What if he fires me? After all, he got rid of his old tutor because she was hitting on him.

What if the other night was a test? What if he was seeing if I would let him touch me?

Whatever his intentions were, I would have, without a doubt, failed. I don't know when something changed between us, but I know that it's becoming impossible to ignore.

Griffin and I are meeting downstairs in our usual spot at the dining table in two hours, which means I will get to stay up here in my pretty little cage for a while longer.

A heaviness weighs on me today, knowing my dad is getting chemo treatment. He has everything he needs, aside from me, but that's okay. As long as he's getting better, that's all that matters. He's going to call me after he's done at his appointment today.

Setting my phone down, with the sound on so I can hear it ring, I grab my book and fall back onto the bed, holding it up above my face to read. As I get lost reading about Liam, singing a song he wrote for the girl he loves, who also happens to be his best friend's little sister, Avery, all of my stressors and problems happily float to the back of my mind.

I wish I could jump into this book and stay there for a while. Where my dad isn't sick and I don't have to make a deal with an annoyingly hot hockey player to stay in school and pay for my dad's treatment. But as my problems drift away and I relax more and more, my eyelids drift shut, and my nap consumes me.

A monstrous, hairy beast with long horns and sharp claws approaches me with soft hazel eyes and a shy smile. With a red rose —my favorite—clasped in its hand, it reaches out and brushes my hair out of my face. Hesitantly, it holds the rose out to me, and I take it. The beast scoops me into his arms, cradling me against his chest, and every worry falls away as he carries me into the dark castle.

As I begin to fall asleep in his warm arms, he shakes my shoulders, and I wish he would stop.

I don't want to get up yet.

"Blair, wake up," the beast growls, deep and vicious, rattling me to my bones.

He shakes my shoulders once more, and I gasp as I fly upright into reality, leaving the dreamworld behind and coming face-to-face with The Beast of the real world. Except this beast isn't scary looking at all. He's a six-foot-five giant with an alluring smile, eyes that you can't look away from, who has a soft demeanor that only shows when he thinks no one else is looking. I suppose, in his own way, he is scary. Or perhaps it's just me who is scared to know more.

"Hey, are you okay?" He reaches out and brushes my cheek.

"What?" I mumble, realizing I've been staring at him this entire time and not saying a single word. "Yeah. I'm fine. W-why are you in my room?"

Crossing my arms, I sit back, pulling out of his touch. I can't ignore the pained look that seems to strike him like a jolt of electricity, his eyes widening and brows furrowing.

He hurries off of my bed and stands up, looking anywhere but at me. "We were supposed to meet downstairs, but you didn't show."

Shit.

"After a few minutes, I just came to check on you." He steps back and turns to walk away, and my heart drops. "But we can reschedule. You should rest."

"Wait. Umm … what time is it?" My mouth is dry as I stall him from leaving, not ready to say goodbye so soon.

He runs his hand through his hair. "A little after four p.m."

Jumping out of bed, I straighten my HEAU hoodie that twisted itself up when I was asleep and adjust my leggings, tugging them back up on my hips. "Dammit. I'm sorry, Griffin. I didn't mean to fall asleep. We can start right now."

He walks around my bed, not stopping until he's only a couple of feet away from me, and finally meets my stare, looking almost straight down into my eyes. "Don't worry about it. I'm feeling pretty good about the assignments anyway. I'll just need your help with editing and formatting next week's essay. I've got it drafted already." He smiles before adding, "Please make it not sound like complete garbage."

"I have a hard time believing that it will sound bad at all. Your other ones have been excellent," I admit, telling him the truth.

Are they perfect? No. But they are definitely passing grade material.

"Yeah, you have to say that." He smirks, rocking forward on the balls of his feet and bringing us even closer together.

I grin. "Actually, you pay me to tell you the truth, and if your essays were terrible, trust me, I would tell you. I might even enjoy doing it."

Humor dances in his smile and eyes as he murmurs, his voice deep and smooth, "Oh, I'm sure you would."

Biting the inside of my cheek, I attempt to kill any blush from warming my face, but I'm afraid I fail miserably. With a hesitant step, I drift toward the door and lean against the eloquent trim of the wall.

He follows me, dragging his feet until he stands in the open threshold. Yawning, he stretches his arms over his head, resting one arm against the doorframe and caging me in ever so slightly. Immediately, I'm reminded of what it felt like to be pressed against the kitchen island, wanting nothing more than for him to touch me.

Forcing my gaze away from him, I stare at my book on the bed, waiting for him to say something ... anything. But as each second ticks by, we seem to drift closer together, and I don't trust myself not to do something about the butterflies he is stirring up inside of me.

"I'm going out tonight, by the way," I announce rather abruptly. Looking up at him again, I watch his hooded eyes widen, and his parted lips seal shut and thin. "So, I probably won't be home until late."

His tongue swipes his bottom lip before he bites down on it. "Oh, really?" he asks, his voice suddenly louder and a little shaky, almost sounding like … jealousy. "And what if I need emergency tutoring?"

The corner of his lips tips up, and a twinkle glimmers in his eyes.

Is he … flirting with me?

Pursing my lips, I challenge him, nervous about pushing it in case this is a real test of my professionalism. "Then, you can call or text me. Although I'm sure whatever you might need can wait until morning."

He shrugs. He looks over my shoulder, and his jaw tics. "What are your plans?"

Sneering with a grin, I roll my eyes. "That is none of your business."

Sighing, he drags his gaze back to me, painstakingly slow until he meets my eyes again, and I inhale sharply at the intensity of his stare and the tightness in his jaw.

"Well, my little prisoner, I'm making it my business. Where are you going?"

Tightening my arms across my chest, I protest, "Like I said, Griffin, it's none of your concern. I don't owe you an explanation."

His jaw tics again, and I can't help but grin at his frustration.

He steps toward me and slides his fingers along my waist, his touch burning an imprint into my skin. He tugs me toward him, and warmth ignites in my core, spreading throughout my entire body.

"Is it a date?"

I swallow hard. I swear it just got fifty degrees hotter in here.

My voice is a weak whisper. "Maybe."

Lowering himself inch by inch, he begins to close the distance between us, and I feel like giggling, screaming, running, and staying in place, all at the same time.

He chuckles deeply. "Oh, yeah? Who is it?"

Standing my ground, I hide any nervousness from my words. "You know him actually. He's nice, funny, easy to get along with, and hot as hell."

He inhales sharply and forces his exhale through gritted teeth. He huffs, breathing heavier than before, and I can't help but feel proud that I'm affecting him at all.

His breath hits my lips. "I'll drive you."

"No need," I pant, my entire body tingling from his nearness, desperate for his touch. "He's picking me up."

His jaw clenches, and anger flashes in his eyes. "Over my dead body. You just give out our address to random guys, huh?"

A giggle slips past my mouth.

"Only cute ones," I whisper, taunting him.

"Blair." He says my name as a warning.

But I can't stop. I love watching the jealousy torment him.

He narrows his eyes at me, and bubbling laughter breaks free.

"What's so funny?" he murmurs and presses his body against mine.

I gasp at the contact as a jolt of pleasure strikes my core, any laughter immediately dissipating. If I don't look away right now, I'm afraid I might launch myself at him. I force my gaze to his chest. But apparently, he doesn't like that.

He grabs my chin and lifts my head up, leaving me no choice but to look directly into his eyes.

"Are you messing with me?" he whispers, his words brushing my lips, taunting me to lean up just two inches more.

Biting back my grin, I answer him in a sultry tone, watching him hang on every word. "I have a hot date tonight … with Lumi."

I see every part of our conversation play back in his mind as his face and body relax.

"Lumi. Hmm." His tight lips break into a grin, and he chuckles. "What an interesting way you chose to explain that to me. Almost like you *wanted* to get a rise out of me," he teases.

Shrugging, I place my hands on his chest and softly guide him away from me. "Maybe I was. Maybe I wasn't. But I do have a date with Lumi, and I need to get ready. So, if you'll excuse me …"

He doesn't move an inch, he just studies me with darkened eyes. "What are you guys going to do?"

He takes a step back, and I inhale, feeling like I can finally start to breathe again.

"A party on campus. He got invited and is bringing me as his plus-one."

He rubs his jaw, and his tone cools. "What party?"

Rolling my eyes, I hold my hand out, pointing toward the door, gesturing for him to leave. "Some baseball one. Any other questions, warden?"

"Baseball one," he mutters under his breath. "That will be all, my little prisoner. See you later."

Without another word, he strides out of the room with pep in his step. I don't have time to read into that right now. I need to get ready. Lumi will be here soon, and I don't even have my costume picked out.

But thankfully, working at the club has left me with all the pieces I could ever need to put together a tastefully slutty costume, and I do just that. An outfit that has me feeling confident, cute, and sexy, all at the same time. I finish my look with smoky eye makeup and a bright red lip.

I wish Griffin could see me in this.

Perhaps in another life, our situation would be different. Maybe it still can. But for tonight, none of that matters. I am just going to go have fun with my friend.

In case I run into Mrs. Potts or Chip downstairs, I throw on a long coat and cinch it at my waist before strolling out of Hawthorne Manor.

After a short show-and-tell of our outfits, Lumi and I head to the party, arriving fashionably late.

As we walk into the brick baseball house, I can't help but feel slightly on edge. I know a lot of the baseball team is close to the football team, and the last thing I want tonight is to run into Grant.

"Oh my God, that's the guy who invited me," Lumi

murmurs into my ear. "I'm going to casually go get a drink next to him. Be right back. Do you want one?"

Nodding, I can't even get a word in before he's walking away and heading to the cute guy by the keg. Awkwardly, I find a wall and tuck myself against it, out of the way. I'll just wait here until Lumi comes back.

To pass the time, I pull my phone out and scroll through socials. A notification pops up at the top of my screen, and I see a text from Grant. My stomach drops.

Grant: What are you doing here?

I type my answer as fast as I can while my rage starts growing inside of me, unfurling into every finger and toe. After tonight, I'm blocking him for good. But in case he is extra crazy, I'm not doing it until I'm at home if he decides to murder me for doing it. It might seem dramatic, but men have killed for less, especially the insane and possessive ones.

Trying to have fun. Why are you texting me? I don't need your permission to be here.

His fingers must be sore from how fast he types out his next message.

Grant: Nor do you need my permission to dress like a whore, but here we are.

Glancing above my phone, I scan the room and search each face, trying to find him. Tucking my phone into my chest bag, I try to ignore him while I keep a keen eye on the room, wondering what corner he's lurking in.

I left my coat in Lumi's car, and now, I feel so exposed, knowing that Grant is watching me. Any stranger looking at me right now is fine, but not him. It makes me feel all icky.

"There you are!" Lumi startles me, and I jump a little as he holds a cup out for me. "Whoa. What's wrong?"

"It's Grant," I grumble.

His eyes widen. "He's here?! It's starting to be real fucking horrifying, Blair. What the hell is his deal?"

Running my hand down my face and my neck, I sigh. "I don't know. But I've decided to block him when I get back to Griffin's."

"Good. As you should because he's a creep." Lumi's face twists with disgust.

Nodding, I take a sip of the beer and do my best to push Grant out of my mind. But it's tough when I can't ignore the aching pit in my stomach that is warning me to run.

defender

A hockey position that is responsible for preventing the other team from scoring, as well as other tasks.

chapter sixteen
griffin

The party is deafening when I walk inside the baseball house behind Malik. I had no intention of coming to a party tonight, but once I knew Blair would be here, there was no way I was staying home. I know how these parties can get sometimes, including how handsy some of the guys are. God knows I've torn enough unwanted guys off of girls in this house before. Blair is not going to become one of them.

I'll keep my distance and behave unless someone requires me not to. I just want to keep an eye on her and make sure she's safe. That's all. *Mostly* all.

After we get drinks—well, Malik, Dean, and Asher get drinks—we go into the living room. I choose to not have any alcohol because I want to be completely sober, keeping an eye on her tonight.

We find a couch in the living room and take it over. I don't love pushing other people around, but the living room is the center of the parties here and a good place where I'll more than likely spot Blair.

After about a hundred people filter in and out of the room, I see her luscious brown hair.

Locking on to my target, I watch her incessantly. There are too many people between us to see her completely, but I can at least see that she's with Lumi and that no one is trying to bother her right now. The group of girls blocking my view of her scatter, and my vision homes in on her, everyone else blurring in comparison.

My heart leaps into my throat. Picking my jaw up off of the floor, I adjust my hips in my seat and wet my lips. My breathing shallows out, and my heartbeat races faster with each second I stare.

How in the hell did I sit in that class with her for weeks and not notice?

She glows like a beacon, beckoning me to her every time she walks into a room. It's like admiring her was written into my DNA, and it was triggered when we spoke for the first time, and now, I'm forever searching for her everywhere I go.

She looks so fucking sexy and beautiful right now.

Thank God I opted to wear jeans with this ensemble instead of the joggers I almost chose because there would be no hiding what she's doing to me right now.

Fucking Christ.

Setting my hands in my lap, I do my best to cover my growing appreciation of her beauty. But it's damn near impossible when the most beautiful girl in the fucking world is twenty feet away from me, wearing fishnet tights, a deep red skirt, and a matching top that has a rose on the front of the corset bra. Her loosely curled hair is in a long, high pony, and I can't stop thinking about running my tongue from the base of her exposed neck to her ear. Her lips are painted red, and I suddenly have a desire to see what that shade would look like painted across my body.

"I need you to punch me in the balls right now," I say to Malik, straight-faced, with no inflection in my tone.

"Spread 'em, baby. Here I come," Malik says and winds his fist up.

"Fuck. Stop. I was mostly kidding." I ground my words out, frustrated on so many levels right now.

"Look, I get it, man. She's hot. Why don't you just go for it?" he asks me as if it could be that simple.

If everything works out perfectly, then, sure, it could be. But what if every wrong thing happens? What if I kiss her and she leaves? I would be fucking devastated.

"I can't. I just can't. Not yet at least. I don't want to run her off and screw everything up. I need her right now," I admit.

He chuckles and glances at my lap. "I mean, I think the entire room can see that."

Biting down on my laugh, I elbow him. "Shut up."

"You've really got it bad for her, huh? I've never seen you like this," he confesses.

My heart thumps harder because I know it's true.

Rolling my head onto the back of the couch, I sigh and admit the truth for the first time out loud. "Yeah."

I can't get her out of my head. Everything reminds me of her. Any coffee shop makes me think of the warm cup she always has in her hands. Every book I see has me wondering if she's read it. Every time I see someone smile,

I think of hers—the shy ones that are often accompanied by reddened cheeks, the big ones that take over her entire face, and the ones she shares only with me.

Her smile is so intoxicating that I never want to see her frown again. I want to take care of her in any and every way. I don't want her worrying about how to pay for school or her dad's medical shit. I want her to be happy and stress-free. I want her to want for nothing. I would happily provide the world to her if she only asks and thank her for letting me.

My mind empties the second her eyes lock on to mine, unable to think of anything but *her*. She tilts her head ever so slightly to the side as she recognizes me. I didn't bother dressing up, so it's not all that hard to figure it out. But I think she's shocked that I'm here at all.

Truthfully, I didn't plan on coming to this party, but there was no way in hell that I was going to be anywhere else tonight, knowing she would be here. And, holy fuck, I'm glad I got to see her in that outfit because it is ruining me right now.

The tiniest smirk forms on her lips as she stares me down, a mix of bewilderment and satisfaction dancing in her eyes. I should go over there and say hello, but a part of me is scared that she'll think it's creepy that I showed up at the place she'd mentioned earlier.

Lifting my arm up, I wave at her and smile.

A few girls that are scattered around her wave back, but I ignore them, only looking at her. Blair raises her hand and wiggles her fingers at me.

Lumi snaps her hand in front of her, and she jumps,

turning to face him. But she steals a glance my way. And another.

They exchange a few words, but I'm way too far away to hear it over this music. Her brow furrows and lips tighten. I want to know what's twisting her face into a scowl. But as fast as it appeared, it's gone.

She looks over at me, and I don't bother averting my gaze. I don't care if she sees me staring right now. She deserves to be gazed upon, and I would happily oblige for eternity.

Even though the lights are dim, I witness my new favorite thing—seeing her blush from anything I do. I'm obsessed with it. I crave it. But only if it happens because of me. I think I might lose it if another guy brings out that redness in her cheeks like I do.

She might be talking to Lumi now, but I know she's still thinking about me because she can't stop sneaking glimpses my way. With every glance over here, my willpower to stay in my seat quickly deteriorates.

"So, what's going on with you two?" Malik leans over and asks me, nodding his head toward Blair.

Crossing my arms over my chest, I swallow hard. I don't know why it's so hard for me to talk about liking her. I've never been one to voice my emotions, especially ones that feel so vulnerable. Anger is easy to feel, and it's safer because you feel it offensively. You are on the attack. You lash out with rage.

But with vulnerability, it's the opposite. I feel like I'm playing defense twenty-four/seven, just waiting to get hurt again.

"Nothing," I answer him without tearing my gaze away from her.

"Umm … that's a lie. But I'll let it slide for right now." He chuckles, and I can't help but smirk as he calls me out.

My grin flattens as I focus on a guy approaching Blair and Lumi. He says something to them, but primarily Blair. He looks familiar, but I can't quite place it.

And then it clicks.

Josh.

He's got a reputation—that's for sure. A rep that has me wanting him as far away from Blair as possible. He laughs overtly hard at something she said, and my eye twitches before my lips twist into a nasty scowl. She smiles politely at him, and he continues to eye-fuck her. He reaches over and touches her arm, brushing his hand against her.

I'm on my feet before realizing it, barreling straight toward them. But I don't care. In seconds, I close the distance between Blair and me.

Slowing my pace, I enter their circle. I step behind her and snake my arm around her waist, flattening my hand against her stomach and pulling her into my chest. Fuck, she fits so perfectly pressed against me.

"What the hell?" she scoffs and turns, her eyes widening so far that I think they might burst.

"There you are. I wasn't sure you were going to make it, babe," I say sweetly down to Blair with absolute ease.

Her brows pinch, and I squint my eyes with a smile, holding her stare and hoping she's getting my point—to stay away from this guy.

Her eyes study mine, and I watch as my plan registers

on her face. Her confusion dissipates, replaced by a smile and twinkling eyes. Her shoulders and body relax into me. She holds my gaze for a second longer before turning back toward the other two, settling further into my arms.

Fuck, I love holding her like this.

She leans her head back and smiles up at me, and I enjoy every second of her undivided attention. With the hand on her stomach, I start brushing over the fabric of the corset with my thumb, back and forth. A shiver runs through her body, and my chest flutters at the reaction.

Josh looks down at the movement and then up at my face, his demeanor immediately shrinking into submission. "Hawthorne. I didn't know you would be here tonight."

Nodding at him, I kiss the top of Blair's head, immediately distracted by how amazing she smells, and rest my head on hers.

I don't miss the opportunity to sneak in a little chirp. "Well, she told me she was coming, and there was no way I was letting her party in this house without me."

"What's that supposed to mean?" he scoffs and takes a sip of his beer.

"It was just a joke," I lie through my teeth, not wanting to get Blair kicked out of the party by pissing off one of the hosts.

He laughs without humor, but does nothing to challenge it further. "Okay, sure. I'll see you guys around."

"Yep," I respond coolly as he walks away, and my shoulders relax the tiniest amount when I know he's gone. Bending down near Blair's ear, I whisper, "You're welcome."

She spins around in my arms, but doesn't back up,

giving me way too much hope that maybe she feels the same as me. She looks straight up at me. "What exactly am I thanking you for?"

"For saving you from Josh," I tell her, leaving out some details I've heard whispered through campus.

He's had a few complaints against him for sexual harassment, but apparently, his dad's money has bought the silence. But there's one person his dad can't protect him from, and that's me.

I don't usually get involved in shit that doesn't actively affect me, but seeing him in action with Blair has me feeling a whole different way about the situation. Maybe it's time to give him a taste of his own medicine. His dad wouldn't be able to save him this time. But I'll worry about that later.

Tonight, I need to focus on Blair and Lumi. I want them to have a safe and fun time. I won't let them drive after seeing how much they've already had to drink. I'll hang around until they're ready to leave.

I don't want to make tonight about me, so as hard as it is, I release Blair from my hold and step back. I plant a kiss on her forehead for two reasons. One, because I wanted to. Two, because without a single word, I let everyone know that she's mine and off-limits. Even if we aren't together, I'm not going to watch guys throw themselves at her all night. And if someone messes with her now, they're doing so at their own risk, knowing she's here with me and there will be consequences.

"I'll be here if you need anything. Have a good night, Blair."

She opens her mouth to say something, but nothing

comes out, and I leave her be, walking back over to my seat next to Malik.

He has a giant smart-ass grin on his face. Sarcasm oozes from his every word as he says, "Yeah, it looks like nothing is going on between you guys at all. A totally normal relationship between a tutor and student."

My phone vibrates, and I check it, finding a two-worded text from Blair that has my heart doing backflips.

Blair: Thank you.

Malik obnoxiously leans over and reads the message.

Keeping my eyes locked on Blair, I elbow him before any stupidity leaks out of his mouth. "Shut up."

He laughs and slaps my knee. "I'll be right back. I'm going to get a drink. Do you want anything?"

Shaking my head, I answer him, "No. I'm good. Thanks though."

"No problem," he says before walking away and disappearing into the kitchen.

Nothing happens by the time he returns with a drink in hand. No one else has tried to be stupid and approach her. Lumi and she seem to be having fun, drinking a lot and dancing.

I can see the changes in her movements as I watch the alcohol hitting her system. She's looser, freely moving her hips and body. It's hypnotizing. I think if the building caught on fire right now, I still wouldn't be able to look away. I would happily burn to ash in this very spot.

The next hour or so is exactly the same—way too many drinks and lots of dancing. Personally, I'm having a great fucking night. I could sit here and watch her until the end of time.

"I'm going to get some water," I tell Malik before dismissing myself to the kitchen.

After managing to find one of the last unused Solo cups, I fill it up with tap water and chug it quickly before refilling it and heading back to my seat.

As I enter the living room, Blair's voice cuts through the music and stops me dead in my tracks.

"Get the fuck out of here, Grant. You have no say in my life anymore."

Anymore? Who is this guy?

As I turn in her direction and she comes into view, my veins pump harder and faster the second I see his hand around her wrist. I storm across the room, and people part ways like water around me to let me through, although I don't know if it's from my size or the anger emanating from me in waves.

Lumi notices me first and looks instantly relieved, his tight shoulders relaxing.

"Can you hold this?" I ask him, holding out my cup of water.

Confused, he says, "S-sure," and takes it from me without hesitation.

With deadly rage, I turn my attention toward the second guy pushing his luck with Blair tonight.

My words rumble from deep in my chest, silencing the conversations around us. "Let. Go. Of. Her," I order him, my voice booming loud and deep.

His heated gaze turns to me, humor dancing in his eyes, but he doesn't let go of her. The skin on her arm around his fingers is stark white from the amount of pressure he's using. I've never felt more rage in my life than I do at this moment.

"We're having a conversation here. Get fucking lost, dude," he scoffs.

And every shred of patience I have *snaps.*

Reaching out, I pinch his wrist in my grip. He yelps like a little bitch as I rip each finger away from Blair's reddened forearm. His fingerprints remain on her, bringing my anger to a whole new level, and as I lift his pinkie, I snap it backward into two, feeling a gnarly pop as he shrieks in pain.

But I'm not done yet.

No one—*no one*—gets to leave marks on her like that.

Releasing his wrist, I grab him by the throat and storm toward the wall behind him, dragging him like a doll as he struggles to stay on his feet. Everyone is gasping around us as I slam him into the wall, pinning him by his throat.

Getting in his face, I make sure he hears me loud and clear. "Don't touch her ever again. Do you understand me?" An animalistic sound tears from deep in my chest.

He looks at me with confusion and shock. His words rasp through my grasp. "Who the hell do you think you are?"

With a haunting chuckle, I squeeze his throat tighter, watching his eyes bulge out of his head. "The person whose hand could break your fucking neck right now if you give me a good enough reason."

He does his best to laugh through my hold, and my vision pulses red.

"Griffin, stop!" Blair's hand flattens against my back, but I don't move a muscle. "Please."

My grip on this prick loosens with her plea.

When I drop my hand to my side, Grant falls a few inches to the ground. I didn't even realize I had lifted him up.

Fuck.

Blair is making me lose my mind.

Malik steps into my peripheral vision. I had no doubt he was beside me seconds after I grabbed this dude, just in case I needed backup.

The guy coughs and looks at her. "You know this guy, huh? Really, Blair?"

Stepping in front of her, I cut his view of her off. "Don't fucking talk to her. Did you not just learn anything?"

I grab his broken pinkie and twist it. He screams out in pain, but any sympathy is long gone.

"I would happily show you again with a different finger if you need a reminder."

"I don't," he growls.

I will give it to him. He never gives up, even when he's fighting a losing war.

"Get out of here," I spit before turning around to Blair.

"Look out!" Lumi shouts and points behind me right before I feel a fist crack into the side of my head.

Blair flies forward into Lumi as someone shoves her.

My vision goes from red to black.

Spinning around, I grab the guy by the neck of his shirt, pull my fist back, and punch him as hard as I can right in the face. A nasty crack vibrates through my hand and cuts through the music, ringing in my ears.

I would be worried, but it's not my hand that hurts; it's his face. Blood is spurting out of his nose, and his hands fly to his face as he starts to sob.

Turning back to Lumi, I ask, "What's his deal?"

He nods and glances at Blair. "It's her ex, and he won't leave her alone. Grant Gustavson."

Why didn't she tell me about this? I could have helped her—

Later. Think about that later.

Giving the man of the hour my undivided attention, I wipe the blood from my knuckles on his forehead and shirt, cleaning them off. "Grant, right?" He nods, and I continue, "Believe it or not, this was me holding back. If I find out you are still bothering Blair, it will not just be your face that I break. Do you understand me now?"

He cups his face, catching the blood that's still oozing from his nose. "Y-yes. Fuck. You're insane!"

My words hiss through my teeth. "Do you know what the definition of *insane* is, Grant? It's doing the same thing over and over and expecting a different result. I gave you perfectly clear instructions not to touch her, yet you did it again and expected a different outcome. So, really, who's the crazy one here? Not me." My words bellow from the deepest part of my chest, a menacing growl. "If you want to see crazy, try shit with her again. *Please* fucking test me. I would love to take some anger out on you."

He remains silent.

"Josh!" I shout over the music.

Josh finds us a moment later, and I tell him, "This guy needs to leave."

Grant looks at me in utter disbelief. "Are you serious? Josh, you cannot kick me out," Grant pathetically begs him.

Josh hesitates, and I fully shift my attention his way, my nostrils flaring and chest puffing with fury. He knows I'm not leaving any room for debate. If Josh says no, he'll have a problem with me, too, and he's smart enough to know that's not something he wants.

"Grant, let's go, dude. I saw you put your hands on her. You can't do that shit," Josh accosts him.

Grant scoffs. "Really? Coming from you?"

Josh doesn't respond. Instead, he grabs Grant, and along with a few other baseball players, he escorts him to the door and throws him out of the house.

"I don't need you to fight my battles, Griffin," Blair slurs behind me, and I turn to find her with glossy eyes and a flushed complexion.

God, she's so goddamn cute, especially all angry and pouty.

"I'm not fighting them for you. I'm fighting them with you," I correct her, teasing her slightly, which only pokes the bear more.

She purses her lips and jabs her finger into my chest. "You are being ... ugh, frustrating!"

She glares at me for a moment before her eyes fall to my lips, and my lips part in response as blood pumps straight to my dick. Her being mad at me should definitely *not* turn me on, right? Although I'm not sure there's much she could do at this point that wouldn't have that effect on me.

Right now, I just need to get her and Lumi home.

Clearly, Blair has had her fill for the night, and by the slightly horrified look on Lumi's face, he wouldn't mind leaving the scene I just created.

"Frustrating? Hmm. Why don't we continue this conversation in the car?" I offer, gesturing her backward with my hands.

She doesn't move a step. Instead, she crosses her arms and stomps her foot. "I'm not going anywhere."

Ignoring her for a moment and sighing, I look at Lumi. "Does she have a purse or a bag we need to track down?"

He shakes his head. "Nope. We don't have anything else. Just my car."

By the sound of his words, I can tell he's still heavily intoxicated from what he had to drink, so he's not getting behind the wheel and driving home.

"Are you cool with crashing at my place? We can get your car tomorrow," I ask.

Blair seems to drift into thought, her face blanking out.

Jesus. How much did she have to drink?

Lumi smiles. "Sleep in Hawthorne Manor? I thought you'd never ask."

Chuckling, I ask, "Hawthorne Manor?"

Lumi's eyes widen, and he glances at Blair. "It's what she calls it."

Why is it adorable that she has a nickname for my house?

"All right." I laugh. "We'll get your car tomorrow then. Let's get out of here. Are you ready?"

Lumi smiles. "Sure am."

Blair rushes a few feet over to me and plants her head

on my chest, wrapping her arms around my waist. My hands fly out to her sides in shock, not touching her.

Slowly, she looks up at me and says, "Thank you."

"Please don't thank me for that," I respond immediately, meaning every single word.

"Griffin ..." She trails off and rocks onto her tiptoes.

Her pupils dilate, and she licks her lips. I don't know if it's the alcohol or not, but I've never seen her so exposed, and I don't mean physically.

I mean the way she's looking at me. There are no barriers between us at this moment, and I never want to go back. I'm addicted. I'm hooked. She's never looked so vulnerable, and my heart constricts in my chest because I know she's only looking at *me* like that. I'm over the fucking moon that she feels safe enough to let her guard down with me.

She inches closer to my lips, and I stay still, gazing down at the only girl who can steal my breath away simply by existing.

She lifts her hand to my jaw and guides my head down, and for some insane reason, I let her. Her eyes drift closed as she wets her lips before they graze against mine.

Every nerve in my body jumps at the contact, and it takes everything in me not to lean into her kiss. I mean, *everything* I have.

Her eyes flutter open, and she looks up at me with parted lips and disappointment.

Whispering only loud enough for her to hear, I say, "I'm not going to kiss you, Blair."

"Why not?" She pouts, and I bite down on my lip, wanting nothing more than to bite down on hers.

"Because you're drunk. I'm not into taking advantage of you, and I don't want a room full of people to see how desperate I am when I finally claim those pretty lips with mine. And I sure as fuck am not risking you waking up tomorrow and regretting it."

Her lips part, and her cheeks burn, turning the same color as her lipstick.

"Come on." I slide my hand around hers and intertwine our fingers.

"W-where are we going?" Blair slurs.

"We're going home, baby," I murmur to her, pulling her tighter against me.

"Thank God. I hate parties," she admits, and I grin.

I have so many questions that I am dying to ask her, and part of me wants to use a bit of her drunkenness to my advantage. She might say things now that she wouldn't admit if she were sober. But I never want her to feel like I'm exploiting her for anything.

She passes out not a minute into the drive home, leaning across the middle console, her head lying on my shoulder. Lumi is quietly singing in the back seat to the radio with his head leaning against the window, drunkenly enjoying the ride as we pull into my driveway. When I shift into park, Lumi perks up, seemingly more sober, and hops out of my truck. Tucking my phone, keys, and wallet into my pockets, I quickly make my way around to the front passenger door and pull it open.

Rustling my keys back out of my pocket, I grab the house one, handing it to Lumi, and whisper, "Can you unlock the door? I'll carry her inside."

Lumi's gaze softens, and he nods with a slight smile before turning away and starting up the stairs.

Looking back down at Blair, I study her for a moment longer. There is something so peaceful about watching her sleep, every worry about her dad and money gone, only a look of relaxation on her beautiful face.

Bending down, I reach over and undo the seat belt. Sliding an arm under her knees and around her back, I lift her out of the truck and cradle her against my chest. The second she lays her palm against my peck and nestles her head against me, my breath hitches.

I don't want to carry her up the steps. I don't want to put her to bed. I want to stay right here with her in my arms. Tilting my head down, I breathe her in as deeply as I can, filling my lungs to capacity.

As I take a step back, I place a gentle kiss on the top of her head and push the door shut with my foot.

The cool air swishes around us as I carry her up the steps toward my front door, which Lumi is now holding open. Stepping inside, I tighten my hold on Blair, not ready to let her go.

"I'll get her upstairs. Feel free to take one of the empty bedrooms on the first floor, unless you want to share with her in her room?" I ask, part of me hoping he chooses the first floor so that I can stay with her tonight and make sure she doesn't puke in her sleep.

He shrugs hesitantly. "I'll probably just stay with her to keep an eye on her."

"Y-yeah. Yeah, that makes sense. Definitely. Someone should definitely keep an eye on her," I ramble, hating myself more and more with each dragging word.

He knowingly smiles as we start walking toward the stairs. "Unless you had other ideas?"

"Nope." The word flies out of my mouth before he can even finish his question. "Not at all. I mean, she would probably want you there anyway."

"Okay, then it's a plan," he states.

I hate this plan.

Silence stretches between us for the rest of the walk to her room, and Lumi gasps as we step inside.

"Holy crap. Can I move in too?"

I smile at his awe.

But as quickly as pride floods my veins, guilt replaces it.

This house is nothing more than pretty decor and elaborate architecture. For how many rooms it has, most are empty of happy memories.

Well, until Blair got here, that is.

"I'm kidding, Griffin. Don't look so scared." He laughs, and I chuckle along with him, allowing him to believe that my fear is of another person living in my house and not of the uncontrollable feelings I'm developing for the girl wrapped in my arms.

Walking over to the bed, I shift her in my grasp and cradle her with one arm as I pull her comforter back. Gently, I lay her down on the bed, and she instantly nuzzles into the pillows.

Memorizing the shape of her relaxed lips, the soft rise and fall of her chest, and the flutter behind her eyelids, I take a step away from her and turn on my heel.

"Good night, Griffin. Thanks for giving us a ride and letting me stay. And beating the shit out of Grant. Lord knows he's had that coming for a while," Lumi says, and the mention of that guy makes my blood pressure spike.

"Speaking of him"—I continue toward the door—"can you let me know if he messes with her anymore?"

He nods. "Yeah, of course. I'm honestly surprised you didn't know who he was or why she hasn't mentioned him. He never stops bugging her. I'm just glad you were there to step in tonight. Grant can be ... unpredictable."

Clenching my jaw, I assure him, "Don't worry about him anymore. I'll handle it from now on."

"Thank God." He chuckles, the kind that holds no humor but rather laced with relief.

"Good night," I say before leaving the room and closing the door behind me.

As I walk into my room, I grab the handle and spin around to close it, but instead I leave it cracked a few inches. Just in case Blair needs me for anything tonight.

"It's like time has lost all continuity. Every second with you outweighs days of life before I met you."

Stephanie Meyer

chapter seventeen
blair

Holy mother of God, my brain is trying to break through my skull. Every step down the stairs is agonizing, and I think I might die if I don't drink ten gallons of water right this second.

"Ughhh." I massage my temples.

This is my first real hangover, and I never want to experience it again. I've never let myself lose control, not like I did last night. Oh my God, I cannot believe I let that happen.

Small moments flash in my mind, and right as I try to grab on to them and home in on the memories, they're gone.

Starting at the beginning of the party, I have a pretty good memory. I remember how surprised I was to walk into the living room and see Griffin on the couch. Especially since only hours before, he had no plan of attending until I mentioned it. Seems rather coincidental.

I remember the baseball guy who was a bit flirty with

me. I also remember Griffin running him off, which was entertaining, to say the least. The energy was a bit weird, and Griffin was insulting him for being a creep, and I don't know if the guy even realized it.

And *oh my God.*

He said he knew I was going and wouldn't let me go alone. Did he mean that? Or was he just keeping the ruse going a little longer so that guy would leave me alone?

My cheeks warm at the thought that Griffin came to that party just for me. Because if he did just go for me, then that means … more? More than simply warden and prisoner. More than student and tutor. More than *friends.* Although I think we might have been more all along, even if we didn't know it.

Stop. You're being ridiculous.

He can go to the party for his own reasons and happen to scare that guy away for completely platonic reasons and then platonically kiss my forehead.

I smack into someone hard as I turn into the kitchen. "Shit."

"Good morning, my little prisoner," Griffin's smooth voice sings in my ears with an undertone of humor.

Squeezing my eyes shut for a moment, I open them again and meet Griffin's dazzling gaze. "You do this a lot? Party?"

He bursts out laughing. "Having a bit of a rough morning? And, no, not if I can help it."

Closing my eyes to avoid the humiliation and bright lights, I groan. "I don't know why anyone would do this. Ever. I am never touching alcohol ever again, I swear."

Peeking out of one eye, I see him grinning from ear to ear, and I open my other eye.

"Is my suffering amusing to you?" I grumble.

He holds my gaze, studying me kindly before mumbling, "Not at all. But I can't help but be slightly entertained, thinking of last night. I can't say I've ever seen you so ... loose?"

Loose? Oh God, what did I do last night?

An image of Griffin looking down at me, only inches from my face, flashes in my mind, warming my body by a thousand degrees.

Did we kiss? Did we ...

"How much of last night do you actually remember?" he asks curiously, leaning against the wall and crossing his ankles.

Racking my brain, I look away and scour as many pieces of the party as I can recall.

That one dude Griffin didn't like—I think his name was Josh.

Griffin watching me with hunger in his eyes.

My stomach twists as the next memory filters in.

Grant. Grant was there too.

My heart races. He grabbed me. And then Griffin ripped him off of me.

And then ... I tried to kiss him.

Oh God.

My eyes widen and fly to his.

Griffin chuckles. "Is that you remembering throwing yourself at me?"

Snapping my stare his way, I scoff, "I would hardly say I threw myself at you. That's a bit of an exaggeration."

He shrugs. "That's not how I remember it. I could barely fight you off."

Cocking my head to the side, I cross my arms and step closer to him. "You are so full of it. I didn't even try to kiss you. I wouldn't have."

Lie. I remember that now, clear as day. I wanted nothing more than to feel his soft lips against mine.

He squints his eyes at me. "Oh, really?"

In one quick movement, he grabs me by the waist, pushes me against the wall, and pins my arms above my head, lowering his face to mine. His warm, minty breath hits me in waves, and I sharply inhale.

"You didn't want to kiss me? Not at all?" His words are pure lust on my lips, beckoning me closer to him.

Rolling my eyes, I glance away from him. But he adjusts my hands, now pinning them with one hand, and catches my chin with the other, forcing me to look back at him.

I pop the *P.* "Nope."

He bites down on his lip and stares into my eyes with such searing intensity that I'm scared I'm going to melt into the wall behind me.

The air around us thickens with tension, like every fiber and dust in the air freezes and anxiously waits for one of us to move, pausing to see who moves first.

"In fact, I barely like you at all," I tell him, unable to keep the smirk from kicking up on my lips, killing my poker face.

"Really? What don't you like about me, Blair?" he asks, closing the distance between us even more.

My body is practically shuddering from his proximity.

Licking my lips, I keep a straight and stern face as I list all the things I downright hate about him. "For one, you are funny. It's distracting, and I very much dislike distractions. Two, you're good at English, but for some reason, you're holding yourself back. Three, you're a hockey player, and the ego is ridiculously enlarged. Four, you're annoyingly hot, and sometimes, it's hard to look away. Another distraction. In total, you are really just a pain in my ass."

"Blair …" His voice, deep and husky, causes tingles to radiate from my head to my toes, pulsing from deep in my core. "I didn't know you had such a disdain for me. Should I list all of the reasons I don't like you?"

His lips are an inch from mine, and my chest is rising and falling so fast that I'm practically panting. Maybe I was throwing myself at him last night because I feel like I'm about to do it all over again.

Slowly, I shake my head. "I think I'd rather not know everything you hate about me."

He smirks. "That's a shame."

His hand grazes my waist, his delicate touch threatening my restraint. I suck in a breath at the contact, and he freezes long enough for me to tell him to stop. But I don't.

His fingers trail up and then down my rib cage until he grabs on to my hip and pulls me flush against him.

Can this level of excitement cause a heart attack? I think I might be close to it.

"Because I have so many things I would like to tell you. Countless reasons why I definitely one thousand percent *don't* like you."

I gulp.

"Like how you always wear one of those cute little bows in your hair when you style half of it up. How you get lost in your books, completely entranced by a good scene that you drift away to another world. Or how you bite down on your lip when you're concentrating on something."

I do not do the lip thing. Right? Oh my God, I think I do. No one has ever pointed that out to me before. And he's noticed my hair ribbons?

I had no idea he paid that much attention to me.

He pauses, and his eyes drop to my lips. My back arches slightly, pressing into him further, and a soft, whimper-like noise leaves me as I feel how perfectly we fit together.

"Wow. You really hate me, huh?" My voice is breathy and desperate, as I'm starved for his touch and his kiss.

His brows furrow, and he whispers, "*So* much."

He tilts his head ever so slightly, and when his lips graze mine, a shock electrifies my entire body, every hair and nerve on edge.

"Blair?" Lumi's voice drops a bomb on our moment, and I jump back. "Oh shit. Oh God." He winces as he turns into the kitchen and finds us nearly kissing. "Ahh! Pretend I wasn't here. I'm *so* sorry!"

"Lumi?" His name is a whisper on my lips as I wonder what the hell he's doing here. But I quickly push the thought out of my mind.

He scurries away, and we burst out laughing into a fit of giggles and smiles.

My heart still thumps loudly in my chest as Griffin pulls away, releasing my hands from above my head.

"I-I'd better go get ready for class." My words are a stuttering mess, and I lower my arms.

His face twists in confusion. "You're actually going this morning?"

"Well, yeah. Why wouldn't I?"

The oven beeps, and he walks over to it and grabs an oven mitt as he says, "Because you are hungover as fuck and should chill in bed and rest."

I take a few steps to the cabinets and grab a glass. "Well, that's not going to help me keep my perfect grades," I say as I wander to the fridge and fill my glass up with nice cold water.

He pulls a muffin pan out of the oven, and the delicious scent of chocolaty, buttery goodness wafts my way, my stomach rumbling in response.

"I am going to owe Mrs. Potts my life for making chocolate chip muffins. My favorite." I swoon and scurry over to the hot pan, eyeballing up the one that I want.

Griffin rubs the back of his neck and leans against the kitchen island. "She didn't make them."

"Well, if she didn't, then who ..." I trail off and look at him.

Griffin looks away shyly, his voice barely audible. "I did."

"You can bake?" I snap, my words racing past my lips in shock.

He glares at me playfully. "Funny. And, yes, I'm an excellent baker. Mrs. Potts taught me."

"Mmm. Good to know. Add it to my list of things I

hate about you. I'm trying to keep a good figure, and you make delicious sweet treats. Not a good combo." I spin around, smiling, and focus on the muffins. "Come on, little buddy. You are all mine."

Popping the hot-as-hell muffin out of the tin, I put it on a paper towel and hold it gently, like my most prized possession. Although, in about ten seconds, I'm going to devour it.

I walk over to Griffin before I can stop myself, stand up on my tiptoes, and kiss him on the cheek before genuinely saying, "Thank you."

"Y-you're welcome," he whispers softly and swallows hard, the apple of his throat bobbing.

As I pull away, I find his cheeks deepening into a pretty red flush, and I memorize the image of a shy Griffin who looks so cute when flustered.

Without saying anything else, I begin walking out of the room, but Griffin stops me.

"Do you guys want to get Lumi's car before class? I'm free for about an hour after if you want to wait too."

"Wait, what?" I ask. "Lumi's car?"

He nods. "Yeah. You both drank like pirates last night, and I wasn't letting either of you get behind the wheel, so I brought you home."

I don't remember that at all.

My brain feels like mush for so many reasons right now, and it's hard to think straight. "I'll ask Lumi and see what he wants to do."

"Sounds good," he answers before pushing off of the island and walking out of the kitchen on the other side of the room, and I can't help the smile spreading onto my lips.

Glancing up at the clock on the wall, I check the time —seven a.m. We usually have to leave by eight forty-five a.m. to get to class. I'd better start getting ready, especially if we are going to get the car beforehand.

After curling loose waves into my hair and doing my makeup, I pin half of my hair up and add a black ribbon. For no particular reason. Just another day. Definitely not because some hockey player says he likes them.

Lumi is ready about an hour before me, and he decides to wander downstairs. When I'm finally ready, I take one last look in the mirror, suddenly nervous about walking out of the room. Do I look cute? Is this a good outfit?

I picked out black tights, a black suede skirt, and a cream oversize sweater. I'm going to wear some black booties with it.

No, this is cute, for sure. Stop doubting yourself. You never have before.

Yeah, well, I wasn't trying to impress someone before.

Grabbing my backpack, I throw it on before I talk myself into changing.

As I get downstairs, I find Griffin and Lumi waiting by the door for me. *Silent.* Both of them staring at me like I caught them talking about something I wasn't supposed to hear.

"What's up?" I ask awkwardly.

Lumi shakes his head aggressively, and Griffin mumbles, "Nothing. Ready?"

"Yeah … you guys are being weird," I tell them as I walk to the door, and Griffin pulls it open for me.

"Because we are weird." Lumi laughs, and Griffin looks at him questioningly.

Trying to ignore that it seems like they have a secret now that I am not a part of, I go to the truck and hop into the passenger front seat.

Griffin gets in and starts the truck, and Lumi jumps in the back.

I wonder what we will cover in class today. Speaking of class, I ask, "Have you been working on your paper? Can I look over it yet?"

Griffin wrings his hands on the wheel. "Yeah, and no."

"Yeah, you've been working on it, and, no, I can't see it? Or, no, you haven't been working on it, and, yes, I can see the blank docs?" I ramble.

"The first one. I'm not very far with it though."

"So then, can I read what you have so far?" My curiosity is overwhelming, and I'm desperate to know more about him.

"No. Definitely not. It's not ready," he says, leaving no room for argument. His secrecy makes me want to read it even more. "Digging up memories and feelings, talking about life, and all my dreams for the future—it just feels so forced, and I hate it. Maybe one day, you can read it, but just not yet."

"Okay, deal," I agree, not wanting to push him further than he's comfortable.

A light bulb goes off in my head on how I can learn more about The Beast himself. I remember the project I did when I started my paper to help me come up with ideas.

Opening my backpack, I pull out my laptop and quickly find the document I'm looking for.

"What are you doing?" Griffin asks as he pulls out of the driveway.

Hitting Send on an email to him, I sigh proudly. "Being the best tutor in the world. I just sent you an assignment. I'll need it back by the end of the day. It's for extra credit for Dr. Schrute."

"What? I want extra credit!" Lumi protests from the back seat.

"Sorry, only for students who are getting tutoring," I lie, wishing he could read my mind so he knew that the extra credit doesn't exist.

"Sweet, thanks!" Griffin says, and my heart twists slightly.

I don't love lying to him, that's for sure. But even if he doesn't send it back to me, it will help him more than he knows. It's basically an outline for his final paper. So, in the end, it'll be worth it, and if he does share it with me, then I'll be able to discover more about him.

Shutting my laptop and zipping it into my bag, I feel a light tug at my hair.

As I sit up, I see Griffin reaching across the middle console.

With his eyes on the road, he murmurs, "Nice bow."

Nice bow. Tell me why it's been hours since he uttered those words to me, and I still can't stop replaying them over and over in my mind. Along with what happened in the kitchen. When did everything shift between us? Was it gradually over time, or was there a singular moment that changed us?

I don't know. But I do know that for the first time, I struggled to focus in class today. I couldn't think of anything aside from Griffin in the seat next to me.

Oh God, what is happening to me? Am I broken? Is this some form of Stockholm syndrome? Regardless, I don't really care what it is. I just need to decide if I like it or not.

I mean, of course I like it, but do I want it to continue, or do I want to end whatever is growing between Griffin and me?

Initially, he wanted me as his tutor because I wasn't into him. But now, it seems like he doesn't mind the idea of me liking him; in fact, he seems to be encouraging it more than anything.

I would say he's testing me, but I know he's not. I could see that clear as day in how he looked at me in the kitchen this morning.

Ugh. I need to get out of my head and focus on my homework.

Hopping up onto my bed, I empty my backpack and

organize my books and notebooks. Looking at my planner, I decide what to work on first. Let's do math. There's no emotion in math. No messy, sexy, wet hair that hangs over stunning hazel eyes. No firm chest and mouthwatering body. It's just numbers and logic. Easy.

Grabbing my notebook, I set it next to me and open my laptop, pulling up the assignment for tonight and getting to work.

My stomach grumbles sometime later, and I check my laptop to see what time it is—eight p.m. I've been doing homework for six straight hours, and now, I'm starving.

Pushing my laptop away, I lean back and stretch my legs out, feeling the stiffness from sitting crisscross for hours ease out of my muscles.

Knock. Knock.

My heart skips a beat.

"Come in," I call out and sit back up as the doorknob twists and the door swings open.

Dear God, no one should be allowed to look that good with wet hair, sweats, a Legends hoodie, and a backward cap. It's ridiculous really, how some people are just gifted with those genes.

"What's up?" I greet him, leaning back on the palms of my hands and crossing my ankles in front of me.

Lifting a packet of paper into the air, he walks over to me and sits beside me on the bed. "Turning in my home-work assignment."

Shit.

"How was practice?" I ask, avoiding talking about the fake assignment I gave him.

He stretches his neck from side to side. "It was good."

Nodding, I flash a smile. "Oh, well, that's good."

I've felt terrible about this all day. I shouldn't have lied to him about the questionnaire.

"Griffin, I have to tell you something." I sit up and return to my crisscross position, clasping my hands in my lap and avoiding his gaze.

He laughs and reaches out, brushing my knee with his hand, pointing at the stack of papers in my lap. "Are you going to tell me that this isn't for extra credit? Because I already know."

I snap my eyes to his as my face drains of warmth, and I extend my legs out in front of me. "What do you mean?"

He leans on his side, bending over my shins, and makes these torturous little circles on my knee. "I went to Dr. Schrute."

"Oh no." The words fall from my lips.

"Oh *yes*. I wanted to find out exactly how long I had to finish this, but he had no idea what I was talking about."

Glancing at the packet, I see every single question on the top page filled in. He reaches over and grabs it, pulling it away from me.

"You can have this on one condition."

Looking back up at him, I whisper, "And what's that?"

He smirks. "You never lie to me again."

The guilt clenching around my heart like a tight fist is reason enough to agree to his term.

"I really am sorry about that. I got a bit carried away. I just wanted to know more about you," I admit. "You might not get extra credit for it from Dr. Schrute, but you get a few bonus points in my book."

"I suppose it wasn't a waste of time after all," he murmurs.

Then, I see it—the glisten in his eyes, the part of his lips, the softness in his gaze, the quickness of his breath, and the way he isn't just looking at me, but *seeing* me as I am at my core.

The words are barely audible as I say, "I won't lie to you again, I promise."

He sets the packet back in my lap with care.

Tucking the papers against my chest, I hold them close, not wanting to give him a chance to change his mind.

"Thank you," I whisper and look into his eyes, showing him how much this means to me.

"You're welcome. And please ..." He hesitates, and the look that flashes in his eyes is one of helpless fear. "Please don't share it with anyone."

Reaching my hand out, I place it over his, wanting to give him a sense of comfort and assurance. "I promise."

He grins and takes a deep breath. "Thank you."

"Thank you for giving this to me." I stroke the back of his hand with my thumb.

He looks down at where we touch and stares at our hands intently. "Blair ..."

Wetting my lips, I study him and see how his chest rises faster and faster with each second. He is made of hard lines and sharp features, but at this moment, I see the softness of his lips, the golden flecks in his eyes, the gentleness in his gaze. His jaw is clenching and unclenching as he seems to be fighting a war inside his mind, and he looks away from me.

"Griffin …" I whisper, and his eyes fly to mine.

I could get lost in his gaze for eternity.

Silence settles between us as invisible strings seem to tug us toward one another. He's looking at me like he's drowning and I'm the breath of air that will save him.

Quickly, he pushes himself off of the bed and stands up. "I should, umm … get going. You have work to do. Good night, Blair," he whispers to me before turning on his heel and walking out of the room, closing the door behind him before I can even respond, leaving me utterly breathless.

A guttural scream tears through the house, twisting my stomach into knots, and I fly to my feet with my book in my hand.

It sounded like … *Griffin.*

"Ahh!" Griffin cries out again, and I rush to my door, hovering my hand above the handle for a second before throwing the door open, preparing to come face-to-face with anything.

Griffin screams again, quieter this time, but still just as heartbreaking. It's coming from his room.

Twisting his doorknob, I rush into his room without a second thought. It could be an intruder. I grip my book tighter in my hand, prepared to wield it as a weapon.

But I don't think that will be necessary.

Griffin's bare chest is rapidly rising and falling as he

thrashes in his sheets, asleep in his bed. He must be having a nightmare. Perhaps I should let myself out and leave him be.

"Ugh!" His deep voice startles me as another scream slashes through the silence.

Striding over to the side of his bed, I murmur his name. "Griffin."

He doesn't react, so I say it a little louder, this time gently reaching out and wiggling his shoulder. "Griffin."

His eyes fly open and land on me. I gasp at the look in his eyes, the utter terror and sadness stretched into every feature. It's startling compared to his usually composed demeanor.

"Hey, you were just having a bad dream," I whisper softly.

He blinks the emotion away, and the haze in his eyes clears as he comes back to reality.

"Blair?" His voice cracks.

"Hi. I'm sorry for intruding. You were ..."

"Screaming?" He fills the word in for me.

I nod.

"I'm sorry for distracting you," he apologizes, and my heart aches.

"There's no need. I just wanted to make sure you were okay," I say.

He nods and sits up in bed, resting his back against the headboard. "I'm fine." His eyes flick down to the book in my hand. "What are you reading?"

"*The Wicked Truth*," I answer, flashing him the earthy-green cover.

Rocking back and forth on my heels, I glance at the door, and his stare mimics mine. "I should let you rest."

As I turn away, his hand flies out and catches my wrist. "Stay."

"What?" My gaze flies to his face.

He's still staring at the door. Slowly, he lifts his eyes to look into mine and clears his throat. "Will you read to me?"

His thumb brushes over the sensitive skin on my wrist, and I whisper, "Yes."

The faintest glimpse of a grin lifts his lips as he slides over in the bed and pats the spot at his side. Sitting on top of the covers, I rest the book in my lap and open it to the page I was on and begin reading.

I feel his gaze burning into me as I recite chapter after chapter of the hauntingly beautiful story to a beautiful, haunted boy until he falls deep asleep. Then, I return to my room and bury myself under my covers with a smile on my face.

In all the time I've spent with Griffin, I've seen the versions of himself that he presents to the world. To his team and friends, he is The Beast, a renowned hockey player with a successful future ahead of him.

I've seen the version of himself that he puts on display for Chip and Mrs. Potts, one that's strong, fearless, and happy. The one he wants them to see so they don't worry about him.

But in the silence, in the moments when he thinks no one is looking, I've seen the real him. The one who has nightmares and finds comfort in being read to. The one who makes a damn good chocolate chip muffin. He is the one who is a friend to everyone, but no one really gets close to him. He keeps them at a distance. Well, everyone besides me.

I've seen him open up more with Malik, and I do not doubt that that's his best friend. But I can see that he keeps him just far enough away to not see behind the curtain.

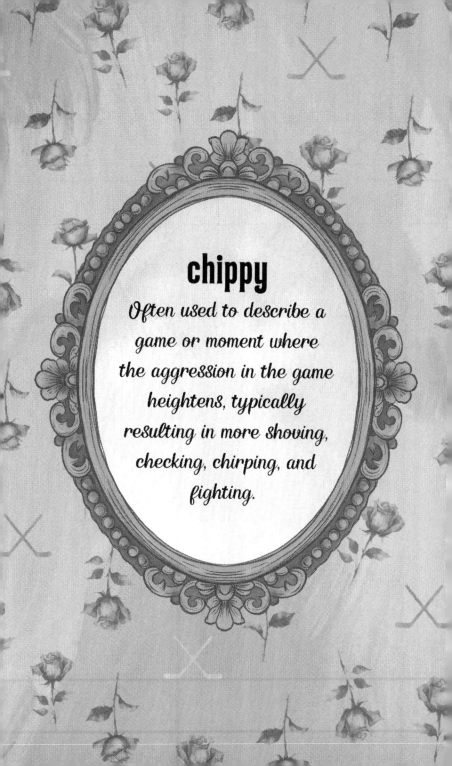

chippy

Often used to describe a game or moment where the aggression in the game heightens, typically resulting in more shoving, checking, chirping, and fighting.

chapter eighteen
griffin

As I approach Blair's bedroom door this morning, my palms are sweating. I have no idea why I'm so nervous about seeing her, but it's killing me. Usually, she is downstairs by now, waiting for me to be ready to go.

Knock. Knock.

No answer.

"Blair, are you about ready to go?" I call out to her through the door.

No answer.

"Blair," I call out again, and again, it goes unanswered. "I'm coming in."

Worry wraps around my throat as I slowly open her door, trying to prepare myself for anything. This is so unlike her. She has never once been late.

Any fear dissipates when I see her in bed, softly snoring, still fast asleep and curled up in her blankets. I should wake her right now before we're really late for class. But I can't. She looks so peaceful, and I can't look away.

She is so beautiful without even trying. With messy bedhead, no makeup, and drool dried on her cheek.

Her alarm sounds again, and I nearly jump out of my skin. She mindlessly turns it off and goes back to sleep.

"Hey, Blair," I whisper and approach her like I would a wild animal, with my hands slightly raised, ready to defend myself if she pounces. "Blair, wake up. We're going to be late."

Her eyes flutter open, and she blinks. Once. Twice. Three times. And she flies up in bed as her eyes bulge out of her head.

"Oh my God! What time is it?" she shouts and searches in the blanket for her phone, finding the time to be much later than she hoped. "Shit. Shit. Shit."

She throws the blankets off of her and slides out of bed, racing toward the wardrobe. Her dainty silk PJ set is all wrinkled from her deep sleep. She yanks out a sweatshirt and leggings before hooking her fingers in her shorts and tugging them down.

"Oh. Okay. Umm," I ramble and spin around to give her privacy as I fight the urge not to sneak a peek her way. "Tell me when you're decent."

"Okay," she says a moment later, and I take that as a signal that she is dressed and turn back around.

"Ready?" My jaw unhinges, and my eyes drop to her chest and the bare skin of her stomach.

Thankfully, she got the leggings on fast enough, or I would have become a puddle on the fucking floor.

"Griffin!" she squeals and yanks the sweatshirt over her head.

"Shit, sorry," I apologize, but don't move. "I thought your *okay* meant, like, *Okay, I'm decent.*"

"No!" she scolds me, laughing.

But I'm frozen, hypnotized by her beauty and her body. I know I saw her practically naked onstage, but that doesn't count because we didn't really know each other then. But now, it's different.

Now, I see how her lacy bra cups her breasts the way my hands are meant to. The way I want to trace every curve of her body with my tongue and memorize every moan and groan that I earn with my touch.

My dick twitches, and I gulp as she settles the sweat-shirt down over her stomach.

"N-now, are you ready?" I ask her again, smirking as she looks up at me with glaring, squinted eyes.

"Yes," she says sassily, grabbing a pair of socks before rushing into her bathroom.

It dawns on me that I've never seen her wearing comfy clothes like this—well, aside from her PJs—and I fucking love it. I would love this outfit even more if it were my sweatshirt she was wearing.

"Give me, like, five minutes, and I'll be downstairs," she announces to me before shutting the door behind her.

"Okay, I'll be in the truck," I tell her, wanting to give her a few minutes of alone time before we leave. "I'll get your bag."

"Thanks," she calls out.

I sling her bag over my shoulder and head downstairs, pulling my phone out of my pocket as I descend the stairs.

As I head toward the door, I make a detour into the kitchen and grab a chocolate chip muffin, paper towel, and water.

When I get into my truck, I set her breakfast on the middle console and text Lumi to grab Blair a coffee because we are running late. I know she usually texts him in the morning if she wants one, and I don't know if she'll remember to this morning with all the chaos.

A minute later, Blair bursts through the front door and heads toward me. Her hair is pulled back in a tight pony-tail, and I find yet another way to appreciate her gorgeous face.

When she throws the passenger door open, she hops into the seat and immediately spots the muffin, eyeballing it with jealousy.

I push it in her direction as she closes the door. "It's yours."

She glances up at me with slightly wide eyes, and I wish she wouldn't be so shocked that I grabbed her break-fast. It's just a muffin and water. Nothing crazy.

"Thank you," she murmurs and studies me like I did to her this morning, hesitant, like you're face-to-face with a predator and unsure of how to act.

"You're welcome. Figured you were hungry," I admit coyly and pull forward, heading down the winding driveway.

"Starving actually. So, an extra thank-you is in order." She smiles, peels the paper away from the muffin, and takes a bite. "Mmmm. Oh my God. This is so good."

"I know," I admit and smirk as I feel her glare warm my face.

"Smart-ass." She giggles and does a little happy food dance that I've never seen before but will now strive to get every time I make her something.

The drive to class is uneventful, aside from Blair doing karaoke to some Taylor Swift songs. After we park, we find Lumi waiting underneath the gazebo decorated with green vines and flowers. I've never really noticed how much detail there is in this school, interior and exterior, until now. Is this the same place where we met Lumi before classes? It must be because that building right there is where we have English. I just don't remember this area being so beautiful.

"You got me a coffee?" Blair squeals with happiness and reaches for Lumi's outstretched hand. "You are a mind reader and a lifesaver. Seriously. I completely forgot."

"Well, it's not me you need to——"

"Should we head inside?" I cut him off and make a cut-it-out gesture, lifting my hand to my neck and shaking it side to side.

Blair looks over at me with big eyes; her face flushes, and I bite down on my lip to stop smiling at how goddamn cute she is when she does that.

"Yeah," Lumi says, holding his elbow out for Blair, who takes it while still maintaining my gaze.

Slowly, she pulls her stare away from mine and strides forward with Lumi. I follow them inside, and we find our seats. A few minutes later, Malik joins us, sitting to my right.

"Hey, sweet cheeks. What's up?" Malik bumps my shoulders, and he settles into his seat.

"Not much. You?" I ask him, chuckling.

Sometimes, he lives in his own world, I swear.

"Nothing to report," he sighs heavily, and I feel like there's more to that than he's letting on.

Blair, checking her phone, grabs my attention, but right as I turn to look, she slams it down on the desk and huffs.

"What's wrong?" I lean over and whisper into her ear.

She shakes her head. "Nothing. It's fine."

Reaching over, I place my hand on top of her thigh. "It's not. It's okay if you don't want to tell me right now. But eventually, I would love to know what is pissing you off so much."

She nods but stays quiet.

"Good morning, class," Dr. Schrute addresses us, but I don't look away from Blair.

Her eyes well up with tears, and my jaw and fists clench. I want to hurt whatever or whoever is doing that to her. I'll kill them. I don't care who it is.

I squeeze her hand, and her shoulders relax slightly.

The silence in the room is ruined when everyone's laptops ding with notifications, including Blair's, which is open on her desk.

She rips her hand from mine and opens the email frantically.

Our classmates start looking around, stopping when they lay eyes on Blair, and I'm starting to feel really fucking uneasy.

Blair clicks on the email, and it's from the school's distribution account. Usually, we receive inclement weather notifications, class cancellations, event information, et cetera, from that email address.

But as the screen loads, I find none of the above.

Instead, it's a video taken of Blair onstage at The Fallen Petal, and the words *the hockey team's favorite slut* are written in the middle of the clip. Blair is dancing onstage, and the guys and I are sitting in the front row.

"Oh my God …" Blair whimpers, slams her laptop shut, and shoves it into her bag before jumping to her feet.

Laughter echoes through the room, and my anger reaches a whole new level.

"Blair, wait," I shout and take off after her, flying down the stairs.

I will ruin whoever did this. I won't just beat them to a pulp. I will destroy their goddamn fucking lives.

I stop at the bottom of the stairs and focus on the class for one second.

I meet their eyes, some smiling, some laughing, some horrified, but the second I open my mouth, their faces fall. "If you share it, if you talk about it, look at it, for fuck's sake, think about it, it will be the last thing that you do. I swear to God."

They nod, practically in unison, as fear finds its way into every one of their faces. Without another second lost on them, I chase after Blair.

"I want to be alone, Griffin!" Blair yells at me as I burst into the hallway, where even more onlookers stare at her, glancing back and forth from their phones.

"Mind your fucking business before I do it for you!" I snap at them, and everyone's heads whip the other way.

She slams to a halt and turns around, and the second I

see her bloodshot, reddened eyes soaked with tears, I crumble to pieces. I want to fix this. I want to make it all go away for her. I want to take the pain and feel it for her. But I can't, and I don't know how to fix this. And the panic building in my chest is making me feel fucking helpless.

"Stop following me," she orders me with a cold tone as tears continue to pour down her cheeks. "Seriously, Griffin. I want to be alone!"

Rubbing my hand down my face, I look away, and my eyes land on the door to a private study room.

Grabbing Blair's hand, I pull her with me, and she willingly follows. Throwing the door open, I find it empty, and I couldn't be happier. Pulling her inside, I shut the door behind us. There are no windows, nothing to let anyone see inside of here. Just us.

"Let me out of here, Griffin." She crosses her arms and glares at me.

"No," I tell her, my heart twisting from the pain etched in her face.

"Then, you leave!" she spits out, crossing her arms.

She can push me away all she wants right now, but I don't care. I'm not leaving her. I, for one, know what it's like to lash out when you're angry.

Rushing over to her, I wrap my arms around her and pull her into my chest, blocking the world from reaching her. "I'm not leaving you, baby. You can try to push me away, but I'm not going anywhere. You want to cry? Cry. You want to hit something? Hit me. You want to scream? Let it out. But I will be here for all of it."

She's rigid, frozen solid, still as can be.

Tucking my head down onto hers, I pull her tighter against me, if that's even possible.

"I'm here, Blair. I'm right here. I won't let anything happen to you. Never again. I will find out who did it, and I will make them pay," I promise her, meaning every word.

I turn slightly and kiss the side of her head, and something deep inside of her explodes.

Sobs heave from her, filling the room around us, and she cries unbearably into my chest. Her body softens, and she melts into me second by second until I'm the only one holding her up. She is falling apart in my hands, and I will carry her pieces until she's ready to put herself back together.

"I hate him," she cries out, and I rub her back.

Him?

No fucking way. Is it her ex? That Grant kid?

"It's okay. It will be okay," I assure her, cradling her head against my chest.

"Everyone saw it, Griffin. *Everyone*," she whimpers.

Carefully, I pull her down to the ground with me. "Come here," I tell her.

She wraps her legs around my hips, and her arms tuck into her chest as I encase my arms around her and pull her as close to me as she can physically get.

"I know, but I will fix it. I will find a way, okay?" My voice cracks, and my throat tightens.

If I have to bribe every person on this campus to delete it and pretend they never saw it, I will. If I have to threaten every person for them to listen, then so be it. Regardless, they'll do it because if they don't, I'll break them into pieces.

She pulls away and looks up at me with a mix of fear and admiration. I brush away the wetness on her cheeks and push the hair out of her face.

"I'm so sorry he did that." I cup her face with my hands and finish wiping her tears away.

She nods slowly. "I'm sorry I ever dated him."

"Yeah, you have terrible taste in guys," I tell her, and she smiles up at me, making my heart jump.

She takes a long inhale before sighing. She's still uncontrollably gasping as her diaphragm spasms from crying, but at least she's breathing and trying to calm herself down.

I drop my hands to her sides, and we sit in silence as our breathing matches up, and I feel her start to unwind in my lap.

"Would it make you feel better if I let you host that dinner with Lumi that you wanted at my house?" I offer the one thing that I think will lift her mood.

Even if I absolutely hate the idea of having guests over, I'll make an exception if it makes her feel better.

Her lips tip up. "It wouldn't hurt anything. But why? You hated that idea."

Biting down my smile, I lean forward and kiss her forehead. "I know. But I'll do it for you."

"Really?" she asks, looking at me with hope.

I have no choice now. "Yes, the house is yours. I know Mrs. Potts will be excited to entertain."

She sits up even taller. "Don't worry; everyone will behave."

I roll my eyes. "That's impossible. You never behave."

She scoffs and jabs a finger into my chest. "Hey! I do too!"

Licking my lips, I smile. "I know you do, my perfect little prisoner."

She glares playfully at me.

"Let's get out of here for the day, huh?" I ask her, holding her stare.

Her eyes widen for a split second as I watch the sadness creep back in for a moment before she nods. "One day of skipping classes will be okay, I suppose."

"You're such a rebel," I tease her.

She pulls her arms out from between us and throws them around me.

Stunned, I freeze as she cradles her head into my neck and whispers, "Thank you."

Kissing her cheek, I say, "Don't thank me for that. There isn't a single other place in the world I would rather be than right here with you."

She presses her lips against the tender skin on my neck, and my heart jolts in response.

She giggles against me before pulling away, and she slowly gets to her feet with the brightest red color on her face, a redness that is not from crying.

Huffing, she lowers her shoulders with her chin raised before opening the door. "After you." She gestures.

I follow her instruction, stepping through the threshold and finding Lumi typing frantically on his phone in the hallway. He looks up, seeing us, and instantly relaxes.

As Blair walks out and steps beside me, she does something that surprises me. She slides her hand around mine, interlocking our fingers together. I don't know if she needs it for extra support right now or if she simply wants to hold my hand. Either way, I don't care as long as she doesn't let go.

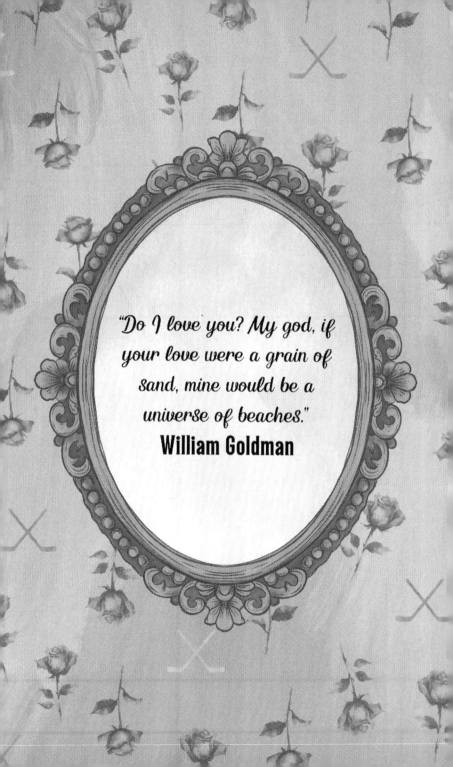

"Do I love you? My god, if your love were a grain of sand, mine would be a universe of beaches."

William Goldman

chapter nineteen
blair

I still can't believe Griffin is letting me do this. When we first discussed it, I thought he would have preferred to have his teeth pulled rather than let us host dinner at his house. I can't imagine why he hates having people over because his house is a work of art and deserves to be seen.

We get to work once Griffin gives us the green light for the party. Mrs. Potts is over the moon about it. She told me that the Hawthornes used to host the utmost elaborate soirees with the most exclusive guest list. Maybe Griffin doesn't like them because of how many he had to attend as a kid.

Our guest list might not consist of senators, royalty, and celebrities, but it is still rather exclusive—only a handful of people got invited. Said guests will be arriving within the hour, and I still need to finish my hair and get dressed. We decided to go all out with the dress code. Even if it's just our close friends, getting dressed up will be fun, and I have the perfect gown. I got it right after I started working at The Fallen Petal as a little retail therapy. I spent way too much on it, but at least now, I have an excuse to wear it.

After loosely curling my hair, I run my fingers through it, opting to leave it all down, cascading down my shoulders. I get dressed and then head downstairs to meet Lumi, who just texted me to let me know he's here. My heels click on the marble floor as I descend the stairs and make my way to the front door, feeling a bit like a queen wandering through her palace.

As I open the door, I find Lumi with his jaw on the floor.

"You look incredible, Blair." He laughs in amazement. "Griffin is going to lose his mind."

Pursing my lips, I smile. "Thank you. You guys look pretty amazing yourselves."

Lumi invited Paul, whom he met at the baseball party. Apparently, they have been hitting it off, and I'm excited to finally meet him.

"Hi, I'm Blair," I introduce myself to Paul, who smiles nervously.

He opens his arms for a hug, and I happily accept.

"I'm Paul. It's great to meet you. I've heard so much from Lumi."

Pulling away, I chuckle. "Oh, I'm sure you have."

He laughs with me. "Good things. I promise."

"Well, come inside and make yourself at home. Feel free to grab a drink in the kitchen. The other guys should be here soon," I inform them while searching outside for any sign of Griffin, but no luck.

We find seats at the dining table, and I spend the next half hour telling Paul funny stories about Lumi while Lumi tries his best not to die of embarrassment. I only tell mildly humiliating ones, like the time he fell into one of the fountains at school because he was on his phone and not paying attention.

My phone vibrates on the table, and I check it to find a text from Griffin.

> Griffin: Hey, I'm sorry we're running a few minutes late. But we are on our way.

"The guys are on their way. Practice must have run late," I fill Lumi and Paul in as I respond to Griffin.

> No problem. Drive safe.

"I'm going to use the bathroom. I'll be right back." I excuse myself from the table.

I go to the bathroom and double-check that my makeup still looks good before doing one final look-over. My red satin gown glides over my body like water flowing over every curve. Thin straps hold up the plunging neckline.

Suddenly, I'm very aware of how much of myself is on display, and even though he's seen me practically naked, I'm more nervous now than I was the night I danced. A shiver runs down my spine because I know Griffin will be here soon, and I wonder if I should change. This dress is probably too much. I should grab one of my usual school outfits—a cute sweater and a skirt.

Actually, maybe I'll just throw on my HEAU hoodie

and leggings. Wiping the little smudge of red lipstick off of my teeth, I leave the bathroom on a mission. I'll say I had a wardrobe malfunction and had to change.

My chest is tightening more and more by the second. I think what I really need is a some fresh air and a deep breath.

Walking past the dining room, I head toward the front door and step outside into the cool evening air, immediately feeling more refreshed. Tilting my head up, I stare up at the darkening sky and inhale deeply.

I hold my breath for a second, then slowly exhale as the hair on the back of my neck stands up. A vicious wave of tingles drifts down my back, making me suddenly uneasy. The type of discomfort you feel when you're being watched. But looking around, I don't see anyone. I'm probably just imagining it.

Descending a few stairs to the first landing, I lean against the golden railing and search the grounds I can see, but I find nothing out of place. Turning my head, I have the same result.

Until I spot Griffin's truck, which is parked far from his usual spot and tucked as far away from the house as possible. I didn't hear them come inside or see them in the dining room when I walked by.

Looking closer, I can tell the vehicle's empty, so they must already be in the house. But why would they go out of their way not to use the front door? Regardless, that means he's here.

Maybe I should head back inside.

I spin around, my dress flowing in the breeze, along with my hair. As I place my hand on the railing and take a step up, the front door opens, and I freeze, my mouth drying and pulse racing.

Griffin steps through the door in a white button-up and dress pants that takes my breath away. His brown hair is perfectly styled in that hot, messy, but somehow still kempt way. His white button-up is undone at the top and tucked into his slim-fitted navy slacks, secured with a belt. I genuinely didn't think he could get more alluring, but I was so very wrong.

As I scan over every inch of him, I can't help but notice him doing the same to me, and I feel myself warm from his burning stare.

"If I knew hosting a dinner meant I got to see you in that dress, I would have agreed to do this long ago," Griffin utters, his voice low and rugged.

Looking up at him, I take another step, trying to find the right thing to say.

"Speechless, my little prisoner? I've never seen you at a loss for words." He smirks and holds his hand out to help me up the last few stairs.

Gulping, I smile and slide my hand into his. "Thank you."

He helps guide me up the last few steps, and when I finally hit the main landing, he lifts my arm into the air and twirls me around.

My chest flutters, and I giggle as I come face-to-face with him. "Thank you again for letting us do this."

His fingers graze my waist, and I inhale sharply. "I doubt there is anything you couldn't convince me of, Blair."

"Who knew the little hockey player could clean up so

well?" I compliment him in the only way I think I know how—teasing him.

He bites down on his bottom lip, smiling, and opens the front door. He guides me past him with his hand, but not before leaning down to my ear and whispering, "There is nothing little about this hockey player."

I am so out of my league when it comes to flirting with Griffin. I think I'm doing good, and then he sweeps me off of my feet with something like that, knocking me off-kilter.

As I walk inside, I spin, glancing down at our hands, and my face falls. "Oh my God. What happened to your hand?"

I didn't notice his knuckles when he stretched his hand out to me on the stairs, but they are red, split, and bruising in a deep array of colors.

Griffin is quiet this time, and when I look back up at him, I find him studying me cautiously, unsure of what to say.

"What happened?" I ask him again, lifting his hand closer to my face for further inspection. "Oh God, Griffin. That has to hurt."

He flexes his fingers. "Not any more than I can handle."

"Was it hockey? You didn't have a game today, and I can't imagine you beating one of your teammates up this bad," I ramble, trying to talk my way to the answer. "The only person I could think of who you'd do this to is Grant."

He stays quiet.

"Oh my God, it was him, wasn't it?" I look up at him, seeing the truth all over his face.

"I won't apologize for hurting him. He deserved it. But I'm sorry I didn't tell you about it first. I just didn't want you to risk you talking me out of it," he admits, and I can't think straight.

Grant has always been clingy, different, and obsessive. For what he did, I wish I could have been there to hit him myself. But I'm more worried now about whether he's going to retaliate. Griffin can't always be by my side, and what happens if Grant corners me when I'm all alone?

"Are you mad at me?" Griffin whispers, each word laced with worry and despair.

Lifting his hand up, I gently press my lips against each one of his knuckles, kissing them tenderly before meeting his eyes. "No, I'm not mad. Of course I'm not mad at you. You did that for me."

He flips his hand over and brushes my cheek with his thumb. "You still look upset."

I answer him honestly, "More like concerned. You don't know Grant. Sometimes, losing only makes him want to win that much more. I'm just scared of what else he might do."

My eyes burn, and I bite back the tears that are forming.

Griffin tilts my head up, forcing me to look at him. "He won't. I made him promise not to fuck with you anymore."

"And did he?" I ask, desperately wanting to hear the word *yes*.

"He did. Repeatedly." His thumb swipes against my bottom lip.

I would say that's reassuring, but I'm not sure Grant's word holds any weight.

"Come on. Forget about him for right now. Let's enjoy the rest of the night."

Taking a deep breath, I sigh, "You're right. He's had enough of our time."

"That's my girl," he coos and holds his hand out, gesturing toward the dining room. "After you."

I step forward and lead the way back to the group. Everyone is lost in conversation, including Malik with Mrs. Potts. I can't imagine what they are possibly discussing.

Something grabs my attention, and I look down to where Malik's hands are clasped on the table. They look exactly like Griffin's. Did he help? Why would he do that?

"Dinner is ready, if you are?" Mrs. Potts addresses the group, and we answer her with a unanimous, "Yes."

Griffin pulls a chair out for me, and Lumi flashes me a smile as I sit down.

Lumi gives me a look that I interpret as, *Where were you two?*

Squinting at him, I roll my eyes, dismissing him.

Griffin sits next to me, and I suddenly realize that this kind of feels like a date. Well, perhaps if it wasn't shared with five other people—Mrs. Potts, Chip, Lumi, Paul, and Malik.

Mrs. Potts serves all of us our food and drinks before sitting down and joining us. She made New York strips, asparagus, and mashed potatoes.

As I start to devour my plate, I am suddenly so upset I haven't asked her to cook dinner before because this is the best meal I have ever had in my entire life. Seriously, it's so good.

"Mrs. Potts, this is incredible," I praise her between bites, and she grins from ear to ear.

"I'm glad you're enjoying it." She beams. "Save a little room for dessert."

"Can I marry you?" I ask her, and Griffin coughs, choking on his food next to me. I look at him, fighting back a smile. "Are you okay?"

"Yep," he responds, taking a sip of his water.

We finish enjoying Mrs. Potts's excellent cooking, including the most decadent crème brûlée for dessert. I am absolutely stuffed by the time I set my fork down next to my empty plate.

After a few minutes of listening to Malik and Griffin talk about hockey and my food baby has rested, I decide I can help clean up. I gather my and Griffin's plates and carry them to the kitchen. I set them down next to the sink before going to get more.

Turning back into the dining room, I come face-to-face with Griffin, who's holding two more plates in his hands.

I smile up at him, and he nods his head at me and continues into the kitchen. I gather the last of the dishes and help Griffin load them into the dishwasher.

"Thank you for helping me," I tell him as I load the final plate.

"Thank you for cleaning," he says, closing the door and starting it.

"Of course. It's the least I could do," I admit truthfully.

"Blair?" Lumi calls out and walks into the kitchen, immediately turning red as he sees Griffin and me talking. "Oh my God, I have the worst timing."

"You sure do," Griffin agrees, and I chuckle.

"Sorry about that." He pauses. "Paul and I are going to head out for the night."

"Okay, I'll walk you out." I can feel Griffin's gaze on me as I turn the corner and head toward the door. "Thank you guys for coming tonight."

"Are you kidding? This was the best. We had way better food than we could ever get in town, and it's in a mansion, for God's sake," Paul babbles, and I can't help but think of how perfect of a match he and Lumi are. "Thank you for having me."

Lumi hugs me as we hit the front door. "I love you. Have a good night. Can't wait to hear all about it."

Pulling away, I glare at him. "I love you too. And nothing is going to happen."

"Uh-huh. You should have seen the way he was looking at you all night. I bet it would take one word from you for him to be on his knees," he whispers, and I shoo him out the door.

"Yeah, yeah. Good night, guys!" I tell them as they walk outside.

"Good night!" Paul says and waves, dragging Lumi along with him.

Shutting the door behind them, I hear Griffin and Malik talking, but can't really make anything out. Walking on the balls of my feet, I quietly stalk back toward the dining room until I can hear what they are saying.

"He got what was coming to him. Thank you again, man. Seriously," Griffin says.

"I'd do anything for you, Griff. You know that. I'm glad she's doing better after what that prick pulled." He hesitates. "But I'd better get going. Are you sure you're good with me taking your truck tonight?"

"Yeah. Just pick me up for practice in the morning," Griffin says, his voice suddenly sounding much closer.

Quickly, I tiptoe back toward the door and put my hand on the handle like I am just closing it as they walk into the hallway.

"My favorite bookworm," Malik calls out and walks toward me.

"Hey, Malik. Thanks for coming tonight." I genuinely thank him. My dislike of him is slowly fading away, especially after tonight.

"No problem. Have a good night, you two. I'll see you in the morning," he tells Griffin before letting himself out.

My feet ache as I rock back and forth on my heels. "I am dying to put on some PJs and cozy socks right now. I'll be right back."

"I think I'll join you," Griffin says, and his eyes widen. "Join as in *also* change into cozy clothes. Not watch you change. Although I wouldn't mind—" He cuts himself off and huffs. "I'm going to change as well."

Pressing my lips together, I chuckle. "Got it. Real smooth."

He laughs and follows me to the stairs, once again

offering me his hand to take, and even though I don't need his help, I slide my hand into his.

He helps me up the stairs and into the east wing, and we part ways at our rooms. The second I'm inside and shut the door behind me, I kick the shoes off and slide down to the floor.

What is he doing to me?

I think I'm losing my mind, or perhaps he's stealing it because he seems to be occupying it more and more every day.

After picking myself up off of the floor, I quickly change into one of my favorite sets—lacy red shorts and a camisole—before heading to see if Mrs. Potts needs help with anything else. But when I get downstairs, the kitchen is empty and spotless.

Opening the fridge, I grab a bottle of water and can't help but notice a container full of chocolate-dipped strawberries. Grabbing two, I take my water and hop onto the kitchen counter to enjoy my little treat.

I bite into the strawberry and practically moan from how good it is. I don't care what anyone says; this is the best dessert. Juicy, fresh strawberries covered in silky chocolate? Unbeatable.

"Can I have one too?" Griffin's deep voice cuts through the silence, making me jump. He's leaning against the entrance into the kitchen, wearing gray sweats and no goddamn shirt.

How long has he been standing there?

Is he not wearing a shirt just to torture me? Because it's working.

"You can have one out of the fridge." I gesture to the

one next to me and grin before pointing at the one on the counter beside me. "That one's mine."

He saunters over to me and grabs my other strawberry, the one I *just* told him he couldn't have. "This one?"

He steps between my legs, forcing them apart, and I sharply inhale. I nod, answering his question, unable to form a single word.

"Open your mouth," he orders me, placing his hand flat on my upper thigh while pressing the berry to my lips.

Holding his stare, I challenge that sexy gleam in his eyes, but he doesn't back down, so I do as he asked.

He pushes the berry into my mouth, and I bite down, chocolate falling right onto my lap. Without hesitation, Griffin sets the strawberry down and grabs the pieces of chocolate from my thighs, tossing them into his mouth with a heated stare.

I'm too shocked to chew my bite, but I force myself to focus and swallow it before I end up choking on it.

"Mmm. That's good," he rasps, and my lips part at the sultriness in his voice. "The chocolate—it's good."

The chocolate, *of course.*

He leans further into me, forcing my hips to open to him completely. I do the only thing I can and secure my legs around his waist.

He places his arms on the counter next to my hips and leans forward, rolling his forehead against mine.

"Blair …" He draws my name out, and the need in his voice draws me closer to him. "What are you doing to me?"

A breathy scoff leaves my lips as I ponder the very same thing about him.

"Someone's coming," he states and pulls away from me before storming out of the room, leaving me a hot and confused puddle on the counter.

A second later, Chip walks into the kitchen with a water bottle in hand. He looks up and smiles at me, and I do my best to act normal and wave back.

I hop off of the counter, grab my now two-half-eaten berries and water, and walk away, trying to sort out what the hell just happened in there. I make my way to my room, just as hot and bothered as I started.

I set my stuff on my nightstand and jump into bed, grabbing my vibrator from the nightstand drawer. I need to get rid of this pent-up energy before I lose my mind. At least then, I'll be able to think a bit clearer.

Sliding under the covers, I slip my shorts off and turn the toy on.

I should have grabbed his face the second he pulled away and kissed him. God, his hand on my thigh has me soaking through my panties.

I've never been this turned on in my life, and it's driving me insane. Pressing the toy against my center, I gasp as the sensation lifts my back off of the bed.

"Ahh," I whimper as I imagine him grabbing my jaw and kissing me.

His hands slide up my sides, lifting my top off and leaving me bare.

Oh God, I can't imagine what his mouth would feel like, sucking on my nipples.

I'm so desperate for release. My orgasm is building fast. I won't last another thirty seconds if I'm lucky.

He picks me up off of the counter and carries me upstairs, sucking on my neck and biting my lip before plunging his tongue into my mouth.

That's all it takes to send me over the cliff with my arms spread wide, welcoming the descent into euphoria.

"Fuck, Griffin." I moan louder than I intended. I slam my mouth closed and ride out my orgasm against the toy as unbelievable pulses of pleasure rock through every cell of my body.

Knock, knock.

"Oh shit." I sit up and turn the vibrator over, frantically searching for the power button. "One second!"

I find it, shut it off, and chuck it into my nightstand before sliding my shorts back on.

"Come in!" I call out, patting my hair down and trying to slow my breathing.

Griffin opens the door, and my eyes widen.

Oh my God, what if he heard me?

"Are you okay?" He looks at me with a furrowed brow.

Shaking my head, I dismiss his concerns. "I'm perfectly fine. Why?"

"You're a bit, uhh ... *flushed*." He emphasizes the last word with a smirk on his full lips.

"Nope. Not at all." I try to change the subject. "Did you need something?"

He grins. "Yes, actually. Here, this is for you."

He walks over to the bed but remains standing and hands me a credit card.

But I just stare at him without taking it.

"What is that?" I ask, wondering why he wants me to do his shopping.

"I'm going to be gone for games this weekend, so I want you to have it in case you need anything."

He holds it closer to me, and this time, I hesitantly take it.

"I don't need this, Griffin," I tell him, knowing I'm not going to use it even if I do need something.

If he insists, I would feel bad, using his money like that.

"It would make me feel better, knowing you have it. I mean it though. Use it for anything. I don't care," he says, holding my gaze.

"Okay," I say, knowing he's not going to let it go until I agree. I set it down beside my water. "Thank you."

"Got to make sure my gir—*tutor* is taken care of." He smirks, and my stomach erupts with butterflies from what he almost said. "Try not to miss me too much."

He backs up to the door as I say, "I won't."

He fake stabs his heart and looks pained as he steps into the hallway. "Ouch. Good night."

"Good night, Griffin." I smile at him as he pulls my door closed.

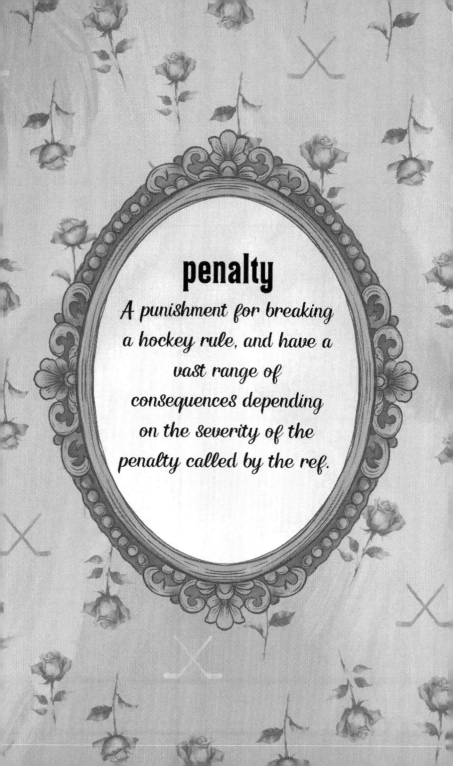

penalty

A punishment for breaking a hockey rule, and have a vast range of consequences depending on the severity of the penalty called by the ref.

chapter twenty
griffin

We had an off week last week for games, but I have been itching to get back on the ice. Especially after this last week with Blair. I need something to help me get some energy out.

When I had her legs around me in the kitchen, I was so close to kissing her and never stopping. Part of me is thankful that Chip interrupted because I was ready to show her exactly how she's been making me feel.

It's been so long since I let anyone get close to me, and it's fucking terrifying. What if something happens to her? That thought alone makes me want to curl into a ball. I hate knowing that I'm opening myself up for pain, but I can't resist my feelings for her any longer. I'd be lying to myself if I said that she isn't already completely inter-twined with my heart. It's been hers since the day we met.

When I return home after this weekend, I will officially ask her out. I don't want there to be any doubt about my intentions. I want to make her mine, and it's as simple as that.

I also got word that the baseball player, Josh, has been released from the team for accusations of sexual assault and that the survivors are pursuing criminal charges. The school is also reviewing his enrollment and should be expelling him any day now for violating the university's policies.

Apparently, someone put a word in with the dean that these accusations were being brushed under the rug, someone whose word carries a lot of weight due to donations to the campus. Someone like *me*. It won't solve the root of the problem, but it's a start.

"Hawthorne," Coach calls out, and I look up at him from the bench in our locker room. "Are you with us?"

I shake out my nerves and the lingering thoughts of Blair and focus on the game ahead. "I'm here, Coach."

He nods. "Good," and directs his attention back to the group. "We've got a big weekend ahead of us—double-header games against our rival school. I know how hungry you guys are for the win."

"Damn straight!" Finn shouts, and cheers echo around us in response.

"Play your game out there. You guys are the best team when you work together and push each other. Leave everything on the ice, be smart, and you'll have nothing to worry about. Let's get out there, boys." He smacks his hand against the clipboard. "Walt, count us down," he says to one of the assistant coaches.

"Legends on three. One. Two. Three," he roars.

We all answer his call, shouting, "Legends!"

We rush down the hallway and line up outside of the board door onto the ice. One of the Knights staff opens the door, and Finn, our starting goalie, leads us out. The second my skates hit the ice, I inhale deeply, feeling excitement radiate across my body.

I grab a puck as I skate by the pile of them on the ice and glide toward the net, dumping it in as I fly past. The team and I continue to get a few shots in for the next minute before setting up our first drill.

We work through our regular warm-up routines, including passing and shooting drills, before heading back to the locker room.

As we skate toward the tunnel, I scan the crowd. I know she's not here, but I can't resist the urge to search for her anyway. I know I'm only going to be gone for the weekend, but I already miss her.

We beat the Knights last night in overtime, four to three. Tonight's game has the potential of being just as close, which means I'm going to need to be on my best behavior so I don't end up in the penalty box, which will put the other team on a power play.

Last night, number ninety-two laid a dirty fucking hit on Asher, and if the opportunity presents itself, I'm going to repay the favor. But I have to play smart and try not to draw attention from the officials.

Lining up for puck drop, I set up next to the player who laid that hit on Ash.

"Watch your back out there," I warn him, putting my stick down next to his.

"Is that right?" He laughs and drops his shoulder into me slightly as we wait for the puck.

Holding his stare, I emphasize every word. "Yeah. I'm coming for you."

The puck drops, stopping him from saying anything back. Asher wins the drop, dishing the puck back between his legs to Dean. He leads us into our offensive zone and passes it to Malik. Malik moves it over to Dean, who swings back and slaps it with his stick, sending it flying toward the goal.

Their goalie manages to get a stick on it, blocking it and kicking it out to the side. One of the Knights players grabs the puck and hangs back, passing it to his teammate behind the net. They are buying time to change a few of their players out, and we do the same, changing lines to get a new group of guys with fresh legs on the ice.

By the end of the first period, neither team scores nor spends any time in the penalty box. We are neck and neck the entire second period too. Thankfully, number ninety-two hasn't done anything to deserve any special attention from me … yet. His time will come. I meant what I said at the beginning of this game—I'm coming for him. I just have to be picky with *when* I do it. I don't want to catch him off guard. I want him to look me in the eyes when I bury him in the ice. He should've been thrown out of the game last night for his hit on Asher. He only got a two-minute minor, and the crowd was outraged by the decision. Everyone in the arena, aside from the refs, knew that he should've been thrown out and received a misconduct to keep his ass off the ice for tonight's game. Because now that the officials didn't penalize him fairly, I will have to do it for them.

We are halfway through the third and final period when the tie is broken, and Dean sinks the puck into the back of the net.

Digging my skates into the ice, I barrel toward him with my stick in the air. "Fuck yeah!"

"Fucking sniper out there!" Asher sings his praises as we pile onto Dean.

Our crowd in the audience goes wild, cheering for us. They might be small, but they are mighty.

We skate past our bench, Dean leading the way, and bump gloves with our teammates before changing out for the puck drop at center ice.

With three minutes left in the game, number ninety-two makes the move that seals his fate. As Dean skates past him next to the boards, he rears back and plows his elbow into his face, taking Dean down instantly. Dean drops to the ice, holding on to his face and rocking back and forth.

Taking off, I race across the ice, digging in as hard as I can. Ninety-two turns and looks at me, his eyes widening with fear. He knows what he did; he should have seen this coming. With as much force as possible, I plow into him, sending him flying headfirst straight into the glass. He crumples into a pile as I tower over him. The second he tries to get back up, I use my stick and shove him back down, over and over.

Another Knights' player flies over to me and grabs me,

pulling me away from him. He throws a punch, but I don't even entertain him. My focus is still locked straight on ninety-two.

He looks up at me through his now-dented cage, and I see blood pouring down his face from his nose.

"That does not look good, bud. You might want to get that checked out, along with your fucking pride," I chirp at him, grinning from ear to ear.

"I'll fucking kill you!" he growls and takes off after me, but a linesman grabs him and drags him away as he lets loose a slew of curse words.

I laugh at him and point, which only pisses him off more. He says something to the ref before shoving him hard. The ref loses his balance and falls painfully to the ice.

"You're out of here!" the official ref yells at ninety-two and makes the hand motion, signaling his official call.

"Are you *fucking* kidding me? I barely touched him!" he whines as the ref escorts him to the benches. "This is fucking bullshit!" He continues to shout as he walks down the tunnel to the locker room, where he'll stay for the remainder of the game.

The Knights player releases me, and I head toward the penalty box. There's no doubt that I'll serve time for that hit. But at least ninety-two fucked up more than me. He's likely to be getting an unsportsmanlike conduct call along with a game misconduct, meaning he won't play the next game.

My guess is correct, and ninety-two rakes up the penalty minutes, helping us keep the score one to zero until the buzzer sounds at the end of the third period. I should send a thank-you card to that prick; after all, he did exactly what I wanted him to do.

After the game, the guys and I decide to have a little celebration at our hotel. Some puck bunny one of the guys knows brought beer to our hotel and snuck it in for us. Dean, Asher, Malik, and I grab a case and hang out in the twins' room.

Popping the cap off the bottle, I take a swig of beer and dig my phone out of my pocket.

Checking my notifications, I see a text from Blair.

Blair: Good game, Warden.

My chest flutters now that I know she might have been watching the game or, at the very least, cared enough to check the outcome.

Thank you. How is my little prisoner?
Missing me yet?

Blair: Nope. Not one bit. Although I will say your bed is so much more comfortable than mine.

She's in my bed? Without me? Fucking hell.

I wonder if I'll be able to smell her in the sheets when I get back. I adjust my hips as I type my response out.

> What do you think you're doing in my bed?

> Blair: I'm finding out how incredible your silk sheets feel against my bare skin.

Fuck. She really is flirting with me right now, isn't she?

I take a few chugs of my beer before setting it down and giving my phone my full, undivided attention.

> Bare skin, huh? What exactly are you wearing in my bed right now?

Text bubbles appear, disappear, and reappear before her next text comes through.

> Blair: Who says I'm wearing anything?

Biting down on my bottom lip, I close my eyes as my cock twitches, and I fight the urge to hop on a plane ride home.

"You good over there, buddy?" Malik asks and raises his beer to me.

Stretching my neck from side to side, I grab my beer and stand up. "Yeah, I'm just a bit tired. I'm going to get some sleep."

Malik smirks at me. "Okay, yeah, sure. You seem *so* tired right now." He laughs. "Just text me when you're done jerking off."

Mockingly saluting him, I chuckle. "You got it. Good night, boys."

"Night, Griff," Asher says, and Dean joins in, "Good night."

The second I'm in the hallway, I rush a few feet down to my room and step inside, pressing the Call button on Blair's contact the second I'm alone.

It rings once, twice, three times, and my heart races with nervousness that she won't pick up.

Shit. Maybe I shouldn't have called. Maybe that's too much.

"Hello?" she answers, her voice soft and cautious.

I flop onto my back on the bed and murmur, "Hey."

She stays quiet, so I take the lead and fill the silence.

"Not wearing anything in my bed, huh?"

She inhales and hesitates. "How else am I supposed to feel how luxurious the sheets are?"

"That's a good point. But do you want to know something? Your sheets are the *exact* same ones as mine," I tell her.

"That's weird because yours are *so* much better," she says, her tone soft and sensual.

"Is that so?" I mumble.

"Is that why you called? To inform me about the similarities of our bedding?" she challenges me, and I love the confidence she seems to be finding behind the phone.

I do the same. "No. I called because I wanted to hear your voice. Send me a selfie of you right now."

She gasps, "Griffin ..." She trails off before hesitantly saying, "I don't send nudes."

"Relax. I don't want you to send that. I want to see what you look like, wrapped up in my bed," I correct her, grabbing my dick through my sweats.

"Hold on," she whispers, and I hear rustling on the phone. "Sent."

Putting her on speaker, I click on her text and the picture.

"*Holy fuck*," I growl, seeing her sexy self in my bed.

She's lying on her stomach, tangled in my golden sheets and comforter, with her messy hair flowing over her shoulders. Her tits are covered from my sheets, spilling over the top of the tightly pressed silk.

Rubbing my hand down my length, I take the phone off speaker and groan. "You are so goddamn perfect, Blair. I wish you were here."

"Yeah?" she asks breathily. "Why's that?"

I love how badly she wants to hear me say it.

"I wish you were here so I could show you how crazy you are driving me. I'm absolutely mad, completely losing my mind, all because of you," I tell her, hearing her sharp inhale from my confession. "I'm tired of lying in my bed every night, knowing you're right across the hall and not by my side. Twenty feet has never felt so far away."

"Griffin ..." she whimpers into the phone, and I can see her pretty lips forming my name in my mind.

"You don't think the same? What about when I had you caged in on the kitchen counter? You didn't want me? You haven't imagined what that first kiss will be like a thousand times over? You haven't fantasized about how good I am going to make you feel when you let me touch you and how I am going to worship every single part of you? You haven't pictured me coming into your room at night, sliding under the covers, and making you mine?"

Her breathing is ragged and heavy.

"Because I have. It's all I fucking think about. You're all I think about." I'm practically panting when I finish.

It's her turn now. I didn't hold back. I laid everything out there. It's her move if she wants to keep this going or end it.

"Do you remember Thursday night when you came into my room and said I looked flushed?" she murmurs.

I nod, wondering where she's going with this. "Yeah, of course I do."

"It's because I thought you'd heard me," she says. "I had just finished ... using my vibrator. I said your name repeatedly before you knocked on the door."

I would give my soul to go back in time and hear that.

"You would've known if I'd heard you, baby. We would've been having this conversation that night instead of now," I tell her, sliding my hand down my pants and gripping my hard shaft.

"I, uhh, wasn't sure it was what you wanted ..." She trails off.

"Fuck, Blair. I want you, only you," I admit to her unabashedly.

Her voice is thick and needy as she says, "I want you too."

Digging my head back into the bed, I groan. "I can't wait to see you tomorrow."

She giggles. "Now, I'm nervous."

"Don't be," I assure her. "It's just me."

"Yeah, just the guy who's paying for my school, my dad's treatment, and bills. What if you think I'm a terrible kisser and kick me out?" She chuckles nervously.

"Blair ..." Her name rolls over my tongue. "I wouldn't do that to you. Even if you are the worst kisser in the world, I don't fucking care. That just means we'll have to practice even more."

The hotel door opens, and Malik walks through, laughing obnoxiously loudly with Dean. They freeze and stare at me with wide eyes. Apparently, Malik forgot about our little deal. I'm going to kill him.

"Oh God, they haven't been there the whole time, right?" Blair asks desperately.

"No, I promise. They just barged in. And are going to leave." I glare at them as I say it.

"I should let you go. I'll see you tomorrow, Griffin," she says before the call ends.

"I swear to God, I am going to murder you two!" I growl and slam my phone onto the bed.

Malik grimaces, and Dean avoids all eye contact.

"I kind of thought you were joking about the jerking-off thing." He laughs. "My bad."

Clenching my jaw, I roll over and bury my erection in the bed.

"We'll give you some space," Dean says, and I can hear the laughter he's holding back in his voice.

"No point now," I sigh.

I could go into the bathroom and finish. I have that photo she sent me and my imagination. But I've gone this long without coming. I can wait another day if it means my release might be by her own hand … or mouth.

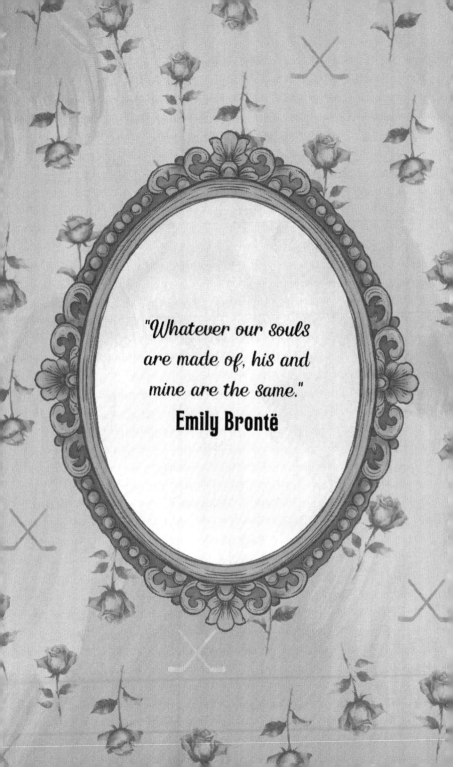

"Whatever our souls
are made of, his and
mine are the same."
Emily Brontë

chapter twenty-one

blair

Griffin returns home today, and after our conversation last night, everything is changing between us, and I'm nervous. I'm also scared where that might leave me in the end if we don't work out. He said he won't kick me out or stop helping me, but he can't know for certain what he will or won't do in the future.

Rolling out of his bed, I grab one of his T-shirts and hold it up to my nose, inhaling deeply. I might have to start stealing his clothes because I can't get enough of how comforting, safe, and serene he smells.

I throw his HEAU Hockey Legends T-shirt on and let it settle onto the tops of my thighs. Grabbing my phone off of the nightstand, I see a text from Mrs. Potts.

> Mrs. Potts: Chip and I are going to run some errands this morning. We should be back early this afternoon.

I type out a quick response so she knows I saw it.

Sounds good. Have fun!

Mrs. Potts: Do you need anything?

No, thank you!

Setting my phone back down, I focus my attention on Griffin's room. It's clean, orderly, and decently decorated. I wonder if that's Griffin's doing or Mrs. Potts's.

I wander out of his room and start down the stairs. I have the entire house to myself. *What should I do?*

As I step onto the landing and turn to head down the rest of the stairs, I freeze in place as a terrible, horrible idea creeps into my mind.

Spinning on my heel, I look across the landing to the set of stairs I've never been up, the ones Griffin banned me from, the ones that lead into the west wing.

My rotten idea comes to life as I approach the double doors calling out to me.

I probably shouldn't do this. It's a major invasion of privacy. But my curiosity gets the best of me as I continue up the stairs and place my hand on one of the golden doorknobs at the double-door entrance. It's probably locked anyway, so it won't matter if I try to turn it.

Twisting my hand, I find no resistance, and the entrance into the unknown opens with little effort.

Deep down, I was hoping that it would be locked. Then, the decision to continue would be out of my hands.

Turning my head, I take one last look behind me and

listen for any noise. No one's home—I know that. I just want to be sure.

Silence is all I find.

Taking a step inside, I'm greeted with cold and stale air, smelling of mustiness. It smells like an old home, vastly different from the rest of the house, which is kept spic and span.

What the hell is he hiding in here?

As I step forward and the door slams behind me, an eerie shiver snakes its way down my spine. Now, I feel like I have the tiniest right to know if Griffin's a creepy serial killer with a murder wing in his house.

I flick the light switch on, and the lights in the hallway illuminate. That dreadful feeling only grows in my chest.

This place is untouched, with dust and cobwebs decorating every surface. It must have been a long time since anyone has come in here. This hallway mirrors ours in the east wing, but it looks completely different. Ours is welcoming and warm; this is cold and screaming at me to leave.

I drift forward, curiousness moving my feet, the silence making me more and more on edge as I approach the first door on my right.

Maybe I should turn back. I can pretend I was never here. I could just ask Griffin what this place is and why no one ever comes here.

But I am already this far in. I'll just take a quick look around and leave. I won't mess with anything. No harm, no foul. Although I am a bit disturbed that Griffin never mentioned this creepy part of the house. The dust has even built up on the doorknobs.

How long has this place been abandoned?

Grabbing just the sides of the doorknob, I twist and push the door open, immediately inhaling dust. I cough hard, trying to clear my lungs.

Once I feel like I can kind of breathe again, I begin looking around.

A blue race car bed sits against one of the walls. The room is decorated exactly how I imagine a young boy would want—toys everywhere, some even strewn on the floor, like they were being played with before freezing in place. Laundry fills a basket in the corner, and I see a little boy's clothes piled high.

I wonder if this was Griffin's childhood room. But I can't imagine why he would have left it untouched for all these years.

It's clear no one has been here in ages. Walking over to the dresser, I drag my finger along the edge, picking up what appears to be an inch of dust that has gathered over time. As my eyes continue to wander over everything, I notice the picture frames, all face-down on top of the dresser.

Lifting one up, I find an image of Griffin. He must be a young teenager in this. But he's not alone. Pictured next to him are two adults, who I assume are his parents, and a little boy, nearly a spitting image of Griffin. It must be his little brother.

He rarely mentions his family, and when he does, he only speaks about when they left him …

My eyes land on the object centered between the face-down picture frames, and my heart drops to the floor.

It takes me all but a moment to realize what this room

is. It takes not a second more for my heart to shatter into pieces on the floor and to understand that Griffin's story about his family leaving him has a meaning far worse than I ever imagined.

Sitting between the frames is a tiny urn with an engraved gold plaque.

It reads, *Gavin Hawthorne, forever in our hearts.*

Oh God.

Mindlessly, I set the picture frame back down as my heart races.

His little brother …

This is his *little brother's* room, not Griffin's.

My stomach churns, and I feel like I might be sick.

He never told me. He never elaborated on his family. I should have asked, but he changed the subject whenever I pushed him about personal stuff or ignored it altogether.

Everything around me freezes, and I seem to run out of the room in slow motion.

I find the next door and open it. As it creaks on the hinges, it reveals a dark office with a gigantic wooden desk at the center and a nameplate on the desk that reads, *Linus Hawthorne.*

I've never questioned that the rest of the house is empty of family photos. The walls are decorated with art rather than memories. I assumed that was just their way of making the space their own, not that perhaps those memories are too painful to remember.

Closing the door, I walk softly, nearly tiptoeing to the next room, feeling incredibly out of place. But I have to know if it's true and see it for myself.

The next room I find makes my worst fear come true.

A king bed decorated in a colorful spread, muted from the years of isolation, sits against the furthest wall, beneath a large window with embroidered drapes. This is the most colorful room in the house, yet it feels tremendously heavy and sad.

A bright purple velvet couch sits in the corner, opposite of two blue chairs, with a rustic table between them.

My eyes spot what I was hoping never to find. And I slam my eyes shut, trying to stop my brain from processing what I see. But it's too late.

No. No. No. No. No.

I force my eyes open, and they land on two urns sitting side by side on the little table.

His family didn't relocate across the country. They didn't start a new life. They didn't move on and forget about their son. They weren't terrible people who abandoned Griffin.

They ... *died.*

I drop to my knees, feeling weak and nauseous.

How did this happen? When? How long has Griffin been mourning his entire family in silence?

My heart shatters at the thought of what he's been through and will forever go through.

I can't imagine losing my dad. He's everything to me. He has been my rock my entire life; losing him would be like losing myself.

My skin crawls as reality becomes more and more real, and I've never felt more sinful in my life, standing in a place that I should have never come in. The west wing was sealed off from the rest of the world, frozen in time.

Oh no, I've made a horrible mistake.

Standing to my feet, I stride out of the room, gently shutting the door behind me. I shouldn't be here. I never should have come in here. This was never for me to see.

Twisting the knob out of the west wing, I throw it open, nearly sprinting at this point, and slam right into Griffin, who has never looked angrier.

Oh God, what have I done?

Backing away, I hold my hands up in surrender as his chest puffs with each quickened breath. His hair falls loosely over his forehead, but it does little to hide what he's feeling.

"What the fuck are you doing?" His tone is cold and emotionless, but his face shows all of the disgust and rage his voice doesn't.

My back hits the door, and a tear strikes my cheek. "Griffin, I'm so sorry. I—"

"What? You didn't mean to? Did you accidentally fall into the west wing? Did you trip up a flight of stairs, through double doors, and into the one place I'd explicitly forbidden you from entering? The one part of my home I don't let anyone see? Is that what you were going to say?" His voice grows louder with each accusation, his eyes reddening by the second and tears welling as his lips twist into a deeper scowl.

His lip quivers, and I heave at the pain I'm causing him.

"Griffin, I'm so sorry," I cry out, my voice shaking uncontrollably as I begin to hyperventilate between sobs. "Please. I'm sorry. It wasn't right for me to go in there. I shouldn't have!"

"You're right, Blair! You fucking shouldn't have!" He

takes a steadying breath as a single tear rolls down his cheek, and as he opens his mouth to speak, my chest tears in two. Calm and dangerously cold, he orders me, "*Get out.*"

"W-what? Griffin, please," I beg, stepping toward him.

He steps away from me and yells, "Get out, Blair!"

I gasp and run as fast as I can to get my phone, which is still in his room. I can't go anywhere. I don't have a vehicle.

I hear Griffin smack the door or the wall or something hard and roar, "Fuck!"

I call Lumi once I reach my phone, and he answers on the first ring.

"Hello?"

I try to take a deep breath, but my diaphragm is still convulsing, and it comes out more like a horrible wail. "Can you pick me up? Right now?"

"What happened?" he asks, his tone instantly worried.

"Later. Please get here," I beg him and run into my room.

"I'm on my way. Be there in less than five," he tells me, and I end the call without a word.

I rip Griffin's shirt off of me and throw it across the room before changing into a hoodie and yoga pants. I slip my tennis shoes on, grab my purse, and try to get downstairs and out of this house as fast as I can.

He needs space.

I need space.

We need to cool off, and that's not going to happen right this second.

Lumi is pulling up when I hit the stairs outside, and I fly down them and into his front seat.

"Oh my God, Blair, what the hell happened?" he shrieks. "What is going on?"

"I'll fill you in. Just drive," I tell him, leaning my head against the window as everything begins crumbling to the ground around me.

"Where?" he asks, pulling forward to loop around the driveway.

"Anywhere but here," I murmur and peek at the front door, searching for Griffin once more before the house is out of view, but he never shows.

My stomach is churning, and I feel like I'm going to throw up. My body feels like it's on fire, so I roll the window down and close my eyes.

I'm dreaming. This must be a horrible dream, and I will wake up at any second now. That's the only scenario I can handle. The alternative is far too devastating.

Tucking my legs into my chest on the seat, I repeatedly hit my forehead on my knee. I fucked up so badly, and I don't know how to fix it.

"What happened?" Lumi whispers, stilling my head.

My face is soaked, my tears dripping onto my pants. My chest hurts so badly right now. It feels like daggers are sticking out of it, and every breath I take makes them slice deeper and deeper into me.

I don't even know how to begin explaining this to him. I can't exactly share all of Griffin's secrets that I'm not even supposed to know about.

"Just take some deep breaths," Lumi murmurs. "I'll drive us around."

Nodding, I rest my cheek on my knee and stare out of the window.

I can't believe his family is really gone. How long ago did it happen? How did it happen? How long has Griffin been suffering in silence?

He might not always have a smile on his face or be a bubbly guy, but I never would have guessed that he's been mourning his entire family.

I knew there had to be a reason he kept everyone at arm's length. I knew there was a story behind the nightmares he had. But I couldn't have ever imagined it being this.

My throat burns like I've swallowed acid, and my heart is cracking every one of my ribs. Gasping, I do my best to calm my hyperventilated breathing, but I fail miserably.

Lumi reaches out and rubs my arm. I don't know what I would have done without him. I would be all alone.

My heart drops into my stomach.

The same way Griffin is right now.

I might have royally messed up. I might not be able to fix it.

But I won't let him go through this alone.

When Grant sent that video to the whole school, Griffin refused to leave my side. He clung on to me, letting me fall apart in his arms. He was my strength, so I could be weak.

When I look over at Lumi, he meets my eye, seemingly reading my mind before I say with utmost certainty, "Turn around."

Lumi's lips tip up into a grin, and he veers around an intersection and speeds away toward Hawthorne Manor.

I'm absolutely terrified. What if this is a mistake? What if he just yells at me to leave? Then, I'll tell him no and stand my ground. I won't let him go through any more pain alone.

Lumi turns onto Griffin's driveway, and my hand is on the door, ready to run.

"Do you want me to wait?" Lumi asks as the house comes into view.

I shake my head as my heart jumps into my throat. "No. I'll be okay."

"Call me later, please. I'm going to need to catch up," Lumi scoffs.

"You got it."

As he approaches the stairs, I throw the door open and jump out before he finishes coming to a stop. Catching my balance, I take off up the stairs as fast as I can. I shouldn't have left him. I should have stayed. But I'm here now, and I'm not going anywhere.

I reach the landing and continue to pump my legs hard, not slowing, even as I get to the top of the stairs and throw one of the front doors open.

I run through the foyer beneath glowing chandeliers. My heart and stomach are a tangled mess as I race through the house. I know where he'll be. I don't have to guess. I don't have to call out to him. I know. I know because I know Griffin. He doesn't want to be alone, and the only ones to keep him company are in urns in the west wing.

As I reach the stairs to the second floor, I spot Griffin,

and as if lightning strikes me, my soul cracks apart, and pain lances through me. He's sitting on the steps to the west wing with his head in his hands, tucked between his knees. Sobs tearing through him.

I did that. I caused that pain to surface.

I'm out of breath, panting heavily, as I ascend the stairs to the landing.

"Go away, Blair," Griffin utters between hitching breaths.

I climb up a step toward him, my voice shaky and barely audible as I say, "No."

His head snaps up to mine, and I somehow fall apart even more. His eyes are downturned, bloodshot, and soaked with tears. Snot drips out of his nose, and his face is splotchy and red.

He scoffs, and a wet, squelching sound reverberates out of him. "No?"

Shaking my head, I swallow hard and take another step, only four remaining between us.

My breathing is ragged, but I try to remain strong. For him. For us. "No. I'm not leaving."

His lip quivers as his chest rises and falls unevenly. "Get out. I want you to leave." His words are choppy and pained.

I take another step, shaking my head. I bite down on my lip, and my ears pound loudly from the blood rushing through my veins, matching the thump of my trembling jaw, as I take another step.

"I'm not leaving you," I tell him as tears fall from my lashes and crash onto the marble floor.

He doesn't say a word. He looks straight ahead with

upturned eyebrows and a shattered heart. I take another step, and he looks straight up at me as my legs graze against his.

"You want to cry? Cry. You want to hit something? Hit me."

He inhales sharply at my words, the same ones he once told me.

"You want to scream? I'll listen. But I'm not leaving you." I hyperventilate. "I *won't* leave you, Griffin."

He gasps as a guttural cry slices through him, echoing down the long, empty corridor. "*Blair.*"

Throwing myself onto the step, I catch him as he launches himself at me, his head crashing to my chest as he shatters to pieces in my arms.

"I'm right here," I sob, holding on to him like my life depends on it. "I'm right here."

I will be his stability so that he can be weak. The same way he was for me. I will hold him in my arms for eternity if that's what it takes for him to find peace.

"I'm so sorry," I apologize and press my wet lips against his disheveled hair. "I shouldn't have gone in there."

He clings to me, his fingers digging into my skin. "I couldn't bear to talk about them. To even think about them. I haven't gone into that wing since the day of the crash. If I never processed it, then they were never really gone." He trails off as he heaves and cries, and we gently rock back and forth. "It was my fault."

His words crack my chest in half.

"You don't have to explain it to me. You don't have to talk about them until you're ready."

"I wanted to tell you. I really did," he cries into my lap. "I just didn't want you to hate me the way I hate myself."

Pulling him tighter against me, I promise these words to him. "I could never hate you, Griffin. No matter what."

He weeps and forces a few long breaths in and out of his quivering lips. "That n-night, they weren't even supposed to be on the road. But I decided to sneak out and go to a dumb high school party. It got busted by the cops." He gasps and buries his head. "The only reason they got in the car that night was to pick me up."

Oh God.

He takes a shuddering breath. "Gavin was only six. He was the happiest, *brightest* kid. Mrs. Potts was gone that night, so my parents brought him along so he wasn't left alone in the house."

My tears drop into his hair, and I press my lips against them as he continues, his words sporadic and broken, "They were hit by a drunk driver. It took hours for the news to reach the cops at the party and then me. *God*, I wished it had been me *so* badly. That guilt … that pain is all-consuming."

He lifts his head from my lap, and I cup his face in my hands and stare into his eyes.

"It's not your fault, Griffin. You were just a kid."

He frowns. "Maybe, one day, I'll believe you."

"Then, I'll say it to you until you do because it's *true*," I cry out, wishing I could take some of that crushing burden from his chest.

He nods ever so slightly, and I can see in his eyes that

he thinks the worst of himself. That what happened really is his fault.

We don't say anything for what feels like minutes or hours. We just look into each other's eyes with no walls or barriers. We give each other the rawest version of ourselves.

Brushing his cheeks with my thumbs, I wipe the wetness away.

"You came back." His whisper cuts through the silence.

Carefully, he sits up, pulling out of my touch, as his breathing and mine begin to even out. Side by side, we look at each other, our broken pieces fitting perfectly together.

Nodding, I look up at him, forcing a glimpse of a smile. "You can't get rid of me that easily. I'm not going anywhere."

Delicately, he reaches out and brushes the fallen hairs from my face before running the back of his fingers against my cheek.

"You found me, the real me. Even the parts I kept buried so deep that I'd forgotten they existed." His words are a whispered confession between us. "I would be lost without you."

Leaning forward, I rest my forehead against his. "I'm right here."

His fingers lift my chin up slightly, and his hand wraps around my side, tugging me further into him.

He pulls away enough to gaze into my eyes before guiding me closer to him with the fingers beneath my chin. His warm breath brushes against my lips, and I inhale.

"I know, and I'm never letting you go again."

He seals his lips against mine.

Everything ... everything we've been through since we met has been leading to this moment. I can feel it, the connection we share; it's tangible. The same way the ocean tides are connected to the moon and life itself is connected to the sun; I am connected to Griffin.

He kisses me tenderly, like if he does it too hard, I might break. But I've come this far. I'm not going anywhere. Pushing back against him, he grunts, grabbing my jaw and sliding his hand into my hair.

As his tongue traces the seam of my lips, I part them, giving him full access. His tongue dips into my mouth, dancing with mine as we find a perfect rhythm. He kisses me like nothing else in the world matters, like the only thing he needs to survive this pain is me.

Our apologies are woven with each press of our lips and gasp for air.

We understand each other without words, but rather the emotion pulsing between us.

His hand tightens at my waist, and as we both come up for air, his forehead rolls against mine. The sound of our heavy breathing is enchanting, like a song I've been dying to hear for so long.

power play

When a team has more
players than their
opponent on the ice as an
outcome of the other team
committing a penalty.

chapter
twenty-two
griffin

I'm still an emotional wreck, waking up this morning, but at least I have Blair by my side. After our kiss yesterday, we came into my room and talked all day long about anything and everything. I told her more about my parents and Gavin. Which was fucking painful. But it was nice to share the good memories with someone, to remember them. Blair told me more about her dad and her mom—who passed from a heart attack at a young age —and what her life was like growing up. I will make sure that those financial struggles she endured will never happen again.

My phone alarm sounds, and I roll over and shut it off, wincing as I look back at Blair, hoping she doesn't wake up. But she's still fast asleep. Mrs. Potts and Chip were scheduled to go on a little adventure this morning to the aquarium, but I'm going to hijack it and take them some-where else.

Over the last few years, I've disregarded them more

than I like to admit. They have been there for me through everything, and I was too scared and closed off to realize that. That changes today.

Slipping out of bed, I quickly get dressed, throwing on one of my Legends sweatshirts and joggers before heading downstairs.

I find Mrs. Potts in the kitchen, packing up a bag of snacks and drinks for her and Chip.

"You're up rather early," she chimes as I rap my fingers on the kitchen counter, loving that she knew I didn't have a game today.

Grinning, I look around to see if Chip is here before I murmur, "How would you feel about not going to the aquarium today?"

She looks at me with a confused stare. "What are you thinking?"

Shrugging, I say, "I thought we could maybe take a trip to the animal shelter. You've always said how beneficial a pet might be for our little Chocolate Chip. I figured it was about time we made that happen."

Her face lights up, her eyes glowing joyfully. "Really?"

It's not like she asked me to get him one before and I said no. I think she never felt comfortable getting one without me, which is my own fault for making her feel like she lives in my house when it's just as much hers.

Nodding, I can't help but beam along with her. "Of course."

She rushes around the kitchen island and throws her arms around me, and I freeze. "He is going to love that so much."

Relaxing, I wrap my arms around her, hugging her

gently. "Good. Should we make it a surprise? I'll leave before you, and then you can pretend you're still going to the aquarium, but instead meet me there?"

She pulls away, nodding frantically. "A perfect plan, Griff."

"All right. When were you guys planning on leaving?"

"In about fifteen minutes. The aquarium opens at eight a.m. Do you know when the shelter opens?" she asks me, simultaneously grabbing her phone. "I'll check quickly." She pauses, looking it up. "Oh, perfect. Eight a.m. So, we can stay right on schedule."

My chest thumps a beat harder at the pure excitement radiating from her. She's the best mom in the world. Chip honestly could not have gotten luckier.

After grabbing a water from the fridge and a banana, I leave for the shelter, desiring to beat them there. When I reach FurEvermore Rescue, I head inside, wanting to talk to the staff quickly before Mrs. Potts and Chip arrive.

"Hi! Welcome in. I'm Amy," one of the workers greets me pleasantly, welcoming me over to the counter. "What brings you in today?"

"Hi. I am actually waiting for two more people to arrive. But I just wanted to start the process because I have no idea what it looks like …" I trail off, hoping she can pick up even a smidgen of what I'm saying.

She smiles. "Are you guys looking to adopt today?"

Nodding, I say, "Ideally, yes. My …"

What do I call Chip? My housemate? My roommate? Guilt tugs at my chest for the label popping into my mind. But I hope wherever Gavin is, he knows that no one can or will ever replace him. He will be my little brother forever, and I will always love him. In a way, I have two brothers—at least, it feels that way. Chip might not share any relation with me, but he's always felt like a little sibling, growing up.

So, I hope Gavin doesn't hate me when I call Chip, "My brother. He has autism and doesn't speak, so we kind of thought that a friend who can't talk might be the perfect companion. They can communicate in their own way."

She frowns kindly. "That's so beautiful. I'm sure we will have the perfect friend for your little brother. What's his name?"

Gavin.

"Chip—well, it's actually Charlie, but we call him Chip," I say.

"That's adorable," she sings, and I hear the door opening behind me, grabbing my attention.

Looking back, I find Mrs. Potts and Chip walking inside. He's beaming brighter than I've ever seen.

Widening my eyes, I smile. "Surprise! Are you excited?"

He nods relentlessly and claps his hands.

"He is *very* excited!" Mrs. Potts smiles.

"Awesome! Well, Chip, let's go find you a new friend!" The worker speaks directly to Chip.

We follow her back into an empty meet-and-greet room.

"All right, what kind of pet are we looking for? Dog? Cat? Big or small?" the worker asks.

Mrs. Potts glances at me, but I gesture my hand out, giving her the floor to decide.

"Probably something on the smaller side. Sometimes, Chip can get overwhelmed, and I think a smaller dog might be best," she answers and looks at me for reassurance.

I nod and agree, "Sounds great."

Leila and Mrs. Potts spend the next few minutes discussing Chip's personality traits and the ones they might be looking for in a dog. After a surprising number of questions, Leila tells us that she has the perfect little guy for us. She dismisses herself from the room and returns a few moments later with a furry friend in her arms.

"This is Rex. He's a Tibetan spaniel. He came to us about two months ago as a stray. We believe he had an owner because he was well cared for. But no one ever came to claim him. He's about three years old."

Rex is the perfect size, not too small and not too big. His floppy ears bounce as Leila lowers him to the ground and lets him off his leash.

"He's a super-friendly boy, and he loves to cuddle. Once you guys become friends, he will be attached at your hip," she informs us, and I can't believe that we haven't done this sooner.

Chip scoots from his chair to the floor, and Rex doesn't waste a second before beelining it straight into Chip's lap.

"Oh! They are fast friends!" Mrs. Potts giggles as Rex licks Chip's face.

Happiness blooms in my chest at the scene playing out in front of me, reminding me of the girl who's asleep in my bed at home—the one who makes me happier than I've ever been.

I bounce my knee up and down, and Mrs. Potts

notices and smiles. She pulls out her phone and types rapidly, seconds before mine vibrates in my pocket.

> Mrs. Potts: I think we've found the one. I'll take it from here. You should go home and fill Blair in on our newest member of the family.

For so many reasons today, my body is filling with joy. Mrs. Potts and Chip are my family, and seeing her say that in her message makes my heart swell. I'm not alone and never have been.

After saying goodbye to Mrs. Potts, Chip, and Rex, I head home to Blair. I just want to be near her, bathe in her presence. She has become such an important part of my life, and I'm tired of holding my feelings back from her. Life is too goddamn short.

As I walk into the house, I find Blair walking down the stairs in her pajamas with messy bedhead and sleepiness in her eyes.

My heart starts pounding in my chest with each step I take toward her. She means fucking everything to me. I'm falling so hard for her, and if she doesn't catch me, I think I might perish on the ground below.

"There you are. I was wondering where you went—"

Cupping her face, I crash my lips into her, kissing her roughly and deeply. She parts her lips, and I take no time tasting her mouth with my tongue, breathing in the minty freshness. Her hands flatten on my chest as she kisses me back with the same intensity.

We pull away, breathing hard, and stare into each other's eyes.

"I'm never going to get enough of you," I whisper into her parted lips.

She smirks and bites down on her bottom lip. "Good. Now, kiss me again."

I claim her lips with mine, and we match every push and pull as we fight for control. Bending down, I hook my hands around her legs and lift her up, wrapping her around my waist without breaking our kiss.

Shifting her weight and locking her against me with an arm around her, I grab her cheek with my free hand, guiding our kiss until we're in sync. Fuck, I never want this to end.

"What were you coming downstairs for?" I murmur, blood rushing to my core.

"Just to see what you were doing. Why?" she asks, kissing me again after answering.

"Just checking before I carry you back upstairs," I groan and plunge my tongue back into her mouth.

Desperation doesn't come close to describing the way I need her.

"If that's okay with you," I whisper, getting her permission before taking a step forward.

She nods and sinks her tongue into my mouth before saying, "Yes, *please*."

"I don't want to rush you," I counter.

Every part of my body hums with desire.

She giggles. "You have no idea how long I've even wanted to kiss you. This isn't a rush. I want this. I want you."

Without another word, I press my lips to hers and carry her up every step, not stopping until I'm standing in front of my bed.

A deep and desperate gasp shudders past my lips as she runs her tongue up the side of my neck and nibbles on my earlobe.

I toss her backward onto the bed, and she shrieks, "Ahh!"

I tower over her, feeling like a man who has been starved for days. "You have no idea how long I've wanted you."

The way she's staring up at me, waiting for me to make a move, is driving me crazy.

"Come here," I growl, and she sits up on her knees.

Grabbing the hem of her top, I lift it up and over her head.

"Can I?" I ask her as I trail my fingertips down the sides of her perfect, full breasts.

Her head rolls back. "Please, dear God, yes, touch me."

Leaning down, I take one of her hardened nipples into my mouth, sucking on it and flicking my tongue over it repeatedly.

She moans softly, and my cock fights against the confines of my pants, begging to be set free. But it's not time yet. I want to focus on her right now.

Cupping her other breast, I massage it with my hand before pinching and rolling her nipple between my thumb and pointer finger. Her back arches as I run my tongue across her chest and take her other nipple into my mouth.

It's not enough. I need more of her, all of her.

"Lie back," I release her from my mouth and slide my hands down to the waistband of her bottoms and panties.

She lifts her hips for me, and I meet her lust-blown pupils and hold them as I slowly slide her clothes down over her hips and off her, leaving her completely bare before me.

Stepping back, I stand to my full height and look down at her, taking in every inch of her body. "You're so fucking beautiful."

She bites down on her bottom lip, grinning.

Quickly, I remove my sweatshirt, tossing it to the floor.

Gently, I grab onto her bent knees and spread her legs apart. "I want to see all of you. Open those legs for me, baby."

She does as I asked, and as she opens up to me, I push my pants to the floor. She's making me too fucking hard, and the constriction is killing me.

Her eyes widen as she watches my pants fall to the floor, and she wets her lips as she stares at my growing erection, still trapped in my boxers.

"I'm not going to fuck you right now, Blair," I tell her honestly. "I meant what I said. I'm not rushing this. I want to take my time and savor every moment."

She juts her bottom lip out, pouting. "*Griffin.*" She rolls her head back and looks at me with hooded eyes, her chest rising and falling with panting breaths.

"You can beg all you want. But it won't change anything," I tell her as I drop down onto one knee in front of the bed. "Don't worry though, my little prisoner; I'm still going to make you come. You'll just be wrapped around my face instead of my waist."

It's the only warning I give her before I run my tongue up her core, tasting her sweet pussy.

"Ahh! Fuck!" she cries out.

Taking just the tip of my tongue, I circle it around her center, teasing her as I skip her clit every time.

"*Griffin.*" She says my name with pure frustration this time, wiggling her hips, desperate for any friction.

Surprisingly, her frustration gives me an idea.

"Stay right there. Don't move a muscle."

"Where are you going?" she whines.

I ignore her question, walk across the hall to her room, and go straight to her nightstand. I pull the drawer open, happy that my assumption of where she keeps her toy is correct. I grab her vibrator and stroll back into my room, nearly drooling from the image of her sprawled out on my bed.

I turn it on and glide it across her thigh as I kneel before her again. She jumps from the contact, then relaxes immediately once she realizes what it is.

Pressing the toy against the crease of her thigh, I give her what she wants, running my tongue up her center and sucking her clit into my mouth, and she calls out my name between moans. After a few moments of the most beautiful sounds leaving her lips, I pull away and run one of my fingers across her wetness before gliding it inside of her and gently adding another.

"God, you're so tight, baby," I groan, feeling her clench around my two fingers.

Sliding the toy up her thigh, I press it against her clit, feeling her jolt from the pleasure.

"Oh fuck! God, that feels *so* good!" she cries out.

I could come just by listening to her.

I pump my fingers in and out of her, syncing up with her gasping breaths, and within seconds, she is tightening around my fingers and begging for release.

"Fuck! Fuck! Fuck! Don't stop!" she begs me, and I continue.

Fuck, you'd have to kill me to get me to stop.

"There you go, baby, just like that. You're doing so good."

My words are her undoing, and she rides my hand as she falls apart at every seam.

"Griffin! Oh! Oh my Gooood!" She pulses around my fingers, over and over, and when her breathing starts to calm, I pull the toy away from her center, granting her reprieve.

She lifts her head up and looks at me, and the darkest red I've seen colors her cheeks. "That. Was. Amazing."

Standing back up, I adjust my length, wanting nothing more than to free myself.

Her eyes widen as they fall to my hand. "Your turn."

She rises to her knees and crawls over to me, flipping her hair to one side of her head.

Fuck, I'm not going to last five seconds.

Her fingers hook into my boxers, and she tugs them down, letting my cock spring free. I moan as it bounces against her cheek, my eyes rolling into the back of my head.

"Oh my God," she mumbles, her eyes bulging from her head as she takes me in.

I stay silent, unable to form a single thought, let alone a word.

She holds my stare as she licks her lips and wraps her fingers around me, pumping me torturously slow.

My eyes disappear into my head again, and my head falls back. "Fuuuck."

The wetness of her tongue swipes across my tip, and I nearly lose it. She sucks me into her mouth and continues to take me deeper and deeper.

"Blair," I whimper loudly, feeling pleasure course through my veins. Her mouth feels so goddamn good. "Hand me the toy."

She starts to pull away from my dick, and I miss her warmth for the second she's gone. She hands me the vibrator, and I turn it on, setting it on the bed.

This time, it's me who pulls away. "Flip over."

She flips onto her back, hanging her head slightly off of the bed, and opens her mouth with a smirk on her lips and a gleam in her eyes.

She guides me back into her mouth, and I step forward, sliding further down her throat. Grabbing the toy, I lean forward and press it against her center, her back arching immediately.

She moans with her mouth full, and it vibrates around me, sending a hot shiver up my back. My balls start to tighten, and I know I'm not going to last much longer. But I'm not letting myself come before her.

Fuck no.

I wet my fingers on her center before sliding them back inside of her, finding that perfect rhythm from before. I can feel her starting to clench around my fingers, and her moans quicken around my cock.

She moans faster and faster, and the moment I feel her come around my hand, I fly over the fucking edge.

"Fuck, baby, I'm coming," I groan and pull out of her mouth, ready to come on her chest, but she grabs me, sucking me back into her mouth as months of built-up desire finally find release. "Fuuuck!" I breathe through my moan as pleasure whips through me in waves.

Slowly, I pull my fingers from her, shut the toy off, and toss it onto the bed. She releases me from her lips, and as I pull her up as she swallows hard.

Cupping her face, she looks into my eyes, out of breath, with flushed cheeks. She's never been sexier.

"Be mine, Blair. Only mine."

Her eyes shimmer, and her lips tip up as she sits up taller. She hovers her mouth an inch from mine and whispers against my lips, "I already am."

I'm picking Blair up after class right now, and even though it's only been a few hours since I've seen her, my heart starts racing the second she walks into view in the parking lot and makes her way over.

I step out of my truck and walk over to her, meeting her halfway, grabbing her backpack, and slinging it over my shoulder.

Leaning down, I steal a quick kiss and throw my arm around her. "Hello, beautiful. How was class?"

"Ehh. Boring. We've been working on the same

chapter for about two weeks now. Some of the students have been struggling, so the professor wants to review some stuff again before moving on," she fills me in. "How was your morning skate?"

I shrug. "Same as usual. Nothing exciting to report."

"That's good. Are you excited for the game tonight?" she asks, looking up at me.

I nod. "Yeah, it should be an easy win. We've crushed this team before, and they haven't been playing that great as of late."

She looks forward with that focused look on her face. "Yeah. I was digging into their stats in class. They've only won three games this season, and the wins were against the worst-ranked teams in your division. Their goalie save percentage is only seventy-six percent, which I found out is not good for a goalie, so as long as you guys get lots of shots in, you shouldn't have a problem. Eventually, you'll beat them."

I slam to a halt and stare at her with admiration and shock. "Umm, hello?"

She turns to me and laughs. "What?"

Reaching out, I poke her forehead. "So *lifelike*, but you must be a robot replacement of my girlfriend. Especially for someone who once told me that hockey was a bunch of oversize humans wearing blades on their feet and chasing after a ball."

Now, she's the one staring at me in shock. "Y-you called me your girlfriend."

"Are you not my girlfriend?" I ask her smoothly and intertwine my fingers with hers.

She looks down, smiling. "Yeah, I guess I am."

Raising our connected hands, I guide her chin up. "You guess? Maybe you just need a little reminder."

Her cheeks burn, and she giggles.

Dropping her hand, I slide the palms of my hands along her jaw and tilt her head toward mine. She looks up at me, and her breath hitches.

Trailing my lips across her cheek, I plant a soft kiss before moving on to the other one. Once she melts into my hands, I slowly press my lips into hers and remind her exactly what we are. I slide my tongue along the seam of her lips, and she parts them. I take full advantage, tasting every inch of her mouth. But before I get too carried away, I pull back and kiss her forehead.

"Did that help?" I ask her, wiping her bottom lip with my thumb.

She nods, then shrugs, biting back a grin. "Ehh, maybe you should try again."

Grabbing her hand, I pull her along with me toward my truck. "Funny."

Opening the passenger door for her, I offer my hand to help her, but she stares me down while getting in on her own.

I laugh. *So stubborn.*

Closing the door behind her, I go around and get in on my side.

Reaching my hand into the back seat, I grab the gift box I've been dying to give her all day, a little something I put together. "This is for you."

"For me?" Her face falls, and she looks up at me with doe eyes.

Placing it in her lap, I say, "Yeah, of course."

She looks down at the gift and then back up at me. "You didn't need to get me anything. I don't have anything for you."

Grinning, I chuckle. "That's why it's a surprise gift, not a gift exchange. It's nothing crazy, just open it."

She carefully lifts the lid and pulls the tissue paper back.

"Griffin!" She swoons and pulls out the Legends jersey with my name on the back.

"I thought you could wear it to the game this weekend," I mumble as she holds it up.

"I would love to!" She leans over the console, puckers her lips, and closes her eyes. "Thank you."

I give her a quick kiss before saying, "There's more."

"More?" she questions before looking back into the box and digging beneath more tissue paper to find the envelope I taped to the bottom. She grabs it and tears it out without looking inside. "Griffin, what is this? I don't want it."

She shoves the envelope at me, and I push it back.

"You don't even know what it is yet."

"I know that it's probably more than I can give back to you," she whispers and looks away.

"Hey." I slide my hand over hers. "I don't want anything back. I just want to see you smile. That's it, *seriously*."

She looks up at me, and I can't resist taking in every tiny detail of her pretty face. She turns her focus back onto the little blue envelope and reaches inside, grabbing the slip of paper.

"Griffin, w-what is this?" she whispers.

331

"It's symbolic, really, because I'll send you the digital version. I just wanted you to be able to open it," I explain as she reads it.

She peers up at me, and I find her eyes welling with tears. "Is this to go visit my dad?"

Nodding, I quietly say, "Yeah. I know you miss him, so I thought that you could fly out and visit him for a few day—"

She throws her arms around me and hugs me tightly. "Thank you."

Kissing her head, I say, "You're welcome."

Our home crowd goes insane, cheering for us as we take the ice for puck drop. I haven't seen Blair in her seat—at least since I snuck a peek at the crowd earlier. I take one last glance where she should be—on the glass and next to our bench.

My chest flutters when I see her. She's on her feet, screaming along with the rest of the crowd. Her eyes find mine immediately, and her lips tip into the biggest smile.

I take a mental snapshot, knowing that in this crowd of thousands, that girl—*my girl*—is smiling just for me.

She does a twirl, showing off her jersey that hangs down to the tops of her thighs. That's it. That's officially my favorite thing to see her in. I personally think she should wear it every damn day. Nothing is as attractive as her wearing my last name, like a sign to the world that she's mine.

The ref blows the whistle, and I force my attention on the game, setting up for puck drop. The second it's airborne, Asher kicks it to Elias, and we take off toward the net. Elias passes it to Malik, who dekes out the defender and flies down the empty lane, handling the puck with finesse. He slides it far left, and the goalie takes the bait, following his movement. But in one quick motion, Malik kicks the puck across the ice and backhands it right into the net between the goalie's leg and his blocker.

"That's what I'm talking about!" I shove Malik and shake his shoulders with praise.

We all cheer for Malik's early goal before skating to the bench to celebrate. Since we haven't been on the ice for very long, Coach keeps our line in, and we set back up at center ice.

Setting momentum is essential, and scoring off of the first possession says a lot about where we plan on taking the rest of the game.

They win the face-off, and I skate backward into their zone, watching the puck while simultaneously staying locked on to the player to my right.

He's given the puck, and I jab my stick at it and poke it away. But his teammate recovers it and throws it back up to the player near the blue line.

They pass it around, trying to make a play to collapse our defense, but they are unsuccessful, and we take possession. We strategically skate it out to the neutral zone and across the center line before chucking it across the rest of the ice toward their goal so we can change our lines up.

Our domination on the ice continues all the way into the middle of the third period. The score is four to zero. Their team is pissed off and just trying to start shit at this point to try to ruin our game.

"Psst, Hawthorne." One of their players tries to get my attention before the ref drops the puck, but I ignore him.

They gain possession and race toward the net, but I manage to stay between our goalie and them the entire time. The guy I'm glued to dumps the puck behind him and skates to my right.

Keeping an eye on him and the puck, I see their next move before it happens and line myself up to smash this guy into the boards.

Digging into the ice, their players send the puck his way, and he catches it on his stick. But it doesn't matter because I crash into him hard as hell and flatten him against the glass.

"Fuck!" the guy cries out as he falls to the ice.

One of their guys immediately rushes me and throws a punch, but I block it with my hand, a smile stretching across my lips. It was a clean hit—a big hit, but still clean.

"Too much of a pussy to fight back?" he chirps at me, but I just shake my head.

"You'll have to do better than that." I laugh and look at his jersey to find his number. *Twelve*.

He gets in my face, and my fists tingle, wanting to smack the stupid off of this guy's face. "I heard a rumor from a buddy of ours. Do you think you could get us a private dance with that tutor of you—"

My hands are wrapped in his jersey, and I swing him

around like a rag doll into the glass before he even finishes his last word.

Pressing my cage against his, I growl, each word hissing between my lips. "Say it again. See what happens."

He laughs as one of the linesmen skates over and pulls us apart.

"All right, guys, don't do anything stupid," he warns us as he skates between us.

"I'll leave that up to this guy. As long as he doesn't open his mouth, we'll both be on our best behavior," I inform him before skating away and resetting for the drop.

I glance over at Blair, and her brows are pinched and worried. I shake my head, letting her know I'm fine.

"Oh, is that *her?*" number twelve, my newest enemy, asks as he skates up to me, positioning himself for the face-off.

"I'm only offering mercy *because* of her right now. But if you look at her again or so much as mention her" —I meet his gaze and watch his face falter when he sees the seriousness in mine—"I will make good on my word."

He shrugs and smiles. "Yeah, well, you can sure try."

The puck falls between the two players on the dot, and they fight to win the battle and get the puck to their teammates.

Number twelve skates in front of me and waves his glove at Blair, sealing his fate.

"What did I just fucking tell you?" I shout at him, and usually, I would say it's lucky for me that the puck glides onto his stick just now, but what I'm about to do to him won't be debated about for penalization.

I throw my stick to the ice and race after him, flicking my gloves to the ground and ripping off my helmet.

Shockingly, he finds the balls to do the same.

His words replay in my head like a rage-fueled mantra as I grab on to the collar of his jersey and smash my fist into his jaw. He grunts in pain, and I swing back, repeatedly landing hit after hit into his face. Pulling back, I drive my fist into his ribs, right between the pads.

He can't even maintain his balance, but I hold him up for the both of us.

Dipping into the pit of anger that always dwells in my chest, I release it, landing relentless blows into his face until red paints my knuckles.

"Do you have anything else to say?" I ask him as a ref steps in and tries to pry my hands off of him.

He stays quiet, and I smile from ear to ear and get in his face one last time. "Let this be a warning. Anyone who talks about her will be lucky if their biggest problem is picking their teeth off of the ice and not being carried out on a stretcher when I'm through with them. Do you understand me?"

He nods, and I release him. He stumbles but eventually catches himself.

I would feel bad, but in my defense, I gave him plenty of warnings not to go there. I told him exactly what would happen if he kept opening his mouth. He just decided to keep going. Now, he faced the consequences.

Malik skates beside me with a shit-eating grin, and I resist the urge to check on Blair. I don't want her to be scared of me or disappointed for taking that too far. But I had to set a precedent that she is off-limits. Word will spread, and if anyone else makes the same mistakes number twelve did tonight, they are a special kind of stupid or cocky enough to think they can beat me.

Malik smacks my ass with his stick and smirks. "I thought she was *just your tutor?*"

Glaring at him, I shake my head before a smile breaks onto my lips. "Yeah, well, she's not. She's my girl. Simple as that."

Malik nods in approval and lifts his stick, pointing at something in the crowd. "Well, I'm happy for you, man. And apparently, so is she."

"What?" I ask as I follow Malik's stick to find Blair on her feet, cheering along with the crowd as they chant my nickname.

"Beeeast! Beeeast!"

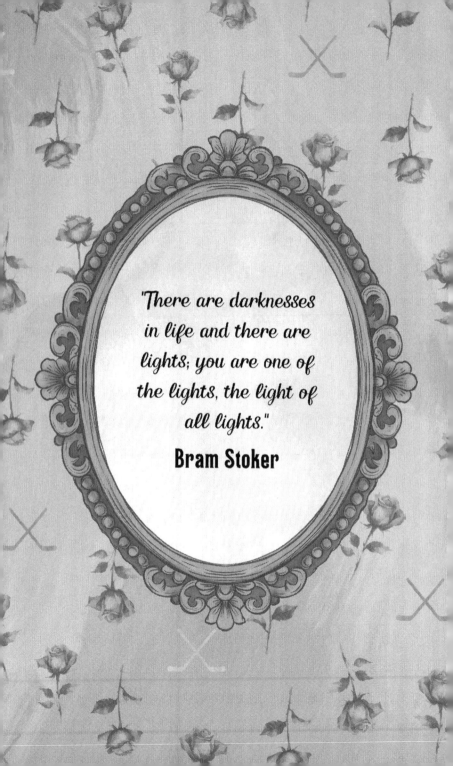

"There are darknesses in life and there are lights; you are one of the lights, the light of all lights."

Bram Stoker

chapter twenty-three
blair

I feel like every girl in the lobby is staring at me as I stand in Griffin's jersey and wait for him after the game. I'm probably just being paranoid, but as I scan the room, I'm starting to feel like it's not paranoia at all.

The door I've seen a few players come through swings open, and Griffin walks out, his face relaxed, but the second he sees me, his lips tip up into the biggest smile, and I can't help but mirror it. A small group of kids and girls dressed in the tightest outfits imaginable swarm him, but he only pays attention to the two kids at his feet, holding up Sharpies and asking him to sign their jerseys.

He says something to them, but I can't quite make it out. Whatever he says makes the kids smile so hard that I worry it might hurt their little faces. He signs both of their little Hawthorne jerseys, and when he's done, they spin around and take off for their parents, happy as ever.

Griffin's eyes lock on to mine as he dismisses the few

girls ogling him like a piece of meat and walks through them, making a beeline straight to me.

"There's my girl," he calls out, still a few feet away from me, and I watch as each of the puck bunnies' faces twist with repulsion.

He drops his bag to the ground and spins his baseball cap around on his wet hair before grabbing my waist, lifting me high above his head, and sliding me down his body, pinning me against his chest.

"Griffin," I squeal as he lowers me just enough to claim my lips with his.

"Mmm," he groans as he releases my mouth and returns me onto my own two feet.

"Are you ready to go?" I ask him, sucking my bottom lip into my mouth, already missing the sensations of his kiss.

He snakes his arm down mine and intertwines our fingers, nodding. "Yeah. Did Lumi already head out?"

I reply, "Yeah, he's going over to see Paul."

Griffin mockingly sticks his bottom lip out. "Oh no, you mean I have you all to myself tonight?"

I giggle as we walk outside, and the cool air feels so good. I know I was just inside a cold rink for hours, but the burning glares from the onlookers in the lobby had me sweating.

"Yeah, I bet you're really beat up about it," I tease him as he leads us to his truck, hand in hand.

The hair on my neck rises, and a cold shiver runs down my back. I feel so uneasy and caught off guard that I don't hear what Griffin says.

"I'm sorry, what?" I ask him to repeat himself.

He pinches his brows. "I just said that I am definitely not upset about it, but forget that. What's wrong?"

Shaking my head, I try to force the concern away. "Nothing. I just ... I don't know. I felt like we were being watched. But it was probably just one of the girls back there who were looking at me like they wanted to kill me."

"They could try. But they'd have to go through me first, and that could prove impossible when it comes to protecting you," he says, soothing all of my anxiety away and making me swoon.

Rolling my eyes, I smile. "So smooth."

He shrugs and opens my door for me, further proving my point.

Once I'm safely inside, he throws his bag in the back and gets into the driver's seat.

He starts the truck, and I reach for the volume immediately and turn it up, hearing one of my favorite songs blare through the speakers.

I start singing along to "The Love I Give" by RHODES. Griffin smiles as he pulls out of the parking lot and takes us home, watching me sing and dance to the music. I continue blessing him with a free concert the entire ride—it's not my fault that great songs keep playing —and he loves every second of it.

Griffin locks up behind us when we get inside, and I start heading upstairs to change.

"Where do you think you're going?" he asks, his voice deep and playful, stopping me dead in my tracks.

Spinning on my heel, I walk backward toward the stairs and answer him with sass dripping from every word, "Going to put pajamas on, *duh.*"

He kicks his shoes off and throws his bag to the floor, stalking toward me like a cat hunting its prey.

"Oh, really? How about we make a deal first?" he mumbles, taking another slow and steady step toward me.

Standing my ground, I can't help but bite on his bait. "And what, my warden, is your offer?"

He glides toward me effortlessly and catches my chin in his hand. "You run. I'll chase you."

"Hmm. And then what?" I ask. My breathing is shallow as heat floods my core.

"That depends." His fingers slip beneath my jersey and lightly grip my waist. "If you beat me to my bedroom, I'll let you change into those cute pajamas. Besides, I love those matching sets you wear."

"And if you win?" My voice is light and airy.

His fingers glide across my stomach before he dips them into my jeans. "If I catch you, then I'm going to strip your clothes from you."

"And then?" I push him, forcing him to say my desires out loud.

He bends down and kisses me gently, tenderly, in the most seductive way. "Then, I will kiss my way up and down every inch of your perfect body."

Well, if that's the case, this race will be over rather quickly. But I think I'll have some fun with it first.

Sticking my hand out between us, I agree to his terms. "Deal."

He smirks at my outstretched hand and removes his fingers from my pants before shaking mine. "All right, my little prisoner. You get a five-second head start. Ready, set, g—"

I tear my hand from his grasp and take off up the stairs.

"Ahh!" I squeal as I grab the railing and race as fast as I possibly can.

Obviously, I would rather him catch me than for me to win, but I still want to beat him to the top of the stairs at least. I'm too competitive to lose by a landslide.

"I guess you get *six* seconds, you cheater. You'd better run fast!" he calls after me before counting down. "Five. Four. Three ..."

I tune him out and fly up the second set of stairs after the landing, bursting through the east wing entrance.

I hear his feet hit the stairs right as I come to a stop in front of his door and turn around, waiting for him.

Moments later, he reaches the double doors, slightly out of breath, with a look of desperation in his eyes that sends tingles from my head to my toes.

"What are you doing?" he questions me as he takes the last few steps my way.

Grabbing the front of my jeans, I undo the button and zipper before pushing them down my legs and pulling them off completely. Without a word, I throw them at my bedroom door before looking back at Griffin.

His eyes eagerly travel up me, from my feet to my eyes, and I can practically feel his gaze caressing every inch of me.

Shrugging, I murmur, "Who said I didn't want you to catch me?"

"*Fuck*," he growls before grabbing my face and slamming his lips into mine.

He pushes the door open behind me and leads us

inside without ever pulling away. With one arm, he secures it around my lower back and lifts me up. Without thought, I wrap my legs around his waist and part his lips with my tongue.

His warm kiss travels to my neck, and he nips at my skin before lapping away the sting.

"Ahh," I whimper as he runs his tongue from the base of my neck to my jaw.

"I need you, Blair, forever." His words are pure ecstasy as he lowers me onto the bed.

Vulnerability is a word I thought I always understood rather well, but until this moment, writhing beneath Griffin's intense gaze, I realize how wrong I was. Nothing comes close to the nakedness I feel right now, and I'm not talking about the amount of clothes I have on. I am talking about how he holds my heart and soul in the palm of his hand, capable of crushing me to smithereens at any moment, if he so desires.

How terrifying of a thought it is to know that someone has so much power in their hands to break you completely. But as scary as it is, I wouldn't want it any other way. I would hand myself over to him time and time again.

He grabs the back of his shirt and tugs it over his head, and I thoroughly enjoy it, not hiding any of my appreciation for his hardworking body.

"I never knew someone could look so good in a Legends jersey," he mutters while grabbing on to my ankles and pulling me until my ass is on the edge of the bed. "I think you might have to keep that on a little longer."

I'll leave it on for eternity if it means he won't ever stop touching me. "I think that can be arranged."

"So formal," he teases. He grabs a pillow from the bed and drops it onto the floor before me.

"We did make a deal after all. I am just accepting your amendment," I say, wanting to punch myself in the face for continuing the formality.

"You're cute when you get all flustered."

He drops onto both knees, and I prop myself onto my elbows to watch him. He slides his hands between my thighs, gently pushing them apart. Biting down onto my thumb, I study his slightest movements.

He presses his lips against the inside of my thigh, right above my knee, and that sensation alone has my core pulsing.

"I hope you aren't in a rush tonight." He trails another kiss upward, lapping my sensitive skin with his tongue before pressing his lips against the same spot. "Because I plan on savoring every second I can."

My panties soak with my arousal. I've never wanted someone as badly as I want him. *Want* isn't even a strong enough word. I need him more than I need air to fucking breathe.

His teeth and tongue continue to nip and lick up my thigh until I'm a panting mess, my hips bucking desperately to feel his tongue against my core.

But he feels like tormenting me first. He hooks his fingers in my panties, and I stretch my legs up as he slides them off.

"I wish you could see how pretty your pussy is. I might

have to fuck you in front of a mirror so you can watch how perfectly we fit together."

My back arches at his words, and I'm so close to snapping and skipping the foreplay. I want him inside of me so pathetically much.

If it wasn't for the fact that I haven't had sex in months, I would rush this and slide onto him without letting him warm me up. But he's girthy as fuck, and his cock is big enough to rearrange my organs. I know that for once in my life, I should slow down and smell the roses— or in this case, let Griffin get my body ready to take him.

He peppers kisses down my other thigh, and I whimper in protest of his slowness, but fuck is it working exactly how he wants. My thighs are dripping with my desperation. Rolling my head back onto the bed, I gasp as he finally gives in and plunges his tongue into my wet desire.

His fingers circle me, and I'm biting my lip so hard that I think I might break skin. I need more. I need to feel *more*. It's like lightning is rippling through my body, bouncing from cell to cell and growing more powerful with every second, desperately looking for the quickest release to explode.

He senses my absolute hunger and appeases me, sliding two fingers into me, and I gasp from the fullness. He hooks them into me and pumps them, slow and steady, in and out. He moves in a fluid and torturous rhythm as his tongue latches on to my clit, and stars decorate the backs of my eyelids. I liquefy under his control. He picks up his pace, and I feel like I might be levitating off of the bed.

"Ahh …" I moan deliriously.

I stiffen up as my core starts clenching around his hand. My gasps and cries fill the room as he works me faster and sucks harder, sending me spiraling into oblivion.

"Grifffffin." His name is a helpless whimper on my lips as I come undone.

He pulls his fingers from me, and I hear him suck them clean. But I can't manage to open my eyelids as my orgasm finishes rocking through me.

Forcing my head up, I open my eyes and gulp at the view before me. Griffin's hand is wrapped around his massive erection, and he strokes himself from base to tip. His engorged cock grazes my inner thigh, and his eyes flutter from the contact. I'll never get over how badly I affect him—that I hold the capability of bringing him to his knees.

Sitting up, I brush my finger across the tip of his cock, swiping through the bead of liquid desire from him before bringing it to my lips and sucking it into my mouth.

"Fuck," he groans, and I push his hand away, replacing it with mine, stroking him slowly.

Adjusting myself, I get on my knees with one hand on the bed in front of him and wiggle my ass in the air as I lean forward and lick his tip before sucking it into my mouth, continuing to circle my tongue.

He threads his hand in my hair as I take him deeper and down my throat. His cock twitches, and my eyes water as he starts fucking my mouth, letting out delirious groans and grunts, giving me all the praise I need.

"Oh my God. You're doing so fucking good, baby," he whines, and my pussy pulses.

He pulls himself from my mouth, and I cough and gasp for air as I blink away my tears and look up into his eyes.

The Fallen Petal taught me how to project sexiness, and I lean into those skills, swaying my hips from side to side.

Opening my mouth again, I stick my tongue out and wait for him to slide his dick back in, but he shakes his head.

"That mouth of yours is going to make me come before we even really begin, and I'm not ready for this to end."

My cheeks burn because I know I was close to making him come just from my mouth alone.

Arching my back, I murmur, "Griffin, I want all of you. *Please*."

He huffs and wets his lips. He grabs my waist and pulls me up onto my knees, and I let him guide me wherever the hell he wants.

He grabs the hem of my jersey and lifts it over my head before tossing it onto the floor, quickly followed by my lacy bra.

He kneels on the bed and orders me, "Lie on your back."

Wetting my lips, I lean back on the bed, and he positions himself between my legs and hovers over me, his hair falling and framing his face like a work of art that I could get lost in.

His arm muscles bulge as he leans down and kisses my neck, trailing his mouth across my collarbone and back up before stalling over my lips for just a moment. His eyes flick up to mine, and as he stretches forward, closing the distance between us, my eyes flutter shut, the anticipation killing me. Trailing his tongue along the seam of my mouth, he kisses me tenderly and slowly.

He tastes me relentlessly, dipping his tongue into my mouth, dancing with mine. Squeezing my thighs against his legs, I grind my hips, desperate to find any friction. He sucks my bottom lip in between his teeth and tugs gently, sending bolts of pleasure through me.

Sitting up, he reaches over to his nightstand, but I stop him before he gets to it.

"I'm on birth control."

He smirks and brushes the hair out of my face before claiming my lips again. "Thank God. I never want to feel anything between us, just you and me."

Tilting my head up, I plunge my tongue into his mouth, taking control. I could never leave this spot. I could happily stay here forever.

He moans, and the vibrations that tingle my lips only egg me on, releasing feral feelings that I didn't know even existed.

"Please," I beg him between kisses and slide a hand between us, grabbing on to his cock. "I need you so badly. Please, Griffin."

He takes his dick into his hand and glides his tip through my soaked pussy. Back and forth, back and forth, he swipes the tip through my center. He pulls back enough to meet my eyes, looking deeply into each one carefully, his gaze twinkling and darkened with lust-blown pupils.

His words are a breathy declaration of his desire. "You're mine, Blair, all mine."

His tip pushes inside of me, and I gasp at the pressure. Griffin stalls, waiting for my signal to move.

"Deep breath, baby," he whispers to me as I wrap my arms around his neck and feel his chest graze my taut nipples. "Yeah, just like that," he encourages me as I start stretching around him, my body molding perfectly to his.

I nod, silently begging for more, and he gives it to me, inch by inch, stretching me more than I ever knew I could.

"Holy fuck, Griffin."

Gently, he pulls out before thrusting forward, slow and steady and intoxicatingly delicious.

His eyes are hooded, and his lips part as he sinks further into me. "You are so fucking tight. You have no idea how good you feel. I want to stay buried inside of you forever."

I am a mess of pants and moans as he continues to praise me, bringing my pleasure to a whole new level.

"You're doing so good, baby. We're almost there," he whispers, and I can't believe he's not bottomed out in me yet.

He lowers his hips, and I moan his name as his balls brush against my ass. "*Griffin.*"

Our breathing fills the room, a symphony of pleasure as he starts moving, thrusting his hips torturously slowly. As I begin relaxing around him and the pleasure outweighs the pressure, I meet his movements, lifting my hips as he plunges deep inside me.

"Oh fuck," he grounds out through his teeth and loses all control.

He sits up and grabs my hips, pulling me flush against

him, drawing back until only his tip remains before slamming back inside of me.

"Griffin!" I shout out, stars forming in my eyes as he fills me to the brim.

He chuckles, deep and sexy, as he fucks me with abandon, each thrust rocking my body higher on the bed.

My mind becomes cloudy, and I am only able to think about one thing and one thing only—him.

We become one fluid movement, and I cry out as his fingers drift over my clit and bring me over the edge.

I scream his name over and over as he continues pounding into me, not letting up as my orgasm tears through me. I'm a puddle of pleasure in his hands, and I don't know where he ends and I begin.

His pace picks up, and I know he's close. His breathing quickens even more, and his thrusts become long and fast.

With a sound like a grunt and a breathless whimper falling past his lips, he buries himself into me to the hilt and comes hard, mumbling my name between moans.

We lie together, our bodies intertwined. After a moment, our breathing evens out, and we come back down to earth. He leans down and kisses my cheek, then the other, before tenderly kissing my lips.

"I lo—" I cut myself off as my heart jumps into my throat, eyes widening at what I almost said, and try to cover up my slip of the tongue. "I *loved* that so much."

He kisses me again. "You have no idea. You've ruined me, Blair. I'm yours for good, and you're stuck with me."

He pulls out of my center, and I wince, knowing I'm going to be sore for a day or two after this.

"I wouldn't mind being your prisoner forever." I giggle and bite down on my lip.

"Good." His smile lights every inch of his face up with a glow I've never seen before. "I'll be right back," he says before backing off of the bed and walking into the bathroom, returning a moment later with a towel in hand.

He crawls back on the bed and cleans me up, and I can't help but swoon at the gesture. No one has ever tended to me after sex. This is new and nice, and I could get used to it.

He helps me to my feet, and I balance on my wobbly knees before dismissing myself to my room to change. "I'm going to go put those PJs on now."

He smiles. "I'll be waiting."

My mind is a scattered mess as I enter my room and slip on panties and pajamas before walking back across the hall to Griffin.

I cannot believe I almost told him that I loved him. What in the actual hell is happening?

I've never once told a guy I loved him, and I sure as hell never almost dropped it after sex. But I don't even want to start processing that can of worms right now.

Griffin's room is empty when I walk inside, and I decide to get comfy in bed while I wait for him to come back from whatever he's doing.

I hear him humming in the hallway, getting louder by the second, and I can't help but smile at the pep in his step when he turns into the room.

My jaw unhinges when I see a tray in his hands.

"I grabbed a few things."

"I see that," I murmur, sliding over in bed to make room for him.

On the wooden tray are Mrs. Potts's delicious chocolate chip cookies, a sandwich cut in half, a bowl of chips, and two glasses of water.

He sets it down in his lap as he slides next to me. "I'm hungry, and I figured you might be too after that workout, so I got us some snacks."

He hands me a glass of water, and I try to say *thank you*, but no sound comes out. Once again, this man has left me speechless.

"Do you want to watch a movie?" he asks me, grabbing the remote off of the nightstand.

He presses a button, and the seventy-inch TV rises up from the floor. I wonder if I'll ever get used to stuff like that.

Nodding, I take a sip of my water and try to wrap my mind around everything, but I fail miserably.

"What are you in the mood for?" he asks me, scrolling through the channels.

I lean over and set my glass of water on the nightstand on my side, finding words to answer him. "Something funny or rom-commie is always my go-to."

"You got it. What about this?" he asks and clicks on the movie *Crazy Rich Asians*, one of my all-time favorites.

"Perfect," I answer him, although I will have to try not to quote the entire film out loud, as I've seen it probably a hundred times.

He moves the tray between us and hands me half of the ham sandwich. "Are you excited to go visit your dad?"

Nodding, I take a bite of the sandwich and swallow

before responding, my eyes burning at the thought. "Yeah, I can't wait. I've been dying to see him."

He looks at me with disbelief. "Why didn't you say anything? I would have flown you out earlier."

Shying away from his gaze, I shrug. "Because I hate the idea of taking money from you."

He sets his sandwich down and grabs my hand, bringing it to his lips and pressing a kiss against each knuckle. "Blair, I want you to have it. I want you to have anything you desire. I'll buy you a private jet so you can see him anytime you wish. It's just money, and nothing compares to watching you light up." He kisses my hand. "I never want you to have to worry again. You were wound up so tightly when we met, and I know you had to stay like that to fight to get where you are, but you can relax now; I've got you."

He reaches out and wipes my cheek. It dawns on me that the burning sensation in my eyes gave way to a downpour of tears. I've never thought about it like that, but he's right. I was so focused on school and work that I never relaxed or took a deep, calming breath. I was so terrified about losing the school of my dreams that I couldn't allow myself any more pain, so I shut out most of the world around me.

I run my hand along his jaw and kiss him, unable to find the strength to say anything. He makes me feel weak in the best of ways. He has become the one place I can be raw and fragile because I know he's right there to support me.

I put my half-eaten sandwich on the tray, and he moves it, setting it on the nightstand before opening his arm for me to snuggle into his side. Leaning into him, I cradle my head in that perfect crook of his neck and breathe him in, resting my hand on his chest.

His fingers dance across mine as we watch the movie in silence. Minutes pass, and neither of us speaks.

"I want to tell you about them. I do." He hesitates, and it takes me a second to realize he's talking about his family. "I just … I'm not ready yet."

Looking up at him, I rest my hand against his cheek, making him look down at me. "That's okay. I'll be here when you are."

His eyes soften at my words, and I realize that I am a goner. I am head over heels in love with The Beast.

Grabbing my phone, I see a few notifications and check my texts. I have one from my dad.

> Dad: I can't wait to see you, sweetie. I am counting down the days.

I leave in a few days, and it's nearly all I think about. I haven't seen him in what feels like forever. Of course, we've FaceTimed and talked, but it's not the same as getting the biggest hug ever.

I check my other texts, and my stomach drops when I see one from Grant with a few photos attached.

> Grant: You cheating whore. You have no shame.

I click on the images and find two pictures of Griffin kissing me in the arena after the game, and my body chills. *I didn't even see him there. Did he take these himself?*

The thought of him being ten feet away from me without my even realizing it has my skin crawling.

Scrolling above the images, I find two more texts.

> Grant: End it. You're mine.

Rage fills me to the core, and I quickly type out a response.

> I'm over your shit, Grant. I'm done with you! You and I will never ever be together. Leave me alone, or I'm going to call the police. This is your only warning.

The second I hit Send, I open his contact and block him as an eerie chill settles deep in my bones.

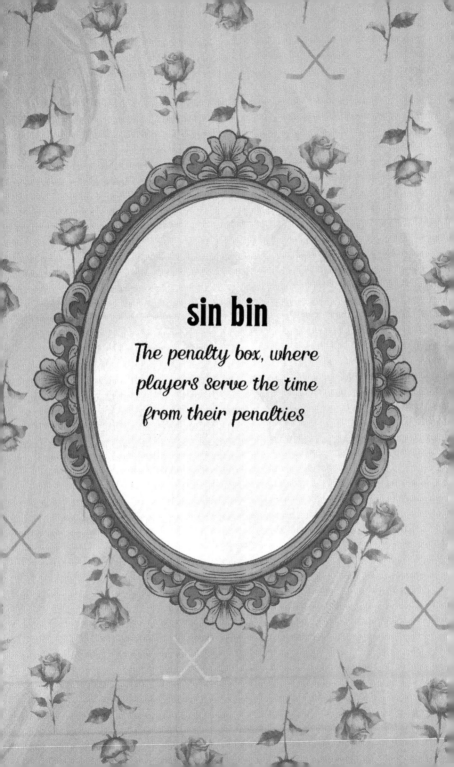

sin bin

*The penalty box, where
players serve the time
from their penalties*

chapter twenty-four
griffin

"Good morning, gorgeous," Lumi sings, handing Blair her usual cup of coffee from Cogsworth.

I was talking with Lumi the other day and gave him a gift card for the kiosk he always gets coffee from. I don't know what his financial situation looks like, but I never want him to struggle enough that he can't bring Blair her coffee. I would do that for her, but it's kind of their thing, and I don't want to impose. So, instead, I gave him a thousand-dollar gift card so that he wouldn't have to worry about it, and neither would I.

They fall into conversation about Paul as we walk down the cobblestones toward class.

"Hey." Blair bumps me with her shoulder as we enter the classroom. "You haven't asked me for a tutoring session lately."

Smiling, I look into the eyes of the reason why and tell her, "Because I don't need them anymore."

She squints her eyes at me and pinches her brows. "Really? Just like that?"

I chuckle. "Not quite. But in a way, yes. I found the root of my problems, and once that happened, everything sorted itself out."

"Huh … care to share more about your break-through?" she murmurs as more students file into class.

Reaching out, I tuck one of her loose, curly strands behind her ear. "One day. But it's because of you that I found it. I couldn't have done it without you."

Her cheeks burn, and she grins bashfully. "Well, that's because I'm an excellent tutor."

"You sure are." I lean down and kiss her forehead.

"Yuck. You lovebirds are giving me a cavity," Malik groans next to me and rubs his temples.

Smacking his hand, I scold him, "You remember what happened to the last guy who had shit to say about her?"

"What do you mean?" Blair asks.

Malik props his head in his hand and leans on his elbow on the desk, directing his full attention her way. But not before addressing me. "First off, I wasn't talking about her. I was referring to you mostly. The Beast seems more like a puppy dog nowadays."

I do my best to keep a straight face, but I can't, and I burst out laughing, along with Blair and Lumi.

He looks at Blair. "Secondly, you were at that game—the one where Griffin practically broke that guy's face. Well, that could be a few different games. But the last home game."

"That was about me?" she asks shyly, her eyes bulging.

Looking forward, I feel weirdly vulnerable at this

moment. I might have kicked that guy's ass right in front of her, but she probably thought it was just some hockey fight.

Malik scoffs, "Are you kidding? The only times I've seen him go completely ballistic are when it's about you. He might have earned his nickname, but he's a whole other monster when it comes to defending you."

Dr. Schrute clears his throat and starts talking to the class about today's lecture.

Blair leans over and whispers in my ear, "My hero."

Now, my cheeks are the ones burning.

After class, Blair and I decide to grab a quick bite to eat at the café before we part ways for the afternoon. I've got to review previous game tapes with our team and coaching staff. Then take the ice for practice for a couple of hours.

As we walk across the campus to the library, I slide my hand over hers, intertwining our fingers. "I heard some stuff about Grant."

Her grip tightens in mine. "What's that?"

"Levi, who's friends with a few of the football players, said that he hasn't been showing up to any classes or practices since our little altercation."

She tenses immediately. "Why?"

"I wish I had an answer for you, but I have no idea, and neither did Levi," I tell her, hating how rigid she has become since I brought him up.

"He's been AWOL," I say, debating on whether telling her was a good idea, but I will never deliberately keep something from her.

"That's … concerning," she murmurs, and I hate the trembling fear in her voice.

"At least he's disappearing," I sigh, hoping it stays that way. Swinging our connected hands between us, I change the subject. "I want to take you on a date."

She snaps her head up at me, grinning. "You do?"

Nodding, I chuckle at her surprise. "Yes, I do. Like a real date. We get dressed up, go out to dinner or a movie, or both."

She becomes giddy, her words joyful. "That sounds amazing. When?"

"Tomorrow night?" I offer, wanting at least a day to plan something nice out.

She steps inside the library, and I follow behind her. "It's a date."

"Good."

She leads us through the silent library, through sky-high shelves and endless titles, until we reach a cozy corner of the gigantic room. She drops her backpack onto the table before turning to me.

"See you after practice?"

"Yeah. Should be done around four, and then I'll come straight here," I tell her, wishing that time would slow down a bit whenever I'm with her.

She stretches up onto her tiptoes, and I lean down, closing the distance, and kiss her, pulling her tighter against me with a hand around her waist.

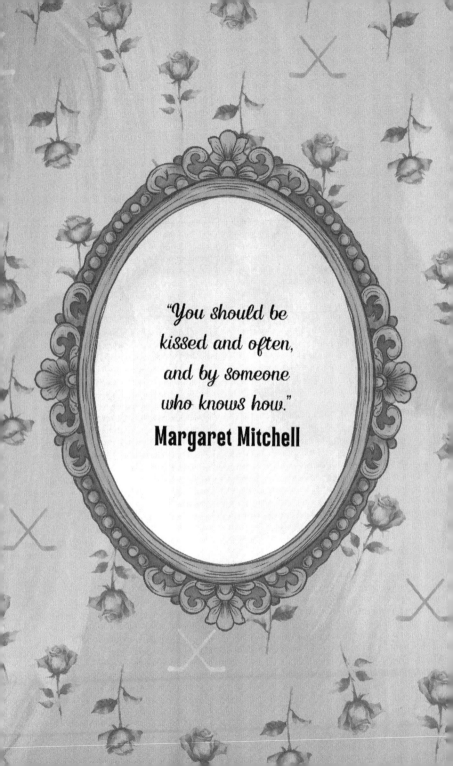

"You should be kissed and often, and by someone who knows how."

Margaret Mitchell

chapter twenty-five

blair

In a matter of three hours, I have finalized my English paper, which isn't due for another week; reviewed my notes from my Econ class; and finished all of my English homework. Griffin should be done in about an hour, so I want to try to create an outline for my History essay, which is due at the end of the week.

Standing out of my chair, I stretch my legs and pull my earbuds out, tucking them into their case before storing them in my bag.

I need to find a few books about the Civil War. This also means I need to figure out where the hell the History section is.

After finding the directory in the center of the room, I walk up the stairs to the second floor and find the shelves that house the books I need. I only have to have three references, and it shouldn't be hard to pull something from any of these.

After grabbing a few different ones, I carry my stack

back downstairs, but not before running into one of the librarians.

"Did you need help with anything, dear?" the kind blonde lady with soft green eyes asks me.

"I think I found everything I need." I smile at her before striding past.

That can be true about more than just these books. In a way, I found everything I need this semester. I found a way to pay for my dream school. I found a way to get Dad the treatment he desperately needs. But perhaps the most shocking discovery was that the one person I thought was just a cocky jock at the beginning of the year has become one of the most important people in my life, and I couldn't imagine not being by his side.

Who knew that HEAU would change my life in so many ways?

As I approach my desk, I page through one of my books, already bored by the reading material. I'm sure history books interest a particular group of people, but I am not part of that group.

When I look up from the book, my stomach falls to the floor, and the books tumble from my hand, crashing down. Every hair on my body stands on end as ice-cold shivers run from my head to my toes, chilling me to the bone.

Hesitantly, I take a step forward. My eyes burn as I see the photos sprawled atop my stuff. Photos that definitely weren't there when I left a few minutes ago. My throat ignites, and tears of fear form in my eyes as I study each image—shots of me outside of Griffin's house, at his hockey games, in my classes, walking on campus, and then the ones that rattle me to my core. Pictures of me in my bedroom of my old house, the one back in my hometown.

Pictures of me from different high school events from my senior year and even images of me here in Evermore before school started.

"Oh my God," I whisper and stammer backward, falling into a firm chest.

An arm snakes around my waist at the exact same time one slides over my mouth, stifling the scream tearing from my lungs. His lips hit my ear, and I shiver in disgust from his touch.

"Can't you see it? How perfect we are together? We're meant to be together, Blair. We always have been."

Run. Break free and run.

As much as I try to urge my body to move, I can't. I'm frozen in place in the arms of my nightmare.

"I'm going to remove my hand. Do not scream. Am I clear?" His voice is cold and calculated.

Nodding, I fight back the tears pooling in my eyes. Should I do what he said? Or should I shout and take off running? I know there's a librarian around here some-where, and there have to be other students too.

But faced with fight or flight, I apparently choose a third *F* option I never considered—failure.

He drops his hand, and I take a deep breath, wiping his touch from my mouth.

"You've always been mine, Blair Bear. These photos are proof of that. I've been in love with you since the first day I met you. But every time I tried to get close to you, you shut me out, not giving me a chance until our senior year. But we both know that didn't last long." His hand on my waist travels lower, his fingers slipping into the top of my skirt. "And then, by some miracle, I ran into you here and we got back together. I thought after spending a little more time with me, you'd realize what I'd always known—that we're soulmates."

I remain silent, rigid as stone, as he continues, "But then you had to go and ruin everything we'd built." His fingers dig into my skin, and I do my best not to react. His words are like knives. "Then, that damn hockey player got in the way. He distracted you, ruined you. You fucked up."

Shaking my head, I lie, doing anything I can to keep Grant under control, "It's nothing, and I'm sorry."

He scoffs, pressing his lips into my neck and kissing me. "Did you let him touch you, Blair?"

"N-no, never," I lie again.

"Hmm," he hums into my ear and sinks his hand further down my skirt. "He didn't touch you here?"

I have to change the topic and make him focus on something else. Slowly, I spin in his grasp, and he removes his hand, sending relief through me. But it's quickly replaced by terror when I meet his eyes.

How can I look into the eyes of a person I've known for years now, but I suddenly don't recognize them or the darkness dwelling inside? Was he good at hiding it? Did I pretend it simply wasn't there?

Maybe I've known all along that something wasn't quite right with Grant, and that's why I ignored him for as long as I did. I mean, I only started going out with him because it seemed like the right decision. He was cute and into me, and honestly, I was just tired of rejecting him. I thought maybe he was right that maybe we would be good together.

He was, in fact, *very* wrong.

"Why are you here, Grant?" I ask him, summoning the strength to reach up and caress his cheek.

"To remind you," he grunts before crashing his lips to mine, and I slam my eyes shut and try not to shove him away.

My body chills instantly, freezing me in place. I make no effort to kiss him back, but I don't pull away. I don't want to make him angrier than he already is.

He draws back and studies me carefully. "It doesn't feel like you mean it."

Silence consumes us as I stare up at him, anticipating his next move.

"Let's go," he snaps, twisting my arm as he walks away, dragging me along with him.

Digging my heels into the ground, I pull back. "What? I'm not going anywhere." He glares at me, and I add, "I have work to do. I'm not finished."

"Leave it. I'll come back and get it later," he says, yanking me forward again.

"I can't just leave my stuff here." My words fumble out of my mouth as my chest tightens and my lungs burn with fear.

He grabs my jaw in his grasp, squeezing hard. "I don't want to hurt you. I really don't. But you *are* coming with me whether you like it or not. I know the perfect place for us to rekindle what *you've* lost."

"Grant, are you out of your mind?" I snap, my words slicing into him as he winces from my tone.

His face falls and twists menacingly. "What did you just say?"

I'm over this. I'm over dealing with him and all of his

games. I'm over the anxiety coursing through my body every time my phone vibrates.

"You can't make me. You don't control me, Grant. I'm not your toy." I emphasize my words confidently and strongly, even if I don't fully feel that right now.

He huffs and slides his backpack off of him and reaches inside. "Well, if I can't persuade you, maybe this can."

As he pulls his hand from the backpack, my eyes lock on to the cold metal—a *gun.*

He hooks the straps on his other arm, holding the gun inside the thin fabric. "If you try to run, I will shoot you. If you scream and someone comes to help, I will shoot *them.* If you do as you're told, no one will get hurt. Okay?"

I whisper as the tears I've held back drop onto my cheeks. "Okay, I'll come with you. Will you tell me where we're going?"

The hope I felt a moment ago vanishes, and I know I only have one choice. If he has gone this mad, this deep into his fantasy, I don't know what he will and won't do, and I don't want to find out what will happen if I tell him no again.

If I play into his wants, he'll relax, get comfortable, and eventually slip up. Then, I'll make my move. But I can't let anyone else get hurt. I won't. I'll wait until we're alone, even if the thought of it churns my stomach.

"The place where we first kissed after we got back together," he whispers, his lips pressed against my ear. "Oh, don't cry. We haven't even gotten to the happiest part yet."

Sniffling, I wipe away the wetness on my cheeks as he

leans his forehead against mine and presses the gun firmly against my stomach. "Tell me you love me."

No.

"I l-lo—" The words fall silent from my lips, and he digs the barrel harder into me.

"Say it like you mean it, Blair Bear, or it doesn't count," he growls.

Closing my eyes, I picture the only person I can imagine saying it to. An image of soft brown hair falling over his hazel eyes warms me, giving me the facade I need to pull this off.

Griffin, "I love you."

He grins and presses his lips against mine. "That was good, almost believable. Now, move."

"Grant, please," I beg one last time, leaning away from him.

He grabs my hair and yanks hard. "Blair, move your sexy little legs before I put a bullet into one of them. I'll be forced to carry you, but at least then you won't be able to run."

Oh my God.

He jerks my hair once more, and my hair falls free from the bow holding it in place. He releases me and brings his hand between us. My black bow is in his hand, crinkled from his fist.

He turns his hand over and opens it, and the ribbon falls, crashing to the floor. "I've always hated these."

michigan

A Michigan is a lacrosse style goal where the player picks the puck up on their stick, skates around the back of the net, and throws it into the net to score.

chapter twenty-six
griffin

"I think you're getting soft, Griff." Dean laughs and skates into me. "You haven't threatened any of us today."

Smiling, I consider showing exactly how wrong he is, but I choose to show him mercy instead. "Just distracted."

"With what?" Malik asks, skating up behind me and slapping my ass with his stick.

Rolling my eyes, I don't even want to say it because I know he's just going to give me shit for it, but I do it anyway. "Blair. I'm taking her out tomorrow, and I want it to be perfect."

"I think it's nice you have something so strong," Asher says, joining our circle.

"Thank you, Asher. At least someone thinks so." I laugh, glaring at Malik.

He holds his hands up in defense. "Look, I lo-lo—oh my God, I can't even say it. I *like* that you seem happier than I've ever seen you. Seriously, I *am* happy for you, but that doesn't mean I won't make fun of you for it the entire time either. I do it out of l-lo-lo—."

The guys burst out laughing, and I can't resist joining in. That was quite the dramatic moment, even for our resident drama king.

"Oh, come on, Malik. You've never been in love?" Asher jabs him in the chest with the hilt of his twig.

Malik shudders and looks away from us with an indiscernible gleam in his eyes. "Yeah, no. Definitely not."

"You just haven't met the right girl," Asher tries to salvage Malik's view of the L-word, but fails.

He laughs hauntingly. "I doubt that's the problem."

Coach blows his whistle, saving Malik from the spotlight. He's the first to skate away, and we follow, heading to where Coach stands on center ice.

"Great work today, boys." He claps his hands once. "In return for your hard work and effort today, I'm cutting you loose early. Enjoy the extra"—he checks his watch— "twenty-six minutes of freedom."

Some of the guys voice their excitement as he lifts his hand in the air. "Legends on three. One. Two. Three."

"Legends!"

Rarely does a practice end early. If anything, we are usually on the ice way longer than planned. But that's what you have to do to be the best.

We head to the locker room, and I take a quick shower, racing through my motions, itching to see Blair. I have no idea how she spends hours upon hours in her studies and then spends even more time buried in a book she's reading just for fun. But it's one of the things I love about her.

She's happy within the pages of a story, content to fill her time with the things she loves. She's independent and confident.

I get dressed and leave most of my shit in my locker, aside from my wallet, keys, and phone, before leaving the arena and heading to the library.

My steps slow as I pass by one of the campus shops, Happily Ever After Floral. Maybe I should stop and get some flowers to surprise her. More than anything, I just want to see that smile of hers. The one that makes my knees weak and heart soar.

Making a quick detour, I walk into the flower shop and purchase a dozen red roses—her favorite. I wonder if she's put it together yet—that all her favorite things keep magically showing up in the house.

It wasn't a coincidence that I made chocolate chip muffins for her. Personally, blueberry muffins are my first choice.

It wasn't a weird coincidence that red roses began decorating all of the tables in the house, including her nightstand and bathroom. It's because I order them in bulk and fill the vases before she wakes.

I snuck into her room one night when she was in the shower and snooped. It might have been a bit immature to rifle through her things, but I wanted to learn more about her without coming on too strong. That was back when we still pretended not to be into each other and to follow the *just tutor and student* guidelines we'd set. I found a questionnaire, the same one she pawned off as extra credit to me, and I took pictures of her answers and studied them thoroughly. Thankfully, she filled it out to help with the layout for her final project.

With the bouquet in hand, I walk through the library and try remembering the path she led me down earlier. Eventually, I manage to find the corner she set up in, spotting it across the walkway between shelves.

Her chair is empty, but I'm sure she's just off, grabbing more books to add to her piles. My heart pumps hard as I approach the table, eager to see her reaction to my little gift.

"What the fuck?"

Setting the roses down on the hardwood table, I pick up one of the pictures of Blair. It's of her in that silk red dress the night we hosted dinner. She's by herself, leaning over the gold railing on the stairs outside my house.

Dropping it, I grab another and another, panic building in my chest and spreading like wildfire through my body, cutting oxygen off to my lungs. My concern snaps into fear as I realize exactly what I'm looking at.

He was at my house, watching her.

Grant isn't just some guy who won't move on. He's fucking stalking her.

Ripping my phone out of my pocket, I immediately call Blair.

After the first ring, a vibration hums on the desk, and my heart drops.

Lumi. I'll call him. Maybe she called him, and they're together, and Grant put these here after she left. Although I know she wouldn't have left all of her stuff behind. But I hold on to the delusion because it's the only thing keeping me together.

Lumi answers on the first ring. "Hey, what's up?"

"Is she with you?" I ask desperately, praying he says yes.

"Blair? No, she said she would be at the library all afternoon. Why—"

I cut him off. There's no time. "Yeah, I'm here at the library. But she's not. And her stuff is covered in creepy fucking pictures that only Grant could have taken. I think he did something, took her—I don't know! But I'm going to kill him when I get my hands on him."

My chest feels like it's cracking open at the thought of her trapped with him.

"I'm at Paul's in the dorms. I'll be there in two minutes."

I hang up and shove my phone into my pocket. I can't wait for him to get here. I need to find her.

"Fuck!" I scream and thread my fingers through my hair. "Think, think! Where would she be? Where would he take her?" I rack my brain, trying to answer my own questions, but I only draw blanks.

I pace back and forth in front of the desk, then ram to a halt as I spot a black ribbon on the floor—her bow.

Picking it up, I cradle it in my hands, pressing it against my lips. *Where are you, baby?*

Tucking the bow gently in my pocket, I remember that Grant's a football player. I take off running, racing out of the library to the field.

I'm going to break every bone in his fucking body. Oh God, she's probably so scared right now. My heart shatters in my chest, and my eyes burn as I close the distance to the field, glad to find that the team is still practicing.

As I rush onto the green, straight in the middle of their play, I start shouting, not giving a single fuck about ruining whatever they're doing.

"Grant Gustavson! Where is he?" I belt out, addressing anybody within earshot.

"Hey!" one of the coaches shouts and runs toward us, but I ignore him.

"You," I growl, recognizing the red-haired kid usually attached to Grant's hip. Grabbing his collar, I lift him up and yell, "Where is he? Where is Grant?"

He cries out, "How would I know? I haven't talked to him in days! Put me down!"

Getting in his face, I sneer my words through my bared teeth. "Do you like playing football? Because if you don't answer me right now, I'm going to make damn sure you won't ever again. He took her. Now, tell me!"

"Hey, let him go!" One of the other football players charges up to me, but the second I look down at him, he plants his feet on the turf and tucks his tail.

"For fuck's sake, Felix, tell him already!" one of the others shouts.

"I don't know, okay?! I would have told someone if I had known he was planning something like that!" He holds his hands up.

Lowering him to the ground, I grab him by the arm. "Where would he take her? Does he have a house? A dorm? You have three seconds before I shatter every bone in your arm."

"Someone stop him! Why are none of you doing anything?" he sobs, looking around at his team.

"Are you kidding me? I've seen what he can do on

skates on slippery ice. I'm not willing to find out what damage he can do on solid ground," someone scoffs.

"Three. Two. One." Tightening my grip, I lift his arm up, and he stops me.

"Wait! Wait! Wait! He has a place he likes to go when he needs to clear his head." He hesitates, thinking. "A tower? A tower with a bell? I've never been there, but he's mentioned that place when talking about Blair before!"

I can see it in my mind, smack dab in the middle of campus. I hear it every day at noon, yet I've never given it a second thought before.

Grabbing him by the throat, I feel the group close tighter around us, but I don't acknowledge them. "If you're lying, I will be back for you. I promise."

Dropping him, I push through the players and take off sprinting, pounding my feet into the ground, willing them, praying for them to move faster.

The second I hit cobblestone, I know I'm getting close. The stone will eventually lead me to the tower.

My throat thickens, and my ears ring.

I can't lose her. I can't fucking live without her. I should've told her I loved her; I shouldn't have held back. But I was so goddamn scared.

After my family died, I sealed myself off from the world. I don't know how or when she broke through every wall I'd built up over the years, but I do know one thing. She's invaded me, heart and soul.

Above the hedges, I spot the bell, hanging still in the air.

My legs and lungs burn, but I don't slow down. Digging into a reserve I didn't know existed, I race down the path, turning right at the opening, and within seconds, I close the twenty feet to the tower.

Throwing open the wooden arched door, I take the first step onto the wooden stairs and call out, "Blair!"

"Gr—" Her voice is muffled, but it's all the strength I need to fuel the fire scorching inside of me.

Taking the steps two at a time, I circle round and round, flying as fast as I can. The stairs come to an end on my last turn, and Blair comes into view. The bell blocks most of her body.

My breath catches, and my knees threaten to give out on me. She gasps when she meets my eyes, heaving and sobbing. Her scrunched face is streaked with makeup and tears.

Pushing myself further onto the platform, I finally see Grant, standing behind her to her left.

I can't breathe. I can't think. I can't—

Images of Blair smiling in my arms flash in my mind. I can hear her laughter in my ears. This is my fault. All of this is my fault.

My brother's innocent stare joins Blair's, then my mother's and father's, and tears spring to my eyes. It's my fault Gavin's gone. It's my fault my parents are gone. Everything bad happening is *my* fault.

If I had never asked her to be my tutor, I never would have gotten her fired, and she never would've moved in with me. If I had stayed in my mansion, hiding my heart from the world, the girl I love wouldn't have a gun aimed at her head.

"Grant, *please* let her go." My words shake with fear, vibrating from the spasming of my chest.

He sniffles, and I realize he's crying too. "Why would I do that? I have her right where I want her."

Focusing all my strength on my legs, I force my right foot to step forward. "Let me take her place. Please."

Blair's sobs, mixed with my agony, fill the tower, bouncing off of the bell and resonating around us.

"See, Blair?" He runs his hand over her hair. "Loving you is a dangerous thing. You make us insane, make us willing to do crazy things just to keep you to ourselves." Grant wipes his tears and snot away with his sleeve as his downturned glare lands on me. "Tell him you hate him, Blair."

Her bottom lip trembles, and she shakes her head from side to side. I will make him pay for what he's doing to her.

He moves the gun to the side of her head and yells, "Tell him! Tell him now!"

"N-n-no," she murmurs, and the shattered pieces of my heart cut into my lungs, releasing all of my air.

Please don't hurt her.

"Ahh!" he grunts. "Always so goddamn stubborn!"

His face twists with anger, and he tightens his hand on his gun before pulling it away from her and pointing it straight at me. I've never felt more content, knowing if he pulls that trigger right now, it's not her being shot. She'll be able to use it as a distraction and run.

He wraps his arm around her neck, pinning her against his chest. "Blair, I swear to God, if you don't tell him how much you hate him right now, I am going to put a bullet in his head."

Forming an O with my mouth, I breathe in deeply,

showing her to do the same, and she follows my lead, taking in a quivering breath.

"Tell me," I say softly, holding her bloodshot stare. "It's okay. Tell me you hate me."

She forces that breath through her nose and inhales again. Her gaze softens as she looks at me the same way she did when I first kissed her. She parts her lips, and I anticipate the three words that will hit me like a punch to the gut.

But she takes a breath and stutters, "G-Griffin." The pain in her voice slices me to the core. "I love you."

Time freezes, the world around us spinning to a halt.

Grant repeatedly yells, "No," and lets out a guttural scream.

Blair looks away from me, focusing her attention on the weapon in his hand, and I see her plan play out in my mind seconds before it happens.

"Ahh!" Grant shrieks and pulls the trigger, but I'm already crouching down and moving toward them at the same time Blair strikes his arm, pushing the trajectory of the bullet straight at the bell.

The round strikes it and deafens us, ringing louder than my ears can bear. Blair elbows him in the ribs, and he hunches over from the blow, loosening his hand on the gun.

Lunging forward, I smack it out of his hand. It goes flying over the short stone wall—the only divider between the platform and a twenty-foot fall to the ground below.

Grabbing Blair, I move her behind me, tucking her safely out of his reach. "Go! Get out of here!"

"You can't have her!" Grant growls and takes advantage of my distraction, crashing his knuckles into my jaw.

"You hit like a bitch," I ground out, grabbing him by the throat.

He smacks my face with a half-clenched fist. He should know me better than that for how much he's been watching us. He won't beat me hand to hand. For fuck's sake, I take punches and give them for a living.

Adrenaline pumps through my veins, and I rear back, releasing my fist like a spring. It finds its target, a gnarly cracking sound erupting as I shatter his nose.

Reaching down, I grab his arm and twist it, fighting it past its breaking point. I snap it in two, and he shrieks in agony.

"I refuse to let her be loved by The Beast," Grant spits out.

"Get it through that thick skull. Underestimating me would be a grave mistake," I challenge him further, my words declaring what I will do to him if he continues.

Sirens wail in the distance, and I release his throat, keeping his arm tightly in my grasp.

"Let me go!" he grunts and tugs hard, leaning back and hurting himself more than I am.

Drawing his arm back, he lunges forward, punching me in the ribs, and I groan.

"We're done playing your games." I shove him hard, and he tumbles backward, bumping into the wall.

"Not until I say so," he grits through his teeth and takes off after me, but I step to the side and move out of the way.

He doesn't anticipate my move as he charges. He trips and flies forward, crashing into the stone barrier headfirst.

He gets to his feet immediately as I step near him, readying myself for his next attack. But it never comes. He grabs his head, now pooling with blood, and wobbles back and forth on his feet. I'm too late when I see what's coming.

He teeters back, losing his balance, and flips over the stone barrier.

He screams out as he falls.

People shout and cry out as he seems to free-fall through the air forever until he crashes to the ground, sounds of cracking bone singing into the air. Rushing over to the edge, I peer at the scene below.

He's still conscious, and his screams haven't stopped; if anything, they've grown louder. Grant's upper body lies on a bush that seems to have softened the impact of his fall. His lower body didn't have the same luck. His legs are twisted, bent into unnatural positions, bones sticking through his pants. Blood decorates the cobblestones beneath him.

"Griffin!" Blair calls out, and I hear her feet slapping against the wood as she soars up the staircase.

"Blair!" I answer her call and race over to the top of the stairs as she pushes off of the final one. "Thank God," I whimper and lift her into my arms the second she reaches me before carefully lowering her back down.

"Are you hurt?" I ask her, pulling away and studying every inch of her for possible injuries.

She shakes her head.

"Did … did he touch you?" The words are poison in my mouth.

Her bottom lip quivers, and she nods. My vision spots with pure fury. I should have shoved him over the edge myself.

My eyes well up as I pull her into me, wrapping my arms around her. She lays her head on my chest, and guilt wraps itself around me like a snake squeezing its prey to death.

"I'm so sorry …" I whisper to her, kissing the top of her head.

She lifts her head up and stares at me with absolute confusion. Confusion burrows into the crease of her brows and frown of her lips. "What do you mean? You came for me and saved me from him."

"Yeah, almost too late." I sniffle, my chest contracting at the thought of what could have happened if we hadn't gotten out of practice early. "I don't know what I'd do without you, baby."

She looks up at me and confidently says, "Good thing you never have to find out."

She stretches onto the tips of her toes, and I lean down.

Closing my eyes, I wait for her kiss, but she presses her lips against my cheeks, one and then the other.

Malik's voice slices through the moment. "Don't attack me!"

He climbs the last few stairs and bends over, placing his hands on his knees, gasping for air.

Blair bursts out laughing at him, and it's so contagious

that I can't help but laugh along with her. But I'm more confused about what the hell he's doing here.

"How did you find me?" I ask him.

He stands up, his face scrunched with exhaustion. "I saw you hauling ass across campus, so I chased after you. Eventually, I got lost, but then I heard screaming, found the gross little accident outside, ran up all of those stairs, and now, I'm here—here to help."

His ramble brings a smile to my face, and I release Blair long enough to pull Malik into an embrace. "Thank you, *seriously*."

He hugs me back. "Ehh, don't mention it. You'd do the same for me."

He's right. I would. He's my best friend, and I'd do anything for him.

Nodding my head, I communicate that through my stare, and he reads it clear as day, nodding back at me.

Pulling out of our embrace, I wrap my arm around Blair and pull her into my side.

We should sort out whatever we need to do downstairs so we can start putting all of this behind us.

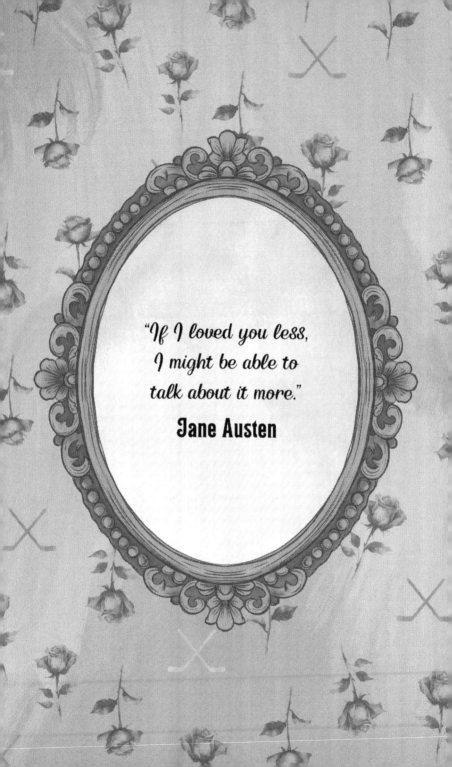

"*If I loved you less, I might be able to talk about it more.*"

Jane Austen

chapter twenty-seven
blair

The aftermath of Grant's attack has been blowing over rather fast. In the two days since he fell from the tower, he's been expelled from HEAU for having a gun on school property, among other obvious reasons. He's also facing criminal charges, including threatening me and others with his firearm, attempted kidnapping, and more. He's facing some serious time, and there's not much he can do to dispute it. The campus is covered in cameras, including everything that happened in the tower.

As far as I know, he's still in the hospital, being treated for his fall. At least this is all finally over. I don't think he'll mess with us again. Griffin says I should get a restraining order against him, and I agree, wanting some kind of rule carved in law that he can't be near me ever again.

I was supposed to be leaving to visit my dad today, but I decided to postpone it for a week in light of what had happened. I filled him in on everything, and he agreed, wanting me to come only after I've decompressed from the situation. He also said I shouldn't leave the area until Grant's legal stuff is finalized, just in case they have any questions or need me to come in for anything.

We have our last English class of the semester today, and I have bittersweet feelings about it. This class changed my life—or at the least, it brought me the one person who did.

"I wish you had let me look over your paper before you turned it in," I say to Griffin as we walk out of this class for the last time.

He slides his hand in mine. "No need. It's perfect."

I chuckle. "Perfect, huh?"

Walking across the cobblestone bricks, we begin making our way to the parking lot Griffin's truck is parked in.

"Oh, yeah. Definitely," he claims.

Nerves dance across my back. "Can I read it?"

His thumb brushes my hand as he stays silent.

"It's okay. I don't need to," I assure him.

As much as I want to read more about his past, present, and ideal future, I don't want to pressure him to open up about it until he's ready. I can wait.

"I want to show you something first," he says, opening my door for me and giving me his hand to help me into his truck.

It takes a lot of restraint not to pepper him with questions when he gets inside. He grabs my hand and brings it to his lips as he starts the truck.

"How do you think you did on the final?" he asks.

Quoting him from earlier, I answer honestly, "*Perfect.*"

He smirks and mocks me, "Really? That's quite an assumption."

With a straight face, I say, "Not an assumption at all. It's just a fact."

He laughs. "O-okay, I can't wait to see it."

"Let me paint the picture for you." I grin. "It will look like one hundred percent."

"So descriptive." He snickers.

We fall into a conversation about his upcoming game against the Minotaurs for the rest of the ride home. He tells me how they are one of the only other teams that rivals their success and has a chance at beating them, breaking their winning streak.

I suppose at the beginning of our agreement, when he wanted to teach me about hockey, he got his wish. Because I am actually starting to understand the jargon when the guys are talking, and it doesn't completely sound like a foreign language.

When we walk inside the house, I remember he has something to show me. Dropping my backpack on the couch, I sit on top of it and fall backward onto the pillows.

"What are you doing?" Griffin laughs and walks over to me, smiling.

I stretch my hands toward him, and he grabs them and gently lifts me, helping me up.

"Come on," he murmurs, his face falling and eyes glossing over as he threads his fingers in mine.

What's wrong?

He leads me up the marble stairs, and as we hit the

landing, I veer left toward the east wing, but he stops me, redirecting me in the opposite direction. My heart leaps into my throat as we climb the stairs to the west wing.

He turns the knob and pushes the door open. "I want to tell you about them. I don't want to push them out of my mind and try to forget. I want to remember them. They deserve that."

My chest clenches, and my eyes burn at his confession. I brush my thumb back and forth on his hand, reminding him I'm right here as we step through the threshold into the past.

He takes a shuddering breath. "Gavin was the brightest kid, and he was always happy."

He opens Gavin's door, and we walk inside. I look at the room with a different understanding than I did before.

"He was just starting hockey, and he was a fucking natural, way better than I was at that age." He chuckles darkly and slams his eyes shut. "Fuck!"

Spinning in front of him, I place my hand on his chest and look up into his haunted eyes. "It's okay. I'm right here."

He brushes my cheek. "You can't argue that they never would have been in the car that night if it wasn't for me being a stupid kid."

"I'm so sorry for what happened, Griffin, but you have to find a way to forgive yourself, or part of you will always remain in here behind those double doors," I whisper and press a kiss into his chest.

A tear falls off of his lashes, rolling down his cheek. "Gavin was all of the goodness in life, as were my parents."

"As are you," I add.

He huffs through his nose, fighting the sorrow from breaking free. Without a word, he leads us out of Gavin's room and down the hall to his parents.

"I couldn't bring myself to touch or move any of their things," he admits, searching the room intently. His eyes gloss over, and I imagine he's remembering moments spent here when they were still alive. "My room was at the end of this hall. After the accident, I moved my stuff, closed this wing off, and never returned"—he looks at me —"until today."

"I'm sorry," I murmur, "for coming here without you. I'm sorry."

He smiles, but it never reaches his eyes. "It's okay. I'm thankful you did."

"You are?" My voice is barely audible.

He nods. "If it wasn't for you, I might have gone even more years without stepping foot in here. You helped me realize that I don't want to forget them. The pain I feel in their absence reminds me of how much I love them."

"That's beautiful," I murmur, wiping my tears away. "I'm proud of you. They would be too."

His nostrils flare, and his brows lift. "They would have loved you."

My chest cracks at his words, and I cup his jaw. Leaning into my touch, he drops his head far enough for me to stretch up and rest my forehead against his.

"I love you," I whisper against his lips.

At my words, his eyes widen and soften, those gold flecks dancing in his enchanting gaze. He takes a shaky breath and exhales with every word. "I love you too."

We spend the entire afternoon in the west wing. He tells me stories, both good and bad, about his family. He tells me of the time he and Gavin filled up water balloons and attacked their parents with them *inside* of the house. He laughs as he tells me how he and Gavin started pranking their parents and that he only did it to see how excited Gavin got when they pulled them off.

He tells me how much his parents loved one another and always displayed their affection proudly. And how his dad used to wake up on Sunday mornings and make his mom breakfast in bed.

I listen for hours as he opens himself up to the past, sharing those intimate memories with me.

Eventually, Mrs. Potts finds us. She walks into his parents' bedroom and sees us sitting on the floor. Her face instantly brightens, and her eyes well with tears.

The way she looks at Griffin is one of pure love, like a mother to a son, and I'm so happy he's had her by his side over the years.

"Dinner's ready," she says, and my jaw nearly drops at the fact that we've been sitting here for nearly six hours.

Griffin gets to his feet and holds his hands out for me, and I take them. Mrs. Potts dismisses herself and heads back downstairs.

"Can we come back?" I ask Griffin as we wander out of the room and down the hallway.

He smiles. "I'd like that."

After dinner, Griffin and I decide to watch a movie in the living room. He grabs cozy blankets and puts on *Sleeping Beauty*. Rex decides to join us and nestles in his dog bed in front of the TV. Mrs. Potts and Chip went out to the theater to see a new movie.

A question that's been lingering on my tongue slips past my lips. "What are we going to do about our deal now?"

He lifts his arm, and I scoot over to his side.

He wraps his arm around me. "What do you mean?"

"Well, our tutoring arrangement was only until the end of the semester, which is nearly over," I admit, a playful formality in my tone.

His face lightens with humor. "Oh, so this was strictly business for you, huh? Now, it's time to move on and leave your post?"

Biting back my smile, I say, "As you can see, I did an excellent job. I think it's only fair if I open my expertise up to other students. After all, you once said it would be a shame for me not to tutor with how great my grades are."

He turns his head, looks at me, and squints. "Oh, really? Now you're agreeing with me?" He stills before striking, moving me onto the couch and laying me down with his hands, his heated stare pinning me in place. "I have a new deal I would like to propose."

Giggling, I ask, "What's that?"

His hair falls onto his forehead as he leans down and steals a kiss. "You stay right where you are and never leave."

Rolling my eyes, I grin. "And what? You expect tutoring sessions for free now that we're together?"

"Of course not. I'll just pay you in more than cash," he whispers, pressing his lips against my jaw.

"I will need to get an actual job at some point to put some extra money in my pocket. I'm not letting you pay for everything," I groan.

Now, he rolls his eyes. "Do you still have that card I gave you?"

I nod.

"There's two hundred thousand dollars in that account. There's your extra money."

Cocking my head to the side, I protest while trying to keep my jaw off of the floor. "First off, that's insane. Secondly, I'm being serious."

"So am I." He doesn't hesitate. "Really, Blair. I don't want you to worry about anything besides school. I have more than enough to share, and I want to share it with you. What's mine is yours."

I'll probably fight him on this later because taking money and gifts has never been my strong suit, especially when it's something I would never be able to reciprocate. But I think he might wear me down because gift-giving seems to be one of his love languages.

"And after school? Will our deal change?" I ask him.

He smirks. "Definitely." He leans down and kisses me tenderly. "Then, I'm going to marry you."

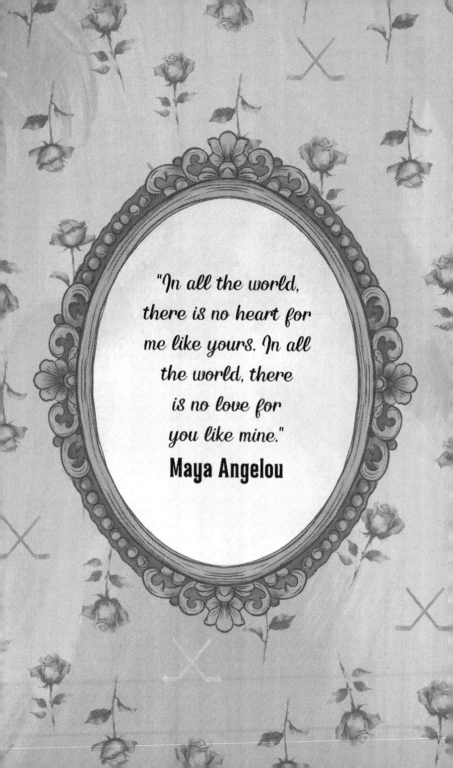

Epilogue

griffin

Blair and Lumi are on their way back from the airport, and I'm already a nervous wreck. They have been gone for four days on a trip to visit Lumi's family. Blair begged me to go with them, and it killed me to say no, but I had to be here to ensure the remodel went smoothly. On top of that, I have practice.

My phone buzzes, and I check it and find a text from Lumi.

> Lumi: We are two minutes out.

"Take a deep breath. You look like you are going to pass out. She's going to love it." Mrs. Potts walks up behind me and pats my shoulder.

Sighing, I run my hand down my face. I hope she's right. I'm so happy that Mrs. Potts and Chip are part of my life. Who knows how I would have ended up if it wasn't for them? They are the glue that kept me together all these years.

I get another text from Lumi and roll my eyes at his message.

Lumi: Pulling into Hawthorne Manor now.

Grabbing the dozen roses off of the counter, I head to greet them. Fuck, I've missed her so much. I know it's only been a few days, but now that I know how life is with her, I dread the days without her.

When I open the front door, a running bundle of energy barrels up the stairs with a shit-eating grin on her face. Gliding down the stairs, I meet her halfway, and she jumps, wrapping herself around my waist.

"Hi!" she sings.

I catch her, strategically shifting the roses to the side so we don't smash them between us.

"Happy birthday, baby," I murmur and lean forward, kissing her soft, supple lips. "How was your trip?"

"*Amazing*. I have so many pictures to show you," she rambles as I carry her up the steps and inside.

Lowering her to her feet, I hand her the bouquet, and she blushes red, like the delicate flowers.

"You didn't have to get me anything." She flicks her eyes up to mine before inhaling the floral aroma deeply.

Without saying another word, I bend down and grab her around the waist, hauling her over my shoulder. Nostalgia smacks me, reminding me of the last time I threw her over my shoulder like this—the night at the club.

She squeals, "Griffin! What are you doing?"

I palm her ass over her leggings. "I have something to show you."

She wiggles, trying to break free as I carry her across the house to the old rec room.

"I couldn't have walked?" She laughs.

Shrugging, I smile. "Yeah, you definitely could have. But that's not nearly as fun."

"Mmhmm, I bet."

Sliding her down my body, I lower her to the ground. "Turn around and close your eyes."

"Why?" she protests, her stubbornness getting the better of her.

I can't contain this secret a second longer. Wrapping my hand around her face, I cover her eyes and open the door in front of us before guiding her inside.

God, I did a damn good job, designing this.

Kicking the door shut, I take a deep breath and kiss the top of her head. "Happy birthday, beautiful."

As I slide my hand away from her face, her gasps fill the space, bouncing up the forty-foot-tall walls of her brand-new library and circling the dainty crystals dangling from the giant chandelier before falling back to our ears.

The circular tower room is covered with floor-to-ceiling bookshelves with windows scattered along the far wall amid the shelves, filling the room with natural light. I took the pleasure of stocking a few of them with some of her favorite books, including a few I also picked out for her. I left the others empty because I wanted her to fill it with what she wanted.

When I glance at her, my heart constricts. Her smile takes over her face, and her eyes are filled with tears as she takes everything in.

In the smack-dab center of the room is an oversize white wooden desk with a vase full of two dozen long-stemmed red roses. I've already scheduled with the campus floral shop to have fresh ones delivered every week and a half so they never seem to die and the petals never fall.

"Griffin ..." she breathes out. "Y-you did this?"

Stepping behind her, I pull her against my chest, forming my body around hers—a perfect fit.

"Did I physically do this? No."

She playfully slaps my hand. "Stop undermining your-self." She spins in my grasp and holds my stare. Her voice is soft and airy. "This is for me?"

Brushing her hair out of her face, I bite down on my lip and nod.

"You're amazing." She snakes her arms around my neck and pulls me down, crashing her lips into mine.

Her tongue plunges into my mouth, and I groan into hers. She slides one of her hands into my hair, digging her fingernails into my skin with the other, and the slight bite sends jolts of pleasure straight to my dick.

Slowly, I ease back from her, not wanting to ruin the sweet moment. But she has other plans. She pulls me forward, sealing our kiss again.

Fucking hell.

Gliding my hands down and over her ass, I lift her up and set her down on her new desk. She draws away, only long enough to outline my jaw with her tongue before trailing her lips down my neck.

"Blair," I pant out.

She smirks. "Yes?"

"What are you doing?" I beg.

She holds my stare as she sassily murmurs, "Is this not part of my present?"

Tilting my head back, I try to find an ounce of restraint, but I'm a goner the second she leans forward and grabs me through my sweats.

It's her birthday after all, and she should get what she wants.

I grab her jaw and kiss her, plunging my tongue into her mouth and reveling in the taste of her. We become a tangle of desperate desire and need, fighting for control with each caress.

"Fuck me," she whimpers into my mouth, and my eyes disappear into the back of my head. "Right now."

Nodding, I shove my tongue back into her mouth while grabbing the bottom of her shirt and ripping it off of her, quickly followed by a sexy red bra.

Dropping to my knees, I scoot to the edge of the desk and suck her nipple into my mouth, tugging at it gently with my teeth. She cries out, and I do it again before worshipping her other one.

Digging my fingers in the waistband of her leggings, I order her to, "Lift your hips."

She listens, and I slide them down her legs, dropping them on top of her bra and shirt on the floor beside me. I bury my face in her pussy, breathing her in before running my tongue across her matching panties. As I grab the thin material, she lifts her ass, and I yank them off of her smooth legs.

"Fuck, you're so goddamn perfect," I growl, grabbing her face and licking her lips. "I'll never get enough of you."

She smirks, and a devilish gleam shimmers in her eyes. "*Good*."

I pull my shirt over my head and drop my sweats, letting my rock-hard erection spring free. "Turn around and put your hands on the desk."

She gulps and hops off of the white wood as she flushes red. Turning around and reaching her arms forward, she holds herself up on the desk.

"Holy fuck. I wish you could see how good you look right now." I fist my cock, pumping myself from base to tip.

She wiggles her hips from side to side. I slap my dick against her ass, and her back arches, exposing that perfect, dripping cunt. Flipping her hair over to one side, she looks back at me nervously.

"Let's see how wet you are," I murmur, sliding my hand between her legs. "Soaking wet already?"

She nods and bites down on her lip.

Using my foot, I spread her legs apart and thrust my cock through her wetness, coating myself in her arousal.

"Are you ready?" I ask her, not wanting to push her to take my length without our usual foreplay.

I would drag this out, but we don't have time. This isn't the only surprise of the day.

She moans, "Yes, *please*, I'm begging you."

Gripping her hip, I pull back enough to line myself up

with her entrance before pushing the tip inside. She clenches around me, and I run my fingers up and down her back, not moving until I feel her relax around me.

"There you go," I whisper and inch deeper inside of her.

"God, you're so fucking big," she whimpers, and my dick twitches in response.

Reaching around her hip, I find her clit, and my fingers massage it in circles. Her head falls forward, and she fills the room with her cries for more, and I give it to her.

She rears back against me, filling herself up and riding me slowly, and it's fucking heaven.

"Take what you want, baby," I continue to rub her center as she stretches out around me, taking me deeper inside of her with each roll of her hips.

She speeds up, riding me faster and faster, and I can barely keep myself standing from the sensations rocking through my body.

"Oh fuck, that feels sooo good," I groan, readying to take control. I'm not going to last much longer at this rate, and I need to make sure she comes. "Now, it's my turn."

Grabbing onto both of her hips, I bottom out inside of her, feeling my balls slap against her, nearly sending me into a spiral.

"Oh! Griffin!" she screams out, and I reach around and cover her mouth with my hand, pulling her flush against me, wanting to feel the vibrations of her cries. "You're so deep right now!"

"And you're doing such a good fucking job taking it," I praise her as I rear back until just my tip remains and slam back inside of her, over and over, until her body gives out to my every desire.

Lowering my hand to her throat, I pull her against me, her back arching as I continue to pound into her pussy.

Holding her against my chest, I glide my other hand down her stomach and find that bundle of nerves that will send her over the edge. She looks up at me with hooded eyes and blown pupils, grunting and moaning incoherently.

I feel her clench around me, and I know she's close. So am I. My balls tighten as I wait for her to fall into oblivion first.

"Oh God, Griffin! I'm going to—oh fuck!" she cries out, her pussy clenching around me as her orgasm tears through her, and that's all it takes to send me over the fucking edge.

"Fuuuck," I pull her tighter against me as I empty every drop of my love into her.

Sliding out of her, I grab my shirt off of the floor and wipe between her thighs, cleaning her up before doing the same to myself and slipping my sweats back on. I know I'm running out of time, trying to keep her all to myself.

"Why are you in such a hurry?" she asks, looking up at me with downturned eyes.

Reassuring her, I rush over and rub my hands up and down her arms. "Because this was just the beginning of your birthday surprises I have planned."

She softens immediately, and in her eyes, I watch as she fights back the protest to tell me I don't need to do anything else. But at least she's learning that I'm going to spoil her cute little ass, no matter what, and telling me not to does little to dissuade me. Because the truth is, she's the greatest thing that's ever happened to me, and I'm not going to let a day go by that I don't remind her just how remarkable she is. Whether it be by my words, actions, or gestures, I'll never let her forget how much she means to me.

If it wasn't for her, I would have never started processing my family's passing. I would have never opened myself up to Mrs. Potts and Chip like I have now, and I definitely wouldn't be lucky enough to say *I love you* to the girl who made it all possible.

I might be called The Beast, but she is the beauty that saved me.

blair

My heart is racing a million miles a minute, my palms are sweating, and butterflies are dancing throughout every part of my body. Griffin has my knees weak and thighs quivering from what we just did in the library.

My library.

My cheeks flush. I still can't believe he built that for me. It's magical and perfect. I can't wait to fill the walls with more of my favorite books and ones I'm dying to read. It's my new playground, and I feel giddy, like a kid on Christmas, at the thought of spending every day holed up and surrounded by old and new stories.

Griffin grabs my hand as we step out of my new

favorite room. My chest swells with the love I feel for Griffin.

He swings our hands between us. "I'm taking you out for dinner tonight. Paul and Lumi are joining us. We're going to a nice Italian restaurant in town."

I should tell him it's my birthday every day if this is what he plans out. I could get used to this.

"What time?" I ask, already imagining the outfit choices I can create and hating every idea so far.

"In about an hour and a half," he answers, and my eyes bulge out of my head.

He smirks and looks away. "Well, our added adventure wasn't on the itinerary."

I laugh, and my face burns as I remember the feel of his hand around my neck and the fire coursing through me. "*Oops*."

He sneaks behind me, dropping my arm and tickling my sides. "Yeah, *oops*. Now, go get ready," he whispers. "I picked something out for you to wear."

Whipping my head around, I gasp as my heart flutters. "You did?"

"It's hanging in your room." He smiles from ear to ear. He gently shoves me up the stairs. "Now go, go, go, or we're going to be late!"

"Okay! I'm going!" I giggle and start running up the stairs to my room.

Lumi is sprawled out on my bed as I walk in. "Finally, I was worried you guys got lost down there."

I can't hide the warmth in my face. "Yeah, yeah …" I trail off as my eyes land on the golden-yellow satin hanging on my wardrobe.

It's the most beautiful dress I've ever seen. Thin spaghetti straps hold it on the hanger, and thicker off-the-shoulder straps hang on the sides. The delicate fabric hangs elegantly, and I'm itching to get into it.

"Yeah, I know, right?" Lumi says, jumping off of the bed and admiring the dress with me. "It's going to look amazing on you."

After a quick touch-up on my curls, I style it half up with my black bow, knowing Griffin will love it. I do my makeup, opting for a faint smoky-brown eye and a soft red lip.

Lumi helps me step into my dress and zips me up. I've never felt more like a princess than I do right now, getting ready to descend the stairs to my prince.

As we exit the east wing, I get a whiff of vanilla, accompanied by the scent of fresh roses. The lights are dimmed, and I reach for the switch, but Lumi slaps my hand away.

"Just keep going," he whispers, escorting me to the top of the stairs.

Watching my feet intently, I make sure I don't trip as we descend to the landing.

Tingles dance over my body, and as I look up, my heart jumps into my throat, and flames ignite behind my eyes.

Griffin stands at the bottom of the staircase, wearing a deep blue suit, in his usual styling—no tie. His hair is brushed back, cascading in waves atop his head.

Behind him stands white-lit marquee letters that spell out *Happy Birthday*. And every countertop is decorated with flowers, endless candles, and gifts.

Paul waits behind the giant letters, Mrs. Potts, Chip, Malik, Asher, and Dean standing beside him.

I don't even realize that Lumi and I have continued down the stairs until Griffin approaches, and my eyes drop to his outstretched hand.

"I thought we might celebrate here tonight." His smooth voice sounds like music to my ears.

I slip my hand in his, and he glides me across the floor toward the little table positioned directly behind the letters. He grabs a glass off of it and hands it to me.

"Happy birthday, baby." He grabs a glass of his own and clinks it against mine.

Unable to contain the smile on my face and the swelling heart in my chest, I take a sip of the champagne.

"Oh, I almost forgot." Griffin sets his glass down and releases my hand. "One more thing."

"Seriously, Griffin, I don't want anything else. You've already done so much."

"Even if the last surprise is me?" The familiar raspy voice of my father sounds behind me, and I nearly drop the glass to the floor as I whip around to see if my imagination is getting the best of me or if he's really here.

"Dad!" I cry out as I lay eyes on my loving and caring father.

"Hey, peanut," he sobs.

I lunge forward and wrap my arms around him, still questioning whether this is real. As I inhale, I breathe in the scent of my childhood, of the man who sacrificed so I could pursue my dreams. I owe him everything, and I love him more than I can ever put into words.

"You look so beautiful. Happiness looks good on you,

sweetie," he whispers into my ear, and the burning sensation spreads from my eyes to my throat.

Squeezing him firmly, I say, "I love you, Dad."

"I love you too," he answers, pulling away and wiping the wetness trailing down his cheeks.

I feel Griffin brush my side as he steps beside me. My dad opens his arms to him, and Griffin hesitates, his eyes glossing over. Reaching out, I touch his hand with mine, reminding him I'm right here.

It's all the assurance he needs to step forward into my dad's embrace. My dad pats his back, and I can watch as every muscle in Griffin's body unwinds, softening from their hug, and it brings tears back into my eyes. I hope that, over time, they can grow close together. Although it looks like they are already off to a great start.

As they pull away, Griffin looks over at Mrs. Potts, giving her some kind of signal, and she walks away. Moments later, music pours into the room around us.

"May I have this dance?" Griffin asks, brushing my hair from my face and offering me his hand.

"Of course." I swoon, intertwining my fingers with his.

He leads me to the open floor in front of the *Happy Birthday* sign.

Sliding his fingers onto my waist, he holds my other hand out at our sides, leading us across the floor as we spin and sway to the music.

Mrs. Potts and Asher join us, followed by Lumi and Paul. I burst out laughing as Malik and Dean start dancing together. The last to drift onto the floor is Chip and my dad, who are becoming fast friends. Rex runs across the floor and happily jumps up around Chip, seemingly dancing with them.

At the beginning of the year, I was fighting each day to stay afloat. I was desperate to hold on to my fantasies and the fairy tale I had manifested for years.

Whether it was fate or perhaps Lumi volunteering me to become Griffin's tutor, I'm forever thankful that we found one another.

Behind his bared teeth and menacing reputation, I discovered so much more than I ever could have dreamed. I might have accepted the challenge of saving The Beast, but in truth, he rescued himself; I simply freed his heart from the west wing, where he'd imprisoned it long ago.

As we rock back and forth, nestled in our embrace, I rest my cheek against Griffin's chest, and he kisses the top of my head.

There is no place I would rather be than right here, surrounded by my favorite people and in the arms of the man I love. I don't know what our future holds or what tribulations we might face, but I don't care. We'll take any challenges head-on, hand in hand, *together*.

Thank you for reading Saving the Beast! If you enjoyed it, please leave a review on Amazon and Goodreads!

Book two is coming February, 2025! Title TBA!

Want to read more from Pru Schuyler while waiting for book two in the HEAU Hockey Legends Series? Check out her backlist below!

Nighthawks Series (new adult pro hockey romance)
Find Me in the Rain
Find Me on the Ice
Find Me Under the Stars
Not My Coach

Mrs. Claus Standalone Duet (adult holiday romance)
Stealing Mrs. Claus
Becoming Mrs. Claus

Wicked Series (young adult mystery/suspense romance)
The Wicked Truth
The Wicked Love
The Wicked Ending

acknowledgements

There are so many people I want and need to thank for helping this book and this series come to life.

First and foremost, I must thank my incredible readers who allow me to live my dreams daily. You are the reason I get to do what I love, and I'll never be able to thank you enough. I couldn't do this without you, and I'm forever grateful for you.

Dante, thank you for being the best husband in the world. Thank you for knowing me better than I know myself and for loving me unconditionally. Thank you for understanding when I have to hole up in my office during impending deadlines. You sacrifice and respect for what I do never goes unnoticed. I love you forever, and more.

Nikki, thank you for loving this concept and encouraging me to write this story. I would be lost without you, and I am so blessed to do this with you. You are the most incredible human, and I'm so proud to write alongside you on this insane journey. Your words are so beautiful and impactful. You have become a part of me, and I will love you forever and ever.

Meagan, you brilliant little ball of sunshine! Thank you for taking the bones of this book and seeing its potential from the very beginning. You leveled this book up in a way I didn't know was possible, and I'm so grateful for the time you dedicated to Blair and Griffin's story. Thank you for picking me up whenever I considered quitting because I didn't believe in myself. You keep me sane in moments of doubt.

Maren, thank you for keeping me in line so I could finish this book on time. Thank you for calling me out when I hadn't written in days and encouraging me to push through to the end. I could not have done this without you. Seriously. And shoutout to MJ for our late-night Zoom sessions that kept me on schedule. You are such an incredible human. Sincerely, Chicken Little.

Mom and Dad, thank you for always encouraging me to follow my passions and being invested in my book career. I couldn't ask for better parents and would not be anywhere near where I am today if it wasn't for both of you.

Jovana, thank you for loving this story and for helping me bring it to life. You are a miracle worker, as always. I'm so grateful for you.

My content teams—arc, street, pr, and social groups, are real-life angels who are helping my stories reach as many readers as possible. I'm forever grateful to everyone who likes, comments, and interacts with me on social media—thank you so much for taking the time to talk about my stories. Your dedication and love are priceless. Communicating with each and every one of you brings me so much joy.

There will never be enough words to truly show my gratitude to everyone who has helped my dreams come true. But I will start with these two—thank you.

about the author

Pru Schuyler is a Top 10 Amazon Best-Selling author, best known for her Nighthawks hockey romance series. She writes *happily ever afters to cry for*, including characters and stories that her readers can truly empathize with. At the heart, her books focus on undying love.

She secretly judges people who get through the day without any caffeine because she consumes an insane amount in order to function. She lives in the Midwest with her adored fur babies and husband. When she isn't getting lost in her writing, she is busy procrastinating by attending her local NAHL games, watching her favorite shows and movies, and spending time with her family at home.

Pru loves to communicate with her readers on her socials.
Instagram: Pruschuylerauthor
Facebook: Pruschuylerauthor
Facebook group: Pru Schuyler's Sweethearts
Website: Pruschuylerauthor.com

Made in United States
Troutdale, OR
11/24/2024

25244198R00270